The ...
of the Lady of the Loch

❧

Through the mist-shrouded waters of an enchanted sea,
the Guardian will be summoned.
The seasons will alter their natural course.
The barriers of time will be broken.

And a woman, with hair of burnished gold,
will be pulled from the depths of Loch Ness.

It is she who will bring the knowledge
and the courage of generations yet unborn.
And a wisdom that will guide
the chosen one out of his darkness.

But the waters will reclaim her once again,
if, after the passage of one full moon,
the immortal she was sent to heal
accepts not the power of Eternal Love.

The Inscription

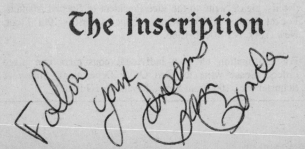

PAM BINDER

The Inscription

SONNET BOOKS

New York London Toronto Sydney Singapore

This book is a work of fiction. Names, characters, places and incidents are products of the author's imagination or are used fictitiously. Any resemblance to actual events or locales or persons, living or dead, is entirely coincidental.

 A Sonnet Book published by
POCKET BOOKS, a division of Simon & Schuster Inc.
1230 Avenue of the Americas, New York, NY 10020

Copyright © 1997 by Pam Binder

Published by arrangement with Goodfellow Press

All rights reserved, including the right to reproduce this book or portions thereof in any form whatsoever. For information address Goodfellow Press, 9502 179th Place NE, Unit 1, Redmond, WA 98052

ISBN: 0-671-04765-5

First Sonnet Books printing January 2000

10 9 8 7 6 5 4 3 2 1

SONNET BOOKS and colophon are trademarks of Simon & Schuster Inc.

Front cover illustration by Paul Bachem

Printed in the U.S.A.

To Jim,
my husband and champion,
and my children: Brock, Scott, and Kelli,
who inherited their father's belief
in honor and loyalty.

and

In memory of Scott and Marit Rhoads.

Acknowledgments

I wish to thank my agent, Liza Dawson; my editors at Pocket Books, Kate Collins and Lauren McKenna; and Pam Goodfellow of Goodfellow Press for her expertise. I am also grateful to the following people, who generously gave of their time to help me with *The Inscription:* Sally Astridge, Matt Buchman, Karen MacLeod, Jennifer McCord, Kay Morrison, Sharon Plowman, May Taylor, Cindy Wyckoff, and John Zobel. I believe my book is richer in texture because of the help of these people.

Chapter

1

❦

Scotland 1566

Once again the mournful wail of bagpipes, followed by a woman's cry for help, had awakened the laird of Urquhart Castle from a sound sleep and drawn him to the mist-shrouded waters of Loch Ness. In the light of the full moon the calm waters glistened like a newly forged sword as he made his way down the path to the shore. The image of the woman who had of late occupied his dreams came unbidden to his mind.

Her hair, the color of burnished gold, hung past her shoulders and the sadness reflected in her eyes made him wonder the cause. Lachlan MacAlpin did not know who she was, only that over the past few days her likeness had lingered in his thoughts well after he was fully awake. Each night this past seven days he had ventured out into the cool air, at first to escape his dreams, and then to pursue them. But tonight would be different. He could feel it.

The haunting music of the bagpipes returned. It was the same tune as the one in his dreams. He felt the hair prickle on the nape of his neck. The sound could be from a lone piper in the Highlands overlooking the loch. He gripped the hilt of his sword.

Waves began to foam to life, crashing against the stone walls of his castle as a shadow moved under the water. He was not afraid of the beastie that lived in the black depths of the loch; it was guardian to his people. But the creature only ventured near the surface when summoned, or when danger threatened those it protected. He knew it was not by chance the Guardian was near. There was a purpose, and as leader he must learn if its appearance was connected to his dreams.

Lightning cracked across the sky and he heard a faint cry for help through the increasing tempo of the bagpipes. There had been a time when he could have ignored such a plea for aid, but that was before he had left those he loved to the mercy of his enemy. The call came again, clear and insistent. He turned toward it. Not far from where he stood he could see someone in the water. A woman. Her cry rose above the growing storm as she fought to stay on the surface of the loch. His premonition had borne fruit, but fate had a way of destroying hope.

Lachlan hastened to remove his sword and tossed it onto the rock ledge. Plunging into the angry waters, he felt the bottom of the loch drop off abruptly to its unknown depths. His pulse quickened as he saw her pulled beyond his reach. Frustration filled him. How fragile life was for these mortals. He was weary of death and longed to become like his sword, strong, emotionless, and unfeeling.

He dove under the water in search of her, but could see little in the murky blackness. Death would not claim this one, he vowed. Surfacing, he saw her only a short distance from him. She was gasping for air. Lightning split the sky and illuminated her face. He lunged toward her. Her long hair and the garments she wore tangled around him. The fear in her eyes disappeared when she reached for him and clung to his neck. Time held its breath. He wrapped his arms around her slender waist before the icy currents dragged them both under the surface.

The numbing cold surrounded him. His lungs burned and the current tried to pull her from his grasp. He held on. She could not survive without his help. Fighting the power of the loch, he kicked free of its hold and broke the surface. He held her head above the waves and swam until he could touch the bottom.

Lachlan stood, shuddering as the crisp wind lashed across his wet skin. She lay cold and still in his arms. Her eyes were closed and her hair was draped over the silken garment that clung to her body. His breath caught in his throat. She was the image of the woman in his dreams. He removed his shirt and wrapped it around her. Reaching for his sword, he slung it over his shoulder and then gently cradled her against him. She shivered in his arms. It felt as though she had molded her body to his.

Cold rain began to fall as he hurried toward the warmth of the castle. This woman from the loch must not die. She had placed her life in his hands. The weight of that responsibility was familiar. His people relied on his wisdom and strength, from the approval of marriage to the fate of anyone who broke their laws. He called an order to the gatekeeper, who ran to obey. The massive door creaked open and torches on the inner walls cast gray shadows as he headed toward the side entrance.

His voice broke through the silence once more and thundered with authority. "Una. I am in need of your help."

He knew his longtime friend would be awake as she slept little these days. As he adjusted the woman in his arms, he could feel the shallow breathing against his chest.

"Rest easy, lass, you are safe." She nestled closer and a wave of protectiveness washed over him. The strength of his reaction surprised him. Lachlan kicked open the door to the cookroom.

Una was busy wiping down a long trestle table. Wisps of gray hair framed her face as she bent over her task.

She turned slowly toward him. He heard her sharp intake of breath as she put the cloth down and wiped her hands on her apron. Una shuffled over to him and touched the woman's face.

"She lives, but death chases her soul. 'Tis a long time since you have brought a lost one to my door. Where was she found?"

"Loch Ness."

Una paused. "The black water claims many who enter its depths. We must make haste."

Lachlan drew the woman against his chest and nodded in the direction of the stairs. "A fire still burns in my chamber."

Una raised an eyebrow. "This is not an injured bird or stay wolfhound you care for, but a grown woman."

"Aye. Advise Marcail her skill as a healer be needed."

He passed Una, climbing the stairs two at a time. She would not question his decision. He had always brought home stray animals and children found abandoned either through neglect of the cruelty of war. Una was ever the one he first looked to for help.

He could hear Una wheeze as she struggled to keep up with him. She was growing older. He could make her days easier until the angel of death claimed her, but he would remain, as he always had. He looked at the lass he carried in his arms. She was as still as the marble statues that lay scattered about the temples of Greece. He drew her to him, hoping to share his warmth.

At the top of the stairs Lachlan pulled open the door to his chamber. He entered and placed her on his bed.

Una's breathing was labored as she came into the room and put her hand on his arm. "You will need to wait in the corridor while I remove the lass' wet clothes."

Lachlan hesitated for a moment, reluctant to leave. He backed toward the door to the hallway. There was a reason the gods had brought her, but their purpose eluded him.

Through the oaken panel door, Lachlan heard Una humming a tune so old the words had been lost over time. He took a deep breath and let it out slowly. Una must believe the woman would survive; if not, there would be silence in his chamber. Una was of the opinion that you let music into your life only when there was something to sing about. He trusted her instincts.

The door opened as Una motioned for Lachlan to reenter the chamber. The woman on the bed cried softly. Worried, he glanced over at Una.

She smiled. "All is well. The lass sleeps, and already her body has warmed. It will be some time before she awakens."

The woman's garments were draped over Una's arm. "I fear her clothes are in such a tattered state that they are beyond repair. But I have never felt their like. The fabric is of the finest silk. The stitches so tiny and prefect, they are almost invisible. She must be a woman of great wealth. There is little more I can do."

"I shall watch over her." He chose to ignore Una's smile.

Lachlan placed a chair by the bed and sat down. A faint glow of color caressed the woman's face. She was beyond his dreams of beauty. And he felt drawn to her in a manner he had never experienced before. He glanced out the window. The angry storm that had raged against the castle walls disappeared as quickly as it materialized. Once again the night was still. He leaned back and closed his eyes. The door to the chamber opened. He heard the sound of a dog padding across the floor.

Una laughed. "Well, if it is not MacDougal, here to keep you company."

The wolfhound trotted over and dropped down at Lachlan's feet. He patted the animal as Una left. It occurred to him that she knew him better than anyone in the castle. For forty-five years she had retained an honored position at Urquhart, and had seen that all ran smoothly when he was away. He sought her counsel on matters that concerned those who lived and worked in the castle.

Lachlan folded his arms across his chest and remembered the time she had learned what he was. He had been gored by a pack of wild boars and she had tended his wounds. Of course, when he had recovered, there were no scars. It was then he had told her that he was immortal. She had been unafraid, a true sign of courage in these superstitious times.

He reached down and scratched MacDougal behind the ear. When Una died, he would see that there was a mass said in her honor. He felt regret constrict his heart as though fingers tightened around it. No matter what he did for them, mortals still died. Of late, he had feared that as a result of all the death that surrounded him, he lacked a soul. His heart might beat in his chest, but he had begun to feel nothing. Lachlan had come to accept it. It was the price he paid for immortality.

The wolfhound raised its head and looked toward the door. It was Marcail. Dressed in a gown of black and gold, she looked regal and as cold as any queen. MacDougal growled.

"Easy, old friend. Marcail will not attack unless provoked." The animal went to stretch out in front of the fire by the hearth, but kept its eyes focused on Marcail.

She raised an eyebrow. "Interesting beast. But, if it were mine, I would not allow it to remain inside the walls of the castle." She nodded in the direction of the bed. "However, there are more important matters to discuss. You have a visitor."

"Una did not have the opportunity to inform you of the woman, yet here you are, at this late hour."

"I would not risk her overhearing our conversation." She motioned for him to follow her into the adjoining chamber.

Lachlan glanced down at the woman who was sleeping in his bed. She shifted, as if in the hold of an inner battle he was unable to fight on her behalf. He reached over and smoothed back her hair from her forehead before joining Marcail.

"Your travels with the Medicis have made you suspicious."

"I prefer to think of it as caution." She turned toward him. "We must decide what is to be done with the woman you pulled from Loch Ness."

"You speak of her as though she was a prize horse to be traded at will. That is unlike you, Marcail."

She fingered the lace at her sleeve and for a brief moment Lachlan saw vulnerability in her eyes.

"We must be careful. Rarely has anyone been pulled from the icy depths of the loch and survived. However, the legend speaks of such an occurrence."

A glimmer of hope, he thought long buried, surfaced. She was alluding to the ancient myth binding his people's history to the loch. It had not struck him until this moment that the woman's appearance was as foretold in the legend.

"You do not believe she could be from a neighboring clan?"

Marcail shook her head slowly.

"One of Subedei's spies sent to infiltrate the castle?"

"Nay, I am certain she is not a spy."

Her words held conviction, and something more. She hid knowledge from him, knowledge of the woman. Lachlan would learn the truth. He let the silence grow between them.

Marcail straightened and raised her chin. "I shall inform the castle that she is from Italy. While on her way to Urquhart, her entourage was set upon and attacked. She was the only one to survive. Elaenor can lend her clothes until suitable garments can be made. Further, she is to be your betrothed."

Lachlan felt the walls close in on him. "An elaborate plan, merely to explain her existence."

Through the window, the full moon shone torchbright in the sky. Her voice was merely a whisper. "It will give us time."

He nodded his head slowly, seeing the logic in Marcail's plan. "And the marriage?"

"Only if you desire it."

*　　*　　*

Pale, rose-colored shafts of morning light burned through the thick mist in the courtyard below. Lachlan welcomed the new day and hoped it would see the woman wake, and thus end his vigil. His thoughts would not let him rest though he longed for the black void of sleep.

He stood in an alcove of narrow windows in his chamber and watched his people make ready the day. They were in high spirits. And why should they not be? The weather had turned warm for a Highland autumn. Foreboding chilled his bones as he remembered the words of the legend.

Through the mist-shrouded waters of an enchanted sea,
the Guardian will be summoned.
The seasons will alter their natural course.
The barriers of time will be broken.

And a woman, with hair of burnished gold,
will be pulled from the depths of Loch Ness.

It is she who will bring the knowledge
and the courage of generations yet unborn.
And a wisdom that will guide
the chosen one out of his darkness.

But the waters will reclaim her once again,
if, after the passage of one full moon,
the immortal she was sent to heal
accepts not the power of Eternal Love.

He put one hand on the stone ledge, feeling the strength of the castle walls beneath his fingers. Those entrusted to his care gave their loyalty to him gladly.

His people resisted change and were suspicious of things that could not be explained. Impenetrable as Urquhart appeared, he knew it could be breached if a weakness were discovered. The woman lying on his bed could well be that weakness. Marcail's explanation of the woman's presence would establish her place in the castle. He would announce their betrothal to the people and the date would be set a year and a day hence. No one would question the Highland tradition of handfasting. The alternative, to say he believed her connected to a legend, would open questions he was not prepared to answer.

MacDougal stirred beside him. The animal had kept vigil with him throughout the night. Lachlan reached down and scratched the wolfhound behind its ear. Lachlan's muscles felt tight and sore from a sleepless night. He longed to be out on the training field, but he would wait until she awoke.

The candle on the table had burned low and flickered as a cool breeze drifted through the open window. He rubbed his eye with the heel of his hand. The easy part had been the plan for the betrothal, the difficult territory lay before him. He would have to convince the woman the plan was sound, not an easy task. Women were not rational creatures, although he would not choose to share his opinion with Marcail.

His intended rolled over on her back and mumbled a few words he did not understand. MacDougal growled, but the dog's tail wagged, disturbing the rushes strewn on the floor.

"Patience, old friend."

She turned toward him and her eyes opened. She moved quickly to the far side of the bed. Her wary gaze lingered on the knife strapped to his waist, and then on the wolfhound.

"Fear not, lass. MacDougal looks fierce enough but has a gentle heart."

As he watched, she gathered the covers closer about her chin. Her hand trembled as she brushed hair from her face and looked around the room.

"Where am I?"

Lachlan held his breath. Her voice was soft and lyrical. He had to lean forward to hear her words. It was almost as though she were speaking to herself, instead of to him, and he could see her fear. Adept at its detection, he had often used this ability to his advantage. But he had no wish to use such tactics on her. His sister had often accused him of shouting out commands when he spoke. He endeavored to keep his voice low.

"You are at the castle. I pulled you from Loch Ness and brought you here. I am Lachlan MacAlpin, of the Clan MacAlpin."

She hesitated. "My name's Amber MacPhee and I was headed here when I fell in." She pressed her fingers against the side of her head and grimaced. "I feel awful."

Lachlan recalled once again the icy currents of the water. Her manner of speech was unfamiliar to him although he had traveled throughout the world, but that alone had not turned his blood as bitter cold as the Highland winds. Her hair shone like molten gold in the light. In the time of the Pharaohs, amber stones were said to have been kissed by the gods. Further proof the legend was coming true, or a coincidence?

The woman, Amber, looked down at the linen nightgown she wore. "Where are my clothes?"

Remembering the feel of her against his skin, his body responded and he cursed himself. He sensed she would not be pleased if she knew the state of her clothing when he had pulled her from the loch. Further, he did not need the distraction.

A knock on the door echoed through the room and brought a welcome diversion. Relief washed over him. He retreated from her question, as well as the others that plagued him, and crossed to the open door with MacDougal close at his heels.

Una stood at the entrance, carrying a tray laden with food. Steam curled from the bowl of soup and the rich aroma floated through the air. Slices of thick, dark bread lay beside the broth. A serving girl was behind Una, balancing a stack of clothes that skimmed the tip of her nose.

Lachlan took the bundle. "Molly, you should be abed waiting for that babe to be born, instead of climbing stairs."

Molly curtsied and fled down the hall.

Lachlan turned to Una. "Did I offend her?"

"Nay, she would prefer not to think of herself as carrying a child, since the father will not claim it."

Behind him a log rolled and shifted in the hearth. He had never understood how a man, knowing he had fathered a child, could abandon the babe. He tore off a piece of bread from the tray, put a chunk in his mouth and gave the rest to MacDougal.

"See that Molly knows she and the bairn will be well cared for." He balanced the bundle of clothes under his arm and reached for another piece of bread. "The woman is awake."

He turned and saw her try to sit up, but the effort was too much and she sank back down on the pillows.

Her hair hung in soft curls at her shoulders. She was still weak, but there was a rose tint to her cheeks. He swallowed. "She looks to be well."

Amber sank lower under the covers and felt the warmth of a full-scale blush sear her cheeks. The intensity of this man's gaze took her breath away. His deep voice echoed through the chamber. Dressed in a green plaid kilt, this man-mountain didn't look so bad himself; if you liked the big, scruffy, bear types with broad shoulders, and piercing blue eyes. She tried to concentrate on breathing normally. It had been her Aunt Dora's idea to come to this medieval reenactment in the first place. Amber had agreed in order to prove to the dear woman that she knew how to have fun. She had not counted on having to interact with anyone, especially someone who looked like . . . him. The panic quieted to a manageable level when she realized she'd have to spend her time finding a way to fish her car out of the loch. But locating her clothes would be her first order of business.

She shifted position on the bed. It crunched like cornflakes. Her head throbbed and her fingers tingled. She couldn't tell whether her bruises were from the fall or from the mattress, but she was alive. In the bone-cold waters of Loch Ness, she'd given up hope, until a man had saved her.

Amber looked more closely. He was probably the one. He had that "savior of the world" look and wore the clothes of a Highland Laird. And his eyes . . . she remembered the determination reflected in them. Lachlan MacAlpin probably had a castle or two tucked away in Scotland as well. Amber could picture them: gray crumbling walls, drafty rooms, and mortgaged to the limit.

She sighed. She was doing it again. The man had just rescued her from drowning and she was already trying to find a chink in his armor. Aunt Dora always said she threw a wall around her heart. Her aunt would be ecstatic over this situation. The sweet woman could play matchmaker faster than tourists flocked to Inverness to catch a glimpse of the Loch Ness Monster.

A woman with gray hair, dressed in period clothes, walked toward her carrying a tray of food. She set it on the table.

"I am Una and by what name are you called, lass?"

"Her name is Amber."

Una's face crinkled up in a smile. "Do not mind our laird's lack of manners. He thinks he must be the authority in all things."

Amber nodded. Her strength was returning with each breath she took, but with it grew a sense of unease she couldn't shake. She combed her fingers through her hair.

"Men are like that."

"Aye, lass, indeed they are." She leaned closer. "Now, it is best you eat and gather your strength." She turned to Lachlan. "The lass needs tending, and you will get in the way."

He walked over to the bed and set the clothes down. "Who tended her through the night?"

"You slept in the chair with that drooling beast at your feet. Now 'tis time for you to leave. Is there not a battle for you to fight, or a knight's head that needs a good bashing?"

Lachlan kissed Una on the cheek. "I shall have help sent to you. Take care your generous heart does not over-task your health."

Una pushed him away. "Be mindful, lad, I could as

well say those words to you. Now, be off and take MacDougal with you. The Lady Marcail has told me of our guest's position in the castle. Angus awaits you in the Chamber of Knowledge."

"Take care, Amber MacPhee. In less time than it takes to string a bow, Una will have you jumping in obedience to the sound of her voice."

"I'll be fine." The words sounded hollow to her own ears.

He rested his hand on the hilt of his blade and stared back at her for so long she could hear herself breathe.

Una straightened the clothes on the bed. "Pay no attention to the laird. 'Tis only men that need guidance. Women are born knowing their own minds."

Amber laughed nervously, and regretted it instantly. Her rib cage was sore. It was possible she had slammed into the steering wheel when the car hit the water. Served her right for not wearing a seat belt.

Lachlan signaled for MacDougal. "Let us leave these women alone, before I feel obliged to defend the honor of all the men in my clan." The dog bounded to his feet and wagged his tail.

The large door closed with a solid thud. Amber thought she would feel relieved when he left, but she was as uneasy as before. The woman called Una was dressed in a long skirt, blouse and shawl in the same tartan pattern Lachlan wore. Both of their brogues were thick, and their clothes fashioned in a style that would fit comfortably into the Renaissance or Middle Ages. If she and her brother, David, hadn't spent their summer with Aunt Dora, Amber would never have been able to understand much of what they were saying.

It was the best reenactment Amber had ever seen.

Her head began to ache again and she pressed her fingers against her temples. The last thing she remembered was the flash of lightning and a tree falling across the road.

She let her gaze wander around the room. Tapestries in vivid reds, blues and greens hung from the walls and herb scented rushes covered the floor. She marveled at how new things looked.

Una's smile seemed to touch every corner of her face. " 'Tis time to eat, lass."

Amber looked at the steaming chicken broth. Globs of fat floated on the surface. Her stomach felt as if it had just flipped over. She managed a smile.

"No, thanks, I'm not hungry. I just want to change back into my clothes and look around."

Una's forehead wrinkled. "The garments you were found in are beyond my skills to repair, but I have brought clothes I hope will be to your liking. It was a brave thing Laird MacAlpin did to pull you from the loch. 'Tis said that those who go in, never come out."

If her aunt, the eternal matchmaker, ever got wind of this guy, she'd be asking him over for dinner. Aunt Dora liked heroes. It would take Amber's complete list of excuses to talk her way out of this one. She looked across to the hearth. Flames blazed and crackled in a stone fireplace as big as her mother's walk-in closet. The noise aggravated her headache. The quicker she was out of here, the better.

"Please, do you have any aspirin? My head feels as if it's going to burst."

Una seemed confused. " 'Tis a word with which I am not familiar." She waved her hand in the air. "But then, there are so many visitors with strange languages that I am forever learning a word or phrase I have never heard before. What is the meaning of the word 'as-pir-een'?"

Amber shook her head slowly. The woman was taking her part far too seriously. "That's okay. I'll try not to think about it."

Maybe the headache would go away if she ate. She reached for a piece of bread and bit into it. It was still warm and reminded her of the bread her aunt cooked on festival days. Una appeared to be waiting for her reaction. Her aunt was like that; food was the answer to everything.

Amber nodded. "Delicious."

The woman's easy smile returned as she offered Amber an earthenware goblet, filled with a deep red wine. "I am glad to hear the words. The laird but wants food and lots of it. Never have I heard him say whether something was to his liking or no. More than once have I thought to stuff a pie with scraps of leather and serve it to him."

Amber waved the goblet away and wondered what the chances were of getting a cup of coffee. "Lachlan sounds like my brother. If you cut the pieces really small and smother the meat pie with a thick gravy, you might get away with it."

"It would never work, lass."

"Actually, it does."

The laugh lines around Una's eyes deepened. "You have a touch of the wee folk in you. Mayhaps it will sweep the somber cobwebs from this castle."

Her expression darkened as she tucked strands of gray hair back in place. " 'Tis a long time since I have heard laughter within these walls."

Una was talking as though this was where she lived, not just a place she came to play a part.

"You've been very kind, but my aunt will be worried if I don't call. May I try on the clothes you brought?"

Una selected items of clothing and handed them to Amber. "If the fit is not right, they can be adjusted."

There were layers of linen slips, a long-sleeved sheath that would drag on the ground when she put it on and a tunic of brown velvet. Amber looked at Una. Obviously they wanted her to blend in when the tourists arrived, but did she really have to wear all this stuff at once? She wondered what would happen if she asked for jeans and a sweatshirt. The atmosphere was pretty formal; best not to press her luck.

"When will the festival start?"

" 'Tis a way off as yet lass, but hurry, or you will get a chill."

Amber slid off the bed. She really couldn't stay too long. Aunt Dora had just recently recovered from pneumonia. It was the reason Amber was in Scotland, and not at her teaching job in Seattle. But her aunt, forever worried that Amber didn't know how to enjoy life, had given her the choice of a date with a neighbor's grandson or the reenactment. It had been an easy decision.

She'd only observed reenactments, she'd never been a part of one before. Maybe when her aunt was stronger they'd come back to this place. She watched Una rummage through a pile of clothes, tossing belts, stockings, shoes and various undergarments onto the bed. It was going to take hours to get dressed. First things first; she needed a phone, and a bathroom.

"Would you mind if I made a telephone call? It's local."

Una stumbled over the word. "Tele . . . and what might that be, lass?"

Amber started to laugh, thinking the woman was joking, and then stopped herself. Una looked serious. She rubbed the back of her neck. "Never mind."

Amber would look for herself once she was dressed. She knew this place had one. She'd called here to make the reservations. But she was too tired to press the point. Now for the next matter. "Is there a bathroom close by?"

"Bathroom?" Una looked confused. "Lass, your words are a mystery to me. Could you explain their meaning?"

Una's confusion seemed completely genuine. Aunt Dora behaved like that sometimes and both women were about the same age. Maybe she could find the bathroom without Una's help.

On the wall opposite the bed she saw an opening to another room. The rushes crunched beneath her bare feet, releasing the smell of rosemary and heather. The next room was only slightly smaller than the bedroom. In the center was a wooden tub filled with water. Linen strips lined the tub and were draped over the sides. On a table next to it lay soap and a stack of neatly folded towels. She picked up one of the bars. It smelled like jasmine. The tub reminded her of the one she'd seen at Leeds Castle, only this one looked as though it were not used for display only.

Una cleared her throat. "I believe I know the meaning of the word you used. My good sense must have been driven to the North Sea, not to have guessed you would be needing relief after the time you spend abed. The laird's mother ordered garderobes, fashioned to her exact specification, to be installed in the upstairs chambers." She nodded in the direction of one of two large alcoves to the right of the fireplace. "But 'tis the Lady Marcail who insisted this bath be prepared for you."

Armor and weapons filled one of the alcoves, but the other held more promise. This reenactment business was going to be, at the very least, an experience she could tell her students. Straw mats covered the terra-cotta tile floor. A vibrant mural depicting Venus rising from the sea was painted across one wall. On the opposite side was a basin with a projecting trough. A raised wooden platform with a hole in the center hugged the wall next to it and a pile of green hay lay neatly stacked in a corner. Amber paused. She was as excited about medieval times as anyone else, but this was a bit too extreme even for her tastes. However, there were no visible alternatives.

She took a deep breath and stepped into the small room. It was obvious Una was proud of this place, yet it was little more than an inside version of an outhouse.

"I want to see the woman, Lachlan. You must let me see her."

"There will be time, later, Mother, when you are stronger." He carried her gently in his arms toward her chambers. It was like holding the wind, cold and as light as air.

Her hand clutched his arm. "This is the same as the other time. You remember my telling you of him? We found his body along the shore of Loch Ness. Strange looking keys were clenched in his hand. He was dead. Very dead. But this woman is not dead. You pulled her free of the icy waters after the Guardian brought her to us. You should have pulled the man out of the loch as well."

"I was in China."

Since her father's death at the hand of Subedei, his mother had become less connected with the present, although her mind vividly recalled the past. The events she spoke of had occurred over sixty years ago.

She sighed. "I think his name was Ford. Yes, that was it. That was the name we found attached to his keys. Ford."

Amber reentered the bathing room and looked around. Una was sitting in a chair facing the fire, reading a book that was bound in leather and etched with gold and red designs.

"A good soaking in the tub will set you to feeling as bright as the sun on a clear day in June. There are linens and soap Lady Marcail brought with her from France. I shall be leaving you. The laird and his men have appetites large enough to empty the biggest pantry, not that they will taste a thing, but I need to make sure there is food, and plenty of it." Una laughed as she stood. She patted Amber on the cheek and handed her the book.

"Take care with it, the laid brought it back with him from one of his travels. He said that I would enjoy the tale of the 'Wife of Bath.'" She winked. "I cannot understand what the lad is talking about. I have had but three husbands. The woman in the story had herself a fine time with five."

Amber smiled and opened the book as Una shuffled out the door. It was *The Canterbury Tales* written in the original Old English style on pages that resembled parchment. She turned to the "Knight's Tale." The condition of the book was remarkable. Her aunt had one similar to this that she kept under a glass case.

The pages of her aunt's book were brittle and cracked with age, and there was an inscription on the inside cover. She imagined this was how her aunt's must have looked when it was hot off the press or, rather, fresh from the copier's hands.

She rubbed her fingers over the hand-tooled leather cover with its gold leaf embedded in the design. Carved in the bottom right-hand corner were the initials "L.M." An uneasiness crept over her. The same initials were carved in the cover of her aunt's book as well. It had to be a coincidence. Probably the work of the bookbinder, or the man who did the intricate designs.

Amber set the book down on the table. The water in the tub was inviting. She pulled the linen gown off, threw it over the chair, and climbed in. She leaned back and closed her eyes. It wasn't as hot as she liked, but still it soothed her aching muscles. Water sloshed against the sides of the tub and the wood crackled in the fireplace.

She wished she could remember how she got here, but there were only pieces to the puzzle, not a complete picture. She'd been thrown from her VW when it hit the water and was caught in a fast-moving current. And she remembered his eyes. She looked into the flames. Maybe she should stay for a couple more days. It would certainly please her aunt. Her thoughts did a fast-forward and she reviewed the goals she'd set for herself. She didn't have time for any type of relationship. It was all she could handle just keeping up with teaching and studying to get her administration credentials. Her head began to throb again.

A breeze rippled across the bathwater. Amber shuddered and sat up. She was alive. That was all the sense she needed to make of this situation. Reaching for the soap, she began rubbing it between her hands until there were thick foamy bubbles between her fingers. The scent of jasmine drifted through the air. She breathed in the rich fragrance deeply before washing her hair.

She closed her eyes and sank back into the warm water. Just a few more minutes and she'd get dressed and find a phone; then her life would be back to normal.

Chapter

2

Amber awoke with a start. Someone had touched her shoulder. Cold water sloshed over the top of the tub as she sat up. She shivered. How long had she been asleep? A very pregnant young woman, perhaps sixteen or seventeen, stood beside the tub. Her skin was pale and there were shadows under her eyes. She'd been crying. Despite the pregnancy, the young woman was skin and bones. Amber had seen this look before at the high school where she taught. She felt sorry for her and smothered the impulse to ask what she could do to help.

"I am Molly, milady, and 'tis sorry I am to awake you. You were so still I thought . . ." Her voice lowered. "I thought you dead."

"Not yet, but I might be if I stay in this tub. I'm freezing." Amber reached for a linen towel and ignored the impulse to ask Molly about the pregnancy. She stepped out of the tub and dried off.

"My name is Amber."

The fire burned down to glowing coals in the hearth. She hadn't seen any electric lights or outlets so there was a good chance this part of the castle hadn't been wired for electricity. Well, she'd never minded camping, and this was pretty close. It wasn't as if she was going to be here very long. Molly seemed rooted to the floor.

"Is anything wrong?"

Molly nodded and then quickly shook her head. "I am to help you dress."

"Okay, I've seen the clothes and I'll welcome the help. But you're looking at me as if I've sprouted a second head."

"Una says I should get used to the strange ways people speak." Molly lowered her voice. " 'Tis not an easy task."

Amber smiled and wrapped the towel around her. She'd never thought of herself as having an accent, but Aunt Dora would say that she always spoke as if she was in a hurry. "I've been told I talk too fast. So, if you need me to repeat myself, just ask."

Molly hesitated. "The others all have pinched faces and sour expressions. You are different."

"I've been told that before. Now let's see about getting me dressed. All of a sudden I'm starving."

Amber walked through the entrance that separated the two rooms. Clothes were heaped on the bed. She took a deep breath. It wasn't going to take hours to get dressed. It would take days. She walked over to the bed.

"Well, Molly, where do we start?"

Shields, gleaming armor, and weapons lined the walls of the Chamber of Knowledge. Lachlan walked over to where a line of square holes were cut into the stone. Rolls of parchment in varying sizes were stacked in each slot. He welcomed the diversion. Only a day had passed since he had rescued the woman from Loch Ness. Already she had unsettled the orderly life in which he lived. He pulled out one of the maps and spread it hastily on the long table. It depicted Urquhart and the surrounding highlands. Angus approached as Lachlan studied the map. The man was almost equal to him in size and strength. He was a trusted friend. There was no other he would wish by his side in battle.

Flames from the candles flickered as Angus pointed to the area where Loch Ness bordered the castle.

"Subedei will bring his forces by water again and attempt to overpower us with his numbers. If our information is correct, he has both the resources and the mercenaries to level Urquhart."

"Revenge runs hot through his blood, but he will not come by water."

Angus nodded. "Aye. 'Tis true. I forget the beastie of Loch Ness has proven to be our greatest ally."

The dampness that permeated the underground chamber chilled him. "I should have been here when Subedei attacked the castle. I was the one he sought."

Angus leaned against the table. "Nay, it is the Council of Seven he vows to destroy for what they did to him. You but saw that the decree was carried out. He knew the price for his actions."

His sworn enemy haunted his thoughts like a specter in the dark corners of a deserted castle. "He raped my sister and left her naked and battered on the streets of Naples."

"Subedei was castrated, according to our laws."

" 'Tis not enough. Were it not for my mother's wishes I would have preferred to cut out his black heart."

"You may yet have the chance. It is said he seeks vengeance for all who had a hand in his punishment.

Zarie, the man who carried out the order, was found hacked to pieces. Subedei's attempts to take Urquhart failed when all his ships and crew sank into the depths of Loch Ness."

Lachlan gripped the hilt of the blade strapped in his belt. He had been in Egypt, fighting as a mercenary, when Subedei stormed Urquhart. Too late he had learned of the fate of his brothers and sisters. Upon his return, his mother had stared at him with the vacant expression of one who had seen her children slaughtered and her husband die in her arms. She had not put the blame on his head, but he could not wash away the guilt. Grief had not taken him. His only emotion had been his vow of revenge. Subedei's message was clear. The Mongol warrior would return to level Urquhart and murder all responsible for what was done to him. This time Lachlan would be here, waiting. Vengeance was sweeter if taken slowly.

Angus' voice echoed through the chamber and brought Lachlan back from his dark thoughts.

"With you as leader, Subedei's forces will be no match for your Highland clans. A fierce lot. Their ancestors drove the Roman legions from their shores. A madman, such as Subedei, will be an easy victory."

Lachlan folded his arms across his chest. Angus had lived five hundred and fifty years longer than he, and fought in battles where the feats of valor had been exaggerated until legends had replaced the harsh truths. It had dulled his friend's ability to judge another's strength. Lachlan's own thirst for battle had pulled him from his responsibilities. His people had paid for his carelessness with their lives. He leaned over the map and studied the terrain until the images blurred before his eyes. His thinking must be clear, if he was to anticipate Subedei's battle plan.

He looked at Angus. "The villages under our protection will be Subedei's first objective. Once he believes our forces are divided, he will attack. Failing, he will use the ploy of retreat to draw us from the castle. Our clans will be slaughtered."

Angus scratched his beard. "You give the man much credit. Maybe too much."

"Subedei trained under Genghis Khan."

The older man shrugged. "We drove the Mongols from our borders when they sought to conquer all of Europe. This time will be no different."

Lachlan stepped closer to the table. "What minstrel's tale have you been listening to that you have the facts so twisted? Europe did not defeat the Mongols. They left because Genghis died, and their princes returned to vie for control of the empire their leader had created. That is what saved Europe."

Angus' brows drew together. "Had I realized, when I sent you to study their culture, that you would return idolizing them, I would have reconsidered."

"I do not honor or praise a man beyond his ability."

"There is such a thing as too much caution, it will alarm your people needlessly. We must seek out our enemy and destroy him before he lays to waste everything that crosses his path."

Lachlan looked at Angus, the men who had led him into his first battle when he was barely strong enough to wield a claymore. Angus was a warrior of unlimited courage. Lachlan shared his friend's recklessness in the heat of war, but if they were to defeat the great Mongol warrior, they must use cunning.

"You have fought with armies whose rules were

governed by lines, maneuvers, and chivalry; generals who believed in wearing down an enemy by battering them head-on. I have fought with the Mongols. They swept through China with the ease your horse tramples the meadow grass under its hooves." He clenched his fists at his sides. "If it is an unwillingness to change that holds you back, say now, and another can take your place. We must be on guard that the battle be not more important than the reason for it."

Angus' voice was defensive. "Our methods have served us well in past wars. I see no reason to change."

The confrontation ahead might easily wipe out a third of their numbers and more still if Subedei's skill as a warrior were underestimated. Lachlan needed to know what each man would risk to preserve his people. Lachlan felt his temper boil to the surface and knew it was fueled by the need to have his friend realize the strength of their enemy. But Angus would have to choose. Their race's continuance depended upon it. He took a knife out of his belt and drove it into the table. The blade quivered between them and marked the invisible line Angus must cross. The metal seemed to glow white hot in the candlelight.

"Take care, friend, that your confidence does not override your wisdom. It will be as I have said."

Angus stared back at him, a look of resolve on his face. His jaw slackened as he bowed his head. "You inherited the role of leader of the Council when your father was killed, but you earned our loyalty by placing our wishes before your own. It will be as you command."

There was no animosity in Angus' voice, no condescending tone, only obedience. They had started in life as mentor and child, but Lachlan was born into the

ruling family. When his father died, their roles had
changed forever. Lachlan pried the blade from the
table. The council looked to him as the leader who
would take them into the next century. His first loyalty was to the good of all. At times he wished he and
Angus were ordinary solders who fought side by side
for a king or queen, or equal terms and for equal
goals. But it was not to be.

"Come, 'tis time for us to join our men."

In the Great Hall, Lachlan leaned against the white-
washed stone wall near the window drinking his ale.
Soon his men would gather for the evening meal, but
for now he could enjoy the quiet. Amber's presence in
Urquhart was already known and her position as his
betrothed made clear. All that remained was to tell
her. He swirled the ale in his tankard and took a drink.
It was warm and bitter. He knew not how she would
react to the proposal of handfasting. The words of the
legend echoed through his mind like the haunting
notes of a bagpipe. She could be the woman in the legend. He drained the ale from his tankard.

The light of the torches glowed on the walls and
kept the evening shadows away. Large oak panel
squares, with the crests of the Highland clans painted
in each, covered the ceiling. The idea belonged to his
sister, Elaenor. He had encouraged her interest in the
task, hoping the research would distract her from her
solitary thoughts. However, the project had failed.
While the ceiling was magnificent, Elaenor still suffered. What Subedei had done to her older sister,
Beatrice, had shaken young Elaenor to the core.

A half dozen men, clad in the MacAlpin plaid,
saluted him as they entered the Great Hall. He nod-

ded and watched as they sat down at one of the long
trestle tables by the fire. These were good men, loyal
and able warriors. Their laughter filled the corners of
the room. Angus entered. His friend was trailed by
barking wolfhounds.

Servants filed into the room carrying foaming
pitchers of ale, trays of steaming salmon, wedges of
cheese, and brown bread. The sound of voices and the
clatter of earthenware blurred together until none
could be distinguished from the other. Lachlan had
the sudden impulse to retreat to the solitude of his
chamber. The vision of the woman who occupied
those quarters halted his thoughts. Amber. She was
well named. Her hair shone like the blaze of a fire, and
her eyes . . . their warmth stirred his blood. He
reached for his tankard. It was empty.

A shout rose above the din. He looked in the direction of the sound. Angus was likely winning another
wager. He saw his red-bearded friend take ale from a
serving maid before approaching him. Angus' smile
spread wide over his face as he filled both their
tankards and set the pitcher on the table. He slapped
Lachlan on the shoulder.

"If given a chance, your men would wager their pay
on the number of eggs to be found in an eagle's nest."

"Aye, and glad for the diversion."

One of the wolfhounds growled and fought another for a meaty bone. The men in the room turned their
attention toward the dogs, laughing and making
wagers as to the outcome. Lachlan watched the struggle. The warmth of the room closed in. He and Angus
were not unlike these beasts. They were tied to this
world, living within the rules that governed it, yet
they were separate. The two worlds could coexist, but

never join in a permanent union. It was one of the laws of his race. He accepted his fate, but lately had begun to question the reasoning behind it. The price of long life left a measure of his kind insane, and alone.

The larger of the wolfhounds let out a howl that vibrated through the Great Hall. It sank its teeth into the neck of the other animal. Blood gathered on the dark fur. The cheers of the men increased in volume until the room was filled with the sound. Abruptly the large dog released its hold and allowed the other to slip away.

A hush fell over the room. Lachlan understood why the beast had not killed its opponent. Death would have been pointless, the animal had won. But he admired the wolfhound, nonetheless. In the heat of battle reason was often overlooked. He wondered if he would always have the strength of will this animal possessed. Of late, he had begun to doubt.

Muffled conversations resumed and the sound of metal coins clinking together, as wagers were settled, filled the room.

Angus wiped his hand on his plaid and took another drink. "What think you of our new guest?"

Lachlan tightened his hold on the tankard, feeling the smooth, cold metal. He had thought of little else. "She is well enough."

"Well enough?" Angus laughed and slapped Lachlan on the back. "Those words are as stuffed with meaning as one of Una's meat pies. 'Twould be my wager that the lass is bonnie, indeed. Mayhaps I should introduce myself to the lady."

Lachlan was surprised at the jealous tone of his voice, but could not stop the words. "The lady is not for you."

"Ease down, lad. 'Twas only a jest. But perhaps this lady will succeed where others have failed."

Lachlan smiled. Angus knew him too well.

His friend shrugged. "Marcail tells me the two of you are betrothed. What thinks the lass of the arrangement?" Angus winked. "A year and a day; much mischief can be made."

Lachlan managed to keep his voice even. "She is not yet aware of our betrothal."

"Perhaps someone has told her and that is why she flees." Angus nodded in the direction of the corridor outside the hall.

Lachlan followed Angus' gaze and saw Amber hurry down the stairs. The gown she wore was a somber brown and ill-fitting. It hid the curves he knew she possessed. Amber paused. She seemed startled and looked around before heading for the door that led to the courtyard, and the loch.

Lachlan knocked over his tankard in his haste to follow her as the words of the legend echoed through his thoughts. . . . *and the waters will reclaim her once again.* He must stop her. Lachlan wished he was able to ignore the legend. But he was forced to take it seriously. Minstrels sang of an immortal race. His race. If one legend were true, how many others? He must detain her. She should be grateful he wanted to keep her safe until the mystery of why she was here was solved.

The air was still and cold in the waning light of the afternoon sun as Lachlan hurried out into the courtyard. Amber was only a short distance from him and stood between his brother, Gavin, and the tutor, Bartholomew. Perhaps his brother had emptied Una's pantry to feed the wolfhounds again. Whatever the reason, he was grateful she had been detained.

"Where is it that you go?" He bellowed out the words and Amber, Gavin and Bartholomew turned toward him.

Amber put her hands on her hips. "Are you in charge here?"

"Aye. But you have not answered my question."

"You people have taken this reenactment business a little too far. I saw this man beating this boy."

Bartholomew, wielding a sapling branch like a sword, walked around Amber. "Your brother refuses to concentrate on his lessons. He will learn along with the rest of the boys of the parish, or feel the sting of laziness."

"Will reading help me fight the Campbells when they raid our cattle?" Gavin turned to Lachlan. "I hate to read."

Amber's nod was emphatic. "Of course you do. I would too if I was beaten into submission."

It was quieter in the castle's henhouse. Lachlan held up his hand to stop their flow of words. "Enough."

Her voice was clear and strong. "I saw this man from the upstairs window. He was hitting your brother with a stick."

"Laird MacAlpin, who is this woman that she questions my authority over Gavin? I was taught by the Benedictine Monks and recommended to you by Queen Mary."

Lachlan was losing patience. "This is the Lady Amber. And I shall see to the confusion." He turned toward her. "You should not concern yourself in this matter."

"Excuse me?"

Bartholomew tapped the switch against the palm of his hand and cleared his throat. "Women are meddlesome creatures. It would be best to leave Gavin's education to those who can understand its importance."

Amber's face flushed with anger. "That does it, you pompous sack of wind. Where did you get your teaching credentials? Through the mail?" She put her arm around Gavin's shoulder.

The boy sucked in a breath of air and his lips whitened as he reached up to push away Amber's hand.

She leaned down. "I'm sorry. I forgot you were hurt. My name's Amber. May I call you Gavin?" When the boy did not respond she continued. "Education is important, but there are many different ways to learn."

The tutor laughed. "Nonsense and fairy smoke. My methods are never questioned in Edinburgh. There is only one way to teach a child and that is with a steady hand." The switch whistled through the still air.

Gavin flinched.

"Does your teacher hit you often?" Amber asked.

Gavin shrugged his shoulders. "I suppose I deserve it."

She straightened and gazed squarely at Lachlan. "You can't agree with Bartholomew. He doesn't care about your brother. If he did, he'd be patient."

"Gavin lacks not for the tending he needs. It is his mind that has been neglected, not his heart."

"What does his mother say about these teaching methods?"

Lachlan looked at Gavin and then back at Amber.

"Our mother is no longer able to shoulder the responsibility."

The look in her eyes became more determined. "Then you condone Bartholomew's treatment?"

His frustration built on the earlier impatience until he felt smothered. He had searched for a proper schoolmaster for Gavin and still felt he had not erred in his selection. "I am satisfied with the boy's progress."

"When it comes to a student, I usually have a lot to say." Amber's hands trembled as she lifted Gavin's shirt. Dried blood crisscrossed the boy's back. She lowered the shirt and faced Lachlan again. "You are patient with that dog you call MacDougal, doesn't your brother deserve the same treatment?"

Lachlan felt a knot form in the pit of his stomach. Only a coward would strike a child. He saw her reach down and hold Gavin's hand. His brother looked back at her. The fear had fled the boy's eyes. She barely reached Lachlan's chest, yet she was openly defying both him and Bartholomew.

He had failed Gavin. His own tutors had been strict and he had experienced the sting of their disapproval, but he had never run from them in fear, nor had they drawn blood. Bartholomew must be more cruel. He took a deep breath. He felt ill-trained to act as parent to his brother in such matters. His anger grew.

Amber's emotions were easy to read. She looked as if she would stand in the courtyard until the waters in Loch Ness froze, before she would give ground. "Bartholomew's methods might be more severe than I had been aware of, but in the end they will prove correct."

She raised an eyebrow. "How can you be so sure

your brother will be all right?" Amber paused and glanced toward the growing shadows in the courtyard. "You can turn a gentle dog mean and vicious by mistreating him. Are children less fragile? To protect himself, a child could harden his heart to all emotion."

Her words cut through his reserve. His father had turned one of their prize wolfhounds so unmanageable with mistreatment it had attacked and killed one of the children in the town. Truth ran clear in her words. He looked down at Gavin. "Why didn't you speak to me of the beatings?"

"The English attack us from the sea and the Loch Ness beastie frightens the villagers."

"All you say is true, but it is not the question I asked."

Amber touched his arm. "It sounds as if Gavin thought you had enough problems. He didn't want to add his own."

Lachlan had been wrong. Anger burned within him like the heat of a banked fire. If Gavin had come to him with tales of Bartholomew's cruelty, he knew his reaction. He would have done nothing. Lachlan had been consumed with defending his castle against an attack from Subedei.

He paced in front of the tutor. "Mistreatment breeds cruelty. Bartholomew, the troublesome mare I allow you to stable has never felt the bite of your whip, yet you beat a child."

Bartholomew flexed the twig between his hands. "I shall not teach a lad who cannot abide to sit still. He is forever losing his place while he reads."

"Your patience with your horse is boundless."

Bartholomew adjusted the sleeves of his tunic. "The mare needs a gentle hand to coax the right mix of loyalty and duty."

"But Gavin is to be beaten?"

"A boy is not a horse."

"Aye, a boy needs more care." Lachlan doubled up his fist and hit Bartholomew in the jaw.

The schoolmaster slumped back. Blood spurted from his mouth. The mask of confidence he had held intact melted away. Lachlan grabbed Bartholomew around the neck. "How does it feel to have fear run through you like molten lead? I shall notify the general assembly of the need for a new parish schoolmaster."

"I . . . I will not hard the boy again, you have my word." He tried to pry Lachlan's fingers from around his throat. "Please, I beg you, let me go." The switch dropped to the ground. "Please."

Lachlan heard someone come up beside him. It was Amber.

"Don't you think strangling this man is a little bit extreme?"

Her voice was as calm as a spring breeze. His life depended upon exacting swift revenge on anyone who hurt those in his care. Yet she was asking for him to try another path. Her touch cooled his anger. She was right. He released his hold on Bartholomew and watched the man rub his jaw and hurry toward the safety of the shadows. The schoolmaster may have thought he had escaped, but Lachlan remembered something Amber had said. He might not allow his wolfhounds to tear Bartholomew limb from limb, as was his desire, but he would make certain the schoolmaster, if the man taught again, would be watched.

The decision made, he looked at Amber as she talked with his brother. He folded his arms across his chest. This woman had been able to cool his temper with her words alone. The similarity to the women of his clan was apparent. She was a woman who spoke clearly what was on her mind.

Gavin stared at him with the trust of the young, yet Lachlan felt he had failed. He walked over to his brother and knelt down in front of him. "Know that I shall take better care to leave you only with those I trust."

Gavin chewed on his lower lip. "Are you going away?"

Lachlan pulled his brother into his arms. He had chosen his words poorly and knew firsthand the emotions his brother felt at the idea of being left behind. Lachlan drew back and looked at Gavin. "Battles will have to come to me, for I will not be leaving Urquhart. When you are old enough to wield a sword, we shall leave together." He looked at Amber again. "You risked much by your interfering."

She smiled. "It's an old habit of mine."

A cool breeze drifted in off the Highlands, bringing the fresh scent of heather. He stood and gazed at the woman he had saved from Loch Ness. Once she set her path to defend his brother, she had never wavered.

Lachlan guided Gavin toward the entrance of the Great Hall. He tousled the boy's hair. "I will have Marcail tend your wounds."

"Shouldn't you take him to the hospital, or have a doctor look at him?" It was apparent to him she doubted his ability to care for his own.

"I would trust Gavin to no other. I have no doubts as to her abilities." Marcail was a physician. She had once held dreams to heal all those who came her way. The Black Death had made her realize her abilities were limited. It had defeated her.

Out of the corner of his eye he saw Amber struggling to keep pace with them as he and Gavin reached the entrance. She kept stepping on the hem of her gown. He would have to ask Una to see to new clothes.

As she approached, she glanced quickly at his brother. "I'm worried Gavin's back will become infected. Are you sure we shouldn't think about taking him to town to see a doctor? Those cuts look deep. I think he needs stitches."

This woman was right to interfere with Bartholomew; however, Marcail was the only physician his kin needed. He suspected Amber would not discourage easily and, thankfully, he had an answer for her. "Marcail has the gift of healing."

He could hear her muttering behind him as he pushed open the double doors and knew the answer was not to her liking. But she would have to be satisfied with it.

A fire blazed in the hearth in the Great Hall. His men were busy about their meal as Una walked toward him, wiping her hands on her apron. "There you are, Gavin. I sent Angus and his men in search of you when you missed the evening meal." She brushed his hair off his forehead. "Where have you been, lad?"

Gavin looked at Lachlan.

Una's forehead wrinkled. "I knew something was amiss when I saw you leave."

He put his arm around Una's shoulder. "I shall explain at length later. As for now I would have Marcail tend the boy."

"I never did like that man, with all his English ways. Always so full of his own imagined importance." Una motioned to Gavin. "Come lad. I have a sweet for you in the cookroom and then we will find the Lady Marcail."

Lachlan nodded toward his brother. It was a sound plan. Una could mother Gavin. Right now that is what he suspected the boy needed. More than likely, his back had already begun to heal.

Una took the boy's hand and disappeared around the corner. He should probably tell their mother what had happened. The muscles in his shoulders tightened. He dismissed the idea. If she understood at all it would upset her; if she couldn't remember who Gavin was it would distress her all the more. He shook the dark thoughts from his mind and glanced over at Amber. She was staring in the direction Una had taken Gavin. "You need not worry. My bother will be well cared for."

Lachlan watched Amber hesitate before she picked up her skirts and walked toward a long table heaped with steaming platters of food. A few of his men noticed her enter and then looked over at him. It was an easy task to decipher their thoughts. A man could lose all sense of time in the watching of her move across a room. And her skin . . . he gripped the hilt of his sword and returned his men's stares until they bent once more over their meal. They would not challenge him. Some out of loyalty, others from fear.

A young serving girl with a tray of fruit pies sidestepped out of the way as Amber passed. Angus made a sweeping gesture with his arm for Amber to sit beside him at the table. His friend looked over at him and winked. Angus was a dead man.

Chapter
3

〰️

A fish with bulging eyes lay on a pewter tray and stared back at Amber. She shifted on the bench and reached for a piece of white cheese. Lachlan sat beside her, engrossed in conversation with a man named Angus. Across from her sat the woman who was supposed to be such a great doctor. Angus had introduced her as Lady Marcail. She was dressed in a blue silk grown trimmed in white fur, with yards of pearls around her neck. Amber couldn't stop looking at her. The woman's costume was a truly brilliant reproduction of a court dress complete with matching headpiece. She looked as if she had about as much emotion as the fish on the platter and no doubt a bedside manner to match. Marcail had said she'd examined Gavin. She had pronounced him healed and that was the end of the discussion.

Amber heard a child's laughter and the excited barking of a dog. Gavin and MacDougal were playing tug-of-war with a torn piece of material. The dog pulled the cloth free, dropped it, and licked Gavin on the face. The boy certainly looked as if he'd recovered. Marcail ignored the commotion. Instead she was concentrating on cutting her food into grain-sized pieces with an oversized fork and a knife that resembled a small dagger. Amber realized Marcail never put one piece into her mouth, and the words "eating disorder" popped into Amber's thoughts.

Voices blended together in the Great Hall as everyone bent over their food and ate with their fingers. Amber looked around at the sea of tartan-clad men. Their clothes looked worn, lived in and comfortable. It was impossible to tell the tourists from the actors.

Angus' voice rang above the hum of chatter. He nodded toward Lachlan and pointed his tankard of ale in the direction of the young woman by the hearth.

"Your sister seeks only the company of books."

Amber followed his gaze. Alone, in a corner by the fireplace, a young teenage girl sat with a book in her lap. She looked as detached from the people in this room as Amber felt.

Lachlan nodded. "Aye, Elaenor's thirst for knowledge shows signs of exceeding even Queen Elizabeth's. Their correspondence keeps the messengers between London and Urquhart in constant business."

"Is Her Majesty, Queen Mary, in favor of the friendship?"

Lachlan took a drink of ale. "She knows not, nor would it be of interest to her, so obsessed is she with her marriage to Lord Darnley. I have been informed that she is with child. That union will come to no good. We must take care the throne of Scotland falls not to Queen Elizabeth. For all her intelligence, I would keep these lands free of English rule."

Angus turned toward Amber, scratched his fire-red beard and smiled. "What think you of our Sovereign?"

She looked from one to the other. They couldn't be

serious. She was pretty sure they were talking about Mary, Queen of Scots. Amber rested her arms on the table. These people were taking this reenactment business to the extreme. They had immersed themselves so deeply in their roles she doubted if they could climb out of the past long enough to carry on a normal conversation. She might as well play along. She took a deep breath and tried to sound serious.

"I think if your Queen's not careful, she'll lose her head."

Angus' laugh was almost deafening. He reached over and slapped Lachlan on the back. "Laird MacAlpin, the lass has wit."

The force of the blow knocked Lachlan forward and he spilled ale over the front of his tartan. He stood and pulled Angus to his feet. "Lady Amber may indeed be quick-witted, but you have the manners of a drunken reaver."

Amber could see the muscles in Lachlan's jaw tense. His emotions were close to the surface. It had been the same when she had told him about Bartholomew. The episode with the tutor was still fresh in her mind. It had not occurred to her, at the time, that the behavior she was witnessing would be commonplace in the medieval and renaissance era. She didn't like this reenactment. It was too real.

She rubbed her temples. Slow down, think this through. She could hear the grating sound of metal fork against pewter plate as Marcail cut her food. She'd asked Lachlan to take Gavin to see a doctor. Her hands trembled, and she clasped them in her lap. He'd said that Marcail had a "gift of healing." He'd not said she was a great physician. The expression had not seemed odd then, it did now.

The smell of animal fats from platters of mutton and beef, musk and flower-scented perfumes, combined with too many people jammed into the Great Hall had suddenly become overpowering. She felt dizzy. It'd been less than twenty-four hours since she'd been pulled from the loch. She was not rational. After all, her body was probably still recovering from a mild case of hypothermia. A glass of cold water or iced tea might help settle her stomach, not to mention her imagination. Maybe she could scrounge something in the kitchen.

Amber touched Lachlan on the arm. "I think I'm going to look for something else to eat."

She left the table and walked in the direction she had seen servants carrying platters of food. Stumbling over bones thrown on the floor, she wove her way around the long tables until she reached the entrance.

Heat poured from the kitchen as Amber opened the door. In the stone fireplace, against smoke-stained walls, two pigs roasted on an iron spit. A white-washed brick oven stood in the corner and she could smell the rich aroma of baking bread. Garlic and dried onions hung from oak beams. The details were amazing. She had to keep reminding herself that this was only a reenactment, like the one she'd seen at Stirling Castle. Aunt Dora would love this place. Of course, her aunt would put up a fuss if they made her wear the clothes; hot, heavy and confining. She wondered why she'd given in so easily.

Her stomach growled, reminding her of the reason she was here. She stepped farther into the kitchen. Una stood behind a trestle table, kneading a mound of brown dough. As she flopped it over, a powdery mist of flour floated into the air.

Una looked up and smiled. "The clothes fit you well."

"Thanks."

The sleeves on her dress felt too tight and the bodice made her feel as if she were encased in shrink-wrap. She promised herself to wear baggy jeans and sweatshirts for a month when she got home.

"Is there something you seek?"

Amber walked over to the table. "My stomach feels as if it's turned upside down. Maybe a piece of bread would help."

Una wiped her hands on her soiled apron and reached for a knife. She cut a slice from the coarse loaf and handed it to Amber.

A chicken scurried past her feet, chased by a man in a kilt and a frayed shirt. The plaid in his costume was so faded, the colors were no longer distinguishable. He wielded a meat cleaver over his head and grabbed the bird around its throat. Flinging the squawking chicken on a table, he brought the blade straight down and whacked off its head. Blood spurted from the neck and flowed into a metal trough at the end of the table.

Amber backed against the stone wall. Her clothes felt tighter and the smells in the close quarters of the room had suddenly become suffocating. This was more authenticity than she could handle. Una looked at her with concern.

"What troubles you, lass? You look as white as new linen."

A small boy, his face encrusted with dirt and soot, brushed past her. He headed toward the hearth and the sizzling meat. He seated himself on a three-legged stool and began to turn the spit. In a matter of seconds sweat dripped down his face.

Amber edged away from the wall. Of course, this was none of her business. Maybe he was getting paid lots of money for his part in the reenactment and would not appreciate her interference. She hesitated. It had never stopped her before.

Una paused in the work of forming dough into braided loaves, seeming to have read Amber's mind. "Daniel will leave when the meat is done. But 'tis better than tending his father's herds in the bitter Highland winds."

So the boy had two choices; freezing or roasting. Maybe she could appeal to reason.

She cleared her throat. "His schoolwork is going to suffer if he's too tired to study." When she became a principal of her own school, she would make sure student activities did not interfere with their lessons.

Una rubbed the side of her face, leaving a smudge of flour. "The boy has no need to learn letters. This be a fine occupation. Because of it, his family has the scraps from the laird's table."

What Una said was not making sense. Unless . . . it was like Lachlan and Angus' conversation. They not only dressed as if they were living in the sixteenth century, they talked and acted like it. And then there was the business with the tutor. The events she'd experienced since she awoke scrolled through her mind. Like pieces of a puzzle, they started to form an answer.

The fire hissed as fresh drippings from the meat splattered onto the coals. She swallowed. The walls seemed to press in on her. Out of the corner of her eye she saw the man wipe the blood on his hands off on his shirt, and then walk over to Una. He pinched off a corner of the dough with his fingers and tossed it into his mouth. His teeth were black and decayed. On the table blood mingled with the dead chicken, fish and vegetables.

"A goblet of wine, lass?"

She shook her head. "I need some air."

Una pointed to an archway next to the fireplace.

Amber picked up her skirts, hurried in that direction and pulled the door open by the rope handle. A welcome rush of cold air swirled around her as she walked out onto the narrow balcony. She took a steadying breath as she looked at the purple heather that spread like a thick blanket over the endless hills and framed the shore on either side of the castle.

Amber closed her eyes, trying to remember. Without turning to her right, she knew there would be a rolling field that led to a road. The grass would be soft and there would be a cluster of alders where she and Steven had made love. She had been eighteen then and he was on vacation with his family. The flood of memories made her feel dizzy, and her legs started to buckle. She opened her eyes and gripped the railing to keep from falling. The cold rough stones cut into the palms of her hands. She knew where she was. She was at Urquhart, a castle that had been blown up in the eighteenth century. Amber was seeing Urquhart as it must have been before time and wars had destroyed it.

She gathered the heavy folds of her dress and walked slowly down the narrow steps to the courtyard. She concentrated on not slipping or falling. A dog barked as she reached the bottom of the steps. The noise grated as she headed toward the gate. She had to get closer to the water. Wide metal strips attached by large bolts crisscrossed the thick wooden door. It was clearly made to protect the people within the walls and to withstand ramming by an enemy. It was also made to keep the inhabitants in. Would she be allowed to leave? She slowed her pace and forced the panic out of her thoughts as she approached the gatekeeper. He was young and looked as if he shared the Viking belief that baths sapped your strength. He looked very strong. She hoped that he wasn't very bright.

He stepped in front of her. "Halt."

What could she say that he would believe? She pasted on a smile and tried to invoke a Highland brogue. "Salmon were left cooling in the loch. Una bid me fetch them for the laird's table."

He returned her smile; a toothy grin on a smooth face. She relaxed and watched him walk over to the levers that controlled the gate. It creaked open. Not wanting to wait in case the young man changed his mind, she ducked under the gate when it was only half open and hurried to the shore.

Her long dress weighed her down. She struggled to keep from losing her balance over the narrow path. Lachlan and Angus had talked about Mary, Queen of Scots, and Elizabeth I. Amber remembered a tour at Holyrood House she'd taken with Aunt Dora. The guide had told them about Mary's marriage to Lord Darnley and her pregnancy. So, if she had her time line straight, Lord Darnley was still alive and Mary hadn't been imprisoned by Elizabeth as yet. The year must be about 1566. She stumbled on an exposed root, but caught herself before she fell. Somehow she had slipped four hundred years into the past.

There was no doubt she was looking at Loch Ness, and no questions that Urquhart stood behind her: tall, powerful and intact. It was no longer the crumbling ruins of the twentieth century. She'd spent her summers as a guide on a tour bus, showing visitors this very spot. She knew the castle's history, knew the date it was first battered by the English and the MacDonalds and knew the year it was blown up to prevent it from serving as a Jacobite base.

The sun was going down behind the rolling hills as she made her way carefully to the shore. If she'd somehow passed into another century when she fell into the water, could she return the same way? Or would it not work a second time? The sensation returned, of bone-numbing water and the searing panic she'd felt when she nearly drowned. She remembered Lachlan pulling her toward warmth and safety. Would she have returned to her own time if he hadn't been there? Or would she have simply died? And why was she here to begin with? She rubbed her temples.

She tried to calm her mind and stop the racing questions by looking out over the gray waters of the loch. The air felt as though it was charged with electricity. The undeniable fact was that she had traveled to another time. The way she saw it, she had two choices. Get hysterical, or stay rational and find a way back.

A third choice surfaced. She considered it. If there was no way back, and she had to stay here, she would have to make a life for herself. Her family would think she had drowned and would go on about their lives. Her throat tightened. There would be no way to let them know she was all right, or for her to know how they were doing.

Amber sat down on a large rock near the shore. She felt warm tears on her cheeks. What would happen to

her aunt? And her brother, David? She brushed the
moisture from her face. He would have to take care of
Aunt Dora. Her students? Tears started again. They'd
hire a new teacher. An empty feeling grew in the pit of
her stomach.

Footsteps crunched over the loose rock-strewn path
behind her and she turned toward the sound. It was
Lachlan.

He stood beside her and gazed toward the water.
"The loch draws you. I, too, feel its pull." He paused.
"Or is there another reason that drives you to seek the
solitude?"

He was closer to the truth than she wanted to face.
She did not like people getting too close. As a child
she had ridden her bicycle to Urquhart at every
opportunity. It was a beautiful place.

"I just need some fresh air."

"Aye, I felt the same. But I fear the pull these waters
have on you will draw you once again to their depths.
And next time I may not be there to carry you to safety."

She looked at him and felt an icy shiver. It was as
though he'd read her thoughts. But there was something else. She saw concern in his eyes and didn't feel
smothered by it.

"I promise to jump in only when you are around."

Amber thought she saw the briefest hint of a smile
cross his face, but when she blinked it was gone. He
should smile more often. On second thought, she
liked him better when he was scowling. She realized
where she was and fought to hide any reaction. She
didn't have time for this. Looking out over the waters,
she tried to think about something else. A small ripple
marred the surface. She smiled, a little, thinking of all
the times she'd seen the same thing happen when she

was talking to the tourists and had led them to think it might be Nessie. It was great for the tour business.

"What amuses you?"

"Oh, I was just thinking of the legend about a creature that is supposed to haunt Loch Ness."

He seemed to draw back from her, his face was lost in the shadows. "There are many legends tied to these waters."

That was an understatement, but she had the overwhelming feeling that somehow an ancient myth was behind her appearance in the sixteenth century. She couldn't quite put her finger on why she felt that way, but the impression was there, nonetheless. Her aunt told and retold any story connected to the loch. Amber had heard them all. There was one that seemed relevant, if only she could remember. Maybe the answer to her return was incorporated in that tale. She stood, nearly tripping over her long skirts.

Lachlan reached out and held her arm until she regained her balance. Her skin felt warm where he touched her. Great, he was the type who pulled out chairs, opened doors and sent roses on Valentines Day. No, on second thought, his type didn't just send flowers, he'd have his private plane take his date to box seats at the opera and then give her flowers.

"I've heard of the Loch Ness monster, but it's a hoax."

"Lady Amber, it is real. It is a creature of an ancient clan that guards the entrance and destroys all who enter its domain."

She shuddered, remembering her experience in the loch. Maybe hysteria was a good option for her predicament, after all. Pushing the feeling down, she straightened.

"I don't scare easily, and I'm not the damsel in distress type. I've never heard of the creature being anything but shy and curious. That is, if you believe in that sort of thing."

His expression was unreadable, his voice devoid of emotion. "The hour is late and our meal grows cold."

He was avoiding her comment. She knew the tactic, she'd used it herself. "Actually, I'm not very hungry. I think I'll go up to the room."

"Una will prepare you something to eat."

"It's not necessary."

"Aye, lass, it is. There is much we have to discuss." She glanced at him. That was a mistake. His mouth was a straight line across his face, but his eyes held a depth of emotion that took her breath away. Her heart pounded in her throat. Amber realized she would have to slow down. She hoped that what he wanted to discuss were the political advantages of Scotland uniting with England. That, she could handle.

The night air was still, surprisingly warm for this time of year, and the waters over Loch Ness were mirror smooth. As she turned toward the castle she heard a splash. Looking over her shoulder she saw a dark shadow move across the water. Something large was swimming just beneath the surface.

"Betrothed?"

"Aye."

Amber chewed on the corner of her lip. Her aunt's dream was for Amber to marry, but the whole concept frightened her. It meant getting to know someone; their likes, dislikes, what made them happy, what made them sad. And then, after investing all that time with someone, you could wake up one morning and find out it was finished. Because love never lasted. Her parents were proof of that theory. After working side by side in archeological digs for twenty-two years, they'd announced their marriage was at an end. They said they no longer loved each other. Her mother had gone back to college to start over.

Amber rubbed her arms to warm them and glanced out the window of the chamber. Despite the warm night she shivered. She was freezing, sitting by the blazing fire.

"Exactly how far do we play this game?"

He regarded her seriously. "It shall be in name only, but will give you a position in the castle equal to Lady Marcail, and my sister, Elaenor. The inhabitants will respect you out of loyalty to their laird."

"And what would be you?"

He paused. "Aye."

"Perfect."

"You do not sound pleased. It is an honor to be my betrothed and will afford you much freedom." He arched his eyebrow. "Or is it that you already have a clan to which you belong? You need only mention the name, and we shall send word of your arrival."

Amber felt tears burn her eyes and shook her head. "There is no one here." The words struck her hard and she clutched the folds of her dress to keep her hands from trembling. She would never see her family again. Amber had taken it for granted that they would always be there for her.

She tried to control the rising panic. On top of everything else, Lachlan's package deal would rob her of her freedom. In Seattle she had all the independence she wanted. She had her own apartment, a job teaching high school, and her own mint condition,

VW bug convertible. And her chance to become a principal. Back home she had the knowledge that she didn't need anyone. She was independent, self-sufficient and completely on her own. It would be different in the sixteenth century.

At Urquhart castle she would be completely dependent on the goodwill of a Highland laird. She forced the tremors from her voice as the word "survival" surfaced in her mind. Amber had to find a way back to the twentieth century. She had to. She just needed time to figure it out.

"How . . . how long do I have, before we'll be expected to get married?"

"We shall follow the custom of handfasting: a year and a day."

Amber straightened. She knew all about the custom. "I thought you said our betrothal would be in name only?"

"And it shall be. However, the Highland clans are familiar with this ritual and there will be fewer questions."

She felt her nails cut into the palms of her hand. He must think she was an airhead. "I know all about handfasting. A couple live together for a year and a day in a sort of trial marriage, and if, by the end of that time, a child isn't conceived, they are allowed to either marry or go their separate ways."

She could feel the panic rise. Amber knew herself too well and was already physically attracted to Lachlan. If she allowed him into her bed and she became pregnant . . . her heart would be lost and inevitably crushed.

"We can't sleep together." Her voice seemed too loud. "Won't your people think it odd?"

"They will not concern themselves with such details."

"Really? Then why are we bothering with this elaborate plan?"

She saw the corner of his mouth turn up in a smile. "There does not appear to be much that escapes your notice."

Amber did not see the humor. "Not much."

He crossed the distance that separated them. "Very well, lass, after the passage of one full moon we shall have a formal betrothal and an engagement of unspecified length. My family is noted for such. As well as separate living quarters."

"Maybe I don't need your protection. Maybe there are people searching for me as we speak." The words rang true. Aunt Dora would be frantic and would have called her brother, parents and the entire population of Inverness.

"You have already stated there was no one. Besides, you would have mentioned them when first you awoke. Do not be concerned that I shall take advantage of our arrangement."

"It's not you I'm concerned about."

He paused, raising an eyebrow.

Her face burned. "That didn't come out right."

Her comment had surprised her as much as it did him. It was not that she felt he would force himself on her. Honor radiated from him as constant as the warmth from the fire. It was this betrothal thing. It would connect the two of them together. She put her hands on the cool panes of the leaded glass.

"I don't know why you are trying to help me."

The rushes crunched beneath his feet as he walked toward her. "All who find their way to Urquhart have my protection."

Amber turned. He had drawn an emotional mask over his features. She decided he probably would be a great poker player, but she suspected there was a hidden agenda. No one was that nice, not even this guy.

"So, what you are saying is that you would immediately ask any stray woman, who you pull out of Loch Ness, to marry you?"

"Nay lass, not all."

She felt as though a giant, prehistoric butterfly, like the ones her parents talked about, had taken flight in the pit of her stomach. Her emotions were starting to careen out of control as Lachlan left the room. She stared at the closed door. In the few relationships she'd been in, she was always the one who set the pace, intensity and duration. Already she felt a difference with Lachlan and it scared her. There was one way to make sure things didn't go any farther. She must find her way home.

Amber returned to the hearth. Okay, so she had somehow managed to travel back in time to 1566 without the aid of a star ship. That was four hundred and thirty-four years into the past and she had no clue how it had happened. She paused. Don't panic, there was an explanation for everything.

First of all, it was probably a dream. She thought of Lachlan, the cookroom and the bathtub. Well, so it's a sensory-packed, Technicolor-type dream, complete with a leading man who had thrown her into a tailspin. The dream theory was as solid as a sieve. Or could it be part of some legend her aunt was always talking about? There were some pretty amazing things that went on in the fantasy world of myths. She shook her head and ruled out the notion. Too far-fetched.

Next idea; time machine. The chance that she

would have noticed if she'd stepped into an H. G.
Wells contraption was pretty good. The only thing
she'd walked into, or rather been thrown into, was
Loch Ness. She remembered the sensation of being
pulled through the water. She snapped her fingers. Of
course, why didn't she think about it before. The
answer was speed. Einstein believed that if you
moved faster than the speed of light you could travel
through time. One of her students had brought her an
article about a physicist, Stephen Hawking, who had
tackled the same theory. The only problem with the
idea was she had fallen into the water, not onto some
futuristic spaceship capable of traveling faster than
the speed of light. The dream theory was starting to
gain ground again. What she needed were facts. And
the only way to get answers was to search Urquhart
for clues.

Old castles were notorious for their hidden chambers. This one was probably no exception. There
should be a lever to a secret room. Amber paced back
and forth in front of the fire. The walls rose to twice
the height of a normal room and were covered in
vibrant tapestries. She'd have better luck predicting
the weather in the Northwest than finding a hidden
chamber.

She rubbed the back of her neck and went into the
adjoining room. In the center was the wooden tub
with fresh dry linens lining the bottom and sides. On
the far wall were two doors. One led to the bathroom
and the other had a wooden bar across it. She smiled.
Perfect. A door with a lock. A great place to start.

The corridor was shrouded in darkness. Lachlan
raised his torch to illuminate the outline of the door

cut into the stone. He had not visited this tomb-like chamber since the summer solstice and the joining ceremony between Sarat and Madeline. With the sudden appearance of Amber in Loch Ness he needed to examine the clan's secrets contained within.

He reached the door and felt above the outline of it on the top edge until his fingers came in contact with a metal bar. He pressed down and stepped back. The door opened slowly, exposing a dark room. Entering, he placed his torch in a wall bracket. The flames cast shadows around the small chamber. Water from a crack in the stone ceiling dripped on the floor in a slow monotonous rhythm. He was directly beneath Loch Ness.

He walked over to a rose-colored marble slab that covered the wall facing the entrance and read the words etched into the stone:

❧

Time is an Illusion
❧

Of all the mysteries and legends that shrouded his people this was the one he had found the least plausible, until now. The Lady Amber had appeared in Loch Ness, and survived the numbing waters. She had not offered an explanation as to her origins.

He looked at a section of the panel where, centuries beyond counting, liquid gold had been poured into small holes in a random pattern. It covered a major portion of the marble. It was a map of the stars and planets, and recorded the year his people had been forced to leave their island home before the water reclaimed it. In the right-hand corner, below the points of gold that flickered in the light, a hole the size of a man's fist had been cut into the marble. In the center was a gold bar. He turned the lever and a panel slid open to expose a hidden compartment. Lachlan brought the torch closer. The marble surface seemed to change from rose-pink to a deep blood red as he examined the small glass vials.

Shadows from the torch stretched out across the floor and deepened in the corners of the room. A chill crept along his spine. One of the vials was missing. He recounted, but came to the same conclusion. The Elixir of Life was used for only two purposes. Once the liquid was swallowed, the process of immortality and the state of suspended sterility were reversed. The second purpose was the ability to summon the Guardian in Loch Ness.

Both uses were forbidden without permission from the Council of Seven, yet it had been done. Someone had entered the chamber, and removed one of the vials. The first purpose he dismissed. His race held on tightly to their immortality. The second would explain Amber's appearance. This was not the first time a missing vial had resulted in an unexpected visitor.

He wiped perspiration from his forehead with the back of his hand. The air was stale, damp and closing in on him. The Guardian of the Loch had the ability to bend the currents of time and pull someone from one century to another.

The steady drip of water in the corner of the chamber echoed through his mind. He closed his eyes, but the sound grew louder. He took one last look around before leaving the chamber. Soon the Council of Seven would gather and they would expect an explanation as to Amber's origins. But he must have proof.

The torch he held cast shadows over the walls of the corridor. This underground labyrinth was neither silent nor asleep. Small red eyes peered out of the darkness at him. Their owners scurried out of his way. Marcail feared these creatures, not because of their appearance, but because of the disease they could bring. His cousin had witnessed the Black Death. Lachlan knew the memories of its destruction still held her prisoner. He would discuss the matter with Angus. Together they could, perhaps, rid the castle of these vermin.

As he entered a narrow corridor he heard a loud thud, a scuffle and then an oath. It was a woman's voice. He headed in that direction, gripping the hilt of his blade. No doubt a servant who had lost her way. He would know the guilt or innocence by looking into her eyes. It would seal her fate.

The tunnels beneath the castle were forbidden to all but the members of his race. In his father's time, the punishment for any attempt to discover the secrets contained behind these walls would be a slow death. The skeletal remains of those who defied his father still remained, as a warning to others.

At the end of the corridor, in the shadows cast by a flickering torch, stood a woman. The Lady Amber. She was brushing dirt from her gown and muttering under her breath when she noticed him. Her face turned as pale as a shroud and her words came out in a rush.

"I . . . I was exploring the castle . . . looking for you."

Her statement was false, of that he was certain. Her expression reflected the inner battle she waged to overcome her fear at being discovered. And she was winning. Most women, indeed many men, would not have recovered their composure as quickly.

The image of the Map of the Stars flashed before his

eyes. His instincts told him he should not rule out the possibility that the chamber had been her destination. A rat scurried over his boot. He sidestepped out of the way.

Her laughter echoed through the tunnels, like a breath of fresh mountain air. He allowed himself to smile. "A disease-infested vermin attacks me, and you find it amusing?"

Her eyes sparkled with contained mischief. "Absolutely. It's comforting to see a big, strong, handsome man like you, frightened by something so small. It makes you seem more . . . human."

He raised his eyebrows. It had been a long time since he had felt human. He quickly swept the dark thoughts from his mind. "I would prefer to say that I was startled."

"You jumped a foot." Her laughing eyes challenged him. "Admit it. You almost dropped your torch."

He could smell the jasmine she'd used in her bath. The heady scent made him a little dizzy. And she met him as an equal. To him, that was the most potent fragrance of all.

"You are a long way from my chamber."

"You changed the subject, but I'll let you get away with it, this time. There's something else I wanted to talk to you about."

Lachlan suddenly felt as though he were a small child who had been caught taking a sweet from Una's cookroom. "And what would that be?"

"It's about the room. Would you mind if we went back now?"

Before he could answer, Amber walked past him toward the dungeons. He could not let her continue in that direction. Although, at present, they were uninhabited, the skeletal remains and the weapons of torture and death were in evidence in the dark cells. Lachlan had freed the prisoners after his father's death, but that had not washed away the guilt he had felt at not being able to stop the killings sooner.

"My chamber is in the opposite direction, lass."

"You keep referring to where I'm sleeping as 'your chamber'."

He followed her up a slight incline toward the stairs. The gentle sway of her gown and the outline of her form disturbed his concentration. "What did you say, lass?"

Amber turned so abruptly he stumbled back on the walkway. Her words came out in a rush. "If I'm going to stay here, I'd like to think that the room I'm sleeping in is mine."

Lachlan cleared his throat. He wished she were not so eager to keep him from her bed. "The chamber is yours. I have already set up my quarters in the west wing. We are betrothed in name only."

Amber relaxed visibly and he was aware of the gentle rise and fall of her breasts in the close fitting gown she wore. He doubted the waters of Loch Ness were cold enough to quench his growing desire. If she had asked, at this moment, for a bathing tub made from solid gold, he would have provided one.

MacDougal gnawed on a bone at Lachlan's feet. Lachlan relaxed in the high-backed carved chair and waited. His new quarters were sparse, but he preferred it this way. The fewer distractions, the sharper his mind. He knew what his father would have done had he found Amber near the chamber of the Map of the Stars. But then, he was not his father.

Loud voices broke the silence and the dog raised its head. The door opened and Bartholomew was pushed forward.

The schoolmaster stumbled awkwardly before regaining his balance. "You sent for me, Lord?"

"Aye." Lachlan allowed the anger he felt to be reflected in the tone of his voice. "Why is it that you are still here?"

Bartholomew bowed low with his arms outstretched. "I thought to plead for mercy, and to ask for a second chance."

The schoolmaster's words rang false and the expression in his eyes sealed his fate. Lachlan had been too distracted with matters of the Council to evaluate properly the man who was to teach his brother. It had taken the observations of an outsider to see through the thin veil Bartholomew had drawn over himself. This was not an honorable man, but Una had told him that Bartholomew was the father of Molly's babe and for her sake, he would reconsider.

He tapped his fingers on the armrest of the chair.

"I shall not speak against you if you seek employment in Inverness or any of the outlying villages. However, you will leave tonight, or you will not leave at all."

Chapter
4

❧

Amber snuggled deeper under the cover. The bed felt lumpier and noisier than she had remembered. She'd tell Aunt Dora about it when she went down for breakfast. She tried to hold onto the dream, but the threads of it were already fading. She stretched. It had something to do with Urquhart and a gorgeous man in a kilt who wanted to marry her . . . and something more.

She yawned, opened her eyes and looked around. Stark, gray stone walls greeted her. Amber sat up and shivered. Terrific, it hadn't been a dream. She tried to steady her breathing and took a deep gulp of cold air. It didn't help. Okay, so she was stuck here until she could find a way back home and she'd proved earlier this evening that she shouldn't wander around the castle. Particularly since she seemed always to be running into Lachlan. She was still recovering from the last encounter. Through the whole experience she'd had the overwhelming urge to pretend to stumble over loose pebbles and fall into his arms. Amber would be willing to bet a month's salary that his muscles were rock solid.

She stared out the window. It was the middle of the

night. Aunt Dora had always used hot milk and nut-meg as a cure for sleeplessness, restlessness, broken hearts, and just about anything else you could think of. Amber usually preferred a book and dark choco-late. Either way she was wide awake. He stomach growled. Okay, so she was awake and hungry. If she was going to deal with this situation, she needed sleep, and food. And not necessarily in that order.

She slid out of bed and winced as her feet hit the floor. There was only a thin layer of rushes by the bed. The floor was ice-cold. She tossed a blanket down to stand on and reached for the clothes piled on a chair nearby. For once she was glad she had numerous lay-ers to put on; at least she'd be warm. She started with the assortment of undergarments, eliminating the ones that required lacing in the back. She pulled the long-sleeved wool dress over her head and looked at the heavy embroidered tunic. Forget it. She'd just have to deal with whatever fashion police were up in the middle of the night.

After slipping on a pair of soft leather shoes, Amber picked up the candle. Before opening the door she glanced in the direction of the adjoining room. Candles lit the interior and their light appeared to focus on the door she'd used earlier. The wooden bolt was back in place and a larger, fiercer-looking lock secured it. The message was obvious. She didn't need the castle to fall on her to get the idea.

Torches flickered in the long corridor outside the room. Portraits of somber men and women lined the walls, like a gallery at a museum. She paused when she reached a dead end. To her left ran another hall-way and to her right she could see a stone staircase.

The comforting smells of baking floated through

the air. It was the back entrance to the kitchen that Molly had told her about. Una must have started cooking early. Amber picked up her skirts and walked casually down the stairs. She heard a squeaking sound. Rats. She shuddered and made a mental note never to come down this passageway again.

At the bottom of the stairs she pushed open the door. Dried herbs and clusters of garlic hung from a beam that ran lengthwise across the kitchen. Thankfully all the fish, meat and fowl from the evening meal had been cleaned up. The kitchen was spotless and smelled of cinnamon and cloves. She took a deep breath.

Candles, perched on a ledge above the fireplace, shed light on the long trestle table that was covered with flour. At the window a young woman, about fifteen or sixteen, sat with her legs tucked underneath her as she gazed out at the night. In her lap she held what looked like a small telescope. She recognized the young woman. It was Elaenor, Lachlan's sister. The telescope seemed an odd interest for a woman in the Middle Ages.

A cat meowed and Amber looked down toward a tabby ball of fur as it noisily lapped milk from a saucer near the stairwell. She bent down to scratch it behind the ear. The animal looked at her and hissed, before darting into the shadows.

"King Arthur does not like to make new friends."

Amber walked past the cold hearth toward the young woman who had spoken.

"Cats don't always like me at first. But I keep trying. I'm Amber."

Elaenor carefully held the telescope, untangled her legs and stood. "I know your name. You are the one my older brother pulled from Loch Ness, and the one he has announced he will marry."

Amber slipped her hands into the folds of her dress, in an attempt to appear casual. She hadn't a clue how a sixteenth century, betrothed woman was supposed to act. The good news was that these were usually marriages of convenience, so she didn't have to appear love struck every time Lachlan came into the room. Although, if she didn't regain some control, that was exactly how she was going to appear.

"You must have a lot of questions about your brother and me."

Elaenor shook her head. "Nay. The reason will be made plain with time. However, I am curious as to why you are awake at this hour. All in the castle have long since gone to bed."

That question was easy. "I couldn't sleep."

Elaenor sat on the table. Her feet dangled over the edge. "I have the same problem. Besides, tonight there were only a few clouds blocking the stars. I did not want to waste it by sleeping."

Angus had said that Elaenor preferred books to people. Amber could understand what the young woman felt. Escaping into a fantasy world had been a big part of her life as a child. She scooted awkwardly onto the table beside Elaenor and almost fell off when her legs tangled in the yards of fabric she wore. She pointed to the telescope.

"It's a good night for watching the stars."

"How is it that you know of such things?"

Amber shifted on the table to make herself more comfortable. She could always say she'd taken her students on a field trip to the observatory at the University of Washington in the twentieth century.

And then help the locals build a witches' bonfire for her. Or she could lie. Actually, a half-truth would work. She searched for the word used to describe Gavin's tutor.

"I'm a schoolmaster . . . ah, schoolmistress, and I read about it in a book." She knew that women in Italy had taught during this time period: her only hope was that Elaenor knew it as well.

Elaenor nodded as though the concept was not a new one to her. "Did you read that Copernicus published his theory stating that the planets revolve around the sun?"

Amber guessed by the way Elaenor was staring at her that the comment was considered controversial in the sixteenth century. What the heck. She figured she could only be burned once at the stake. Amber adjusted her skirts. "I think I've heard something like that."

"He also believes the planets and stars are driven by spirits." Elaenor looked down at her telescope. "What do you believe?"

Amber let her breath out slowly. She'd be willing to bet that everyone steered clear of Lachlan's sister. Elaenor went straight to the point. It was a little unsettling. She smiled. People like Lachlan's sister were a lot more interesting. In order to answer the young woman's question she should stick with the accepted theories of this time, so as not to bring down any suspicions on herself. Or she could eliminate a few superstitions. She chose the second option. Maybe it was time to take a few chances.

"I believe the planets move around the sun. The other part seems a bit far-fetched."

Elaenor set her telescope aside, jumped down from the table and picked up a poker from the fireplace. She stirred the dying embers until they crackled into flames. "I think so, as well."

"Where did you learn so much about astronomy?"

"Lachlan sent me to London with the Lady Marcail. They wanted me to develop interests outside of the books in my brother's library. Instead, I disguised myself as a boy and attended classes at Trinity College."

Amber took a fresh look at Elaenor. The history books she's read seemed to think women of this time period were content to sit at home, weaving tapestries until their fingers bled.

"That's terrific. Who gave you the idea?"

"The Lady Marcail. She was able to accomplish it when she decided to become a physician. I felt I could as well."

So, Marcail was a doctor. It explained Lachlan's confidence, but a picture of leeches and bloodletting came to mind. Amber made the decision to change the subject. "How long did it take before you were discovered?"

"Two years."

"And weren't Marcail and your brother worried?"

Elaenor shrugged. "Oh, Marcail discovered where I was right away and convinced Lachlan it would do no harm. She thought it was a grand adventure." Elaenor lowered her voice. "I think it was what she had in mind all along."

Amber slid off the table, reached for a stick from a woodpile and tossed it into the hearth. She smiled. "What about Lachlan?"

"That was different. He was a little sad. He thinks I should spend more time with people. But then, after talking to me for a time, he muttered something about warriors needing intelligent leaders and walked away. He feels responsible, somehow . . . but he is not to blame." Her voice trailed off and she stared at the fire for a moment before she continued. "How can I waste my time with people when there is so much to learn? Knowledge is the real power. It can never be taken away from you."

Amber put her hand on Elaenor's shoulder, suspecting the young woman was attempting to fill an emotional void in her life by immersing herself in books. It sounded as though Lachlan was trying to reach her, but he didn't know how. "Do you feel alone?"

"At times." Elaenor's mood changed abruptly and she turned her head to the side. "Do you smell something burning?"

Amber looked at the brick oven. "It smells like burnt sugar."

"Oh, no, it is my shortbread." Elaenor grabbed a long wooden paddle which hung on a hook by the wall. She opened the oven door, shoved in the paddle and pulled out a charred cake.

Amber glanced down at the smoking confection. "Well, I guess we'll just have to start again."

"I am always burning something. Everyone in the castle says it is because my mind is so full of ideas that I cannot concentrate on the things that are important."

"I think it's your ideas which are important. You can always make more shortbread."

"I was baking it for Lachlan. It is his favorite."

Amber had a feeling that Lachlan would like the shortbread regardless of how it tasted, but it was important to Elaenor that it was perfect.

"There's time to make more before Una needs her kitchen."

"Do you really think so? Wait right here, I shall get more flour." Elaenor disappeared through a doorway to the pantry.

The candles flickered over the mantel and Amber saw a shadow in the stairway. It was probably King Arthur coming to finish his milk. Maybe the cat needed a little coaxing. She walked toward the stairs and recognized Lachlan in the shadows. She wondered how long he'd been standing there.

"I would have thought your explorations under the castle would have satisfied you for the night, but as it happens, I am glad they did not." He nodded in the direction Elaenor had gone. "There are not many in the castle who would befriend her. Few can understand a woman's interest in learning."

"Probably because she knows more than they do, and that's intimidating." Amber could hear Elaenor rummaging around in the pantry. She motioned for Lachlan to follow her.

He ducked under the doorway and inspected the burnt pastry. Leaning over, he broke a piece off and popped it into his mouth. As he spoke, his voice seemed to reach the four corners of the kitchen. "Delicious. A sweet fit for the gods."

Out of the corner of her eye Amber saw Elaenor emerge from the pantry, carrying a sack of flour. A smile covered the young woman's face. For all his gruffness Lachlan clearly had a soft spot for his younger sister.

"Do you really think it is good? It looks and smells terrible."

Lachlan reached for another chunk. "Looks do not always tell the full story. I know of none better in the Highlands."

Amber watched the two of them. She'd seen Lachlan walk around the castle with his emotionless mask firmly in place, but he was a marshmallow when it came to his family. She doubted whether he even realized how much they meant to him. He was too busy being everyone's protector. She suddenly thought of her brother, David. He was going to Washington State University and was not any better than she at keeping in touch. She remembered when she'd made cookies for them to eat at teatime. Her dog wouldn't touch them, but David ate every last one. Of course, the next day he cut off one of her braids while she slept. Amber felt tears form in her eyes. She was going to miss David.

A crash announced Angus' arrival as he stumbled into the room. "May the gods take that blasted cat of Lady Elaenor's. It tripped me."

Lachlan folded his arms across his chest. "More likely it was your own feet that caused you to lose your balance. It appears the whole castle is awake."

Angus tugged at his beard. "I have word of Subedei."

Amber noticed Lachlan's instant change in mood. He grabbed the remaining shortbread and motioned for Angus to follow him. At the entrance he paused and turned around. He looked as though he wanted to say something, but instead he nodded and then was gone. Amber watched him leave. The impenetrable wall built around his emotions was an illusion. She wondered what he would be like without his barriers.

Elaenor tugged on her sleeve. "Please, would you help me to clean up the cookroom?"

Amber followed Elaenor's gaze. It was lighter outside. In a few hours the kitchen would be in full swing. "Let's get to work."

Una came through the door from the courtyard, carrying pails of steaming milk. She seemed to ignore the mess as she set the buckets on the table. "I see that you have made another batch of shortbread for your brother."

Elaenor smiled. "He said it was 'fit for the gods.' "

Una turned and winked at Amber. " 'Tis sure I am the lad said as much and more."

Amber watched as Una brought order back to the kitchen. She was surprised that everyone had accepted her as though she were a distant relative who'd come for a visit. They'd welcomed her, offered their protection, been kind to her, and brought her into their confidence. She wanted to believe there were people like this in the world. Certainly Aunt Dora would have done the same if a stranger had washed up on her doorstep. But what would happen if they found out she was from the future?

She remembered reading about the Salem witch trials in school. Beginning with accusations against ten young women, nineteen had been hanged and one pressed to death before the governor stopped the hysteria. An outbreak of disease, or the death of a child, would result in a town looking for a witch to blame.

Amber shuddered. She'd dropped into a past with as many superstitions as those that had plagued Salem a century later. If she didn't want to suffer the fate of those young women, she'd have to be careful. Keeping busy would help.

Books lined one wall in the well-lit chamber where Lachlan sat hunched over a parchment map. Subedei was indeed on the march, and had left a path of destruction in his wake. He must be stopped. A knock pulled him from his thoughts.

"Enter."

Una stalked into the room. Wisps of hair escaped from under her cap. She held a wooden spoon in one hand and a slate board in the other. "You must do something about Lady Amber."

All had been well when they had shared a meal in the Great Hall this morning. She had mentioned that too liberal an amount of salt was used in the preparation of the meal, but that was all.

"What is it that should be done?"

Una was clearly unsettled. "Come and see for yourself."

The woman turned and left the room as abruptly as she had entered. He pushed away from the table and resigned himself to what was to come.

Una rarely lost her temper, except when the boundaries of her territory were threatened. He followed her down the corridor that led to the Great Hall. All was quiet as he entered the chamber. Too quiet. Una had not stopped, but kept her hurried pace.

Once in Una's domain, Lachlan paused. There was an odd feel to the cookroom.

Una tapped her foot on the ground and folded her arms across her chest. "A few hours ago, Lady Amber paid me a visit. She said that she could help make **my** work easier. I agreed out of respect for you."

Lachlan cringed. He knew that tone; it did not bode well. "Continue."

"She has moved all the platters, utensils, foodstuffs, crates, pots, wood, herbs, flour . . ."

"Stop. For what purpose has she rearranged these items?"

Una poked him with her spoon. "She said if I started at the shelf by the door with all the items that began with an 'A,' and worked my way to the pantry on the far wall, ending with all the items that began with a 'Z,' I would know where to find things." Una sighed impatiently. "I knew the location of my supplies before Lady Amber arrived. Since this woman has organized my cookroom, I cannot find a thing. Until you have this matter settled, and I have my cookroom back the way I want, bread will not be baked from these ovens, fish, venison, and fowl will not be dressed for the fire pit . . ."

Lachlan interrupted her, holding up his hand. "I understand. You have made your point. I shall see to it."

The expression around Una's eyes softened. "Be gentle with the lass. She is away from her family and only seeks to fill the empty space left in her heart."

He scratched his beard. Women. He would never understand them. A moment ago Una was breathing fire hot as any dragon's. But in the blink of an eye, she had softened toward Amber. He shook his head. At times, like these, he believed that men had only the power women allowed them to have.

"Amber, there is something we must discuss." Lachlan had spent the better part of the day searching for her and had found her in the solar with what might be every book in the castle. She sat perched on a chair as if ready for flight. He hesitated and waved his hand over the uneven stacks of books. "Is there a reason for this?" He had not meant his question to sound so abrupt, but she smelled of that damned jasmine.

She folded her hands in her lap. "I don't see how anyone can find things when they're scattered all over the castle. So I decided to put all the books in one room. The only thing I haven't yet determined is whether to sort them on the shelves by author, or by title. Do you have a suggestion?"

He did. But he was sure that burning the lot of them was not an option she would favor.

"The task you have set for yourself is vast."

"I'm good at organizing. And I'm bored to death. Should I help Una in the kitchen? I can make desserts, but that ends my cooking talents. Sew? Hemming a dress would probably take me all day. And I haven't the faintest idea how to milk a cow, pluck chickens, herd sheep . . ."

"Enough. You need not concern yourself with any of this. Lady Amber, you are my betrothed." He wished he could take back the words. She began to tap her foot. It appeared the number of females in the castle whom he had offended was growing. Amber's frown deepened. Now he knew why Angus had remained a bachelor.

"What is it that would interest you?" The silence grew so heavy that he could almost feel it when she spoke.

"I want to teach."

The words hung in the air. Schoolmasters were men. The question of from where she came loomed like a dark shadow between them. And then he remembered his journeys to Italy. It was not unusual for there to be women tutors in that country. Wherever Amber came from perhaps it was the same.

Lachlan heard his brother running down the hall, chased by a string of wolfhounds. The lad had too much time on his hands since Bartholomew's dismissal. He paused. A brilliant idea formed. He clasped his hands behind his back. "I have decided you shall teach Gavin his letters."

Her eyes grew wider. "But I only teach . . . well, maybe it would work." She seemed to be talking to herself more than to him. "All right, but I'll have to put these books away first. And if I'm going to teach your brother, we will need a schoolroom. This place would be perfect. A lot of light, shelves for materials and easy access to the outside. Gavin will love it."

Lachlan was not so sure. The lad hated doing his lessons. "There is one condition." He wondered how he had been talked into being a mediator between two women. It appeared doomed from the beginning.

Her expression grew serious. "And what would that be?"

He softened his voice. "You must cease interfering in Una's cookroom and you must allow her to put everything back the way it was before you decided to 'help.' Una takes pride in her duties at keeping the castle running smoothly."

"And when I invaded the cookroom she felt I was taking over." Amber took a deep breath. "That was stupid of me. Would it help if I offered to put things back the way they were?"

"Perhaps."

"You really dislike seeing people upset." Amber reached up and kissed him on the cheek. "Don't worry. Your secret's safe with me. You're a good man, Lachlan MacAlpin. Even if your beard is a little scratchy."

She whisked away from him and began straightening the solar. He felt his beard. Scratchy?

* * *

As the door to the solar closed, Amber felt the walls closing in. "Teach?" She slammed a leather bound book on the shelf. "I already have a teaching job. It's in Seattle, in the twentieth century, in a building with hot and cold running water, real bathrooms and electricity."

She'd said the words out loud. It didn't matter. No one was around to hear her and it felt good to vent her frustration. She paused. This was crazy. She had to get back to the life that awaited her in her own time.

A shadow passed over the bookshelves. It wasn't from the sun. The angle was wrong. Lachlan? Possible. For a large man, he had the remarkable ability to enter a room without being heard. Panic held her frozen to the floor. How could she explain the things she'd said? Amber tightened her hold on the remaining book in her hand, as though it were a life raft, and turned slowly. She was not alone.

In the center of the room stood a frail woman who looked to be in her late eighties or nineties. Her features were delicate and her snow-white hair hung in gentle waves past her waist. The gown she wore was embroidered with Celtic symbols and the style resembled those worn in Greece thousands of years ago. The figure of the woman remained so still, and the clothes so outdated, Amber thought she might be looking at a ghost. She let out the breath she'd been holding and made a mental note to be scared later. At least a ghost didn't talk and therefore, couldn't repeat what she'd said.

"I am called Diedra, mother to Lachlan MacAlpin."

Amber nodded and decided to hope the woman's hearing wasn't as clear and strong as her voice. In any event, she was now face to face with her potential mother-in-law. She felt nervous, and that was silly as she was betrothed in name only.

Diedra motioned for Amber to follow her through the door into a small enclosed garden outside. Amber complied. She hoped Lachlan's mother believed the story that Amber was from Italy. If not, she would have to think of another plausible explanation. She didn't want anyone becoming suspicious. The known world to the people in the sixteenth century was not that extensive. Amber could pick a country that hadn't been discovered as yet, and naturally an exotic country would have equally exotic words. It could work. The voice of reason told her she would have had a better chance if Diedra was a ghost.

Amber shielded her eyes from the sun and followed Diedra to the far corner of the garden. Explaining how electricity worked might be easier than talking to a potential mother-in-law. Lachlan's details of their betrothal had been sketchy, to say the least. The story he was telling was that they'd met in Italy and fallen in love at first sight. Amber had told him she didn't believe in such a thing and he'd said her comment was beside the point. That had ended the discussion.

Lachlan's mother slowed down. She stopped beside a lattice-work fence enclosing a single grave. Amber shivered as the original idea resurfaced, that she was dealing with a ghost.

Diedra pointed to the pink marble headstone. Ivy clung to the smooth sides and wound in lacy softness around the large marker. Amber moved closer in order to read the name printed in block letters: FORD. That was an odd name for this century. But then, she'd never given much thought to where names originated. Maybe the ancestors of the man who'd invented the Model T Ford had been from Scotland.

"You are deep in thought. Does the name 'Ford' hold meaning to you?"

Amber straightened and shook her head. She didn't trust her voice. Her aunt always said Amber would never make a good poker player. If her expression didn't give away the cards she held, the inflection in her voice did.

Diedra shook her head slowly and her shoulders slumped forward. The woman seemed to grow older and more frail. "You are afraid. You shouldn't be, you can't be. It shall not work if you are." She held her hand out to Amber and opened her palm.

Amber swayed against the fence. Keys. Were they hers? She focused. No, her car was a Volkswagen. And cradled in the woman's hand was a set to a twentieth-century Ford automobile. The make of the car was stamped on the metal. Someone had time traveled before her. And died.

The sun streamed in through the window and warmed the small alcove where Amber sat beside Gavin. It was the mildest fall she'd ever remembered, but she wasn't going to complain. It put everyone in a good mood and people talked more when things were going well. A week had passed since she'd seen the grave. At first Amber had feared that whomever had traveled through time had been killed, but that hadn't been the case. Una had answered many questions and Elaenor had filled in the rest.

A few years ago the man had been found washed up on the shore clutching the keys Amber had seen in Diedra's hand. The inhabitants of the castle had assumed he'd fallen in and drowned. It was very possible. The waters of Loch Ness were reportedly thirty-two degrees Fahrenheit. Too cold to survive long without a dry suit. The man must have traveled back in time in much the same way she had, but he hadn't been as lucky. No one had been there to pull him out. All her hope of returning had faded with that knowledge. She had survived Loch Ness once, there was no way of knowing if she would be able to do it a second time. And she wasn't even sure if jumping in the water would transport her back. She rubbed her temples. There were still too many unanswered questions.

As each day sped by, she settled more into a routine and she could feel a sort of resignation seep through her. Her parents had taught her that one of the reasons mankind survived was because of his adaptability. She'd never needed that skill more than now.

She watched Gavin read aloud from one of the stories in *The Canterbury Tales*. It was the "Squire's Tale." When she was a little girl, her aunt had read these stories aloud to her each night before she went to bed. At first she'd agreed to teach Gavin because she couldn't think of anything better to do. Teaching an eight year old, who had a dislike for school in the first place, did not sound appealing. She was a high school teacher. However, it hadn't been so bad. In fact, of late, she had begun to rethink her decision to quit classroom teaching to become a principal. Maybe it was seeing Lachlan talking to his men or showing Gavin how to hold a bow that had influenced her. He used his time as if each moment counted. Her life in Seattle, was such a blur of activity she barely stopped long enough to notice the seasons. Maybe when she returned home . . . Amber shook her head. She needed to concentrate on the present.

She rubbed her shoulder. Every morning, right before she awoke, in the fleeting moments between dreams and awareness, she thought she had returned to the twentieth century. But it never happened. And learning about the man called Ford had made the possibility of her returning to her own time seem remote. So she filled her days with teaching. When Gavin was unavailable she continued to search the castle for answers to her many questions. Although she had found none, she was becoming well acquainted with Urquhart.

Gavin nudged her. "The knight in the 'Squire's Tale' gave King Cambuskan four gifts. I would choose the sword which could slay any beast, known or unknown. It would cut through even the hardest rock. Which gift would you favor?"

Amber smiled and tousled the curls on the boy's head. She knew he'd like this story. It was always fun pretending what you would do with the magical gifts. She leaned back in her chair.

"Let's see. One of the gifts was a brass horse which could fly faster than the wind. Another was a mirror that could inform the owner of the thoughts of both friends and enemies." She smiled. "On second thought, I do not want to know what people are thinking, so I'll rule that one out. I know. What do you think about the ring?"

Gavin tilted his head and looked down at MacDougal who slept at his feet. "This magical ring would give me the power to understand any language, even MacDougal's?"

Amber nodded.

"Then that's what I shall have."

She smiled. Gavin had protested that he hated to read. She suspected his tutor had made him study from books that were both too advanced for the eight year old, as well as ones that would have bored the more industrious student. When she discovered he could read, but was just convinced he couldn't learn, she tried a simple method she used with her high school students. The trick was to find a book that would follow their interests. Before they realized it, they would be involved in the story. Usually after reading the book their confidence in their ability to finish a project gave them encouragement to tackle other things. Gavin had made a connection with the hero in the story and was concerned about what would happen next. It was a good sign.

"You have not asked me what gift it is I would choose."

She looked up with surprise. Lachlan was leaning against the wall with his arms folded across his chest; watching her. She felt the hairs on the back of her neck prickle. She should be used to it by now, he was always appearing out of the blue when she least expected it. Not that she minded, in fact, she was beginning to look forward to his visits.

He pushed away from the wall and walked toward her. "The mirror. That is what I would choose. Not to use it to see into the thoughts of a person, but to foretell the future."

Gavin nodded. "I know the reason. It is so that you can predict when Subedei will attack."

"Aye, lad. That would be very useful information. But I do not need a magic mirror to foretell Angus' humor if you are absent from the training field."

Gavin closed his book, scraped his chair on the

wood floor and stood. "Angus was to help me with my crossbow. I hope he will not change his mind."

He handed *The Canterbury Tales* to Amber and whispered something to Lachlan before running down the hallway.

Lachlan raised an eyebrow as Gavin turned a corner and disappeared. This was not the first time he heard that Amber had made a difference in someone's life. Elaenor had mentioned it, and now his brother. He sat down in the vacant chair and stretched out his legs.

She hugged the book closer to her. "What did he say to you?"

He wondered how Amber would react to what Gavin had said. "My brother wants to keep you."

"Like a pet?"

"Nay, lass, but the question still lies heavy. What am I to do with you?"

"Do with me?" Her voice was laced with a sour note. "You're talking about me as if I were a book on the wrong shelf."

He shifted uncomfortably in his chair and decided he had better not tell her that her comparison had hit the mark. He swallowed. "I expressed myself poorly."

She tapped lightly on the book. "True, but I have the basic idea. You want to take care of me. That's not necessary. In fact, maybe we should reconsider the whole betrothal thing."

Lachlan sighed. He was no closer to discovering whether or not it was the Guardian who had brought Amber to these shores the night he pulled her from Loch Ness. If the legend had come to pass, Amber would return in a very short span of time. The thought disturbed him. Each day he would seek her out on some pretext or other. He smiled. She had an opinion about everything. If she were not connected to the legend, the betrothal would not be necessary. A few of his men had already expressed an interest in her. They would keep their distance, but not if the betrothal was absolved. He did not like to think of that, nor for that matter, of Amber with another man.

He heard the soft tap of Amber's foot on the stone floor.

"Do you always take this long to answer a simple yes or no question?"

He needed the wisdom of the gods to form the right words to say to her. That it was important flashed in his mind as sharp as the point of his sword. "The answer as to whether or not we should be betrothed is not an easy one. There is a rank and order to things. An unattached female makes everyone uneasy. I would not put you at risk." There was truth in his words. He hoped she could hear them.

He heard laughter and saw Elaenor running down the hallway toward him. It had been a long time since he had seen his sister in such a happy state. There was little doubt that the friendship Amber offered was responsible.

Elaenor stopped short. "Angus announced there will be a festival in Inverness to celebrate the bountiful harvest as well as the unseasonably good weather. He also suggested that you would be willing to take us."

Lachlan stood. "Did he now? I have not the time to indulge in such things. There shall be other festivals."

"There will not be another until next year." Elaenor looked at Amber. "Tell Lachlan he has to take us."

He turned just in time to see the expression on Amber's face. He was doomed.

"Your brother wants to take care of us." Amber

emphasized the last few words as if they were a challenge. She glared straight at him, pinning him to the wall with her words. "Seeing to our happiness would come under that heading. I'm sure he will be happy to take us to the festival."

Elaenor hugged him and then kissed him on the cheek. "You are wonderful to us, Brother."

He watched helplessly as she grabbed Amber's hand and walked down the hallway. Amber turned to wave at him. He had the distinct impression that he was no longer master of his castle.

Chapter
5

❦

The creaking of leather mingled with the rhythmic sound of the horses' over the travel-worn road. Amber clung to the saddle of her mare. Lachlan led the group. She decided he was in his King of the Hill role today, aloof, distant and still wondering how he got talked into taking them all to the festival. Amber was glad he wasn't talking to her. She had begun to enjoy his company too much.

Lachlan was followed closely by Angus, Gavin and Elaenor. A half dozen men rode behind Amber, no doubt ready to pick up the pieces if she fell off her horse. They were all going to Inverness. How ironic. She'd spent most of her first day in the sixteenth century trying to convince herself that the people at Urquhart were reenacting a Renaissance or medieval festival. Now that was exactly where she was headed, but she was the one playing dress-up instead of Lachlan and his clan.

Through the occasional break in the dense foliage, Amber caught a glimpse of the waters of Loch Ness in the morning light. She knew this stretch of road through Fairy Glen. During her three summers working as a tour guide on a blue and white bus painted with the pictures of a smiling Nessie, she'd traveled this road twice a day. The green serpent-like creature had been sprawled along the length of the bus. She wondered if the shadow she'd seen under the water that first night really was the Loch Ness monster. She looked out over the water. In four hundred years the trees would be thinned out so the tourists would have a better view of the water and of the elusive creature that haunted the loch. She wished she were riding in the air-conditioned bus, instead of on the back of a horse. Every muscle in her body ached.

The sound of a solitary eagle's cry as it flew overhead pierced the tranquility. It was completely alone. That was not so terrible, was it? Amber had felt the same way in Seattle. She felt she could accomplish more when she was alone. And, after all, she had her independence and her job. What more did she need? She straightened in the saddle. She didn't like having time to think. Amber wanted her own life back. The life that wouldn't allow her the luxury of reflection. She tried to adjust into a more comfortable position on top of her horse, but gave up. Una had produced a trunk full of clothes for her to wear, but the material was heavy and most of the gowns drab in color. She wondered how much trouble she'd get into if she tried to show someone how to make slacks.

Her long, heavy dress was bunched up, she was beginning to sweat and she was hungry. It seemed to be taking forever to travel on horseback the eight to ten miles from Urquhart to Inverness. To make this occasion even more perfect, she would be sore for days. Just one more thing she'd have to endure.

She knew she was wallowing, no, fully submerged

in self-pity. It felt good. She deserved it. The last few weeks had been spent trying to make the most of her situation, either by teaching Gavin and Elaenor, or trying to find out how she'd arrived in the sixteenth century. Convincing herself she had the opportunity of a lifetime to observe medieval life firsthand was not working. Where'd it get her? On top of a smelly, flea-bitten horse and no closer to finding a way home.

The animal whinnied and tossed its head. Amber looked up. They'd stopped. Now what? They couldn't have arrived in Inverness yet. They had not passed the spot where she knew a haunted house would stand one day. A messenger approached Lachlan and handed something to him. She saw him glance at the folded piece of paper before giving it to Elaenor. The young woman ripped the seal open and began to read. When she'd finished she looked in the direction of the loch and then back down at the letter. Amber was too far away to hear their whispered conversation, but Lachlan seemed upset. His sister reached over and kissed him on the cheek before turning her horse around.

Elaenor reined in her horse as she approached Amber. "I must return to Urquhart at once. This letter is from a close friend of mine. Elizabeth wrote to me about a theory we share. I have to test it. I must not delay in my research."

Amber had noticed that in just the short time she'd been at Urquhart, Elaenor ate little, slept less and was always bent over a book or manuscript of some kind. Amber's horse leaned its head down and began to nibble on the tall grass by the side of the road. She pulled on the reins, but the horse just shook its head and resumed eating. If she had a sugar cube or carrot, she would eat it herself before she'd give it to the beast. She hoped she was better with humans.

If ever there was someone who needed a holiday, it was Lachlan's sister. "You were looking forward to the festival."

Elaenor took the letter out of the folds of her dress. "You don't understand."

Amber knew Elaenor wasn't talking about the ingredients in shortbread. If she ever got back to Seattle, she'd dispel the notion that women of this time period were content to sit around and do needlepoint. But the young woman still needed to take a break.

"Your mind will work better if you take time to relax. Can't your theory wait until after the festival?"

Elaenor looked down at the letter in her hand. She seemed to be weighing her options. "Lachlan did say he would help me gain access to the old records if I attended the festival."

Amber smiled. At least he didn't think his sister's interests were frivolous. She leaned over and patted the mare's neck.

"Why don't you consider your research postponed for a day, instead of canceled. Besides, I need help with my horse. It seems she has decided to be the one in control."

Elaenor laughed and gazed once again in the direction of Loch Ness. "You are right. I do so want to go to Inverness. The mystery has waited this long; I doubt that another day or two will matter." She reached over and squeezed Amber's hand. "I have been the cause of too much delay. It is time to resume our journey."

The waters of Loch Ness reflected the clear mid-morning sky. Its jagged shoreline was softened by alders and lush underbrush. Amber walked beside Elaenor and waited for the young woman to speak. Ever since Lachlan's sister had received the letter, she'd been lost in her own thoughts. Amber understood the need to sort out things on one's own and didn't interrupt her.

Elaenor sat on a fallen tree that was picked clean of branches and leaves by the harsh Highland winds. She adjusted her skirts and motioned for Amber to join her.

"The men will give us a short rest."

Amber laughed and rubbed the back of her legs. "I think I'll stand. I can't decide if I'm glad we're taking a break, or if I'd just as soon finish the ride on my bony horse quickly."

A golden eagle flew overhead. Its cry rang over the hills as powerful wings propelled the bird in effortless slow motion toward the opposite shore. Amber watched its flight. It had been a long while since she'd had the luxury to just watch a bird fly without feeling she was wasting her time.

Elaenor picked up a small pebble and threw it into the water.

"You have an endless supply of time to spend with Gavin and me. And, we are most grateful." Elaenor hesitated. "Lachlan needs someone to show him how to laugh."

Amber cleared her throat to keep from smiling. "I think he likes being the serious type. He's quite accomplished at it, too."

Elaenor twirled the intricate silver ring on her finger. "He was not always as you see him now. I worry that he grows further and further away from us." She looked over at Amber. "Please, before it is too late."

Amber heard the shrill sounds of the eagle in the distance. Its cry echoed, mingling with Elaenor's plea. Okay, so the man was obviously a workaholic. If he lived in the twentieth century he'd be a CEO of a major corporation, and a candidate for bypass surgery at age forty-five. Elaenor's eyes glistened with tears as Amber sank down beside the young woman and put her arm around the girl's shoulder. What was it about her that all someone had to do was say "please" and she would give in?

"Okay, I'll do it, but there are no guarantees. I can only try."

Elaenor nodded slowly. "I know."

A command to mount the horse pierced the quiet. It was time to leave. Darn, they hadn't been forgotten. She stood and motioned for Elaenor.

"Don't worry, everything will be all right."

Elaenor's face brightened into a smile and she whispered a thank-you before moving to her horse.

Amber was not in as big a hurry. One of Lachlan's men had helped her dismount from her horse and there would no doubt be someone there to help her remount the beast from hell. And to top off the day, she'd just made a promise she didn't know how she was going to keep.

Elaenor and Gavin rode ahead of Amber along the narrow path to a place where water splashed and churned over the smooth rocks in an inlet off the River Ness. It was an eerie feeling to be on the outskirts of town and still have none of the buildings look familiar. Lachlan led the procession into Inverness. A handful of his men were behind her. Banners in gold, red and blue fluttered on poles surrounding the field. The festival was in full swing.

Lachlan raised his arm signaling for them to stop and she reined in her mount. It appeared that he intended to leave their horses by the river and walk the rest of the way to town. A quarter mile at the most but it would seem like five in her long dress. She raised herself in the saddle to get a better view and nearly lost her balance. As she righted herself the horse turned its head and stared at her.

Amber straightened. "What are you looking at?"

Up ahead Lachlan and the party dismounted. Gavin and Elaenor slid to the ground and waved to her before handing their reins to Angus. They hurried toward what looked like a Punch-and-Judy show. Behind her Amber heard the sound of metal and leather as the men followed Lachlan's command. Well, she'd climbed on this beast, getting off should be a snap.

The sun warmed her face as she unhooked her knee from the saddle and readjusted her weight. Parts of her felt numb. The same person who had invented women's corsets had probably been consulted on sidesaddles. Amber took her foot out of the stirrup and jumped to the ground. She fell forward, landing face first. Something sharp poked her. Amber pushed herself to a sitting position and rubbed her chin. It was sore to the touch and felt as though she'd scraped off a layer or two of skin. Terrific. Her face had zeroed in on the one protruding rock in the vicinity.

The men who had ridden behind her hurried to her side, but backed away as if on cure when Lachlan's shadow blocked the sun. He smelled of leather, horse, and impatience. A scowl covered his face. Something had set him off. Most likely something she'd done, or failed to do. He'd probably wanted to help her down off the monster horse, and she'd robbed him of the opportunity to play the chivalrous knight. Good.

"You have injured yourself. You should have waited for my aid."

She ignored the hand he offered and struggled to her feet. Her loss of pride at her clumsiness hurt worse than the bruises. She had always considered herself coordinated, had even played soccer in college on a scholarship. She brushed away loose grass and twigs.

"I thought I could handle getting off the beast."

"Her name is Guinevere. And you should not be afraid to ask for my help."

He shouted to his men. "Secure the horses." The sound of his voice startled a covey of quail in a nearby bush. They flew off.

Amber watched as his men hurried to obey his commands. Great, they would follow him through the proverbial gates of hell, and he was releasing his frustrations with her on them.

"Do you always have to shout so loud? I think the sound of your voice carried all the way to Urquhart Castle."

He faced away from her, his back an impenetrable wall. "You need not concern yourself in such matters."

She counted to ten, in Latin. An accomplishment her parents had insisted upon. But even struggling over the ancient language hadn't succeeded in calming her down. "I just don't think you need to yell to get your point across."

He ignored her. This man was hopeless. Keeping her promise to Elaenor was going to be next to impossible if Amber couldn't prevent Lachlan from taking himself too seriously. An idea formed that would both show him it was not a good idea to ignore her as well as distract him from his tirade. She rummaged through the leather bag Una had packed and pulled out a thick slice of cheese, wrapped in a cloth. Amber uncovered it, broke off a chunk and walked over to him. She tapped him on the shoulder, interrupting his latest string of command. So much the better.

As he turned around, his brows drew together in a line across his face. A snarling pit bull would look cute next to this man. And Elaenor wanted her to turn him into a fun-loving lapdog? Impossible. She reached for his hand and placed the cheese in his open palm.

"Put this in your mouth, it will keep it occupied."

He frowned. "No one has ever talked to me thus."

As fierce as he was trying to look she noticed his expression change. The man was trying not to smile. She pressed her point. "Everyone is afraid to disagree with their laird. You say, 'jump' and they say, 'how high.' Don't expect me to do the same."

He made a slight bow. When he raised his head, the corners of his mouth were definitely turned up in a smile.

Amber relaxed. Maybe there was hope for him yet. She headed in the direction she'd seen Elaenor and Gavin go. The aroma of fresh baked bread and pies laced with cinnamon floated through the morning breeze. Shouts of children's laughter mingled with the lively notes of a fiddle. The festival was in full swing and she was going to have a good time. She looked over her shoulder. Lachlan was watching her. Amber suppressed the impulse to wave at him and decided the trip on the beast might have been worth it after all.

Gray stone buildings obstructed the light and warmth of the afternoon sun as Lachlan walked beside Angus in silence. Their horses' hooves clattered over the cobblestones and drowned out the laughter and merriment of the festival crowd at Inverness. A vision of Amber as she listened to Gavin reading aloud from *The Canterbury Tales* came to mind. The tranquil scene had made him forget who he was for a time.

As he turned a corner he saw the Rose and Thistle Inn. The shouts of men and the words of a bawdy song drifted toward him. Angus slapped him on the back and pointed in the direction of a sign that creaked and swayed in the afternoon breeze.

" 'Tis a welcome sight, laddie, after the long ride from Urquhart. I shall secure our accommodations and a warm meal."

Angus tossed the reins of his horse to a boy about Gavin's age before entering the inn. Lachlan hesitated. The boy was dressed in little more than dirty rags. Cupping the boy's chin, he tilted the lad's face toward him.

"By what name are you called?"

"Thomas, sire." His voice rang clear and strong.

A man burst from the tavern, stumbled and then passed out on the dusty road. His plaid was indistinguishable; his face scarred by the harsh life he had lived. The bright colors and laughter of the festival could not hide the poverty and despair that claimed many in the Highlands. Lachlan reached into the leather pouch strapped to his belt and pulled out a coin. He placed it in the boy's hand.

"Take care of the horses. Now, off with you."

Thomas led the horses to a stable behind the tavern. He looked to be a sturdy lad with a spirit that had not been crushed by hard times. If Lachlan discovered the boy was without family or clan, he would take him back to Urquhart.

Lachlan entered the tavern, brushing the dust from the road off his plaid. Dim light filtered through the dirt-encrusted windows and rested in the pub where men crowded together in hushed conversation. A young woman, her clothes as faded and worn as the oak beams that crisscrossed the ceiling overhead, offered him a tankard of ale. He accepted the drink, tossed her a coin and looked around.

In a dark corner Angus was already playing a solitary game of chess. Lachlan walked over to him.

"Chess is a game best played with two."

His friend kept his head bent over the ivory pieces. "This way I always win. Rooms to accommodate all those you have brought with you are secured. It took a heavy purse, but the deed is done." He paused. "My informants tell me that Subedei passed this way no more then a few days ago."

Lachlan drew out a rough bench and set his tankard down on the table. A memory of the funeral fire that consumed the bodies of his father, brothers, and sisters before they were admitted to their watery grave blurred his vision. His voice was barely above a whisper. "Where did Subedei take residence?"

"At the inn on Doomsdale road."

"The street leading to the gallows on Castle Hill. 'Tis a fit place for my enemy."

Angus picked up the knight. "This game grows tiresome as does the wait for Subedei. There is much at stake. Why does he wait so long?"

"I suspect he uses the time to hire as many mercenaries as he can before he attempts to storm Urquhart by land. Subedei was ill-prepared when last he attempted to take the castle. He will not make the same mistake twice. Spread the word that I shall double any purse Subedei offers."

"It will be done. Do you think we shall become like the Mongol and your father: killing in order to feel alive?"

Lachlan tensed. The thought had come to his mind many times as well.

A few men at the bar began to clap to an ageless tune as the serving woman danced around and around to the lively rhythm. One by one those in the tavern joined in, shouting, laughing and stomping their feet. The sound vibrated through the tavern. He took a drink. The ale had lost its flavor and the tavern noises faded as events from a not-so-distant past flooded his mind.

The image of a small village in China, in the year 1500, filled his vision. He could hear the sound of metal striking metal. The smell of burning incense permeated the air beyond the garden walls of Subedei's residence. Here, laws did not apply.

In the courtyard two men were fighting. Subedei's head was shaved clean, his chest was bare, and he wore the loose-fitting trousers of the Mongols. The opponent was dressed similarly, but was a smaller man in both size and strength. Lachlan, an invited guest, watched them follow a series of steps, thrusts and parries calculated to penetrate the other's defense.

Although Subedei was quicker to deflect any advance, and swifter still to attack, there was no urgency to the interchange, no passion, no violence. The sound of their blades rang through the enclosure and surged through Lachlan like the blood through his veins. The muscles in his arms tightened. He focused on the two who battled before him. It would be over soon. His turn would be next.

Subedei glanced briefly in his direction, and Lachlan felt the fingers of death curl around his soul. A smile creased Subedei's normally expressionless face, before he turned his attention back to the man he fought. Something was wrong. Lachlan sensed the change. What had begun as a friendly diversion to fill the hours of the day had turned ominous. In less time than it took to draw blade from scabbard a laugh tore from the Mongol's throat. Subedei knocked his opponent's weapon to the ground and impaled his victim with his sword. Pulling his blade free, he pushed the man to the ground and turned toward Lachlan.

Subedei's smile was predatory as he wiped the dying man's blood from his blade. "Death is an elixir. There is no power that is equal to it."

The smell of blood filled Lachlan's senses and his heart thundered in his chest. He could feel his strength build until a red haze clouded his vision. A single purpose lay before him. Kill.

A scream shattered the insanity that held Lachlan prisoner. He saw the man Subedei had wounded choke on his own blood, and reach out toward him. The effort drained the last of what was left of the man's life. His eyes remained open as his hand dropped to the battle-stained ground. Lachlan backed away, trying to push the sound of the man's screams from his mind.

Subedei had killed for no other reason than the pleasure of it and Lachlan was about to do the same. He had to get away from this madness before it consumed him. His father had only to hold a sword in his hand, and the need to kill would overwhelm all reason; killing, for its own sake, regardless of who crossed his path. Toward the end, the castle dungeons had been filled with those who died a slow and torturous death at the hands of his father. No one was safe, even his own wife and children feared him when he held a sword; and for good reason.

While Lachlan stood watching the death scene before him, the blade in his hand grew heavy. It seemed to possess its own strength. It took all his will to force the sword into its scabbard.

"I will not fight you. I have no cause to battle to the death."

Subedei shrugged and bowed slightly toward him. "One day you may have." He smiled. "You stood absorbed in the battle I fought. Savoring each moment as it sped by, until death filled the air. I saw the look in your eyes. You were mad with the fever that affects a few of our kind. Treat it not as a curse, Lachlan, but relish it, embrace it. Let it grow within you."

Lachlan clenched his fists. "We are not the same, you and I."

Subedei laughed as he sheathed his sword. "True. I know what I am. Join me and together we could bring the world to its knees."

Raucous laughter and the clanking of tankards brought him back to the present. The sound of Angus' voice interrupted his thoughts and pulled him from the dark memories that had begun to haunt both his days and his nights. But, as always, he could not shake the feeling that had come over him when he saw Subedei plunge his sword into the man's chest. Lachlan had enjoyed watching the man die. No, it was more than that. He needed to see the man die. And his only regret was that it had not been his sword that had dealt the killing blow. That was the madness and the curse of his people. It had been the same for his father, who had killed one of his own sons to satisfy his unquenchable thirst. His stomach churned and the taste of bile filled his mouth.

"Lachlan."

He raised his head and looked at Angus. There was a worried expression on his friend's face. "Lachlan, has the dream returned?"

"Aye."

Angus nodded slowly. "You are not your father."

Lachlan was not so sure. For some time he had felt powerless to fight the blood lust that had consumed his father and Subedei. Words of the legend floated through his mind like a soothing balm: *Through the mist-shrouded waters of an enchanted sea, the Guardian will be summoned. The seasons will alter their natural course, the barriers of time will be broken, and a woman, with hair of burnished gold, will be pulled from the depths of Loch Ness.*

If it were true, and Amber were indeed the woman mentioned, he might be spared. But he knew not how she could reverse the effects of what he believed had already infected his blood.

He raised his tankard and took a drink of the cool ale. "What think you of the legend of the Lady of the Loch?" .

Angus shrugged. "I believe the ancients created the story to offer false hope. Our path is predestined. Those who believe otherwise are fools. Why is it that you ask?"

His friend's words rang clear with their logic.

" 'Tis only the appearance of Amber in Loch Ness and warm weather in October. I but wondered at the coincidence."

"That is all it is, laddie."

Lachlan felt a dark gloom settle over him. "Aye." He motioned for his friend to follow him toward the door.

Angus put his hand on Lachlan's shoulder. "Believe me when I say you are not your father. The insanity will pass you by."

Lachlan took a deep breath. "I pray it will be as you say."

Bright sunlight greeted him as he stepped into the narrow street. The notes of a fiddle in a nearby alley bounced off the stone building. The sound began as soft as a breeze, but the urgent tempo increased with each sweep of the man's bow, until the tune was a frantic blur. Instead of the music soothing him, it called to his mind the face of the man Subedei had killed. A boy's shout could be heard above the din. Thomas. So, the lad was still here. With his enemy on the march, it would be more merciful to leave Thomas in Inverness. At least here he had a chance for survival. At Urquhart, if Subedei's mercenaries prevailed, the lad would be cut down with the rest of the castle's inhabitants.

Angus nudged him in the ribs. "You cannot be glum on such a warm afternoon. You are in need of a distraction, before your expression grows as dark as the depths of the loch. The games have started. This time you will not be the only Highlander to best all challengers. I intend to enter as well."

Lachlan allowed his friend to guide him toward the center of the celebrations, but he could not shake the dark foreboding that claimed him. There was a difference between his father and himself. There had to be.

The midday sun seemed to shimmer off the bolts of silk, brocade, and velvet rolled and stacked on tables. The goods were crowded together with others being hawked by the merchants. Amber wove through the crush of people whose conversations hummed like bees around a honeycomb. There were booths filled with cinnamon sticks, ostrich feathers, vegetables, fresh breads, pastries, and ready-made clothes. It was the marketplace she'd been told existed when Inverness was an important trading city. Behind her was the bridge over the River Ness and on the hill was Inverness Castle. By her calculations she was standing on the spot where the Town House would be one day.

Four dirt-smudged boys raced past her, laughing and pushing each other in their excitement to reach one of the tables piled high with sweets. She smiled. The warm sun felt good against her face. The mood of the children was infectious.

She could hear the fast pace of a fiddler's music. The people around her appeared to be heading in the direction of the sound. She allowed herself to be buoyed forward on a wave of people dressed in faded tartans and worn dresses. Their faces were bright with anticipation. Conversations mixed with the laughter of small children as the young ones darted through the crowd toward the center of the clearing.

The easy laughter of the townspeople turned to whispers as the soft notes of a flute rose in the air to add its music to that of the fiddle. The crowds formed a semicircle around a crate-sized box covered in black velvet on three sides and resting on pole-like stilts.

The side that faced the audience was open, exposing painted castle turrets and a meadow in the background. Ribbons, the colors of a rainbow, shimmered from the corners and fluttered in the warm breeze. It was the Punch-and-Judy show she'd seen earlier. Amber paused, breathing in the excitement drenched moment, wanting to hold it as she did her breath. She noticed Lachlan standing on the perimeter of the crowd. His expression reflected the anticipation she felt. He seemed content to enjoy the entertainment alone. She started toward him, but at that moment the crowd surged forward again.

A trumpet sounded. A man dressed as a court jester in yellow and purple satin announced the play was about to begin. It was like the time she'd been on a roller-coaster ride at the amusement park. All the people had screamed, laughed, and shut their eyes. They'd shared a combination of anticipation and exhilaration. Amber noticed Elaenor working her way through the crowd. When the young woman stood beside Amber she nudged her.

"Having a good time?"

Elaenor smiled.

The man beat slowly on a drum, increasing the tempo until the air seemed to vibrate around them. He came to an abrupt stop. As he did two hand puppets popped into view. One was dressed as a king, the other a knight. Their faces were painted in vivid colors, their noses long and exaggerated. Each took a bow and then they began to chase each other around the stage, engaging in mock fights to resounding cheers.

Amber leaned closer with the crowd toward the performance. The puppet that was dressed like King

Henry VIII stabbed the knight over and over. The regal figure faced them. "He will not die. He will not die." The puppet appeared more frustrated than surprised. The tale reminded her of one her aunt used to talk about. This was probably where the legend had started, with the imagination of a skilled storyteller and the enthusiastic response of his audience.

The violence of the scene seemed surreal when acted out by the puppets and reminded her of the Road Runner cartoons. She felt herself being caught up in the make-believe world that was created. The shrill words of the puppet and the laughter surrounding the performance echoed over the grass fields. She found herself joining in until her sides ached. It felt wonderful.

Amber felt someone touch her on the shoulder. She turned. Lachlan's expression, a somber contrast to the rest of the people, hit her like a cold shower.

He leaned closer. "I would talk with you."

"Okay, I think it's almost over." She turned back to the performance, trying to concentrate on what the puppets were saying. Something about living forever.

"I would speak with you, now."

Elaenor poked her in the ribs and whispered. "Remember your promise?"

Amber felt a twinge of guilt. She looked at Lachlan. "What did you want to talk about? Any chance my horse ran away?"

He shook his head, putting his hand on her waist as he guided her from the crowd. Amber decided that tall men in kilts did not have a sense of humor, after all.

She followed him to a table heaped with breads and fruit pastries. Behind her the crowd roared. Turning she saw water being thrown on those nearest the stage.

Lachlan handed the round-faced woman behind the mound of pastries a coin and picked up a juicy turnover. He nodded toward the Punch-and-Judy show. "It is the story of Jonah and the Whale."

"Well, I'm certainly glad you saved me from that performance. It would be terrible if I had too much fun at the festival."

She knew she sounded like a petulant child, but actually it felt pretty good to voice her disappointment. He probably didn't understand the concept of sarcasm, anyway.

He shrugged and took a bite of his dessert. "The performance will repeat itself on the morrow."

She could smell fruit, sugar and flour. If she couldn't watch the performance, she could at least eat. She held out her hand, palm up. "How about a loan?"

He raised his eyebrow.

This was embarrassing. Her attempt at humor had failed miserably and she was still faced with the dilemma of having no money, something she hated. The last time she remembered asking anyone for money was when she was sixteen. Dependency on a man was irritating. If she ever returned to the twentieth century, and her students talked about how wonderfully romantic the middle ages were, she'd flunk them.

She cleared her throat and decide to swallow her pride. After all, there weren't a lot of job opportunities in this century. "Could I have money to buy a pie?" Ugh, that sounded awkward.

He hesitated, and then removed a leather pouch from his belt and handed it to her. "I was thoughtless.

You are in need of coin and I should have remembered. This is yours; spend it however you see fit. More will be available to you whenever you desire it." He nodded to the woman. "Sara's pies are the best in the Highlands."

It was as though he had sensed her embarrassment. But she still couldn't shake the uneasiness she felt at taking his money. She put her hand on his arm. "It's hard for me. I don't want you to feel obligated to give me things."

He smiled. "What is the difficulty? You are my betrothed. It is my responsibility to see that you have all you desire."

A vision of the oversized bed in her room entered her thoughts uninvited. Her face warmed considerably. She reminded herself that the arrangement was in name only, but the image remained. Amber could feel the muscles on his arms tense beneath her fingers and wondered if he was having the same thoughts. She decided that touching him was probably not such a good idea and backed away.

"As I was saying. If I thought I earned the money, it would be easier to take it. I'm Gavin's schoolmaster. What if you paid me a certain amount each month?" She was babbling out of control and hoped he hadn't noticed.

His eyes crinkled in a smile. "Agreed."

Okay, so he had noticed. She reached for one of the pies. It was warm and stuffed with some kind of red berry. She licked the crumbs from her finger. "By the way, how did the first Punch-and-Judy story end?"

"It is of no consequence. The motioneers and minstrels keep the legend of an immortal clan alive. The tale is best forgotten."

"Personally, I believe in unicorns, mermaids and . . ." She stopped herself from saying "men from outer space" and took a bite of the pastry instead.

Lachlan finished his pie. "Myths are for children. The more the legend of the immortal knight is told, the more people will think of it as based in truth."

"No, they won't. Not really. People just like to dream."

She had tried to bury her dreams, but they were still there, just waiting for the time when they were needed. Lachlan was too serious and wound tighter than the grandfather clock in her aunt's front room. It was as though he consciously tried to put barriers up around himself. She leaned forward.

"Without the fantasies, life is sometimes too real. There has to be some fantasy or legend you believe in."

He straightened and his expression darkened. "Even if what you say is true, believing in it would change nothing." He dusted the crumbs from his hands and headed toward two men who wrestled to the cheers of a small crowd of people.

Amber watched him walk slowly away. She doubted he took time to notice rainbows or the first flowers of spring. Those things had not been important to her . . . until now. The juice from the pastry oozed through her fingers. She thought of an idea. A long-standing tradition of graduating seniors came to mind. It was hard to look on the doom-and-gloom side of life when food was flying through the air.

"Lachlan, do you have one more minute?"

Chapter
6

Lachlan turned around. A fresh pie sailed through the air and splattered on his face. Berries clung to his hair, chunks of crust stuck to his bread and juice drizzled down his chin. He stared at her. His eyebrows seemed to knit together. Amber heard the woman behind the pastries gasp and noticed Gavin and MacDougal, coming toward her.

Lachlan wiped the dripping juice from his face. "I would have the reason."

The woman leaned forward. "The fat is in the fire now, milady."

Amber shrugged. "I'm not worried."

Looking concerned, Gavin stood beside her and frowned. "Are you sure?"

She took a deep breath. "Pretty sure."

Lachlan crossed the distance that separated them and looked down at her. "I would have my question answered."

MacDougal sniffed around their feet, looking for pie crumbs. She scratched the animal behind his ear. The distraction gave her time to think. She had forgotten for a few seconds that she was not in the twentieth century. What would happen to someone who pelted a laird with a pie? She looked over at Sara who was trying to appear busy with a new customer. She probably figured her master would be able to handle a disrespectful subject all by himself. The other people either hadn't noticed, or were choosing to look the other way.

Lachlan folded his arms across his chest. "Well?"

"Well, what? You were acting like the end of the world was about thirty minutes away. I decided you needed something else to think about."

He raised an eyebrow. "That is your reason for covering me with berries?"

"You are not completely covered, and besides you were taking yourself too seriously."

He licked the juice off his lips. "Do you always try to change that of which you disapprove?"

She nodded her head and smiled. "Pretty much."

"It is a dangerous trait." He attempted to pull chunks of sticky fruit out of his beard.

Amber reached up and flicked a piece of piecrust off his shoulder. "But, it worked."

"True enough. But I am thinking that in the future when I do something that displeases you, I would prefer you just tell me."

"Food gets your attention."

"Aye, it does at that." He looked at her speculatively. "What is to be done with you?"

There was a difference in the tenor of his voice. It no longer reminded her of an impending storm. She returned his gaze. The corners around his eyes had softened and he was actually smiling. It took her completely by surprise.

"Your method of getting my attention put to waste

one of Sara's pies, and turned my beard as red as Marcail's roses. The stain will be with me until May Day." He motioned to Gavin. "There is a stream nearby. I am in need of water to wash this off my face."

Gavin reached for a bucket near Sara's table. He raced down a path into the woods, with the dog close behind.

Sara put more pies out on the table. "Don't you be worrying about the sweets, milord. The juice will come out with a good scrubbing." She shoved a linen towel into Amber's hand. "You are lucky the laird has a generous spirit. His father would have had you whipped." Her expression darkened. "Or worse."

Amber hesitated. Now, there was a happy thought. Lachlan stood as still as an oak tree as she reached up and began cleaning the juice out of his beard. The hair was sticky and matted together. There was a fierce scowl on his face, but his eyes held the glint of laughter. She felt her courage return.

"Have you ever considered shaving?"

Out of the corner of her eye, Amber saw Sara back away from the table.

"My beard is as much a part of me as the Highlands."

Amber remembered a teacher at her school who'd shaved his mustache when he'd lost a bet. It had taken the man a month to recover. She didn't understand men's obsession with facial hair, but then, they didn't understand a woman's love of chocolate.

Gavin returned with the water. It sloshed over the sides of the bucket as he tried to lift it.

Lachlan poured the water over his head, then shook himself. Droplets of water sprayed the air. "So you would have me change my serious ways and remove my beard as well? You ask much."

"I just thought it would be easier to get the stain out if you cut off your beard."

He advanced toward her. " 'Tis more than that."

Amber backed toward the mound of pastry on the table, putting distance between herself and Lachlan. There was a mischievous look about him that warmed her heart and heightened her awareness of him. She felt the back of the table through the layers of material she wore.

"Okay, I admit it. I hate your beard. There, I've said it. It makes you appear like a menacing bear instead of a man. What are you going to do about it?"

His laughter startled her. Then without warning, he reached behind her and grabbed a handful of berries from an earthenware bowl. The juice oozed through his fingers. He winked.

"And I hate the tunic Una gave you to wear. The color does not suit you."

Before she could react, Lachlan dumped the berries onto the front of her dress. She felt the juice soaking through to her skin.

He folded his arms across his chest, looking thoroughly pleased with himself. "They have improved your appearance."

She grimaced to herself. Of course he would think that. Her dress was plastered to her chest. Well, this game was not over. She pasted on her sweetest smile and reached for the berries. He grabbed for her hand, but it was too late.

Amber spread a fresh layer of fruit over his face.

"I yield." Lachlan ducked as a fruit pie sailed past his head. Amber had lethal aim. His beard was now as red as Angus'. MacDougal sat beside her, barking at him as though Lachlan were a vanquished enemy. Gavin cheered as Sara handed Amber another pastry. His brother gave a triumphant yell, then called to the dog. The animal bounded to his feet and chased after Gavin in the direction of men who were engaged in a stone tossing contest. Obviously, Gavin had decided the entertainment his older brother provided was over. Traitors, the lot of them.

Lachlan tried to brush the berries off his shirt, but only succeeded in spreading the fruit over a wider surface. Covered in juice herself, the blasted woman held a pie balanced on the tips of her fingers, looking arrogant, victorious and . . . delicious. He smiled, feeling the sun warm on his back and the laughter and hum of activity around him. He adjusted his plaid on his shoulder and purposefully circled Amber in a wide arc. He wanted to prolong the moment, and the feeling. Besides, her expression told him if he made the slightest move toward another pie, she was ready with one of her own. Battle had never been this much fun. Her eyes, filled with laughter, almost robbed him of breath. He did not care the forces that brought her to him, only that she was here with him now.

"Brother?"

Elaenor's voice broke through his thoughts. She ran toward him, but stopped abruptly when she saw Amber. His sister's mouth formed a perfect circle and her eyes turned from him, to Amber, and back.

"Her dress is in ruins. What has happened?"

Out of the corner of his eyes he saw Amber hand the pastry back to Sara and walk toward him. His sister was not far from the truth. Amber's dress was covered with large patches of red berry juice. He was pleased.

Amber brushed her arm against him. She did it in a

way that seemed as natural as breathing. Her touch made him feel as though they shared a secret. He took a deep breath. The air around him felt as it did the night before a battle, heavy with anticipation.

Licking the berry juice off her fingers, she looked over at Elaenor. "How was the performance?"

A moment ago he had not thought it possible for his sister's face to look more confused. He had been wrong. He searched Amber's expression for any regret over missing the puppet show. Whatever had been there in the past had vanished. However, not wanting to chance fate, and before Elaenor could untie her tongue and answer, he reached for his leather coin pouch. It jingled as he put it in Amber's hand.

"Purchase whatever you desire. All I ask is that the color be bright."

She smiled and turned toward the area of the festival where vendors hawked their wares.

Someone slapped him on the back. He turned. "Angus."

His friend scratched the whiskers on his neck and nodded toward Amber. "From the look of you, she would be a welcome addition to our troops. Her aim is true. What did you say that caused such action?"

"You assume I am the cause."

Angus raised his eyebrow.

Lachlan would get little sympathy from his friend. He watched Amber walk toward a cluster of women who haggled over the price of a live chicken. She glanced over her shoulder and waved.

Angus smiled. "A bonnie lass, that one. Careful lad, your heart shows in your eyes."

"She is my betrothed."

Angus' laughter was deep. "You no more believe

those words than those who say that Darnley makes a good king."

"There is a vast difference between the two."

"Aye, we can do nothing about Darnley."

Lachlan straightened. "Mark well, any decision regarding the Lady Amber will be mine alone." He felt a slight increase in his pulse. The possessiveness he felt surprised him.

Angus stepped back and held his arms out. "Ease down, lad, I meant nothing by the remark. She is a woman of no small character. The castle still hums with how she exposed the cruelty of Gavin's tutor. I am pleased. You have tasted more honey than a hive full of bees these past years. 'Tis time you settled upon one."

Lachlan took a ragged breath, trying to cool his temper. It grew harder to control with each day's passing. He wished his manner was more like his friend's. Hoping to change the course of the conversation he motioned for Angus to join him, and headed in the direction of a path that led to the River Ness. He rubbed his chest. The juice of the berries soaking through his shirt felt sticky on his skin. His beard was matted together.

"You have not mentioned Myra of late, Angus. How does she fare these days?"

His friend fell in beside him, his steps sounding heavy on the well trod path. "Myra is well enough, but too weak to travel. I shall return in the spring and stay with her until she dies."

Lachlan heard the pain in his friend's voice. He was looking toward the growth of trees and light underbrush as if searching for an answer. He put his hand on Angus' shoulder.

"I am sorry."

Angus shrugged. "The years have been good to Myra and me. All things die."

"Except us."

Angus' voice was little more than a whisper. "Aye, except us."

The water sparkled through the trees and a squirrel ran along a fallen log. That Angus loved his Myra there was little doubt, but Lachlan had not expected his friend to feel such loss at her passing. He had been taught from the beginning that their kind were incapable of mourning those who died before them. Lachlan tore off a small twig, reached for the blade he kept strapped to his calf, and sliced off slivers of wood. He trimmed the blunted end into a point. Angus' reaction was unsettling and comforting at the same time. A vision of Amber throwing a fruit-filled pie at him made him smile. The woman he had pulled from Loch Ness had a way about her that distracted him, and made him feel whole. Perhaps that was what Angus had found with Myra.

He tossed the stick into the grass, sheathed his knife and walked to the water's edge. Removing his clothes, he plunged into the freezing river. Breaking the surface he shook the water out of his hair. It felt like an icy wind flowed through his veins, but his skin was free of the sticky fruit. He hurried back to shore.

Angus handed him his clothes. "It might be well to cut off your beard, and start anew."

Lachlan wrapped his plaid around his waist and over his shoulder. "It would please the Lady Amber if I rid my face of the beard. She is not in favor of it."

"That would be reason enough for me."

"Is there nothing you would not do for a woman?"

Angus rubbed his beard. "Nay, lad. Not for a woman I want."

Lachlan bent over and picked up his belt and weapons. Of course, Angus was thinking with his heart, not his head. His love for Myra clouded reason. Lachlan strapped his sword in place.

"There are things that take precedence. And what of war?"

"Your zeal for battle exceeds my own. But you head the Council of Seven, and all know you take the responsibility as your birthright."

Lachlan watched a fish swim close to the surface. Its scales glittered like newly made chain mail. The trout was locked in the confines of the pond's dimensions. He felt the same, drowning in traditions blurred by the passage of time. There were moments when he wanted to accomplish so much, to break out of the rules that governed his people. He picked up a smooth stone and skimmed it across the water. The ripples spread and multiplied.

"What if I were to take a bride?"

Angus' expression was serious. "To join to produce children with an outsider is forbidden. But a marriage might be allowed, as long as the joining ceremony and Elixir of Life were not part of the bargain. And how would you explain to the Lady Amber, that, while she grew old, you stayed as you are now? A man who appears to be thirty and some years?"

The wind rustling through the trees blended with the muffled sound of the festival. The world seemed out of focus to him in that moment, more illusion than reality. He picked up a handful of small rocks and felt their rough edges in his palm.

"Perhaps it should be considered."

Angus' sharp intake of breath could be heard over the rustling of the leaves. "Rebellious words."

Lachlan felt the worn edges of the leather-wrapped hilt of his sword. "History is marked by those who have, at times, resorted to traitorous acts in order to bring about change. You were not allowed to marry Myra, even though I know the love you have for her is great."

The lines across Angus' forehead deepened. "Not great enough to give up my immortality. Perhaps, in time, you can encourage change for those who seek it."

"Encourage it? I shall order it be allowed. We live as if isolated, keeping to ourselves like a secret society, allowing only certain of our number to venture beyond our boundaries."

Angus put his hand on Lachlan's shoulder. "I see the years have not mellowed your temper."

"My survival is dependent on keeping my mind alert. You would best remember that as well." He looked past the quiet woods. "These festivals are too tame for my taste."

Shouts broke through the laughter of the celebrations. Lachlan turned toward the sound. They headed back up the path.

"Hurry. Already the sunlight fades and we have yet to join the game."

"Of what nature? Jousting, fencing?"

Lachlan called over his shoulder. " 'Tis more of a challenge than that."

The room over the Rose and Thistle Tavern was well lit. Amber stood at the window, staring into the black darkness of the night sky as the seamstress, Grizel, altered her gown. All the celebrations of the festival had moved inside. As soon as she was finished getting dressed, she intended to get something to eat downstairs.

"I don't know why I let you talk me into buying this dress." She glanced over at Elaenor, who sat perched on the bed, a Cheshire cat grin plastered over her face.

"Lachlan will love your new red gown."

"What little there is of it."

Amber stared back at her reflection in the small wood-framed mirror on the wall,. The words, "plunging neckline," came instantly to mind. She was revealing cleavage she didn't know she had. During her travel back in time, she must have lost some crucial brain cells. Here she was, standing in the middle of a room, as Grizel worked on a dress Amber should never have bought in the first place.

She should have selected an outfit slightly more practical. Of course, she did need something to wear after Lachlan ruined the front of her tunic and there hadn't been that many dresses to chose from at the festival.

Who was she trying to kid? She had picked out this particular number to see if Lachlan's eyes would pop out when he caught a glimpse of her. But the dress was too big, and had to be taken in. She flinched as the old woman stabbed her skin with the needle. The seamstress was bent over with age, her face weatherworn and creased with wrinkles. But her eyes held a warm glow and her voice was gentle and kind.

"Sorry, milady, m' hands are not as nimble as once they were." Grizel grimaced as she pushed herself off the floor. " 'Tis done. Will that be all? There is a lass in the village whose birthing time draws near. She asks for m'soothing herbs."

The old woman had done a good job in a short period of time. This dress was easily the most beautiful garment Amber had ever worn. Even for her prom, she'd worn a black, formless sheath with a high neck and cap sleeves. Her father had approved, and her mother had remarked that it was a dress she could easily shorten and wear to work.

"Lass, I'll be going now."

Amber shook herself free from her thoughts and reached for the bag of coins Lachlan had given her.

Grizel shook her head. "Nay, you are the laird's betrothed and I owe him a debt that is beyond price. He comes to see us often, and we want for nothing."

She picked up her needles and thread and slowly hobbled toward the door.

When she had left, Amber turned to Elaenor.

"I wanted to pay her. She worked hard, and life can't be easy for a woman her age. Do you know what she was talking about?"

Elaenor slid off the bed. There was a note of hatred in her voice as she spoke. "Aye, I know well the reason. Some years past, when I was but little more than the age Gavin is now, men came to rid the Highlands of witches."

Amber felt her blood turn to ice. "Go on."

Elaenor lit another candle and set it on a table against the wall. "The men who claimed to be doing God's work had tortured and burned one woman. It was claimed that she could turn the milk of a cow sour by her touch. Grizel and her daughter were accused of having the power to bring the dead back to life with their herbs and potions. When Lachlan received word of what was occurring, he was not pleased."

The silence in the room deepened, broken only by sounds of merriment from below. Amber felt the moments tick by. "Please continue."

"My brother freed all the women who were accused and ended the slaughter before it could worsen."

Amber remembered what she'd learned about this age of superstition. The people involved were fanatical, and wouldn't have given up so easily. "Didn't they send more men?"

Elaenor shook her head. "Lachlan does not allow intolerance. No one fears the witch-hunters here. He has seen to it. His power reaches the royal courts. They will send no one to replace those he . . . dealt with."

"And what of Grizel?"

"He discovered that Grizel had been crippled under the torturer's hand, and her daughter blinded. He offered to bring them to the castle, but they wanted to stay in Inverness." Elaenor smiled. "Lachlan has a kind heart, no matter how hard he tries to hide it. He has never forgotten Grizel and her daughter. He provided a cottage in the village and visits them often." She stood, as though wanting to change the subject. "But why are we speaking of such things? My brother will be anxious to see your new gown."

Amber smoothed the material over her waist. Lachlan didn't share the superstitious views of the rest of this time period. In fact, he'd taken an additional step and actually defended those accused. A dangerous position in itself. But it meant that he would be her strongest ally if anyone ever accused her. As each day passed she felt the desire to tell him the truth increase. Of course, even if he was tolerant, there was no way he could grasp the notion of what she was saying.

Elaenor smiled. "If we do not join those downstairs soon, Lachlan will have departed."

Amber linked her arm through Elaenor's and guided her to the door. "Is your brother aware of your matchmaking tendencies?"

Yellow torchlight changed the ale in Lachlan's tankard to a dark gold. It reminded him of Amber's hair. He drained the tankard and looked about the crowded tavern. His mind was truly addled. Must everything remind him of her? He remembered seeing a child frown at the festival, and had thought Amber might enjoy telling the lad a story to cheer him; he heard laughter and wondered what she might be doing at that moment, or what she might be thinking. Elaenor had sent him a message that Amber had bought a new gown and would be joining him for the evening meal. And here he sat, waiting. If he be in such a desperate need of the company of a woman, there were many in this village who would welcome him and without putting demands on his time.

A hush fell over the tavern. He raised his head to determine what had caused such a distraction. His sister was approaching arm in arm with Amber. He stood. The heat in the tavern closed around him as she drew nearer. The gown accentuated her charms: her full breasts, narrow waist, and the sway of her hips. Lachlan's pulse raced. He stood, his palms were sweating. He longed to caress her skin, to feel her naked body against his. She smiled and his heart stopped. He could not breathe nor speak words that he would trust. Stumbling backward, he sought the comfort of the cool night air.

Amber flinched as the tavern door slammed shut. She glanced at Elaenor. "Is something wrong?"

The young woman smiled. "From the expression on my brother's face, I would say he finds your gown more than suitable."

Morning sunlight glistened on the dew-covered grass. Amber, drawn by the cheers of the crowd, saw a juggler tossing bright colored balls in the air and a fire-eater performing next to him. Along the field adjoining the River Ness, men were playing a game that resembled a cross between American soccer and rugby. She wondered how soon it would be before women joined in these games. Centuries, no doubt. Too bad. She would have enjoyed the exercise and thought Elaenor might as well. Of course the trick would be to find something to wear that was easy to run in and would not cause a scandal.

Amber hadn't been able to talk Elaenor into coming to the festival this morning. She had said she needed to finish her letter to her friend, Elizabeth, but promised to come later. Even so, Elaenor had insisted that Amber wear the red dress. She smiled, remembering Lachlan's reaction. There was a moment when their eyes met . . . her face grew warm. She was acting like a schoolgirl with her first crush. It was unsettling.

A dog barked. A half-dozen boys raced toward her. Gavin led the pack. Their clothes were splattered with dirt and their faces flushed from running. They laughed and wrestled playfully.

Gavin stopped in front of her and handed her a sprig of wild heather. The stem was bent and the bloom wilted, but he presented it to her as though it were a long-stemmed rose. "This is for you."

She took the flower from him, inhaling its fragrance. The unexpected gesture brought tears to her eyes. "Thank you. Would you like me to tell you all a story?"

He nodded, smiling so hard his dimples showed. He turned and whispered to his friends. "I told them you tell better stories than Torquil the minstrel."

She laughed. "I don't know about that, but I'll give it a try."

Amber led them to a small, grass-covered mound not far from the river. Shielding her eyes from the sun, she searched for Lachlan. He was nowhere in sight. Disappointed, she turned her attention back to Gavin and his friends.

One of the boys tugged on her gown. He was the smallest of the bunch with big brown eyes and chubby cheeks. She resisted the urge to put her arm around him. Boys this age felt they were too old for hugs.

Gavin's words tumbled out in a rush. "Peter wants to know what the story will be."

Amber rubbed her chin, deep in thought. She could tell them a few tales of the wonders of her century. She looked up at the sky and pointed.

"I'll tell you about a man who walked on the moon."

All the boys smiled. Amber eased herself down on the grass as they crowded in, focusing their attention on her. She began the story of Neil Armstrong, feeling a warm glow wash over her. It was the same sensation as when she'd first started teaching. It'd been a long time since she'd felt this good about her chosen profession. As she was quoting Armstrong's words, "one small step for man, one giant leap for mankind," a leather ball seemed to fly from the sky. It landed beside her. The boys leaped to their feet, cheering and shouting.

Gavin pointed to a half-dozen men who were running straight for them. "We are in their way. We'd better move."

She stood, dusted the loose grass from her dress and saw Lachlan running toward them. His chest was bare, his face was caked with mud and his eyes were focused on the ball that lay near her feet. Her heart beat out of control. He looked even more handsome today than he had last night.

Shouts of competition rang through the air as an opposing team of men ran from the opposite direction. The men had resumed the game they'd begun yesterday. A surge of exhilaration swept through her. It had been months since she'd played.

Amber ignored Gavin's pleas to leave the area. Instead, she picked up the ball, raised it over her head and threw it an equal distance from both groups. Her college soccer coach had bragged that she had a strong and accurate throw in. The distance was not as good as it used to be, but not bad, if she did say so herself. Both teams veered in the direction the ball had taken. Lachlan reached it first. Muscles flexed, he looked over at her. He wore that expression all men have when they're trying to impress a woman, and kicked the ball halfway across the meadow. She covered her mouth with her hand to smother a laugh. Some things would always be the same, thank goodness.

Gavin's eyes were wide and his mouth open as he turned toward her. "Where did you learn the skill to throw?"

She'd be willing to bet a year's teacher's salary not too many women, in this century, could throw a ball as far as she just had. But before she could think of a plausible explanation, Gavin's attention was diverted to the game. He'd forgotten all about the throw and the story. She smiled. Children were easily distracted.

She put her hand on his shoulder. "Why don't you run along and watch your brother?"

Gavin hugged her. "I promise I shall listen twice as hard tomorrow." He bolted for the field, followed by his friends.

It didn't matter what century you were from, children were all the same. She smiled, watching the boys run along the sidelines. They had removed their shirts, no doubt in imitation of the men on the field. She noticed Gavin's back had healed without leaving any scars from Bartholomew's beating. She was little surprised, but maybe the boy's wounds hadn't been as deep as she had first thought. Hopefully any emotional injuries had healed as well.

She took a deep breath of the fragrant air and turned to watch Lachlan. He was in the lead, and looking strong and athletic. The morning had turned warm suddenly. She brushed her hair back from her shoulder and watched him. There was something about him that was different, something that set him apart. She couldn't identify it, or why she enjoyed watching him. It must be the kilt.

The notes of a fiddle drifted toward her and she followed the sound. The relaxed atmosphere of the festival, as well as the warm October sun, conjured up the image of Camelot. A place where anything was possible and love was forever. Amber sighed and smiled at the daydreams that swirled in her head. There might be more of her Aunt Dora's romantic nature in her than she thought. However, in the past, when a potential Prince Charming appeared, she had discovered his armor was tarnished. Her aunt always reminded her that she would have to kiss a lot of frogs before she found her prince. Amber had almost given up hope. Almost.

She headed in the direction of the music. A small gathering surrounded the fiddler; the tune was quick and lively. A circle dance began to form, increasing in size as people joined in. Those not participating clapped their hands in time to the music, while others sat on the grass nearby. Amber looked back toward where the men were playing. The game must be over. Lachlan was heading in her direction.

Out of the corner of her eye she saw Elaenor run toward her. Amber smiled. "I thought you had a letter to write."

"I did, but I heard the music, and remembered what you said about not losing myself in my books. Please, will you join in the dance with me?"

Before Amber could answer that she hadn't a clue how to perform the complicated steps, or any dance steps for that matter, Elaenor had pulled her into the midst of the group. The music stopped as the fiddler accepted a tankard of ale. He handed it back as he wiped his mouth with the back of his hand. The lull afforded Amber sufficient time for panic to set in.

"Elaenor, I can't do this."

Elaenor looked distracted. "Did you say something?" Amber wondered if it would do any good to tell her she hadn't the faintest idea what she was doing and decided, probably not.

The fiddler began a new tune, more lively than the last. The notes seemed to fly through the air, infusing new energy into the dancers. Many more joined in and several people in the crowd began to sing. Amber caught a few of the lines. Something about a man and a woman. Was there ever any other kind of song? On the perimeter of the group she saw Lachlan staring at her.

He smiled and she felt the heat rise on her face. Terrific. Last night, when she felt in control and beautiful, he hadn't said a word. In the light of day, when she couldn't keep her eyes off him, he'd decided to stay. Good thing the music was loud, it would drown out the thundering beat of her heart.

It was time to escape. She turned to Elaenor. "I never learned how to dance. I think I'll sit this one out." The remark was sort of true. She'd never been taught any medieval Scottish folk dances in physical education class, or anywhere else for that matter.

"I shall teach you."

She was trapped. Elaenor was determined to have a good time.

Elaenor reached out to her. "Hold my hand, and the hand of the person next to you."

Amber did as she was told. "Now what?"

"The women will dance in one direction, while the men form a circle on the inside and dance the opposite way."

No sooner were the words out of Elaenor's mouth than the women started to move. Amber looked down at Elaenor's feet and tried to mimic the dance. They kept on the balls of their feet. Step behind, step in front, step and stamp, stamp. The movements were not as difficult as Amber had first thought and soon the steps became automatic.

She felt the exhilaration that always came to her when she exercised. Tension melted away as the dancers matched the tempo of their steps to the fiddler's music.

A loud yell brought the men into the center of the circle. They were greeted with an answering shout from the women. Lachlan was among the men. His expression was unreadable as he kept in step with the other male dancers. Closer and closer he came, until he brushed against her shoulder, circled, and then faced her again. He looked at her and smiled.

She missed a step in her confusion. "What a mess."

The deep sound of his laughter seemed to vibrate through her. He placed his hand on her waist and she could feel the warmth of his touch.

The tempo of the music increased. Each note blended into another. The townspeople swirled around her in a blur of smiling faces. She watched the world spin past as she held onto Lachlan's arms, feeling the strength of his muscles beneath her fingers. He drew her closer. Her heart beat a little faster. She shouldn't feel such a strong attraction to him. He was too tall, and his eyes were too blue.

The sound of a second fiddle joined the first, its notes clear and quick. Lachlan's hand was on the small of her back, and he was bending toward her. Had they stopped dancing? She couldn't tell. He leaned down and kissed her lightly on the lips. His touch was warm and his voice a whisper.

"You should always wear the color red."

"Last night . . ."

He traced the line of her chin with his thumb. "I dared not stay. I find that it is hard to breathe when I am near you. But, away from you, I lose the reason to breathe."

Chapter
7

❧

Amber walked along the River Ness, watching the sun glisten over the water. The music and the dance she'd shared with Lachlan were only a memory. The walk would help clear her head. Angus had pulled Lachlan away from her to continue their game. She looked over her shoulder. He was shoving past an opponent for control of the ball, but paused long enough to wave to her. The gesture almost cost him the advantage he'd gained. She smiled to herself.

Angus, whether he knew it or not, had saved the day. A few more minutes in Lachlan's arms and she would have been melted butter. He wanted her and she wanted him. And if the two of them slept together, what would happen next? In the twentieth century the scenario was simple. It broke down into five words; meeting, dating, lust, friendship and commitment. Of course, it didn't always happen in that order, and the last two were tricky, but she'd always felt it was important to know the stages. In the Middle Ages she had a feeling there might be a few more rules. And then there was always her aunt's explanation of love. She'd said that a person just knew when it was going to work. It was not necessary to examine the pros and cons, or list the number of things you had in common. But her aunt was an incurable romantic.

A flock of birds flew overhead in a slow, relaxed flight. She headed in the direction of a line of thatched-roof houses that overlooked the River Ness. The homes were in the same general location as Aunt Dora's bed-and-breakfast inn. Her aunt had told her that their ancestors dated back to this time period, and had lived along the water. Of course, her aunt's people were fishermen and weavers. She smiled, wondering if in one of these houses there was a MacPhee. It might be fun to see if there was any family resemblance. But it would have to wait until after the festival, because the present homes looked deserted. Amber saw a small fenced area where a half-dozen cattle grazed aimlessly. In front of one of the houses hung fish on wooden spits above an open fire.

The seamstress, Grizel, carrying a basket under her arm, hurried into one of the homes. She seemed to be the only person around. There was an unnatural stillness in the air.

A scream pierced the quiet. It emanated from the house she'd seen Grizel enter only moments before. Amber froze. She wiped her palms against her dress and looked back in the direction of the festival. The sound of the woman's screams had not reached that far, but had been muffled by the celebrations. She should go for help. Amber heard the cry again. It tore through her. She took a deep breath. It sounded as if someone was dying or being killed. That did it. She must stop thinking and find out what was wrong. She picked up her skirts and ran toward the house.

She pulled open the door and peered inside the cottage. The shutters were closed tightly against the sun and fresh air. A single candle flickered on a table beside a bed where a pregnant woman lay moaning. Amber pulled back. There was no doubt it was Molly, the young woman she'd met on her first day at the castle. Beside her knelt Grizel. Tears stained the old woman's face. She looked up at Amber and brushed away the tears with the back of her hand.

"And what be your concern in this place?"

Amber averted her gaze from the bed. The old woman was giving her an excuse to run. This was none of her business. She backed toward the door and felt the wood against her spine. More than a year ago, one of her students had tearfully confessed to being pregnant. Amber had convinced herself that she should not become involved with other people's problems.

Grizel was the same woman Lachlan had saved from a witch's fiery death. He could have gone along his way, confident that he'd done a good deed, and left the survivors to fend for themselves. But he hadn't. The sixteenth century was supposed to be barbaric in comparison to her own time, yet Lachlan practiced a level of caring that she had only bragged she possessed.

She swallowed. When her student had told her about the pregnancy, Amber had rationalized that she was a teacher, not a counselor. She hadn't wanted to get involved with their lives, or know what happened to them once they'd left her classroom. But all the girl had asked her to do was come along with her to the abortion clinic. She couldn't even remember the student's name. Amber stepped away from the door.

"I heard a woman scream, and thought I could help."

"This be Molly Grant." Grizel made a quick movement of her head toward the pregnant woman. "Help be welcome this day."

Amber's smile quivered. "We've met."

Having a baby in this century was life-threatening for both mother and child. There were bound to be complications. Amber's total experience concerning the mysteries of childbirth came from books and an eighth grade video entitled, *How a Baby is Born.* Every girl in her class had vowed never to have a child after watching that tape. She hoped the midwife was good at giving directions.

"I'll do what I can."

Grizel reached for a goblet on a nearby table. She held it toward her. "Can you not smell the stench through the sweet wine?"

Amber repressed a shudder. "That's awful. What is it?"

Grizel shook her head and looked at the liquid. "Savory, ground with pennyroyal, and the scent of something I cannot identify. Molly has tried to rid herself of the babe."

The walls in the small, one-room house seemed to close in on Amber. She took a deep breath of the warm stale air and gagged. She was in over her head.

Molly screamed and clutched at the coverlet.

The old woman set the goblet down and reached for a cloth in a basin of water. She gently sponged the girl's damp forehead. "There is much to do, and little time."

Amber forced herself to walk over to the bed. Molly's eyes were clouded with pain. Amber knelt beside the midwife.

Molly raised herself on one arm and reached for Amber. The young woman's fingers tightened around her hand.

"Bartholomew isn't who he claims to be." Her eyes closed as, briefly, a spasm shuddered through her. "I followed him through the castle's underground tunnels. He was angry with me. I told him I wouldn't tell. How could I? I love him."

The midwife smoothed the young woman's damp hair away from her face as lovingly as if Molly had been a small child.

Grizel nodded. "The devil's own tempted this one. I knew the father of her child would not take her with him, but until this moment I knew not his name." She turned to Amber. "Please, stay with Molly. There is a matter that needs tending. I shall see that my daughter is here with you, until I return. Although blind, she is a skilled midwife."

The old woman stood. "Not many would offer to help on the day of a festival."

She opened the door and departed, leaving Amber alone with Molly in the small cottage. Amber's hand trembled as she took the linen towel and wiped the girl's neck and face.

"Everything will be all right. It has to be."

Shouts rang over the field by the River Ness in the fading light. Soon it would be too dark to play the game. Lachlan watched as Angus shouldered his way into the center of a group fighting for control of the ball. His friend, who was playing for the opposing team, burst from the circle of men and kicked the ball free from his attackers. It headed toward a goal line marked with a flag bearing the MacAlpin colors, and went in. The score was now even. He smiled. It was a welcome change to hear laughter on a field instead of the screams of battle.

Lachlan reached for the wooden bucket and took a long drink of the cool water before pouring it over himself. The teams this day were evenly matched. Only a few broken bones that would be in need of tending. Lachlan nodded to Gavin and handed him the bucket. "Angus has played well."

Gavin set the empty bucket down beside him. "You would be the one to catch him."

"Aye, the same thought came to my mind."

"Why do you and Angus not share the same team? You could win easily."

"There is no pleasure in a game, if it be readily won." Lachlan looked into the crowd of townspeople lingering around the booths and traveling minstrels. "When last did you see Amber?"

Gavin turned the bucket over and sat on the upturned end. "She told us we could watch you and Angus. Was I supposed to stay near her?"

Lachlan shook his head. "Nay, Gavin. Perhaps she has gone back to the inn."

A man and a woman were arguing in a grove of trees nearby. Although their words were not clear, the anger and frustration rang out. As he watched, the woman turned her back on the man and folded her arms across her chest. There was a smile of satisfaction on her face as the man pleaded with her. Lachlan remembered the dance he shared with Amber. She was strong-willed and intelligent, of that there was little double. But he believed she would never play a man for the fool as did the woman in the grove. If Amber wanted something, she would ask.

Someone touched his arm and he turned. It was Grizel.

She motioned for Gavin to leave. Lachlan could

read the urgency in her eyes. The old woman would only seek him out on matters of importance. He knew that Gavin would not budge until given an order from him. Lachlan sensed he should set a task for the boy, lest he feel dismissed because of his youth. He put his hand on his brother's shoulder.

"Grizel seeks a word with me and it comes to mind that I have not seen MacDougal in some time. Make sure that the beast has not eaten all the pies in its reach. It is important the dog does not make the townspeople sorry we attended their festival. If there are damages, assure them that the MacAlpins will make it right."

Gavin puffed out his chest. "No one will regret our being here. I shall see to it." The boy ran toward the brightly-colored booths.

Grizel stuffed a strand of hair back in her cap. "You have a way with the lad. If he grows to be a man worthy of your clan colors, you alone will be responsible."

Lachlan folded his arms across his chest and waited. Grizel would come to the reason she was here in her own time.

Tears glistened in her eyes. "Molly's time has come."

"The child is early."

Grizel nodded. "Aye, true enough."

"How will she fare?"

The midwife shook her head.

He heard the sound of men cheering and knew the game was at an end. A celebration would fill the taverns this night, while Molly and her child's life lay in the balance. The sights and sounds of the festival dulled before him. "Was an accident the cause to bring about the early birth?"

"No accident. 'Twas learning that her man would neither wed her, nor take her with him, that drove her to it."

"Speak not around the truth. What is the cause?"

Grizel wiped the tears from her face with the back of her hand. "Molly tried to rid herself of the child."

"The Church forbids killing of an unborn babe."

"That may be the truth of it, but the knowledge is still used when need be."

He had heard of such things in his travels. Whispered secrets that were not meant for a man to hear. These matters involved women and were not his concern. But to end a life? The notion troubled him.

"Were you the one who gave her such knowledge?"

Her voice lowered. "You know me, Lord. I bring life into the world, not take it away. 'Twas a mixture of savory and pennyroyal cloaked in a red wine that was the cause. A dangerous concoction for a woman so far along with child. I've seen many a birth. Such a mistake usually means the woman's death. I know not where Molly got the brew."

Lachlan looked away from the midwife's tear-stained face toward Angus and the men on the field. They were headed toward the center of town. He could join them and be welcome, but in truth all desire had fled when he had learned of Molly's condition.

It was for the sake of her child, Bartholomew had been given a second chance. Lachlan had found a small cottage where the family could begin their life together. When last he saw Molly, she was making preparations for her marriage. It was for her, and for her unborn child, that Lachlan had swallowed his anger toward the man. He felt it rise with renewed strength to the surface and turned to Grizel.

"I shall bring Bartholomew back. Comfort Molly that she will have a father for her bairn if the child survives, and a husband, regardless the outcome."

Grizel shrugged. "She has little chance of surviving the night. But the news that the wretch she loves will be coming back may give her the hope she needs to cling to life. I have left Molly with the Lady Amber. Your betrothed is inexperienced, but has a good heart." Grizel nodded before turning down the path and heading toward a cluster of white-washed houses.

Lachlan gazed at the clear blue sky. Someone was in need and Amber had flown to the rescue like an eagle protecting her nest. The last time he had seen Amber she was surrounded by Gavin and his friends. Instead of enjoying the festival, she had put that aside to help another. Lachlan gathered his clothes and headed to the inn where his horse was stabled. He made a vow to bring Bartholomew to Molly.

Lachlan guided his horse, Rowan, through a highland mist that rolled over the gentle sloping hills. A family traveling to the festival had provided the necessary information. They said they had seen a man of Bartholomew's description heading in this direction. He pulled on the reins and Rowan slowed to a standstill. Cloud cover blocked out the night sky. The farther he had traveled from Inverness, the more severe the weather had become.

Lachlan dismounted and led the animal toward where he suspected Bartholomew's camp to be. He had always prided himself on his judgment of character. But with Bartholomew he had listened to the words, not looked into the man's eyes for the truth. The tutor had vowed, falsely of course, that he would take Molly to wife. Now, it was necessary to force the marriage.

Rowan tossed his head and whinnied. Lachlan heard the answering sound of another horse drift toward him, and stroked the coarse hair on Rowan's neck to quiet him.

"If that be Bartholomew's mare, a ceremony will yet take place before the babe is born."

The mist thinned as he reached the crest of a hill and saw a horse grazing. Smoke curled from a fire. Illuminated in the meager light were two men.

Lachlan tied the reins around the trunk of an alder. What were these men doing on this land, made his in battle? Had they come for the festival, or had they another purpose in mind?

The clouds parted revealing the moon in its first quarter. Nearly two weeks had passed since he had pulled Amber from Loch Ness. Words of the legend whispered to him . . . *But the waters will reclaim her once again, if, after the passage of one full moon, the immortal she was sent to heal accepts not the power of eternal love.* The legend was a reality. He could no longer deny it. On his return to Urquhart he must discover the mystery behind the stolen vial and the purpose behind its disappearance. He must also decide if he had the courage to let Amber into his heart.

He paused when he reached the camp. One man lay on the ground in a pool of blood, the other, as yet unaware of Lachlan's presence, stood near the fire. He recognized Bartholomew in the firelight. The schoolmaster bent down and started searching through a traveler's pack.

Lachlan edged closer. He would not underestimate Bartholomew. The tutor lacked honor to have behaved as he had, and men, such as he, were not bound by the same code. The sword belonging to the man on the ground was still in its scabbard. If there had been a fight, the blade would have been drawn. Further, the sound of metal striking metal would have carried on the wind. He felt certain the man had been attacked in his sleep. Lachlan clenched his fist. He had given the schoolmaster more chances than he had given any man. This would be the last.

He stepped out into the clearing. "Have you added murder and thievery to your list of offenses?"

Bartholomew swung around. He dropped the bag of coins and drew his sword. "Ah, so you have come to fetch me. The trip is wasted. As for that," Bartholomew nodded toward the man on the ground, "he attacked me. I defended myself."

"The lies come easily. 'Tis clear he never drew his sword. And now you steal from him as well."

Bartholomew shrugged insolently. "A dead man has no need of coin."

Lachlan noted the change in his demeanor. This man was different from the one who had sought the position as Gavin's tutor. He was aware that he was seeing the man's true character.

" 'Tis a poor choice Molly made in you." Lachlan circled around him.

"I shall wager the MacAlpin skill with a blade is like the Highland mist, no substance for all its reputation." He lunged at Lachlan. "I'll not return to Inverness."

Lachlan stepped back, drew his sword smoothly, and blocked Bartholomew's attack. "Aye, that you will."

The moonlight glittered off forged steel as blade made contact with claymore The ring of metal echoed over the hills. Lachlan forced himself to remember his purpose. It would be an easy task to drive his blade through Bartholomew's heart, but he had vowed to return the tutor to Molly. Lachlan drove Bartholomew toward the mare with a series of controlled parries. The horse, alarmed by the sound and movement, pulled on her tether and sidestepped out of the way.

Lachlan saw fear in the schoolmaster's eyes and beads of perspiration form on his brow. Now was the moment to strike. The force of his attack knocked Bartholomew's sword out of his hand. It clattered to the ground.

"I care not the condition you be in when we return to Urquhart, but for Molly's sake I will bring you back alive. She carries your child."

Bartholomew's voice faltered. "I'll not be tied to a woman's skirts, my bones rotting on Scottish soil. As for the child, I care not. And take warning, I have friends who will not look favorably on my ill-treatment."

Lachlan sheathed his sword. "Talk with you is wasted. Your threats hold little substance." He doubled his fist and hit Bartholomew in the jaw. A bone cracked and blood spurted from the tutor's mouth. He stumbled against the mare and grabbed at her mane before crumbling to the ground.

Lachlan checked that the tutor still lived. Better Molly be alone than take Bartholomew as husband. He had promised to bring the father of her child back to Urquhart and then he would be tried for his crimes.

Stars filtered through the clouds and the moon cast a white glow over the Highlands. Lachlan stepped over Bartholomew to look at the man on the ground. The man rested on his elbow and stared back at him.

A cough racked the man and he doubled over and

winced, putting his hand on his stomach. His shirt was soaked with blood. "The name is O'Donnell."

Lachlan leaned over and helped the man to his feet. There could be only one explanation why the man was still alive, after spilling enough blood to drain Angus himself. He would have more than the legend to discuss with Marcail, on his return.

The first light of dawn began to edge over the horizon in the still morning. Amber rubbed her eyes and sank down beside the shore of the River Ness. She dipped her hand in the water and splashed it over her face, then lay back on the damp grass. She'd never been this tired before. A twig snapped. Whoever was coming would have to walk over her because she wasn't moving. She felt, rather than saw, someone kneel down beside her and opened her eyes. It was Lachlan.

" 'Tis a heavy burden you bear this day."

Even in the gray morning light she saw the sadness in the lines on his face. So he knew about Molly. Her voice trembled. "There was nothing I could do. They just died. I should have been able to do something."

"Marcail has performed the duties of midwife and said if the mother lacked the will to live, she would not survive childbirth. Molly had given up long before she took the herbs that would rid her body of the child."

She felt the burning tears in her throat. "Why?"

He lay beside her and cradled her against his chest. His voice was little more than a whisper in her ear. "The father of her babe would not recognize his responsibilities. Raising a wee lass or laddie without the blessing of marriage would have condemned the child to a lifetime of ridicule and shame. She took the only course she felt was left open to her."

The warmth of his arms quieted her trembling, but not her tears. "I saw the baby, Lachlan. He was so small."

Lachlan turned her face toward him. His fingers were gentle as he wiped tears from her eyes. "I should have been there with you, instead of looking for Bartholomew."

Amber touched the side of his face. It hurt him to see others in pain, although he ignored his own. She tried to keep the tears out of her voice. "What you did was more important."

"Your act of kindness required courage."

She shook her head slowly. "What I did wasn't courageous. It was something I had to do. I've spent my life running away from becoming too involved in other people's lives, or getting too close. I can't run away anymore. I don't want to."

"You judge yourself harshly. It takes time to know ourselves and determine the type of person we wish to become."

The crisp notes of a fiddle broke through the quiet dawn. It came from the direction of the house where Molly and her baby had died. Amber sat up.

He brushed her hair away from her forehead. "Molly's family and friends have come to watch over her and the child until the burial. There will be dancing, weeping, and singing until the sun goes down over the Highlands." He stood, reached for her hand, and kissed her fingertips. "Come, it is time we returned to Urquhart. There are clothes Elaenor purchased for you at the tavern if you wish to be rid of the gown."

She looked down at her stained dress. Her hands shook. The blood of Molly and her baby were a deep red against the fabric. The reality of their death threatened to smother her.

"My dress . . . their blood is on my dress. It's . . . ruined. It's all ruined." Tears spilled down her face and sobs racked her body.

"I shall have a dozen gowns ordered to replace this one."

His body was warm and comforting and his words meant to soothe her, but he didn't understand.

"I don't care about the dress. It can be replaced. But not Molly, not her baby." She looked at him and searched for a sign that he understood what she was feeling. Amber saw concern in his eyes, and perhaps love, but he didn't understand her sense of loss. The realization hit her as if it were a physical blow.

Lachlan's clansmen were riding a short distance behind them as they approached the entrance to Urquhart. Together they rode through the massive wooden gate. He'd not spoken to Amber on their journey from Inverness. For the first time she realized what her aunt had meant when she'd said conversation was not important, it was what was left unsaid that held the substance.

Urquhart, shrouded in a mist, had a surreal white glow. It was as though all the ghosts of the past had merged together and blanketed the castle. The image of Molly as she lay dying and her stillborn baby had occupied Amber's thoughts on the journey from Inverness. She prayed that the young girl and her child had found peace.

Amber was startled by a sudden crashing noise.

Near the main entrance a half-dozen wagons stood, overflowing with furniture, rolled tapestries, and leather-bound chests. What looked to be the frame of a bed lay in a pile of twisted wood on the ground. Servants dressed in short tunics and pants in shades of greens and browns crowded around the broken pieces. A slender man stood before them. He was wearing light-colored hose, gold ruffled pants that only reached the tops of his thighs and a wide-shouldered royal blue satin short jacket with lace at the collar and sleeves. To Amber he resembled a peacock in a covey of mud hens.

Lachlan turned in his saddle to face her. "Theseus has arrived. I fear he has brought the entire contents of his castle and all his servants as well."

"Who's Theseus?"

"A guest."

Amber smiled to herself. Well, so much for asking a direct question and receiving the bare minimum in return. She took a closer look, remembering that the tour guide at Leeds Castle had mentioned that King Henry the VIII, along with others of the nobility, might often bring furniture with them when they traveled. She hadn't taken the guide literally, thinking that history, in the retelling, had been exaggerated. Judging by the confusion in the courtyard, the guide had been right.

Lachlan reined in his horse, dismounted and motioned for the others in their party to do the same. At his command, men ran to hold their mounts and Angus joined him in whispered conversation.

MacDougal barked excitedly at the newcomers. From Amber's vantage point on her horse, she saw the wolfhound race for the back entrance of the kitchen followed closely by Gavin and Elaenor. She stretched her tired muscles and watched the two young people disappear into the castle. She looked over at Lachlan and Angus. They were engrossed in a discussion that involved a lot of grunting and head nodding. From the serious expressions on their faces, she was just as glad she couldn't hear what was being said.

The shouts of the attending men competed with the sound of squawking chickens in the yard as, one by one, the horses were led to the stable. The sound of a voice filled with terror caused her to look over her shoulder. Bartholomew. A chill ran through her. His hands were tied behind his back, and he stood next to Angus. Beside the schoolmaster was a body slumped over a black horse. She shuddered. More death. A gray cloud, on its path across the sun, darkened the sky. Amber's hands trembled and she grabbed the saddle horn to still them.

"The ground at Urquhart is harder than the sweet grass near Inverness. Let me assist you, lest you fall again." Lachlan was standing next to her horse with his arms outstretched. His voice was low.

Amber reached out and let him help her down. She held onto his arm and realized she didn't want to let go.

"I'd forgotten about Bartholomew. What are you going to do with him?"

Lachlan looked over at the schoolmaster. "The man will be tried for his crimes."

Amber followed his gaze. Two of Lachlan's men carried a body on a makeshift stretcher. She shuddered. She'd been so tired when they had started their journey from Inverness she hadn't paid any attention to who was riding with them. "Who killed that man? Was it Bartholomew?"

"O'Donnell still lives, although Bartholomew did attempt to murder and then rob him in his sleep." Lachlan put his hand over hers and his eyes darkened. "The schoolmaster will have much to answer for when he is tried."

Remembering Molly, she felt a tightness in her throat. The woman had loved Bartholomew. She'd said so with her dying breath. Her feelings for the schoolmaster had been so intense and absorbing that Molly hadn't seen, or had not wanted to see, that he'd never keep the promises he made. Blinded by his education and his station, the young woman had not been able to tell reality from fantasy. Amber didn't want the kind of blinding love that only allowed you to see the outer shell of the person, instead of what was in their heart.

Pushing the troubling thoughts from her mind, she played the hours she spent with Molly through her head like the fast-forward button on her VCR. There must have been something she could have done to save her. Grizel had said she'd suspected the girl had taken pennyroyal to abort the child. Amber admitted she knew next to nothing about childbirth, but Molly was almost to term. The baby should have had a chance. She remembered Grizel being a little surprised that the child was born dead. The pennyroyal may well have been laced with poison. MacDougal, the wolfhound, barked, bringing her thoughts back to the present.

Lachlan tightened his grip on her hand. "What troubles you lass? Your thoughts are far away."

"I was just thinking about Molly. What will you do with Bartholomew?"

The muscles in Lachlan's face tightened. "He will be

held in the dungeon until the judgment. I have decided the trial will be long in coming. Bartholomew needs time to realize the weight of what he has done."

Amber remembered holding the lifeless baby in her arms and the look of despair in Molly's face before she died. This was one time when she was not going to interfere. She watched the limp figure of O'Donnell being carried to the entrance of the Great Hall. Bloodstains covered his shirt and contrasted vividly with the almost blue white of his skin. Her legs did not feel as though they had the strength to hold her upright. The violence of this century was one thing the historians had depicted very accurately. Bartholomew may not have killed O'Donnell outright, but she doubted he'd survive long. She didn't remember seeing any bandages to stop the bleeding. What the man needed was the emergency ward at a hospital, but he'd probably get leeches. She had failed Molly. Could she do any better with O'Donnell?

She nodded in the direction they had carried the man on the stretcher. "Lachlan, where are they taking him?"

"There is life in him still. I shall have Marcail see to him. Two days and he will be fully recovered."

Amber watched the torches being lit on the inner walls of the castle. The flames tried feebly to burn through the mist-encased courtyard. "He appears more dead than alive. You think it will take him only two days to recover?"

"Aye."

Conversation with Lachlan was at times very frustrating. She had the feeling that he only told her what he wanted her to know. Nothing more, nothing less. And what she wanted to know was how he could predict exactly how long it would take for a critically injured man to recover.

He motioned abruptly to Angus and the men surrounding Bartholomew. "Take him away. I shall see to him later."

The schoolmaster struggled against those who began to drag him forward. As he passed where she stood in shocked silence, a look of unmasked hatred was evident in his eyes.

Lachlan's voice was low and his hand rested lightly on the hilt of his sword. "Enjoy well the freedom in the cell you share with the rats. It will be the last comfort you shall have. After you are judged, you will deal with me."

The fight drained away from Bartholomew as he was dragged to the dungeon by two of Lachlan's men.

Gavin provided a welcome interruption. "Lachlan." The boy raced into the courtyard, yanked on his brother's tartan and whispered something in his ear.

"Aye, I will go to our mother at once." Lachlan turned toward Amber. "Lady Diedra requests that I speak with her. There are arrangements to be made for the Council members who have arrived in my absence. Angus shall escort you to your rooms."

He covered the distance to the Great Hall with long hurried strides, leaving Amber in the midst of shouting men, barking dogs, restless horses, and dozens of strangers. Everyone appeared to have somewhere to go, or some duty to perform. Except for her. Well, she could at least check on the man named O'Donnell. It would give her a focus. She needed something to keep her mind from dwelling on Molly and her baby.

Angus appeared at her side, waiting patiently to fulfill his duty to Lachlan. She'd known dogs that weren't this loyal. Clearly, there was no way she could take a step without the big man on her heels, but then, she doubted he would mind if she wanted to volunteer to help an injured man.

"I'd like to see what I could do to help O'Donnell."

Angus frowned slightly. "Nay, lass, 'tis not a task the laird would wish you to perform."

"And why not? Didn't Lachlan say I should be given as much freedom as Marcail or Elaenor? We're betrothed after all, and I think I should be allowed to check on an injured man if I want to."

A hint of a smile crossed Angus' mouth. She knew she was no more betrothed to Lachlan than Angus was, but the entire population of the castle had bought the story. If she were a betting person, she'd wager than Angus was only going along with the fairy tale because of Lachlan.

"Well then, lass, since you are intent on this course, be warned, it will not be a pleasant sight." Angus pointed in the direction Lachlan's men had taken the stretcher.

Amber reached up, kissed him on the cheek, gathered her skirts, and headed in the direction Angus indicated. She could hear him tsk, tsking behind her. Okay, so maybe she should have just said thank you, and left it at that. She'd have to remember next time that this century was so formal it made Jane Austen's era look like Sodom and Gomorrah.

Chapter

8

❧

$\mathcal{L}$ady Diedra ordered candles to be kept lit both day and night and their light spilled into the hallway as Lachlan entered. These surroundings were all too familiar. The walls and bedcoverings were draped in red silk. A framed portrait of his mother and shields of varying sizes and shapes glimmered over the mantel. His mother stood across the room from the crackling fire by the window that looked out onto the sunlit waters of the loch.

Her hair, gray as the clouds over the Highlands before a heavy rain, hung past her waist. She wore a white velvet tunic over a linen shift. Celtic symbols and letters were sewn on the hem and sleeves with gold thread. In the six years since her husband and children's death at the hands of Subedei, this was the only style of garment she would wear.

He remembered her words the day she had first shown it to him. "I wore this very gown when I was wed to your father and drank the Elixir of Life. It will be what I wear when I die."

Lachlan felt as if his legs were somehow rooted to the floor, like an ancient tree, free only to observe, but never to take part in the events that swirled around him. He was helpless to change what he knew was happening. His mother longed for death to take her.

It was the custom of his race, once the Council of Seven granted approval for a couple to marry, that they would drink the elixir that reversed their immortality. Within two to three years the sterility was reversed. It was expected that seven children would be born in remembrance of the seven original families who had escaped after their island home was destroyed. Some felt the loss of their immortality was too high a price to pay for the gift of being able to have children. It had not been so for his parents. At least, there was a time he believed this to be true. They would begin to age, but, it was at a slower rate than mortals. It was not unusual to be able to live another one hundred to one hundred and fifty years after taking the elixir.

However, after the deaths in his family his mother had aged more rapidly. Her stare held the vacant air of one who had already left this world for another. He felt the old anger rise to the surface. Lachlan had not been there to protect them. He closed his eyes to try and quiet the self-accusations.

The warmth of the chamber was suffocating. He shifted his weight and waited for his mother to acknowledge his presence as memories drifted back to him. Although she had been vibrant and full of energy when he was a lad, and had followed his father on the battlefield wielding her own sword, his childhood was little different from Gavin's. His parents, like many others of his race, left their children to raise themselves.

He joined her at the narrow window. It was

believed that the only way a child learned was from the harsh methods used by tutors such as Bartholomew. He thought of Amber reading aloud to Gavin, and of her befriending Elaenor. She used a gentle touch and Gavin had blossomed under her care. Elaenor, too, had emerged from the shadows that held her in the grip of sadness. Amber had shown him that, indeed, change was possible.

His mother turned and stared at him, as though realizing for the first time that he was beside her. Her eyes were lifeless and her voice did not hold the strength he had remembered as a lad.

"Do not give up your birthright."

It was the same thing she had said to him during each visit. She regretted the loss of her immortality in order to marry and bear children. He wondered if that was how it had to be with his kind. Would they regret it so much that they ceased to live long before their hearts stopped beating? Was it the reason Angus had not asked to relinquish his immortality? Lachlan knew he loved Myra, but perhaps not enough.

He put his arm around his mother's waist and helped her to the bed. Each day she was thinner. He glanced over at a tray of food. It looked untouched. What Una had told him appeared to be true. His mother was slowly starving herself to death.

She sat down and smoothed the material of her gown. "You have an interest in the Lady Amber?"

Lachlan remembered the night he found his mother outside Amber's chamber. He crossed to the window, picked up a chair and brought it over to the bed. Lachlan wanted to delay the onslaught of questions he knew to be forthcoming and wagered she knew more about the lives in the castle than he did. The knowledge did not sit well. He was not prepared to speak of his feelings for Amber. In truth, he did not know how she might fit into his life.

He sat down and decided to evade the direct question. "We have often provided a safe haven for those in need."

She reached for a book that lay on the table and opened it with care. The pages were framed in gold, blue and red intertwining flowers. Her eyes seemed to hold a depth of compassion he had rarely seen and he wondered at the cause. Then as suddenly as the emotion had crossed her face, it vanished. She closed the book and set it down.

"I can no longer see to read the words, but my mind has not dulled so much that I am unable to tell when my son avoids my question. I ask it only because I would warn you."

He leaned back. His mother rarely took an interest in the events in his life. "Do not be afraid to speak the questions you wish to ask."

She laced her fingers together in her lap and stared at them. "Your father was direct as well. It was what first drew me to him." A smile crossed her face. "That, and his strength of will."

A sudden gust of wind blew against the window and rattled the leaded glass panes. The sound was so loud in his ears he could barely hear her next words.

"I loved your father and enjoyed our time together." She paused and glanced toward the hearth where flames curled around the wood, and smoke drifted upward through the chimney.

She only remembered the times before his father was taken by the madness. She turned back to him.

"Although the children I bore with him will ensure

our race continues, there are times when I regret the impulsiveness to end my immortality."

"Mother, you have lived the span of twenty lifetimes. Surely that is enough, even for us."

Her eyes opened wider and there was anger in their depths. "Should twenty be enough, if thirty were possible? I would return to the time before I drank the elixir and refuse your father."

A cloud blocked the light of the sun, transforming the room into shades of blood red. He looked at the wasted figure on the bed. She spoke of her children as obligations she had been required to produce. He wondered if others of his race shared her view. She seemed to take the love she professed for his father as little consequence when compared with her immortality. He hoped that the regret he heard in her voice was a result of the madness holding her prisoner and did not reflect her true feelings.

"Gavin told me you wished to speak with me."

"I am told Subedei marches once again toward Urquhart. Has he not taken enough from us?"

Lachlan stared at the flames in the hearth. "I should have had him executed for his crime, instead of allowing your wishes to be fulfilled."

Her voice became shrill and frantic. "He raped your sister, Beatrice, tore her heart from her body, and left her in the streets of Naples. I demanded my rights as mother to my eldest daughter. I called on the justice of the ancients, and a judgment was passed down that would assure he remembered what he had done to my child for the rest of his immortal life."

"We had him castrated, but Subedei is not one to retreat into the woods, whimpering like a wounded animal. He is a man who will seek vengeance. We must prepare for battle, as he comes for all who presided over his judgment."

She nodded weakly and sank back on the pillows, her eyes once more vacant and lifeless. "There is a greater battle you have not spoken of, my son. One for which there is no defense. I blame myself, for I saw the beginnings of the insanity that is the curse of our people before I wed your father. I had thought I could both change him and prevent the madness from occurring in our children. But where I have failed, this woman may succeed. I know why Amber has come to you."

He was startled at her swift change in subject. At first he was unclear as to her meaning, and then he recalled the missing vial. He had not thought to ask his mother if she possessed knowledge of what had happened. Although she was lost in her own grief, there was still much he could learn from her.

The candles flickered and cast shadows in the chamber. Someone had opened a door. Marcail appeared dressed in a gown as black as the depths of Loch Ness.

His mother turned and her fingers trembled as she pointed toward Marcail. The effort drained the last shreds of her strength and she closed her eyes.

Marcail fingered the pearls at her throat. "Your mother, how does she fare?"

"It is as it always has been."

"Angus has told me that we have another visitor and asks that I administer to him."

Lachlan barely heard Marcail as the words his mother had spoken, and her accusation, brought into sharp focus the answer he had sought. The woman standing before him was responsible for Amber's appearance in Loch Ness. But eager as he was for a confirmation, a more pressing matter awaited.

"O'Donnell is one of us." He awaited her reaction.

"You are sure he is of our kind? Perhaps Bartholomew did not injure him as severely as you thought. I have known men with extraordinary ability to heal."

"Bartholomew was not satisfied with a single wound to the heart. No mortal could survive the damage that he inflicted on O'Donnell."

Marcail hesitated as though she weighed her decision. When finally she raised her eyes to his, they were cloaked in her familiar emotionless stare. "I shall see to him."

A fire crackled cheerfully in the Great Hall and warmed the chill in the night air. The sound was drowned out by the clanking of metal plates and utensils. The bright colors of the clothes worn by the noblemen mixed with the muted tones of the clansmen. Lachlan drained the contents of ale from his goblet and set it down. His kind had come for the meeting of the Council of Seven and mingled with the Highlanders. Lachlan searched the faces in the crowd, but could not find the woman he sought. He pushed the goblet away and adjusted his plaid over his shoulder.

Before Amber had arrived, his path was clear; defeat all those who opposed him and protect his lands and people. Of late he found himself wondering what it would be like to allow a woman into his heart. Was there truth in what Angus said? Had the thirst for battle taken precedence over all else?

Marcail motioned for him to join her. The flames in the hearth licked and curled over the wood logs like angry waves over a rock strewn shore. He stood. It was time for him to attend to his duties.

He wove his way around the long trestle tables of men bent over their evening meal. A few lifted their heads as he passed and nodded before resuming the business of eating and drinking. Their conversations buzzed like bees in a hive. He paused. Marcail was talking to the twins, Artemis and Theseus. They were wearing the garb of Spanish nobles and stood with Marcail near the window at the far end of the Great Hall. Although they were in a corner, it seemed as though the light of the torches that lined the walls focused on them.

Marcail put her hand on his arm. "Our friends have just returned from the New World. For a time they were with Cortez."

Theseus shook his head. Fine powder from his wig floated to the floor.

"The riches we have tasted with Cortez are beyond belief. We found the people, called Aztecs, both gentle and fierce. They also possess the knowledge to turn dry, desolate land into a lush and fertile paradise with irrigation methods that call to mind the accomplishments of the ancient Egyptians." He frowned. "The Aztecs are doomed, of course."

Theseus seemed to shake away the shadows that had crossed his expression. He held up a small canvas sack. "But all the riches from the New World do not glitter. This strange substance is called 'chocolate.' My good friend Montezuma drank a dark, bittersweet liquid made from these beans. He drained a golden goblet full of it each night before he went into his harem. Imagine, the man had the ability to satisfy over one hundred women."

Theseus spoke loudly enough for the closest of the men to overhead his statement and their laughter rang out. This was followed by more merriment, as the tale was repeated. The men cheered. The volume of the noise increased with each tankard of ale drunk. Those assembled were in good spirits. If one of Theseus' stories had been the cause, he meant to encourage more.

He knew his friend, however, and watched him pull on the ties of the bag he held. It appeared that something caused the Spaniard to tell this type of story. Usually he was only interested in proven facts. But in time Theseus would come to his purpose.

When the room had quieted enough for Lachlan to make himself heard once more, he pressed Theseus to continue. "You say Montezuma satisfied one hundred women in one night? A difficult tale to believe."

Theseus straightened his wig. "I had hoped with age you would develop a sense of romance. As always, you require matters of the heart to be examined as you would analyze strategies for conquest."

Lachlan could hear muffled laughter in the background. His men would not risk his anger if they believed he had taken offense. In truth, he had not. He put his hand over his heart.

"You wound me deeply, but a man cannot change that which he has become."

The twin called Artemis jabbed Lachlan in the ribs. "On the contrary, friend, we have heard that you have changed a great deal. The arrangement you have with a Lady Amber and the rather unusual way she came into your life is a subject of constant discussion. Una has also informed us that you have ordered a gown made to replace one that was ruined. You have more romance in your soul than you will admit."

He lowered his voice so no one other than the four of them would hear. "But that is your affair, as long as it goes no further than a pretense of a promise of marriage. We can ill afford to lose you as head of the Council."

Artemis waved a lace handkerchief. "But as for my brother's outburst, ignore the fellow. He has high hopes for this chocolate concoction that was named 'food for the gods.' Theseus has given some of the stuff to Una to prepare." He laughed. "You have no need of it, but I think it will take more than one goblet full to improve my brother's luck with the women at court."

Lachlan turned toward the fire. These men were older than he, older than Marcail, and yet they retained a lightness of spirit. They were free to follow their quest to explore the world. At this moment he felt as though he had lived centuries, instead of only ninety-five years.

Marcail cleared her throat. "I have heard the Spanish monks have forbidden women the drink. They say it is too potent an aphrodisiac for them. A typical response." Her voice took on an authoritative tone. "There are more important matters to discuss."

"You would make a grand ruler." Artemis fluffed the lace at his sleeve. "Ever ready to steer the rabble back to the business at hand."

Marcail's voice softened as she turned to Artemis. "All our people appreciate the commitment you and your brother have made to search for our kind in the New World. I know well the reason you avoid the subject, and only spin tales of nonsense and fantasy for our amusement."

She motioned for them to follow her to an alcove, where their conversations could not be overheard.

Lachlan agreed. In a castle occupied by so many, secrets were as hard to keep as a tankard of ale from a thirsty clansman.

She lowered her voice and addressed Lachlan. "Have you heard that none of our kind were found in the New World? This is the third time we have sent out emissaries and failed."

So, here at last was the reason why Theseus had babbled on about a mysterious food, instead of coming to the point about this new land. He too would have avoided facing the discovery. But perhaps they were mistaken.

He regarded the twins. "I do not find that unusual. After all, our bodies are not marked. A pity the ancients did not think of a way to remedy the situation. Instead, we have to rely on family histories and investigate any reports of mortals retaining their youth beyond what may be expected. We also must seek out those who survive a seemingly fatal wound."

Theseus took a pipe from within the folds of his shirt. "True enough. But you are missing the meat of the story. Because of the reports of human sacrifice in the New World, we thought our kind might have evolved in that land, as we did around the Nile. We survived the Egyptians' insatiable hunger to appease their gods with human blood by developing a way for our bodies to restore themselves. However successful the ancients were at prolonging life, they failed in the end. Our enemies discovered we cannot continue if our heads are severed or our hearts are torn from our bodies."

Artemis took over the tale. "In the New World, the method of killing for the sacrificial altar is to have the victim's heart cut out of his body and burned. It is doubtful any of our race survived amongst the Aztecs.

Further, the last known birth of a child from an immortal couple was in your family. Our line will die out with Gavin, your brother."

Lachlan was suddenly aware of the noises in the Great Hall. They resounded in his ears and he wondered if his people might be racing toward extinction. Perhaps, one day, only one of his race would remain, to become like the beast that swam in Loch Ness; alone and the last of its kind.

The loneliness would become unbearable, the responsibilities overwhelming. His people kept safe the history of mankind that dated back thousands of years. They allowed ruins to be discovered and the lost writings to be unearthed, as man moved farther away from superstition and into the time of illumination. There was still so much left to do, so much to be explained.

The path before his people was clear. "If children are the concern, then revisit the rules surrounding marriage and the problem is solved. Those who wish to marry should do so when they desire it and with the person of their own choosing. In the case of my sister, Diane, by the time the Council had sanctioned a mate it was too late. Subedei cut her heart out of her chest when he attacked Urquhart."

Artemis nodded. "Your words are true, but it is not an easy task to convince the Council of Seven to change tradition. Besides, there are not many who would give up their immortality to have children and face the eventuality of death. It is too great a price. When Diane expressed her desire to join, it was difficult to find a man who willingly would give up so much."

"There was such a man." Lachlan remembered Diane's tears. "But he was denied."

Theseus drew on his pipe and let the smoke out slowly. "The man you speak of was not of our race. He was mortal. The laws are clear, as you know well. We cannot join with them. It is against the teachings of the ancients. The children born of such a union would not be immortal."

"The warning is three thousand years old and has long since taken on a life of its own. Nothing is proven."

Marcail smoothed her gown. "All you say is true enough. But the risk is too great. It is our duty to produce children who will carry on our race." She shrugged. "We have long relished the idea of living dangerously, as warriors. We have the ability and time to accumulate great stores of knowledge, to help others. We can be killed. We can die. Soon we shall be like the tales of Arthur and his Knights of the Round Table. No one will know what part was legend and what part was fantasy, there will be none of us left to tell the story. Those of us who are willing must drink the elixir and produce children to carry on our heritage."

Lachlan heard the plaintive music of a fiddle through the haunting words Marcail spoke. There was a quality of deep regret in her voice tonight.

She touched his arm. "I need to see O'Donnell. Are you aware the Lady Amber assisted Una in the cleansing of the man's wounds? Ah . . . I see you were not. Well, there was no harm done. He appeared as any man would who had been stabbed. You were right, however, in believing he was one of us. Already O'Donnell has begun to heal."

"The Lady Amber is determined to become acquainted with all corners of my life."

"Of that you can rest assured. Be certain of the

place you wish her to occupy, and then pray to the gods she desires it as well. She is a woman who values her freedom."

"As do you."

A smile softened her expression. She nodded, turned from him, and then threaded her way through the Great Hall toward the stairs. She held her head high. People made a path for her to pass as though it were expected, commanded. Since Marcail had arrived at Urquhart she kept to herself and only associated with others when necessary. Yet willingly she spent time watching over O'Donnell. The first few hours had been necessary to assure them he was an immortal, but after the rapid healing had begun, the need no longer existed. Marcail was not acting predictably, but then neither were Amber and Elaenor.

Why was he not surrounded by women whose only interests were the gown they would wear, or the men they would ensnare for a husband. For that company, he would have to visit the court. He had indeed spent time there, which was one of the reasons for his return to the Highlands.

The sound of the music swelled, echoing off the walls. He saw Marcail pause at the bottom of the stairs to speak with Amber. He stepped closer to get a better view. The noise and activity in the Great Hall faded into the background as he focused on her and felt the rapid beat of his heart. She was dressed in a gown of gold cloth that shimmered with each breath she took, and each step. Her hair, unbound and free of headdress, flowed in waves on her creamy white shoulders. He rubbed the back of his neck and tried to gain control of his irregular breathing. This time he would not run.

*　　*　　*

Amber watched Marcail walk purposefully up the stairs. The woman had asked to borrow the book, *Canterbury Tales*, in order to read aloud to O'Donnell. Amber didn't mind; in fact, it sounded like a good idea. The only thing that surprised her was that Marcail had asked not just for the book, but for her help as well. When she and Una had cleaned and dressed the man's wounds, Marcail had insisted she would tend to O'Donnell without further help.

Now Marcail was asking Amber to visit her in her chamber. She paused. That was odd, but then there was a lot about life in this castle that was not ringing true. She'd try and make sense of it later. Right now she was too interested in doing something about her hunger, and seeing Lachlan.

She was always surprised by the size of the Great Hall. A high school basketball court could fit comfortably in the room. It was jammed with people enjoying the evening meal and talking amongst themselves. She felt apart from them. There had been moments with Lachlan when she'd believed she could learn to fit in, become part of his world. She'd even taken special care in choosing a dress she thought he might like. But the idea was crazy.

Long trestle tables lined the room, overflowing with platters of salmon and haddock. She had the sudden impulse to sneak back to her room. She doubted she'd be missed. Amber picked up her skirts and turned to retrace her steps, then stopped when she heard her name. Over her shoulder she saw Elaenor run toward her. The young woman's smile was a welcome sight.

Elaenor lowered her voice. "If I have to be trapped here with all these people, I shall need someone interesting to talk to. Do you think we can go outside?"

Amber smiled. "Let me guess. The sky is clear, and you want to try locating a planet or two with your telescope."

"True, but that is only part of the reason. I want to share with you my letter from Elizabeth." Her expression reflected her frustration. "Lachlan insists I stay and meet everyone."

"No problem. I'm a master at making an appearance at social gatherings, and then slipping out the back way when no one is looking." She intertwined her arm in Elaenor's, glad the young woman wanted to share the contents of the letter. It was a good sign and one she hoped signaled that Elaenor was trying to widen her circle of friends.

The music of the fiddlers filled the Great Hall. Tables scraped against the wood floor as several men pushed them to the sides of the room. A circle dance began in the central space that was formed. Amber headed toward one of the tables heaped with food. The Scots were the most music-loving people she'd ever met. They were capable of being the most fierce warriors in history and, at the same time, the most generous of people. Amber sat down. It was hard not to want to be part of their life. She tore off a piece of venison, then put it between slices of crusty bread. Taking a bite of the juicy sandwich, she was surprised by how good it tasted. She looked toward the kitchen and remembered the first night she'd arrived. The smells had overwhelmed her and made her stomach turn. She must be more used to things than she thought. The food smelled good. She wondered if Daniel was turning meat over the fire tonight. Maybe she could tutor the boy alongside Gavin.

Elaenor was dancing with a tall, lanky young man

who was dressed in a brocade jacket and tight fitting pants. The young woman appeared, at least for now, to have abandoned her desire to search the skies for stars and to talk about the letter. Both could wait. Elaenor glanced at Amber and nodded in the direction of the young man she was with. Her expression was universal. Amber smiled in silent approval. Tomorrow they would have even more to talk about.

A wave of conversation buzzed around her, mingling with the music and laughter. She had thought life in this century would be boring. It was far from it. Across the sea of faces she searched for Lachlan. Her pulse rate increased. She attempted to return his gaze, but he had resumed speaking with two companions, men who had probably invented the phrase, "overdressed." If she didn't know any better she'd think Lachlan was playing hard to get or intentionally ignoring her. Perfect. Just what she didn't need right now . . . space.

She'd thought that being around people would help take her mind off Molly and the baby, but it hadn't. Everyone was leaving her alone. More to the point. Lachlan was leaving her alone. And after the festival . . . okay, fine, she didn't need a gargoyle to fall on her head. If he didn't want her, she didn't want him. While they were in Inverness he was probably just being nice, but she hated the way her heart ached. Amber wished she could guard against it. But it was too late. She grabbed what was left of her dinner and stood.

Out of the corner of her eye Amber noticed Lachlan staring in her direction as she left the table and headed toward the stairs. His expression was unguarded, his eyes dark with desire. Her heart beat faster as she suppressed a smile. He did want her.

The connection between them was as strong as the pull from the currents of Loch Ness that had brought her here. It took all her strength to leave. She wanted to feel his arms around her, to have him comfort her and love her.

That whole fantasy might prove to be a little tough, since the big lug chose this moment to give her the silent treatment. True, his expression spoke volumes, but this time, in this relationship, she wanted it all. The right words, emotions, commitment, actions; in other words, she wanted the fairy tale.

The light from the torches cast finger-like shadows down the hall. Amber shivered, opened the door to her room and hurried in. A fire and the light of a half dozen candles welcomed her.

She drew a chair closer to the hearth and sat down, watching the flames curl around the logs. She was right to leave all the noise and distractions. She needed time to think, to sort out her feelings. A gentle rain pelted against the windowpanes. All she needed was a cup of hot chocolate and a good book and the world would right itself again. It had always been her solution in the past.

A rush of warm, suffocating air greeted Marcail as she pulled open the door to her chamber and entered. Candles guarded against the shadows of the night, but they were of poor quality. They offered meager light in exchange for their share of smoke. She would talk to Una and advise her to use the tapers from Italy. Marcail paused on her way to open the window. O'Donnell lay unconscious on her bed. Amber and Una had worked hard to clean and bandage the man's

wounds. Her thoughts turned to the woman Lachlan
pulled from the water.

The Lady Diedra knew the events surrounding the
night Amber was pulled from the loch. She must have
told her son about Marcail's role. It was for the best.
He already suspected Amber was tied to the legend,
and soon he would know all.

Marcail herself had poured the elixir into the water,
while repeating the legend of the Lady of the Loch.
The Guardian had never failed when summoned.
However, it did not always end in success. She
remembered the man they had called "Ford." Marcail
had not been able to pull him out of the water in time.
A pity. He may have been able to teach them a great
deal. Regret and guilt still warred within her.

Amber, however, had survived. She must concentrate on that. Marcail could only hope her interpreta-
tion of the legend was accurate, and that Lachlan
would quickly come under its spell. The next full
moon was less than a fortnight away. What she was
unsure of was whether the Guardian had delivered a
mortal or an immortal woman.

It was a problem easily solved, and easier proven.
However, for now she would concentrate on
O'Donnell and give the task of determining Amber's
race to Angus. She tucked the book, *The Canterbury
Tales*, under her arm and looked at the man.

He was of medium height and frame, with shoulder
length hair that looked as though it had been cut with
the blunt end of a knife. His features were of no consequence. He was someone who would blend easily
into a crowd. She was suddenly curious as to the color
of his eyes. The idea came to her that they might be
green. Nonsense. She pulled herself up straighter and

crossed to the alcove next to the hearth. A foolish notion, what matter the color of his eyes?

She opened the double window, took a deep breath of the cool night breeze and sat down on a cushioned bench under the sill. That was indeed better. Una had sealed the chamber as tight as a tomb. Marcail had spent more time than she could remember explaining to Una the importance of fresh air and sunshine when tending the injured or sick. The woman clung to the old ways as though they were written on tablets of gold.

Marcail remembered a time when she shared Una's view. But she had the advantage of having lived over five lifetimes. She had gathered information on the art of healing from China, and Istanbul, comparing what she had learned with the physicians in London, Paris and Madrid.

She looked down at the leather-bound book, with its ornate gold leaf–engraved designs. She had not thought about her early quest to search out all knowledge surrounding medicine in a long while. She opened the book and turned to the story she wished to read. It mattered not. The world had an abundance of physicians, and if there was one less . . .

Chapter
9

❧

Lachlan walked down the winding stairway leading to the cookroom. He could hear someone opening cupboard doors and rummaging through the shelves. As he entered, a draft caused the candles on the long trestle table to flicker.

A figure wrapped in a green plaid was searching the cupboard built into the wall by the fireplace. Even in the shadows he recognized her. The death of Molly and her baby had affected Amber greatly.

" 'Tis an odd time of night to be filling your stomach. Come, I shall escort you back to your chamber."

Amber pulled the blanket more securely around her. "I'm not hungry. I'm looking for chocolate. It usually helps."

Lachlan took a deep breath to steady himself. He had awakened from a restless sleep; the words his mother had spoken still haunted his dreams. She knew about the legend, as did all his kind. But, in her frame of mind, what part was reality, what part fantasy? Walking through the dark corridors he had found himself outside Amber's chamber. When he discovered she was gone, he had been frantic, as the words of the old tale echoed through his mind. Seeing her again made him realize how precious she had become to him in the last two weeks. He could not lose her, but he knew not how to hold on.

Now he discovered she had been searching for something to eat in the middle of the night. Had she asked, he would have awakened the entire castle and had them search for whatever it was she wanted. Lachlan put his arm around her shoulders and turned her to face him. She trembled beneath his touch. "I shall take you to your chamber and wake Una to find whatever it is you desire."

"Chocolate." She shrugged out of his reach. "Actually a candy bar, or hot fudge over coffee-flavored ice cream would be perfect." She opened a cupboard next to the windows.

He pulled a chair from under the table and sat down. The word she spoke was similar to the one used by Theseus earlier tonight. Was she, too, from the New World? He would find out when she was ready, but now she was troubled, and he would know the reason. This woman was not unlike his sister. If something was on her mind, it would take patience to pull it from her. He folded his arms across his chest. It was going to be a long night.

Amber slammed the door shut, grabbed one of the candles on the table and headed for the pantry next to the stairs. He rested his head against the high back of the chair, taking pleasure in merely watching her. If he had any sense he would return to his warm bed and let this woman upturn everything in the room. Let her deal with Una's anger in the morning.

She burst from the pantry and put the candle and a small canvas sack on the table. "I've found cocoa beans. Now where does Una keep the sugar and milk? It shouldn't be too hard to crush them into a powder. I wonder if I need to roast them first? Could you start a fire?"

He reached out his hand and grasped her wrist. Beneath his fingers her pulse raced as if she had been running. "I shall build you a fire and help you make whatever this concoction is, but first tell me what troubles you."

Tears pooled in her eyes and slid slowly down her cheeks. "Molly, the baby and . . . I couldn't help them. I thought I could. Can you believe the arrogance? I really thought I could make the difference." She wiped her face. "It hurts too much to think about."

He gathered her in his arms, held her against his chest and kissed her lightly on the top of her head.

"And I don't belong here."

"We belong together."

Lachlan felt the force of his words linger in the air. He wished he could speak soothing words to her that would take away her pain. But all he could do was hold her. He hoped it was enough. She clung to him as her tears seeped through his shirt to his skin. Slowly, as time silently passed by, the tears subsided.

She pulled away from him. Her expression had changed from grief to confusion as if she struggled with the weight of the world.

"You didn't say one word to me this evening. One minute you're holding me, saying you can't draw breath without me, or that we were meant for each other and the next you're ignoring me."

"You ran from me before I had the chance."

She shook her head. "That's beside the point, and you know it. If you have feelings for me, and I don't mean the friendship or caretaker kind, but real heart-stopping, mind-altering type feelings, then we should explore them. You need to be honest with me."

He gently tucked a wisp of hair behind her ear. "I am a fool."

Amber smiled. "True."

The door to the kitchen flew open. Elaenor and a young man ran in holding hands and laughing. They stopped abruptly.

Elaenor looked from Lachlan to Amber and then back again. "I am sorry, we shall leave." She leaned over to her companion and whispered something in his ear before she turned to Lachlan. "The night is clear. Richard and I were trying to distinguish the stars from the planets."

Lachlan folded his arms across his chest. "Indeed."

He looked at his sister. The blush of excitement had faded. She should fear him. He recognized the boy. Richard was the son of John Tuscony and had traveled from Egypt with Artemis. He might be one of the immortals, but he would be lucky to survive this night.

Marcail had warned him of this day when Elaenor had returned from London. But his sister was still young and her thoughts were always turned toward accumulating knowledge. He had convinced himself this day was far off. A touch on his arm made him look down. It was Amber.

She smiled toward Elaenor and Richard. "So, what do you have in the bag?"

Elaenor turned to her, reaching into the cloth sack the young man held.

"Richard said this fruit is called an orange, and they grow in the lands around the Nile." She peeled back the rough outer skin and took a bite of the fruit. "It is delicious."

"I am not hungry, Sister, and I think 'twas not the sky you were exploring."

Elaenor's eyes seemed to widen and Richard's face turned pale.

"You are unkind, Brother, to think as such." Her smile had faded to a thin line. "However, what you suggest has merit." She turned and kissed Richard on the cheek. He blushed as red as Angus' beard and backed toward the door.

Lachlan could hear Amber's soft laughter. His sister stood with her hands on her hips, defiantly. Richard, however, looked as though he expected to be run through with a sword. Lachlan suspected his sister had kissed the lad in open defiance. He was beginning to think rebellion was a trait all women possessed.

They all awaited his response. He knew, too, he had not handled this well. Elaenor had never been like other young women. He had known, almost from the beginning, that his sister had disguised herself as a lad, and enrolled in Trinity College. He had chosen to say nothing. Lachlan had assured himself she was safe. A professor at the college watched over her. But women needed to be protected.

"How could you accuse me, Brother?"

He looked at the two women. Amber's eyes seemed to accuse him as well. His sister was right. He remembered the reports he had received from his friend at Trinity. After Elaenor's identity was discovered, she had still kept the lads at arm's length. He wished his memory had returned sooner, for the humble pie he was about to eat would be hard to swallow.

"Elaenor will not go." Lachlan slammed his fist on the trestle table. Plates rattled and goblets of wine tipped, spilling their contents over the linen cloth. His men averted their eyes.

Marcail leaned toward him. "Your sister will be well cared for. You shall, of course, send all the men you can spare to escort her to London."

At this moment Elaenor was in her chamber making ready for her journey. Fear for her safety caused his hands to tremble. She was the only sister he had left. Lachlan cared not that Elizabeth was the Queen of England. In the past he had made monarchs wait at his convenience. This would be one of those times.

"We shall send a message and inform Elizabeth that Elaenor shall be detained until I can accompany her myself."

Marcail fingered the pearls at her throat. "You know Elaenor must leave at once, in order to discourage the queen from pursuing this new course she has set."

Lachlan had read the contents of the letter and well knew the dangers. Elizabeth was an intelligent woman. She would be able to ferret out the truth of Amber's origins. That accomplished, it would only stimulate her curiosity more. It would be a matter of little time before his race would be discovered.

He had preached to his people that they must work for the good of all. Lachlan could ask no less of himself. Elaenor must leave as quickly as possible. She, alone, would be able to dissuade the queen from pursuing the theories written in the letter.

The sun was breaking over the horizon as Amber opened the wooden shutters in Elaenor's room. It promised to be a clear warm day. Amber took a moment to try to figure out how Aunt Dora would have broached the subject of the birds and the bees. Of course, Elaenor had mentioned that Marcail had told her all the essential facts, but there might still be a few details that Amber could fill in.

In the early morning light Amber could see the grove where she and Steven had made love. Her aunt had known something had changed the instant Amber walked in the door. The dear woman put on a pot of tea and they'd talked straight through until morning. Aunt Dora never raised her voice, never lectured in that condescending tone her parents always used, but listened to her instead. The normal questions regarding protection were raised and the consequences of teen pregnancy. And in the end, when Amber had asked her how she'd known, thinking perhaps it was the afterglow of lovemaking shining in her eyes, Dora had said it was the look of guilt in her expression.

Her aunt had taken a sip of tea, then explained that with deep and eternal love there was no guilt or regret, only fulfillment of one's self. But she'd also cautioned that love, like a rose, took time to nurture and grow. Amber brushed a tear from her eye as the memory faded.

In the room behind her she heard Elaenor packing clothes. She crossed to the bed and sat down. The young woman was throwing dresses, ribbons and undergarments into a large trunk. Elaenor had just told her she was planning a trip with Richard, no matter that the excuse was to visit a friend.

"I'll bet you could get someone to pack for you if you asked."

That was an understatement. Urquhart Castle was jammed with servants.

"I cannot wait. Lachlan has said my escort will be

ready within the hour to accompany Richard and his family to London."

Amber counted to ten to calm herself. She had the sudden impulse to lock Elaenor in her room.

"Does your brother know what you're doing?" Might as well get to the point; after all, Mr. Wonderful was waiting.

Elaenor tossed an embroidered headdress on the pile of clothes. "Yes, he knows. He said he would chop off Richard's head if we were to lie with one another."

Amber smiled. It was a typical big brother response. However, the threats her own brother made in high school had never stopped her. She felt her frustration increase. "Have you known Richard very long?"

"We were in a class together when I was going to school in London." The lid to the trunk clicked shut. "Do you think I should bring my jewelry?"

This young woman needed a chaperone. One who had her eyes wide open. "What if I go with you?"

"And leave my brother? Nay, that cannot be. He needs you. Even if he has not yet come to realize it." Elaenor frowned and walked over to the bed to sit beside Amber. "What troubles you? I will be very safe on my journey to London. Lachlan is seeing to every detail."

The knowledge was not reassuring. Amber had been on a picnic with Steven's family when the two of them had become "lost."

Amber held Elaenor's hands in hers. "When I was about your age, I met someone very much like Richard. I realized later that a young man's vision of love is not the same as a woman's."

Elaenor raised an eyebrow. "Do you believe I will become Richard's mistress?"

Lachlan's sister was direct. The image of Molly gave Amber the courage to continue. "I want you to be careful, that's all." She cleared her throat. "You are still very young."

"You are worried about my becoming pregnant. You need not be. Even if I were interested in Richard, in that way, I have no fear of becoming with child."

Amber squeezed Elaenor's hand gently and resisted the temptation to start ranting and raving. "Do you plan to use some form of protection to prevent the conception?"

"I have heard of such things. The Lady Marcail said that the Egyptians were particularly skilled in that area. But there is no need to worry about me. It is not possible for me to conceive." Elaenor smiled. "Besides, I have changed my mind about Richard. He is unable to point out even the easiest of the constellations in the sky. Can you imagine such ignorance? Such a man would be of little challenge."

Amber smiled but couldn't shake the feeling that she had missed something. Elaenor was an intelligent sixteen year old, which made what she'd said even more confusing. It was not that Elaenor did not think she'd get pregnant. The young woman believed she couldn't, until she decided the time was right. Amber was probably overreacting. At least Elaenor appeared to be not as romantically attached to Richard as she'd seemed last night. Maybe she should change the subject.

"Where is it that you're going, again?"

"To see Elizabeth." Elaenor went over to an empty trunk and resumed her packing. "When I discovered Richard and his family were returning to London, I decided, that instead of writing Elizabeth of my response to her letter, I would talk of it in person."

A log shifted and rolled to the lip of the hearth. Amber crossed to the fire and pushed it back in place with an iron poker. This woman Elaenor wrote to was interested in the sciences. Only the rich, or those of royal birth, educated their daughters. There were also the eccentrics, a category she decided, which fit the MacAlpin Clan. She dusted off her hands.

"I have to ask. Any chance this Elizabeth you keep talking about is none other than the one who rules England."

"Who else?" She pulled out a letter that was tucked in her sleeve and unfolded it. "Elizabeth is interested in the stars as much as I am. Did you know that before she became queen, her life was in jeopardy? Fearful, she sought the advice of a man who could read the future in the stars. He predicted not only would her life be spared, but that she would be a great ruler. It was then her interest turned toward the constellations."

"You have something in common. It is a good place to start a friendship."

Elaenor smiled and handed Amber the letter. "I would like you to read it and give me your opinion."

Amber stepped away from the hearth and took the note. Across the page, in bold handwriting, was a message from Elizabeth I. She smiled to herself, wanting to savor the moment. This woman would become one of the greatest rulers of all time and she, Amber MacPhee, was reading one of her letters. She felt light-headed.

The message was a short one. The ruler of England did not believe in wasting words. Each one held its own weight.

Dear Elaenor,

We have consulted with our astrologer and he confirms your theory that time is not solid and can be controlled. He further informs us that someone from the future is here.

E.

The words echoed over and over in Amber's mind and the letter quivered in her hand.

Elaenor touched her shoulder. "Is something wrong?"

Amber handed the letter back. "No. But I'm a little shaky. It must be because I didn't sleep well last night." She cleared her throat. "As for the letter . . . the idea is hard to believe."

"I agree." Elaenor laughed. "However, that is why I like her so. Elizabeth is always eager to explore all possibilities, especially if someone says it cannot be accomplished."

A knock on the door interrupted them and Elaenor's eyes widened. "That will be Una. It is time for me to leave." She turned to Amber. "I will miss you."

Amber hugged the young woman. She was going to miss her as well. "Your life will be so rich with adventures; do not be in a hurry to experience them all at once."

Elaenor smiled. "I shall remember each event and write to you of all that happens."

Richard's carriage pulled away from the castle followed by Lachlan's personal guard and wagons loaded with furniture and clothes. Amber left the second-floor window and headed for Marcail's room. The words in the letter repeated themselves over and over in her thoughts. If Elaenor didn't suspect that Amber was the person Elizabeth's astrologer spoke of, she soon would.

However, even if Elaenor made the connection, it was a long journey from Inverness to London and back again. Amber would have that much time to formulate a reason for her presence here, or find a way to return to her own time.

How could she, when she'd been here for some weeks and was no closer than when she first arrived? Guilt raced through her. If she were honest with herself, she would have to say she hadn't really tried and Lachlan was the cause.

She hesitated as she entered Marcail's room. The injured man, O'Donnell, lay on the bed asleep and Marcail sat on a chair beside him. Amber felt she was intruding on the quiet scene, and backed toward the door.

Marcail motioned to her. "Please warm yourself by the fire."

Rays of morning sunlight shimmered over Marcail's gown. She was dressed more for an evening at court than at the bedside of a man recovering from sword wounds.

Marcail nodded. "I am glad you have come. I have finished reading Chaucer's 'Knight's Tale' and am halfway through the 'Wife of Bath.' He treats marriage seriously in his poetry. I find that curious."

Amber walked forward slowly. Tapestries covered the floor as well as the walls. A vibrant mural, depicting a storm at sea, was painted over the hearth. Red and white dragons and two lovers sharing a cup by a well were incorporated into the scene. She recognized the tragic story of Tristan and Isolde, one of her favorite legends. She paused in front of Marcail.

Marcail drummed lightly on the cover of the book. "I have heard you read aloud to Gavin. There is an unusual lilt to your voice and the quality of it pulls the interest of whoever passes."

Amber turned her attention to O'Donnell. She could hear his even breathing. What would Marcail say if she knew that the "unusual lilt" was from the twentieth century Pacific Northwest?

O'Donnell mumbled incoherently in his sleep. Amber listened intently but couldn't understand the words. She'd thought at first, because of his Irish name, that maybe he spoke a form of Gaelic. But that wasn't it. At least it wasn't any version she'd ever heard.

Marcail looked at her. "It would please me if you would read to him while I rest. You can see his condition is much improved since you tended him last."

Amber nodded in agreement. The man's color was good. He looked as though the bleeding had stopped, and he was resting comfortably. Hardly what she would have expected after seeing those wounds. She hadn't thought he'd survive at all. Then she remembered Lachlan's prediction.

He'd not only said O'Donnell would survive, but that he'd recover in forty-eight hours. An uneasiness ran through her until she felt a shiver run up her spine. Maybe it was a lucky guess. But now, here was Marcail wanting her to read to him. It struck her that it was a modern concept to think those in a coma might be aware of the conversations going on around them.

The corners of Marcail's mouth gently turned into a smile. "I can almost hear your thoughts."

Amber hoped not.

Marcail rose from the chair in one fluid motion and walked over to her. "If you are like all the others in the castle, you are wondering why I read to a man held in a deep sleep."

For the first time Amber noticed how tired Marcail appeared. Urquhart was packed with servants, yet it was Marcail who was by O'Donnell's side.

"I don't think reading to him is a waste of time. I think he can hear you."

Marcail's voice lowered. "I do as well. Then, it is settled." She gazed at Amber before handing her the book. "I have marked the page. Do not fear, there is little chance he will awake before my return. I have but one matter to see to before I take my rest." She hesitated. "Have you ever loved someone?"

The image of Lachlan popped into Amber's mind. She forced it from her thoughts and gripped the book tighter, feeling the smooth leather against her fingers.

"I haven't known Lachlan that long."

"Perhaps not, but he was the first person you thought of. Time, you will find, has no claim where love is concerned. I pray you will experience the type of love of which minstrels sing. Unlike Tristan and Isolde, it continues to elude me." She glanced over at O'Donnell for a long moment. "But perhaps there are things that are of more importance."

Marcail turned and left abruptly. Amber felt relief that she would not have to examine her feelings for Lachlan further, but regret that Marcail had left. The woman was intuitive as well as intelligent and someone Amber would like to know better.

Amber walked over to the cushioned bench by the window, sat down and opened to the page marked with a white satin ribbon. Last night O'Donnell wasn't breathing. You couldn't wash a man's wounds and bandage him without noticing a little detail like that. He'd also been ice-cold to the touch. She remembered thinking he was dead, so why bother with bandages.

Today, however, he was resting comfortably as though all he'd suffered was a scratch. If these people were so hale and hearty, why would someone who had been stabbed repeatedly survive, but a woman giving birth die? Of course, Grizel had thought Molly was poisoned. She shuddered, remembering Bartholomew's expression before they dragged him to the dungeon. There was a missing piece to this puzzle.

The fire crackled in the hearth and she turned to stare at the flames, wanting to think of something else. The bright colors and lively sounds of the festival at Inverness floated through her mind. But as the pleasant memories surfaced, so did the questions. There was more that had seemed strange at the time. She sat back abruptly and the book dropped to the ground

The Punch-and-Judy show. Lachlan had laughed along with the rest of the crowd when the puppets began their performance, but when they reenacted the story of the Immortal Knight, his mood had changed. She'd decided, at the time, that he was taking the performance too literally. After all, enchanted beings who could not die were just one of the myths she herself had heard when she was a child. But there was more to it than that. He had not merely disliked the play, he'd hated it.

He was angry because the story was being told at all, and the excuse he gave was weak, at best. He'd objected to the retelling of that legend, but saw nothing wrong with Jonah and the Whale. So, she reasoned, it was not that he disliked legends in general, but the one about the immortal knight in particular.

Amber looked at O'Donnell. Fresh linen bandages wrapped the man's chest. No sign that blood was seeping through them. It was absurd to think this man was like the hero in the story, but it would be easy enough to lift the cloth and examine the wounds.

And find what? The question screamed through her thoughts. She was starting to think like her aunt, seeing trolls, water monsters and men who lived forever at every turn. All she would find, if she removed the bandages, was that she'd reopened the man's wounds. She decided her imagination would not be running this wild if she hadn't seen Gavin's back when he was playing with the other boys at the festival. Obviously Bartholomew hadn't beat Gavin as hard as she had at first thought.

Amber bent down and retrieved the book. She needed to concentrate on why she was here, and give her imagination a break before she did something she'd regret. She opened to the page Marcail had marked and stared at the words for so long they blurred before her eyes. Her aunt might give credence to all manner of fairy folk, but her parents were scientists who spent their lives digging for the pots and pans of lost civilizations. They thought that even the most far-fetched legend or myth had a basis in truth. Her aunt felt the same. Until this moment, however, she'd never made the connection between Aunt Dora's love of legends, and her parents passion for ancient civilizations.

Even if all the myths held some kernel of truth, there still remained vast areas that were embellished.

Therefore, a legend could grow around a man who lived longer than was normal, and the people might begin to think he had special powers.

She sat straighter. That had to be it. She repeated the theory in her head and felt, as her parents must have when they dug in ancient ruins, that under the next rock lay the clue that would make sense of it all.

In the windowless chamber Marcail took her place at the black, marble table reserved for members of the Council of Seven. Despite the gathered immortals, the silence in the candlelit room was almost a presence. They waited for Lachlan.

They had come from the four corners of the world to discuss the impending danger of Subedei's arrival. The twins sat at the far end of the table and whispered together. Kuan Yin, wrapped in a gown of gossamer blue silk, sat beside them in quiet meditation. The woman was a living legend in China and was revered for her boundless compassion and loving kindness. Beside Kuan Yin sat Hsi Wang Mu, dressed in red silk with red phoenix and white cranes embroidered on the cloth. Marcail admired the women greatly for their efforts to lead through example, and had heard it said they felt a deep sorrow at the evil they had seen in Subedei's actions. They had known him before the bloodlust consumed him. She knew they still struggled to find a cure, but the insatiable need to kill was never reversed once it took hold.

A bitter taste rose in her mouth. The ancients had discovered the secrets of eternal youth, but the cost was too high. It would have been better if they had not interfered, and allowed their race to survive the brutality of those times as best they might. But they had not. For some, that which made them immortal could also turn them insane. It struck randomly. At times it left whole families intact, while at others it infected only a few members.

The words of the legend of the Lady of the Loch filtered through her mind ... *a wisdom that will guide the chosen one out of his darkness.* It was Marcail, herself, who had summoned the Guardian. But time was running out. If the Lady Amber, did not alter the course of insanity that Marcail sensed had begun to infect Lachlan, their race would destroy itself. He alone had the strength of mind and body to put the good of all above his own desires and lead their kind into the next centuries. But if the insanity took hold of him, as it had Subedei, a battle between the two would rage that would destroy both sides.

She folded her hands in her lap and fought the waves of fatigue that swept over her. She should have rested while she had the opportunity, instead of speaking to Angus regarding the Lady Amber, but the matter they had discussed was important.

Lachlan entered with Zambodo at his side. Their animated conversation seemed intense. She knew Lachlan respected the man's knowledge of battle strategy. Zambodo had lived more centuries than he could count. A great warrior, he had lost his hand in a battle against Subedei's forces and so had a special score to settle. The ancients had been unable to discover a way for the body to rejuvenate an appendage once it was severed.

Zambodo was from Africa and preferred the warmth and culture of his own country to all else. Still, he had come to Urquhart out of respect for Lachlan. It was by no accident that Lachlan MacAlpin had been chosen, first as member, then as leader of the

Council. He had the intellect of Socrates, and the reasoning abilities of Solomon.

A hush fell over the chamber that was felt more than heard, as Lachlan sat.

"Subedei marches for Urquhart. We all know why he comes. When it was discovered that he raped my sister, the council ordered him castrated. I ratified the decision. The ancients believed it would render a man penitent and weak. They were wrong. Subedei intends to kill us all. I would not jeopardize others. I alone shoulder the responsibility. Leave, while you still can."

A murmur vibrated through the chamber. Angus stepped away from the back row to be heard.

"You are our chosen leader and our friend. The decision to punish Subedei in the old way was not yours alone. We stand together, because alone we perish. Subedei will attack and we shall prepare for his arrival." He paused and his expression grew dark. "Of more importance is what our brothers, Artemis and Theseus, have to say of their travels to the New World."

Lachlan rested his hands on the table. "They have returned from the New World with disturbing news. If our race is to survive, there must be children. If not, we will become like the mists of the Highlands; having neither substance nor soul. Or we can open the books of the ancients, reexamine what has been kept hidden, and begin again."

Angus' voice rose above the loud rumblings of conversation. "The ancients had their reasons for keeping certain truths from all but the Council of Seven."

Lachlan looked out over the sea of faces. They believed he would be wise enough to make decisions for them and that as long as the ancients' laws were not altered, all would be well. His race could live to see the great, great grandchildren of the kings and queens they fought for rise to power, yet they resisted change. If he was to succeed in saving his people, he must use patience.

He motioned to Artemis and Theseus. "Please tell of the outcome of your search for our people in the New World."

Lachlan returned to his own thoughts as the Spaniards told their tale. His people believed they could defeat Subedei as they had before. Lachlan did not agree. His enemy's bloodlust ran deep. They could not easily defeat a man who lived only in order to kill.

However, the matter of perpetuating the race needed to be addressed. Hopefully the report the twins gave would dispel the illusion that there were immortals enough to continue the race.

He both heard and felt the rise in the level of conversation as his people responded to the report. Lachlan would wait for the tempers and frustrations to run their course before he called them back to order. It was a bitter drink to swallow that a few must give up their immortality, for the sake of the greater good. He stood once more, waiting for the swell of emotions to subside.

"It accomplishes nothing to condemn or seek revenge on those in the New World who may have brutally murdered our kind. The decision we face is: in what direction do we continue? Without children, our kind will perish. I propose we look into our hearts. If one of us should choose a mate who is not of our race, but mortal, I ask you to consider the match worthy. The ancients claimed that a union with a mortal would not produce children of our kind. I believe we must test that theory."

Chapter
10

❧

Every bone in Marcail's body ached as she willed her feet toward her chamber. She had not felt this weary since her days tending the sick during the great plague that swept Europe in the fourteenth century. Lachlan was to be admired for his courageous proposal. Although many raised a voice in protest, she knew they would consider his words. Her race grew weary, as did she, of the confining rules which dictated who would be worthy and who would not. It had made her wish for the courage to declare a desire to wed a mortal man.

Lachlan had not expected her to ask permission to enter into a joining ceremony. The expression on his face told her that. But once she had made her decision, the matter was settled. The council was reluctant at first. She had served over three hundred years and when she married a replacement for her position on the Council would have to be found. That, however, was a small price to pay for their race's continuance. They had made suggestions for a mate. She had, however, already made her selection.

She pushed the door to her chamber open and

leaned against the wall. The tapers had burned down low; the night air cooled the room. O'Donnell rested quietly on the bed. The Lady Amber was asleep. All was as it should be.

A dog barked. Marcail looked down the dimly lit hallway and saw MacDougal, the wolfhound, race toward her with Gavin close behind. The animal trotted in, sniffed the ground, her shoes, and then went over to the foot of the bed where he settled down and rested his head on his paws. Gavin stared at her, his eyes wide. He squared his shoulders and tightened the line of his mouth.

Marcail knew this child was wary of her and knew well the reason. She avoided all those who tried to come too near. In her self-imposed isolation, she had become abrupt and distant. However, for all that he must be feeling, he struggled to conquer the emotion. She admired the lad's strength of will. With Lachlan's advice to guide him, he would grow into a worthy man. But for now, he was still just a child and must be taught. There were certain expectations when someone was recovering from an injury, even if that person be immortal.

"That vermin-infested animal has no place in this chamber."

Gavin met her gaze. "MacDougal belongs to me. He bathes more often than anyone in the castle."

The barrier around her heart weakened. This lad stood his ground in defense of his dog. She walked over and stroked the fur on MacDougal's head. His coat was indeed well cared for. She looked over at Gavin. "And are you as clean?"

Gavin folded his arms across his chest in a gesture that reminded her of Lachlan. "MacDougal and I bathe together. The Lady Amber says washing will help prevent me from getting sick. MacDougal as well."

Curious. The woman's views were not common in this part of the world. This theme kept playing over and over, just under the surface, as though it held hidden meaning. *It is she who will bring the knowledge and the courage of generations yet unborn.*

She would not think on it tonight, there were other matters more pressing. She noticed that the young woman slept as soundly as O'Donnell through all the commotion. Marcail understood the level of exhaustion that would allow a person to sleep through any sound. She had often been able to rest in a protected shelter while a battle raged around her. She picked up the book that had dropped to the floor at the Lady Amber's feet and shook her gently on the shoulder.

Amber stretched and opened her eyes. She looked toward the bed. "Is O'Donnell all right?"

"He is indeed. You have done a great service by reading to him this night, but you have missed the meal in the Great Hall. I have told Una to send food to your chamber."

"Thank you." Amber yawned. "Gavin, what are you doing up so late?"

The boy motioned to O'Donnell. "I wanted to help Marcail read to him. I think he will like the "Knight's Tale." Lachlan said O'Donnell is . . ." Gavin paused and looked at Marcail.

She put her hand on the boy's shoulder and pressed lightly to caution him. ". . . a great warrior. Is that not correct?"

He nodded slowly. "Aye."

Thank the gods, the boy realized what he was about to say.

Amber stood and kissed Gavin on the top of his head. "I'm glad you're here to help Marcail read. She looks as tired as I feel."

Gavin's face glowed with pride. "I shall read the 'Knight's Tale.' I have been practicing."

Marcail watched Amber smile before she turned and left the chamber. In a few words Amber had managed to let Gavin know his importance to her. The boy was beaming with pride. Marcail had been on this earth for hundreds of years and thought she knew all there was of life to learn. It was time she began to show Gavin the love she felt for him. It would not make him weak, but give him confidence. She hoped now, more than ever, the test Angus planned would prove Amber immortal. Their race could be only the richer for Amber's contributions.

She felt Gavin tug on her sleeve. Marcail walked over to the bench by the window and patted a place next to her. "Would you like to begin the story?"

"Aye." His voice was eager and his eyes lit up as though she had offered a sweet rather than a book for his enjoyment. He indicated O'Donnell. "Can he hear us?"

She smiled. "We shall have to ask him when he awakes."

Gavin snuggled against her. She put her arm around him and pulled him close. Her heart warmed. She had forgotten the forgiving nature of children. In Lachlan's correspondence he had described Gavin as a child who hated to learn, and would rather spend his day practicing with sword and ax than in a classroom. She knew well Bartholomew's failure to teach the lad. Yet Amber had unlocked the scholar hidden within. An intelligent mind could be nurtured and taught the skills necessary to survive. Yes, she would be most curious as to the outcome of Angus' test.

The inner courtyard was bathed in sunlight as Lachlan removed his shirt and tightened his plaid around his waist. His men were putting away their weapons. He dismissed the notion that they were lazy and reminded himself they were able warriors. Yet he found the further he tested his physical endurance, the more alive he felt. He took a breath of the sweet-smelling autumn air and swung his sword above his head. Over the past year he had increased the length of each day's training. Once more he needed to have a heavier blade forged. He heard the familiar sound of a weapon being pulled from its scabbard and turned to see Angus.

His friend lunged toward him. "I knew I would find you here."

Lachlan deflected the thrust. The force rang along the blade and through his hands. He smiled. Angus was a worthy opponent. "You are late this morning."

Angus sidestepped Lachlan's counterattack. "Marcail and I were trying to discover the mystery that surrounds Lady Amber." He nodded in the direction of the entrance near the cookroom.

Lachlan saw Amber sitting on a bench reading to Gavin. He paused, his concentration temporarily broken. The afternoon sun seemed to focus all its light in her hair. How long had she been sitting nearby? He felt a sudden burning sensation on his arm and looked down. Angus had cut him with his blade. Droplets of blood formed over the wound. He had allowed himself to be distracted. He lunged forward.

Angus blocked the attack. "Amber is a pleasant

diversion, but there is a strangeness that lingers around her."

His friend was indeed close to the truth. He made contact with Angus' blade and drove him back. "You and I shall outlive most men one hundred times over, and yet you call her strange? She has been under our protection these past few weeks. Why the sudden need to discover her origins?"

"Have you considered that she might be immortal?"

Lachlan's pulse quickened. "It is unlikely." He held his sword out before him.

Angus attacked. "Do you never tire of fighting?"

Blade struck blade, the clamor ringing off the walls of the courtyard as the force of the blows resounded through Lachlan's grip. He knocked the sword out of Angus' hand and it clattered to the ground. "I do not see the need to refute my love of battle."

His friend reached down and retrieved his weapon. "You more than love battle, Lachlan, you need it. Take care you fill your life with more than a hunger for the fight. There has not been a time when I would choose my blade over the smile of a lass."

Lachlan tightened his grip on the hilt of his sword and looked across at Amber. "You make the choice sound simple. It is not." He sheathed his blade. "She is unlike other women."

"Aye, on that we are agreed. Our own are treated as equals and she behaves as though she were raised in the same manner. It is not hard to see she is as well-educated and outspoken as any man. The perfect companion for one of us. But maybe too perfect. Is that why you are afraid to discover her origins?"

"I fear only that I shall be drawn into your wild plans."

Angus raised an eyebrow. "Marcail says O'Donnell's wounds are healing without a scar. The test would be a simple one, with little bloodshed."

"I do not want her harmed." Lachlan felt the anger well inside him. He let his eyes linger on her, feeling a protectiveness surge through his blood. "She is not immortal. You have my word."

"How can you be so convinced? The depth of her knowledge and self-confidence are uncommon qualities in mortal women. What other explanation could there be?"

"Question her if you are so determined, but upon your life, harm her not."

A rider entered the courtyard and Lachlan turned toward him, welcoming the distraction. Dust swirled around the horse's hooves as the man brought his animal to an abrupt halt. He shouted to Lachlan as he dismounted.

"The Campbells have again raided your cattle."

The rider's arrival was timely. Lachlan relished the challenge. "How many are missing?"

"Ten, maybe more."

A sudden scream pierced the air. Lachlan turned abruptly to see Amber and Gavin sprawled on the ground. He caught the glint of metal as Angus stood and brushed off his tartan.

Lachlan covered the distance, pushed Angus aside and helped first Amber and then his brother to their feet. She was holding tight to her hand. Blood oozed through her fingers.

Gavin paced back and forth in nervous concern. Amber turned to him. "Don't worry. I'm fine."

Lachlan felt an instant surge of anger and let it build unchecked until he could hear it thunder through him.

Angus adjusted his sword. "I am sorry, lass. I stumbled."

Lachlan grabbed Angus around the throat. The words tore through him as he shouted each one. "She is cut."

Amber tore cloth from her undergarment and awkwardly wrapped the wound. "It was an accident."

"By the gods, it was no accident." Lachlan doubled up his fist and hit Angus in the face. The man crumbled to the ground. "That, too, was an accident. I meant to break his neck."

Amber put her bandaged hand on Lachlan's arm and the contact was like cool water over heated skin. It brought him out of the haze that held him in its grasp. The words of the legend of the Lady of the Loch rolled through his mind like the mist over Loch Ness. She could not have the power to turn him from the fate that had taken his father and now consumed Subedei. Surely, nothing could. Even his mother had tried and failed.

Her fingers pressed his arm. "Excuse me, but I'm bleeding here. You and Angus can fight over whether or not it was an accident later. I'll need stitches, and I'm assuming I'll have to find something vile to use, and that it will hurt a lot." She motioned to Gavin to gather their books.

Lachlan addressed his brother. "See to Angus and have Una tend him. She still has not forgiven him for eating all her pies when first he arrived. I shall seek out Marcail to look after the Lady Amber." He picked her up in his arms. She flinched when her injured hand brushed against him.

The extent of her pain pierced through him like a blade. He pulled her gently to him, suppressing the anger he felt toward Angus as he walked into the castle. It was a new sensation for him to be able to temper his rage. He wondered if it was Amber's doing. But even legends contained flaws. He doubted his reprieve from madness would be permanent. Perhaps, if he could not escape his father's destiny, he could delay its inevitable progress.

Lachlan ran the sharpening stone over the edge of his blade in the smoky workroom of the castle blacksmith. He concentrated on the familiar grating sound and the patience needed to complete his task, but it did not block out that which he so wished to forget.

The image of Amber as she watched Marcail stitch the wound on her hand was still fresh in his mind. Amber would not show pain and had detached herself from what was happening. She had carried on a conversation with him the entire time. He recalled not the words, just the tone. He had behaved in such a manner when he was flogged on a ship bound for the Spice Islands. Knowing he would recover had not dulled the pain, so he had concentrated on reciting aloud the tale of the Iliad and the Odyssey. Marcail had told him to let Amber rest, but when his work here was finished, he meant to seek her out to see for himself how well she fared. Then he would investigate the report of stolen cattle.

He heard someone enter and knew without turning it was Angus. The man cleared his throat.

"The stitches may not have been necessary."

Lachlan turned. "She asked for needle and thread. Would an immortal request such?"

Angus leaned against the rough wood door of the blacksmith's quarters and picked at the splinters. "A wound of such size would heal before I found the needle."

"Precisely." Lachlan put the stone down and grabbed a rag from the rim of a bucket. He wiped the fragments of dust off the blade and listened to the drizzling rain.

"Are you of a mind to use that sword on my flesh?"

Lachlan glanced at his friend and discovered he was no longer angry. The man only searched for the truth. Amber had, in fact, possessed traits common to immortal women. He did not approve of his methods, but Marcail had admitted to her part in the plan. Lachlan had expected better from the healer.

He smiled, remembering the look on Amber's face when he'd vowed to banish Angus and Marcail for their deed. Amber had shaken her finger at him, as though he were a naughty child, and told him to grow up. If she were part of the legend, then in truth, the gods surely had outdone themselves with this woman.

Lachlan raised his blade and tested the sharpness with his thumb. It sliced a layer of skin and drew a small droplet of blood. He wiped the cut on his plaid and turned to Angus. The man stood as quiet and as stoic as the marble statues in Greece. He knew Angus longed for some acknowledgment.

"I have need of your help."

Angus straightened, clenched his fist, and crossed his arm over his chest. He bowed. "Name it, Lord."

The formal title chilled Lachlan's bones. Angus spoke out of respect, and from the need to be pardoned, but Lachlan was in greater need of friends than followers.

"A rider claimed the Campbells were responsible

for the raid on our cattle. They are well aware of the sure retaliation I will pour down on their heads if these allegations are true. In the past, Clan Campbell's judgment may have been in question, but not their intelligence."

"It sounds as though you doubt the scout's information."

"Aye." Lachlan clasped Angus on the shoulder. "Before I strike, I will find the truth. You and I shall ride out at first light."

"It will be as you wish."

The sky began to darken. Lachlan crossed to the window. Lightning split the gloom.

Angus pushed away from the door. "Did you not feel it, my friend?"

"Aye." He glanced toward the castle wing that housed O'Donnell. "The time is at hand." He sheathed his sword and motioned for Angus to follow him.

The door to Marcail's chamber was ajar as Lachlan entered the quiet room. Amber was reading aloud, while Marcail sat and gazed at O'Donnell. He saw the uncertainty reflected in Marcail's eyes. He wondered at the cause and why she allowed Amber to remain. O'Donnell lay on the bed as still as death, his hands were folded across his chest and his eyes moved under their lids. He was only moments away from returning to them.

The law was clear. "Lady Amber, you must leave. At once."

She opened her mouth to protest.

He raised his hand to silence her words. No mortal had witnessed the Return to Life. His kind believed the knowledge was too dangerous. He trusted Amber, but his kind would not, and he had to honor their wishes and respect their fears.

"Leave, Amber. Please."

Amber pressed herself against the wall as the last of the people hurried through the door. She had bandaged O'Donnell's wounds and read to him until her voice was hoarse, but was not allowed to see him wake up. She dusted imaginary lint off her clothes, and off her pride. There was probably some rule, or custom, about visitors to a man who'd just recovered from life-threatening wounds. Nothing to get worked up about.

Before the chaos began she and Marcail were having a quiet chat about herbal remedies and increased life spans. Suddenly she was being unceremoniously ushered out the door. Immediately the parade had begun. Angus, followed by Gavin, the twins she'd seen the other night, and last, but not least, an assortment of people who looked as though they were representatives of the United Nations. Amber doubted all of them would fit into Marcail's room. A sardine in a can would have more space to move around.

Amber walked aimlessly down a torch lit corridor in an attempt to fill the hours before Una served dinner. Three days had crept by since Lachlan left Urquhart in search of those who had stolen his cattle. She'd spent her free time thinking about each moment they had spent together. It only made her miss him more. Amber had not realized how dull the castle was without him stomping about.

She rubbed the palm of her hand. The stitches were

beginning to itch. A sign of healing, her aunt always said. Marcail had done a great job. Amber would only have a small scar, but stitching up the cut had hurt like crazy. She'd turned down the wine Marcail had laced with some sort of painkiller, trying to act brave in front of Lachlan. Amber smiled remembering how much he had fussed over her. It was almost worth the injury. Almost.

Amber paused. She was lost. The hallway stretched into a dark void. Terrific. The torchlights wavered, casting dancing shadows along the walls. Oh, well, if she didn't reach a familiar wing, she'd just look out the window. Her rooms faced Loch Ness, so it should be easy to find her way back. Anyway, she had time on her hands since everyone was busy with O'Donnell. The man had recovered in exactly forty-eight hours as Lachlan had predicted. Once more she felt uneasy.

The flames in the wall sconces flickered. This time she felt a cold breeze. Wandering around a dark castle at night was probably not such a good idea. More than likely all these corridors and vacant rooms were jammed full of ghosts.

The corridor turned. She followed it, then paused. Portraits, the size of the big screen televisions in the Seattle sports bars, lined the walls. The people in the paintings were clothed in a manner that spanned both centuries and countries. A man dressed as a Roman warrior rode in a chariot pulled by a team of four white horses. Beside him, in a separate portrait, a woman in a full suit of armor fought a Bengal tiger.

On this remote wall, in the Highlands of Scotland, was a history of the world. Someone had gone to a lot of trouble to complete such a gallery. She noticed a portrait of a fierce looking Mongol warrior, and another of a Samurai. The corridor was so long she couldn't see the end and paintings took up every available space.

As she examined the faces and costumes of each person a common thread emerged. These were all people in the prime of their lives and they were all warriors. Nearing the end of the hall she saw a man standing in the shadows in front of one of the portraits. It was Lachlan.

"You have ventured far from your chamber." His voice sounded hollow and distant.

Her heart beat faster at the sight of him after so many days. As she walked toward him she fought the impulse to run into his arms, uncertain of his response. She rubbed the palm of her hand.

"You were gone quite a while."

"Aye. My business took longer than expected." He reached for her hand. "Are you still in pain from your injury?"

She shook her head. "No, but I'll have a scar to remember Angus by."

"He was wrong to injure you in such a way."

"Lachlan, it was an accident."

" 'Tis true enough." His words trailed off.

Amber watched him search for something more to say. "How long do you think it will be before O'Donnell will be well again?"

Lachlan's eyebrows scrunched together and then he smiled. "Oh, I understand your meaning. You wish to know if he still remains confined to bed?"

Amber nodded. She figured that if he knew in hours how long it would take for the man to recover from a life-threatening wound, Lachlan would certainly be able to make a calculated guess as to when O'Donnell could get out of bed.

"He has challenged Marcail to a game of chess, and plans to test his skill with my men on the practice field in the morning."

She sucked in a breath of air so quickly she began to choke.

"Lass, be you ill?"

"Ill no, confused yes."

"And what is it that confuses you?"

She rubbed her temples. "You can't be serious. He had dire wounds. I know because I saw them myself. So how can O'Donnell even think about prancing about with a sword?"

"I doubt that he prances. And as for his recovery, the Irish are a hardy bunch."

This was crazy. A critically injured man not only survived and recovered in forty-eight hours, but planned to have a vigorous workout in a matter of days. And Lachlan didn't think it was strange? Well she did.

She shook her head. "Never mind, let's talk about something else. The portraits for instance. These people are all about the same age. Was that on purpose?"

"You are the first to remark on it."

Somehow she doubted that.

"It is a tradition of my clan to have a portrait commissioned in the year of their thirty-fifth birthday."

"None after?"

Lachlan shook his head.

She took another look around the hall. "Do you have any idea why this kind of tradition was started?"

"Aye." He hesitated. "It was the belief of my ancestors that it was not until they reached the age of thirty-five that the true nature of their character showed in their faces."

Amber was curious. Her own time was only beginning to see value and beauty in men and women as they grew older. This seemed like an advanced concept and she agreed. "Do you have a portrait somewhere, or aren't you thirty-five as yet?"

His laugher echoed down the corridor and took her by surprise. "Aye, lass, my portrait hangs in the next hall." He tapped her on the tip of her nose. "And what is your age, my beauty?"

The way he was smiling at her took her breath away. "I turned twenty-eight on June nineteenth." She needed to switch to more neutral territory. "Can you tell me about these people?"

"Aye. You may ask any question that pleases you."

Amber indicated the portrait Lachlan had been looking at earlier. It showed a warrior in a suit of gleaming armor.

He tensed visibly. "That is my father. My mother is on the opposite wall a short distance farther down. I am told he would travel from one battlefield to the next, sometimes for years, before returning to the home of his birth. He would enter a town or village he had heard was embroiled in conflict, investigate the problem, and then fight on the side he felt had the just cause."

The words he spoke sounded hollow to her, as though they held little meaning to him.

"I think I would have liked him." Lachlan's expression turned so dark she backed away. "What's wrong?"

He shook his head. " 'Tis nothing. Come, I shall show you the picture of my mother."

He put his arm around her waist and guided her across the hall to another portrait.

The contact of his hand on her waist made her lose focus. Amber looked up at him. That was a mistake. The harsh expression he'd worn was gone. She felt herself go soft inside. At any second her brain would turn to mush.

"How did your parents meet?"

" 'Twas a story made into a minstrel's tale. My father wounded my mother in a battle."

"You mean they fought each other? I thought you said your father did battle only to protect the innocent?"

He nodded in the direction of his father's portrait. "Nay, what I said was that he fought on the side he felt just. My mother often did the same. On the day they met, they were opposing each other. Clad in chain mail, her head covered by a helmet and wielding a sword, my father did not recognize her as a woman until he wounded her and her helmet was knocked off as she fell. 'Twas said the moment he looked on her, his heart was lost."

A gentle rain misted through an open window at the end of the hallway and drizzled onto the wood planks of the floor. He crossed the corridor to close the shutters, latching them together with a metal bar. "The hour is late. Una will not allow the rest of the castle to eat until I arrive."

"Another MacAlpin custom?"

"Nay, fair maiden, 'tis a rule Una has decreed. And as long as she is in charge of the cookroom, no one dares defy her command. A few have tried and were denied food until she thought them sufficiently repentant."

"And what did you do to get in her good graces?"

A shadow passed over his face. "I was hunting in

the Highlands and came across a village which had been burned and looted. Alongside the men who had fought to defend their families lay the dead. Babies in their mothers' arms, children, the old and the crippled. The dwellings were still smoking. A woman staggered toward me holding the limp, dead body of her boy child. It was Una." The muscles in Lachlan's jaw tensed as he turned toward the window. "She has been with my family ever since."

Amber closed her eyes to shut out the mental image he'd painted. "Did you ever find out who was responsible?"

"Aye."

"And?" She opened her eyes and saw he was still turned away.

"They are all dead."

Amber crossed over to him. An expression of raw pain covered his face. It startled her. The revenge he'd brought down on those who'd massacred the village might have shocked someone living in the twentieth century, but in the sixteenth, it was expected. She put her hand on his arm.

"You did what you had to do. It happened a long time ago, and you need to put it behind you."

"Two days ago I came across a village where the dead were left to rot in their own blood."

Amber swayed against the wall. "What are you talking about?"

"My enemy, Subedei, took more than my cattle." Lachlan's voice seemed hollow. "The Mongol was not satisfied with murdering the inhabitants in the village. One man who survived told me that Subedei impaled the villagers on long poles, and watched them die a slow death."

She tasted bile. The extent of some men's cruelty to others unnerved her. "Dear God, no. What kind of monster would . . ."

"My father was such a monster . . . and I fear the same madness awaits me."

Amber struggled to get her trembling under control. Lachlan had been there. He had seen firsthand the horror of which she could only imagine, and the fear that must have run like a brush fire through the village. However, the expression in his eyes told of a deeper fear. She needed to find the right words to help him fight this battle.

"Lachlan, from what you've said, your father and Subedei have done unthinkable things, but that does not mean you will as well. I know you."

The cruelty she heard in his laugh startled her and his mouth turned up in a grim line. "You do not know me at all. I will become like my father."

A chill shivered through her. She shook herself free from its grasp. It was essential for Lachlan that she keep a level head. Amber reached for all the psychology she'd learned from the high school counselors.

"Just because your father did terrible things doesn't mean you automatically will do them." She turned his face toward her. "You have a choice. You need to take control of your life and choose your own path. Besides, I won't let you turn into a beast."

He brushed a wisp of hair off her forehead before cradling her against him. "I pray your belief in me will prevail."

Chapter
11

❧

Stuffing a chunk of Una's freshly baked bread in his mouth, Lachlan warmed himself by the cookroom hearth. He watched as she kneaded a sticky lump of dough. Sleep had eluded him last night, after he had escorted Amber to her chambers. Wandering restlessly through the castle as all others slept had given him time to think. He had no illusion about his wakeful state, or the reason for it. Amber was the cause. Last night, in the corridor lined with portraits, the words she had spoken held strength and conviction. Although others had told him he might escape his father's madness, Amber said he had the power within himself to change. When he had looked into her eyes, he believed it as well.

Thoughts of the way she would touch his arm when she wanted to get his attention, or to coax him out of ill-humor, drifted through his mind. And her smile; it lit up her face and his heart.

"Lad, you are far away this morn."

Una's words pulled him to the present and to another concern. Marcail. On the night that O'Donnell had returned to them, Marcail had told Lachlan she had chosen the Irishman. He respected her decision, but he would not give his sanction until he knew more of the man. He pushed away from the hearth.

"O'Donnell was not in his chamber. Have you seen him?"

Una clucked her tongue as she added flour to the dough. "I fixed him a bowl of porridge. He mentioned he was headed toward the courtyard to practice his game of chess. The Lady Marcail trounced him well last night after he awoke."

"O'Donnell will need more than practice to beat Marcail at chess. He will need the intervention of the ancient gods."

She laughed and brushed a wisp of gray hair off her face. "Aye, lad, the Lady Marcail is a match for any man. I sense many are scared away before it gets interesting." She winked. "But this man is different, and is much like you. The greater the challenge, the more satisfying the prize."

"You have known me for too long."

Her expression grew serious. "True enough, we go back a ways, you and I."

Her skin was lined with age, but her eyes were as clear and bright as when he first rescued her from the ruins that had once been her village. There were many years between them. It was not the first time he regretted their speed. Still he did not regret telling her about himself and his race. He lowered his voice. "Truly, the loss was mine that we never became more than friends."

She rubbed the small of her back and closed her eyes. Pain marred her features. She looked at him and the full impact of her age and weariness struck him. He put his hand on hers.

"Why do you not answer me?"

"The answer was always as clear as rainwater. A woman needs to know that she is more than wanted. She must be as necessary to her man as sun and water are to the heather in the Highlands. In those days, you needed no one." She squeezed his hand and nodded in the direction of the staircase. "But I have watched you with the Lady Amber. There is a difference about you when she is around."

She shook a flour-smudged finger at him. "And don't be telling me you feel responsible for her because you pulled her from the loch or some such nonsense. You are in love with her, Lachlan MacAlpin. And it scares you more than the affliction that cursed your father in his last days."

"You read more into my actions than is there."

"Nay, lad, I do not."

"Even if what you say is true, she deserves something I am unable to offer. Our high council does not agree with me that there is a difference between the future and the past. As yet, I cannot give her the child I believe she longs for."

She punched the dough with her fist. "Your responsibilities are too heavy for one man to carry." Her voice was a soft whisper. "Be off with you. I feel a lecture bubbling to the surface, and unless you want to hear its full force . . ."

He reached over and brushed a tear from her cheek. "Madam, I would sooner face the cannons of the English queen than your words of rebuff."

"Well spoken. Promise me you will not take your feelings for the Lady Amber lightly."

"Aye, I shall consider it. But you well know . . ."

She interrupted him. "What I know, Lachlan

MacAlpin, is that if ever there was a man who needed the touch of a woman to make him whole, it is you."

He shrugged. "You worry overmuch."

"And who else but me would have the patience?"

He bent over and kissed her on the cheek. "I do not know why you have put up with me for so long."

" 'Tis a wonder to me as well. Now, off with you."

Una shaped the dough into loaves and began to hum an old Celtic tune. It was her way of closing the conversation between them. He felt a tightness around his heart as he tore off another chunk of warm bread and crossed to the door that led outside. The unspoken words between them cut him deeply. There was a time when he had tried to return, in kind, the feelings she had for him. He wished she were not so perceptive, but she had known the limits of his love and turned him away. Una, in her fragile mortal body, needed someone with whom she could cherish each moment as though there would not be another to take its place. She was wise to cast him aside.

He stepped into the courtyard. The air was cool and brisk after the warmth of the cookroom. He hoped it would clear his troubled thoughts, but knew the only solution was to attack another problem.

As he paused, the courtyard started to churn to life. A maid carried a bowl of grain and a stable boy yawned and stretched as he headed toward the horses. The day was beginning.

Ribbons of pale morning light stretched across the horizon as Lachlan went in search of O'Donnell. The man was not hard to find. He sat, leaning against a stone wall, a chessboard balanced on his knees. So, this was the man Marcail chose over all others. O'Donnell was not yet aware of her decision and might still refuse her. He doubted the likelihood of that outcome. Marcail was seldom denied what she sought.

Chickens clucked and squawked as the maid tossed a handful of grain in their direction. Lachlan walked over to O'Donnell. He did not question that Marcail had given the matter much thought, but he did wonder at her choice. She was acting impulsively. It was not the Marcail he knew. Although she had committed to drinking the elixir, there were no assurances O'Donnell would do the same. There were a few incidents where one person had fulfilled his vow and drunk the Elixir of Life, only to learn that the one chosen had changed his mind. Of course the penalty for such a breach of conduct was death. He would not allow such a fate to happen to Marcail. Lachlan would find out the mettle of the Irishman before he consented to the match.

"I have heard the Lady Marcail beat you at a game of chess."

"Not one game, but three. The last was almost over before it began." O'Donnell picked up one of the chess pieces carved from translucent rose marble. "She took my Queen."

"She usually does if it is left unprotected."

"You have played chess with the Lady Marcail?"

"Only when cornered."

O'Donnell's laughter was spontaneous and loud. A few chickens flapped their wings and screeched in protest at the disturbance to their daily routine. It startled Lachlan as well. The man had a sense of humor. Good, he would need one.

O'Donnell rubbed his thumb over the smooth curves of the chess piece in his hand. "You are right. I did leave the lady unprotected and let my eagerness overshadow my judgment." He put the piece back on the board. "The Lady plays the game as she experiences life, with a shield of protection as thick as the wall of your castle."

Lachlan sat down. "Even if she loses her first line of defense, she knows of another that will protect her at all cost."

"Do we speak of Marcail or of chess?"

Lachlan turned his head toward O'Donnell and held the man's gaze until the air was thick with tension. "I speak of both."

"You need not concern yourself with my conduct around the Lady Marcail. I have deep feelings for her."

"And why should I not be concerned? I know you not, and think now that I should have left you for the wolves."

O'Donnell tapped one of the pieces lightly on the board. "Not a pleasant thought for a man who would not have been able to defend himself against such an attack."

"Better that, than Marcail lose her heart to a man who is but passing through."

O'Donnell stood so abruptly the chess pieces clattered to the ground. He drew his sword.

"I have killed for less offense."

Lachlan rose to his feet slowly as he appraised the man. He let his hand fall to the hilt of his sword. A red haze clouded his vision. The image of the man who stood before him, dead from his blade, appeared so strong he could smell the blood. He tightened his grip on the hilt and the thin thread of sanity he still possessed. He took a long calming breath of air, and thought of Amber. O'Donnell was prepared to risk his own life to defend his intentions toward Marcail. The man had passed the first test.

O'Donnell wiped the sweat from his upper lip. "I came only to seek Marcail's love. If she refuses me at this time, I shall wait. Stand and fight me and I will prove, with blood, the words I speak are true."

A cool breeze swirled the dry leaves in the courtyard. On the other side of the stables a dog barked. Shouts of his men on the practice field nearby combined with the sound of metal striking metal as the mock battles began. Lachlan gazed at the man before him. O'Donnell was traveling to Urquhart when Bartholomew had surprised him, yet Lachlan had no knowledge of him until several days ago.

"Sheath your sword. I have no need to fight you. How is it that you know Marcail?"

"I have known the lady for more centuries than I care to recall. When I first met her my hair was dyed black and hung past my shoulders. My right eye was covered with a patch. She thought me quite the rogue." He grinned. "We had ourselves a time."

Perhaps Marcail was not as impulsive as he had first thought. "She said she had never seen you before the night I brought you to the castle. How is it that she did not recognize you?"

O'Donnell lowered his voice. "The last time we were together we did not part on the best of terms. She discovered me in bed with another woman." He shrugged. "I tried to explain."

Laughter burst from Lachlan as though it had been long contained and he clasped O'Donnell on the shoulder. "You are lucky she did not run you through."

He grimaced. "She did."

"I should think that would have given her sufficient reason to remember you."

O'Donnell smiled. "A woman's mind does not often take the most logical course. She has loved me before, and it has taken me two hundred years to realize that she is the only one I want in my life. I will not leave without her." He closed his eyes and tilted his head toward the sky. "Did you ever wonder how long you were capable of loving someone?"

The sounds in the courtyard closed in on Lachlan until he could no longer distinguish one from the other. He felt suffocated. The words he spoke were little more than a whisper. "With every waking moment." He looked over at O'Donnell. "You are that sure of your love for Marcail?"

"I would not be here, otherwise."

Lachlan gazed in the direction of the water. Love was to him not unlike the Highland mist. It rolled off the loch so thick you could feel its embrace, while at other times it was hard to grasp. "I envy you."

MacDougal bounded toward him, with Gavin close behind. His brother tugged on his sleeve. "The Lady Amber asks that you meet us in two hours in the meadow."

Last night Lachlan had agreed to spend more time with her and his brother. He had not thought she meant to start today. "I shall not be finished with . . ."

Gavin looked doubtful. "Amber said two hours would be a long enough time for you to play with your sword."

Lachlan heard O'Donnell's laughter and silenced him with a glance. He turned back to Gavin. "Did she really use the word, 'play'?"

"Aye. And she said if you were not in the meadow, she would convince Una to serve you only bread and water for a week."

O'Donnell slapped Lachlan on the shoulder. "From what Marcail tells me about the Lady Amber, she could convince a fish to jump into the net."

Gavin motioned to his wolfhound and they raced toward the entrance to the cookroom. Once they had disappeared from sight, Lachlan crossed his arms over his chest and looked to where his men trained. They could do without him for one day. They might even benefit from being on their own without his supervision. It would teach them to rely on each other as well as draw on their own strength for leadership. Aye, his being absent from the training field for a half a day would be good for his men.

Lachlan leaned against the tree and looked at the sky through the branches. The leaves reminded him of the molten vats of gold he had seen in his travels to Egypt, and the fire in Amber's hair. He smiled and looked at her, as she and Gavin raced through the field with a ball between them. As skilled as any man he had ever seen, Amber played a game of keep away with his brother. Lachlan reached for a slice of crusty bread from the assortment of food Amber had brought along. She'd called it a "picnic." He tore off a hunk and put it into his mouth, throwing the crumbs on the ground for the birds. He marveled at the peaceful feeling.

He reached into his sporran, took out a piece of wood and rubbed it with his thumb. The carving was almost finished. He liked working with his hands; it helped free his mind to discover new solutions to old problems, and Amber was a mystery he needed to solve. He unsheathed his knife and shaved a rough spot on the wood. He looked over at Amber and Gavin. She had grabbed the boy under his arms and was spinning him around. They ran toward him and collapsed on the blanket at his feet, laughing and out of breath.

Gavin reached for the water and Amber stretched out on the ground and put her hands behind her head.

Then she sat up with her legs crossed in front of her. "It feels great to run again. Una shortened my skirt, otherwise I would never have been able to keep up with your brother. He's fast." She smiled at Gavin. "For a boy."

Gavin let out a dramatic moan. "She has wounded me." He covered his heart with his hand, stood and spun around before collapsing to the ground.

Amber leaned toward Lachlan. "Your brother has a real flair for the dramatic. Did you teach him that?"

"Happily, no. 'Tis Artemis' doing. The man has entertained many of the queens and kings of Europe."

"Gavin is a fast learner when he finds a subject he likes. I think there are many things he can do."

Her eyes mirrored her happy mood and his heart felt lighter just looking at her. He reached out and tucked a strand of hair behind her ear. Her face turned the color of fresh rosebuds in the courtyard garden. He smiled, pleased at her response to his touch. "Gavin needs to learn to become a warrior first, then he can choose whatever else is of interest to him."

"Do I really get to choose?"

Lachlan nodded. He took a small nick out of the carving. "However, Angus awaits you on the training field."

Gavin's eyes widened. "I forgot." He looked toward the castle.

Amber handed him a meat pie. "You have to eat first."

The boy kissed her on the cheek, grabbed the food and ran down the path leading to Urquhart.

Lachlan watched Amber shield her eyes from the sun with one hand. She had come out of nowhere and settled into his life as though she belonged.

"You have a loving way with my brother."

Amber hugged her legs to her chest. "He's a great boy."

"True, but he tries the very depths of a person's patience. You seem to welcome the challenge. I have yet to find a fault in you."

She rested her cheek on her knees. "You're wrong. I have a special place in my heart for kids who are struggling, but those who appear to be doing okay, I've ignored. Sometimes they need just as much encouragement. It's something I have to work on."

Lachlan reached for a slice of cheese and handed it to her. The carving dropped from his lap to the ground.

Amber picked it up, turning it around in the palm of her hand. "This looks like a brachiosaurus. Long neck, short legs and big body. I think they lived in deep water."

Her statement seemed more to herself than to him and her eyes looked troubled. Lachlan put his knife in his belt, taking time to steady himself. She had described the Guardian.

"Have you seen this creature you speak of?"

She handed the carving back. "It sounds crazy, but I think I felt it when I was in the water. Or something like it."

He gazed at the carving before putting it back in his sporran. Stories from his childhood that surrounded the creature came swirling back. They were Gavin's favorites as well, which was why Lachlan was making a replica for his brother. The Guardian had followed some of the kind to Urquhart when they left their home and had remained to protect them.

A cool breeze drifted over the meadows and moved through the tall grass. Lachlan reached over and turned Amber's face toward him.

"Can you speak about how you came to be in Loch Ness?"

He felt her tremble, but she did not pull away.

Amber couldn't read him. He seemed like a person who wanted to experience life only on the surface. It was almost as though he was afraid, or unwilling, to go deeper. A bird chirped in the tree, as if asking why she cared one way or another. But she did; she also wanted to trust him. He was waiting patiently for her to speak. It occurred to her how comfortable she felt with him at this moment.

"So you want to know how I came to Urquhart?" She smiled. "Well, I was . . . near Loch Ness . . . and saw lightning flash across the night sky. The next thing I remember was crashing into the water. I thought I saw a shadow that resembled the carving you have. Then you pulled me to safety."

He stood and brushed the twigs and leaves off his tartan. "I find I no longer care why you have come to be here or what brought you to me. If a sorcerer were to conjure the woman of my dreams, it would be you."

Amber's heart beat so fast her hand shook. In only a short time her attraction for Lachlan had grown to mean a great deal to her. She felt safe whenever he was near and empty when he was not. If she didn't get back to her own time soon, her heart would be completely lost. But she knew she no longer wanted to return. She wanted to stay. With Lachlan.

He pulled her to her feet and smiled. "Your thoughts are a great distance away. Were they of me?"

He was actually smiling at her. Her aunt used to say of Amber that whatever was in her heart was written on her face. It was a trait she hated now more than ever. She was not ready to pour her heart out to him. She looked at the rolling hills and decided to bluff. "I was planning Gavin's next lesson."

Lachlan touched the tip of her nose with his finger. "The two of us should play a game of chess. I would be able to read your next move just by looking into your eyes. You guard your heart as fiercely as I do mine."

Ivy covered the interior walls of the enclosed garden, and a fine mist lightly touched the weeds entangled in the few remaining rosebushes. The afternoon sun highlighted the neglect. Marcail bent down and cupped her hand around a red bud and inhaled the sweet fragrance. She closed her eyes and let the intoxicating scent swirl around her. It gave her encouragement to fulfill the task she had set for herself.

O'Donnell sat on a marble bench near a fountain, with his back to her. Una had said that he was an artist and had sought out the gardens. She questioned his choice. The place was desolate. Perhaps she might live permanently at Urquhart and restore the roses. There was a time when this had been Diedra's favorite retreat, but Subedei had robbed Lachlan's mother of more than her husband and three of her children. He had taken her will to live.

Their race had its violent side, but so did the mortals amongst whom they lived. They did not stop living when one of their own was taken, and neither would she. The gift of bringing children into the world was worth the risk.

Marcail paused behind O'Donnell. She needed to find the right words to convince him to give up his immortality and marry her. She would appeal to his sense of duty to perpetuate their kind. Did he even care about such things? She would soon know. Her theory had appeared sound when first she conceived it. The plan was to marry without love; the only condition of the union was to produce children. There would, therefore, be no expectations, no disappointments. And if he refused her . . .

"Please sit with me."

O'Donnell continued to sketch on a large parchment, making clean strokes across the page with a piece of charcoal. Marcail was disappointed at losing the element of surprise. She had wanted to be in control and to keep him off balance when she made her proposal, but the man was not startled by her appearance. She had already lost ground and the subject had not been broached.

He stood and turned to face her. She felt her breath catch and willed herself to be calm. He was tall, lean, clean-shaven and his hair was cropped short. The white linen shirt he wore was crisp, and the plaid he had borrowed from Lachlan looked newly made. His appearance had improved greatly. Marcail took a step back. Her plan was foolish. This man would never consider her proposal. He looked as though he relished life. He did not appear to be the kind of man who would give up his immortality without a struggle.

"You did not see me approach. How did you know?"

He made a sweeping flourish with his arm. "I recognized you by your perfume."

Marcail felt her courage return. He had taken notice of her scent. A good sign.

He sat back down on the bench. "You use a heavy hand with the fragrance."

She closed her eyes and forced her voice to remain calm. She needed this man. It made no difference what type of fragrance she wore. For all she cared, he could hold his nose while he performed his duty to produce children. She opened her eyes, saw him grinning at her over his shoulder and chose to ignore the way his smile touched her heart. It was familiar and somehow it caught her unaware.

The sun, long hidden behind the clouds, warmed the garden and sent golden rays of light into the enclosure.

O'Donnell held out his hand. "I want to show you what I have been drawing this day."

Marcail swept by him and sat down on the bench. She knew that the increase in her heartbeat arose from her concern that he would refuse her proposal, nothing more. The walls protected her from the breeze and the garden warmed under the attention of the sun. She folded her hands.

"This garden cries from neglect, and its beauty is choked out, what is there to capture?"

She bit her lips. Her words sounded sharp to her. She should have just fluttered her eyelashes and remarked that she would love to see his drawings.

O'Donnell smiled. "I do not draw what is on the surface, but what is inside the soul."

Marcail looked down at a sketch of the garden. Rosebushes covered with healthy blooms stood in neat well-kept rows. There was a bench like the one on which she and O'Donnell sat. The ivy on the walls was cut back to reveal a painted mural. She touched one of the flowers he had drawn. The depth of his talent surprised her. She had watched Michelangelo sculpt warmth into cold marble as he created the work he called *David*, but O'Donnell possessed the same ability to breathe life into his sketches.

She spoke slowly. "You are a gifted artist."

He raised an eyebrow and then bent over his sketches. "I have had many years of practice."

She looked at his profile wishing there was a way to determine how long he had lived. If it had been long enough, he might consider the proposal she offered. Her heart beat faster as a feeling she had seen him before resurfaced. She shook her head slightly, dismissing the notion.

"You cannot ignore your talent. If I practiced for centuries, I could perhaps draw a flower that would be recognizable, but, I agree, you go well beyond the surface. That is something that cannot be learned or taught."

"I accept your praise, but you give me more than I deserve."

"Why do you say that?"

"Because I only sketch what I like."

Marcail looked back down at the picture. "Rosebushes?"

He nodded. "I like rosebushes very much. But there is more." He reached for a dark leather folder that rested against the bench, untied the straps and drew out a thick packet. He put it in her lap. The first drawing was of a woman dressed in a white toga. Her face was obscured by her long dark hair as she bent over a wounded man. In the distance was a picture of a mountain range.

Marcail leaned forward. The images on the page came to life for her, and her hand trembled as she outlined the strokes of the mountains in the background.

"This looks familiar to me."

"It should. It is of you during the battle of Thermopylae between the Greeks and Persians. By day you searched for food and herbs to help the sick and at night you took care of the wounded. You slept and ate little during that time."

She looked at him with renewed interest. She had told no one of that battle. "I remember, but how did you know?"

"I was there. It was the first time I saw you."

Marcail felt the air around her grow still as she watched him turn the page. A dried rosebud, its petals brittle with age, slipped out. She picked it up.

O'Donnell reached for her hand and touched her fingers. "After you tended my wounds you thought I had died, so you picked a wild rose, removed the thorns, and placed it on my body."

She clutched the folds of her gown. It was a long time ago, but she could still hear the screams of those dead and dying in her dreams. She felt his fingers tighten gently around her hand. Memories flooded back. A traitor among the Greeks had showed the Persians a way through the defense line. She wiped the tears that started to brim in her eyes.

"I'm sorry. I don't remember you."

"It is all right. I pride myself on disguises and my ability to blend into a crowd. If I'm recognized or noticed I move on."

She had heard of the existence of men like

O'Donnell who were the chroniclers of history. Her
hopes for a union with him began to fade. If he was
like Artemis and Theseus he was content with his life,
and would not be willing. He reopened his portfolio,
handling the sheets with care.

Each scene brought back events of her life and the
times when all she could think about was increasing
her knowledge to help others. She knew she could
never re-create the gift of long life that her people had,
but she thought she could at least ease the suffering
and improve the quality of life for the mortals. It was
a happy time, filled with hope and laughter. A time
when she smiled. The memories warmed her. She
must content herself with that.

He turned a page to reveal the picture of a pit
carved out of the ground, near what looked like the
Thames River. It was a mass grave. The memory of the
Black Death that ravaged through so many countries
loomed before her. She pressed her hand to her stomach. She could still see the faces of the plague's victims
and hear their pleas for help.

"I do not like to remember." She stood. "Why is it
that you have drawn so many pictures of me?"

He packed the book back in a leather satchel. "It is
not only of you that I draw. I cannot express what I see
and feel in words, so I record history with my drawings. I thought they might be useful one day."

Marcail had not thought she was capable of feeling
again, yet O'Donnell had touched her soul. She
clasped her hands together, afraid of the awakening
emotions he had evoked. She needed to get to a safe,
neutral ground and cleared her throat.

"Was the purpose of your trip to Scotland to record
the life of our Queen Mary?"

"Not exactly." O'Donnell reached behind her and snapped the stem of a rose. "This time I had planned to see you."

Her eyes widened. "What?"

"You changed. After you had administered to those who died during the Black Death, you stopped enjoying life. You existed, but you weren't alive." He removed the thorns from the stem and handed her the flower.

The delicate scent calmed her as it always did. She looked at the ivy that wove like lace over the stone wall.

"How can you fight something you cannot see? For centuries I learned as much about healing as possible. I gained knowledge from many cultures, yet I was helpless against the plague. I envy your ability to see beauty even in a neglected garden."

O'Donnell put his hands on her shoulders and turned her toward him. "Are you not curious as to why you were the subject in these drawings?"

"You record history. I made it my business to be always right in the middle of things."

He touched her cheek. "I am in love with you."

Marcail drew back. "That is impossible. You do not know me." If he did love her, she could easily accomplish her goal and he would agree to join with her, but this man deserved someone who would return his love. She did not know if she had the ability.

"Will you not ask me to give up my immortality, and join with you in wedded bliss?"

"How did you guess my purpose?"

O'Donnell laughed. "I am an observer of people and quite good at discovering what is in a person's heart. Besides, I learned the fine art of slipping unnoticed into a crowd. I overheard Artemis and Theseus last night say how courageous they thought you were for sacrificing your immortality to have children. The only thing I was not sure of was who your choice would be."

"But why did you think you were the one?"

"I did not. I only hoped. And when you came into the garden I felt encouraged."

Marcail pulled away. "Why then?"

"I knew you overheard my telling Una I was coming here."

"That does not explain your suspicions."

O'Donnell scratched the side of his face. "You forget, I have been watching you for a long time. Whenever you were interested in a man, you would splash large quantities of the rose fragrance all over yourself."

"Perhaps I just wanted you in my bed."

He raised an eyebrow. "True, there is always that."

Marcail's hand trembled as she fingered the pearls at her throat. She had entered the garden hoping to convince O'Donnell to join with her, and had discovered he was agreeable to the proposal. No, anxious, was more to the point.

O'Donnell pulled her close. He was about to kiss her. She closed her eyes and let herself drift on the sensations and smells his nearness evoked. His warm breath caressed her lips as she felt him kiss her neck and the base of her throat. He whispered words that had been part of a long forgotten dream. A dream of longing, desire and . . . betrayal.

Her eyes snapped open. "It is you." She pulled back and slapped him across the face.

Chapter
12

❧

Amber passed through the rose garden on her way to the loch and immediately wished she had not. In the corner stood Marcail and O'Donnell. Marcail's hands were on her hips. She looked at O'Donnell as if he were a bug she wanted to squash. He paced back and forth in front of her like a lawyer before the jury box. It looked suspiciously like a lovers' quarrel, and it appeared that O'Donnell was losing. She smiled and slipped through the door that led to the water. Marcail wouldn't need her help. Amber, however, could sure use Marcail's.

The longer Amber stayed in this century, the more confused she became. And every time she thought of her state of unrest, an image of Lachlan came to her. Her plan was to go for a walk in the fresh air to cool her overactive imagination. It was not working. She was starting to compare Lachlan with Superman, and the action hero was losing.

The sound of clanking metal and the shouts of men could be heard in the direction of the training field. Lachlan would be occupied. It would give her a chance to sort things out.

She walked through the gate. The loch waters sparkled like prisms in the afternoon sun. Birds trilled in the willow trees that dipped their branches gently into the calm water. The breeze, that offered more the promise of spring than the reflection of autumn, fluttered through her hair. She had never experienced such a warm November. A soft wind moved the interwoven ribbons of clouds nearer. The weather in Scotland changed its mind many times in the course of a day. It used to be a source of irritation, but she found she was starting to relish the unexpected.

A splash, and the sound of a man swearing, pulled her out of her tranquil thoughts. Amber was not alone. Lachlan was here before her. She could leave right now and he would never know. Coward. Her aunt was right. Whenever Amber sensed a man was getting too close, she ran. Well, not this time.

She wound her way down the narrow path toward the cluster of trees where she'd heard his voice. She was going to meet the challenge head-on. If he broke her heart . . . she'd drown him.

Parting the branches heavily laden with leaves, Amber peered around for Lachlan. He was at the edge of the water. His chest was bare and his tartan was wrapped loosely around his waist. Muscles rippled and flexed across his back as he bent over and splashed water on his face. He looked good. Great, in fact. The afternoon sun was suddenly a little warmer. She frowned. Calm down; she'd seen men with bare chests before. This was not a big deal.

At that moment she slipped on loose gravel and nearly fell. She straightened, deciding her brother was right. She definitely could not walk and chew gum at the same time. Or, in this case, walk and think the kind of thoughts she was thinking.

Lachlan straightened. "Have you injured yourself?"

Well, at least he didn't say, "again." "No, I just lost my balance. It must be the shoes."

Amber could feel the heat of a blush sear her to the roots of her hair. Her voice had actually cracked. She felt like a schoolgirl who had a crush on a football star and found herself unexpectedly talking to him.

She focused on ducking under the branches and not on the fact that he was staring at her. Her face felt warm and she started to sweat. Perfect. He looked gorgeous and she was a mess. She picked a leaf out of her hair.

"I thought you'd be on the training field." Terrific. Now she was making boring conversation. Someone should just shoot her.

"Perhaps tomorrow. Today there is a matter that needs my attention."

In the short time she'd been at Urquhart, this was only the second time he'd skipped an opportunity to train. The first had been the picnic. His workout schedule bordered on the obsessive. But whatever the reason for his day off, she was glad.

"What are you doing?"

" 'Tis time I removed my beard."

That didn't make any sense. She shielded her eyes from the sun and looked at him. "You said it was as much a part of you as the Highlands."

"Your memory is sound."

She remembered everything he said, everything he did, every touch. And there was that imagination of hers again, running amok. She straightened her skirts and tried to plaster a neutral expression on her face. "Why, exactly, are you shaving?"

"A man can change."

She felt the prehistoric butterflies take off in her stomach. This was dangerous ground; a man who wanted to change. She would have no defense against such a creature.

"What if I don't want you to change?"

"Your eyes tell a different tale. Besides, you have said you hate my beard." Lachlan turned back toward the lake, knelt down on the ground and took his dagger out of its scabbard. He began to shorten the beard, taking chunks of hair and discarding them on the ground. He was using his reflection in the water as a mirror, but his image blurred as each breeze stirred ripples on the lake.

She stepped closer to him. "That's it?"

"No, lass. 'Tis more. There is nothing I would not do for the woman I care for."

Amber watched him scrape the hair off his face in long, slow, even strokes. The air grew still and silent. She could hear her heart beating. If he was trying to impress her, he was succeeding. She saw him flinch and noticed blood on his face.

He cupped water in his hand and splashed it on the wound. Then he smiled. " 'Tis a hard task you have asked of me."

"And you're doing a very poor job of it, might I add." Her voice sounded deep and husky in her ears.

He winked. "Am I to assume you could perform the service?"

By the mischievous expression on his face, she knew the blasted man had not missed a thing. Okay, if he wanted her to shave him, she'd oblige. She crossed the distance that separated them, reached for the dagger and knelt down beside him. The blade was heavier than she'd imagined. The hilt was wrapped in leather and retained the warmth of his hand. She brought the blade to his face and began to scrape away the last remnants of his beard, following the contours of his jawline to his chin. She reached down and dipped the knife in the loch. "This would be easier with warm water."

"It will be warm enough soon."

The strings that tied her bodice in back were too tight. As she maneuvered into position Amber fought the heavy material of her dress. She straddled his legs, feeling the flex of his muscles on her bare skin and the heat of his thigh through the wool tartan.

He raised his eyebrow and rested his hands on her waist. "You have performed this task before?"

She swallowed. "Hold still."

"Impossible."

Her hand trembled as she willed it under control and removed the hair from around his mouth. His skin felt warm against her fingertips. As she leaned closer to him she felt her layers of defense melt away. Lachlan possessed a level of caring and integrity that few would ever attain. It was just that he cloaked them under the word responsibility. She paused and took a deep breath.

"This isn't as easy as it looks. It's going to take a while."

He took the knife from her hand and laid it down on the grass. "That is my intent, as well."

Amber looked into his eyes as his gaze lowered to her mouth. Brushing his lips against the hollow of her neck, he moved his hands under her dress along her bare thighs. She shuddered as waves of heat swept over her, and the pressure of his lips on her mouth increased. The intensity and urgency of his passion tugged at her heart.

The realization drifted toward her that there was no other place, or time, she'd rather be than in his arms. She pulled back, wanting to slow down and enjoy each sensual moment with him.

"Lachlan, my love, we have all day."

His smile spread slowly across his face in sudden awareness. "Aye, lass, and the night as well."

Her lips parted as he kissed her and her tongue sought the deep recesses of his mouth.

His breathing was ragged. He unwrapped his plaid from around his waist and spread it on the ground. She forgot to breathe. His naked body was a bronze contrast to the deep green tartan. He reclined and the muscles in his shoulders and arms flexed as he reached out his hand toward her. His eyes were dark with unmasked desire.

"Stay with me."

She placed her hand in his and joined him on the soft wool. The tight bodice of her dress loosened and the layers of clothes disappeared. His body rested against the length of her. His skin heated hers. Leaning toward her, he rested his hand lightly on her stomach. His tongue circled around her nipple in slow, feather-like strokes before he bent down and took it in his mouth. His long hair draped over her as she arched toward him and wrapped her arms around his neck, pulling him closer.

She was fully immersed in the smell of earth and grass and man. Around her the air warmed as he entered and slowly thrust within her. The lyrical music of bagpipes floated in her mind and time slowed with each tender kiss, each caress.

*   *   *

Despite the warm breeze rustling through the pines outside Amber's window, she pulled the wool blanket up over her bare shoulders. The door opened.

Amber tightened her grip on the blanket as she saw Lachlan enter. He was carrying a tray with a bowl of oranges and two goblets of foamy liquid. His shirt was open, his tartan was hastily wrapped around his hips and his hair hung loose to his shoulders. Memories of his body pressed against her and the gentle words he'd spoken flooded her senses. Her breath caught. It had seemed so natural to be with him, to let him make love to her, but now doubts flooded back. If she were in the twentieth century she'd know what her options would be the morning after.

Lachlan put the tray on the bed and sat down beside it. She could see the question in his eyes. He looked as uncertain as she felt and cleared his throat.

"A friend of mine mentioned a drink called chocolatl. It resembled the word you used that night in the cookroom. You said you favored oranges as well."

He was trying to please her, to soften the moment that followed the first time two people made love. It was working. The tension flowed out of her. She had not misunderstood the words he'd spoken last night, or the passion in his touch. The blanket fell from around her shoulders. She walked over to sit on the bed opposite him, with the tray between them. Tucking her legs under her, she reached for an orange and began peeling it. Lachlan was watching her with an intensity that took her breath away.

He popped a slice of orange in his mouth. "I learned there are . . . certain benefits to this drink. Are you not curious?"

"Does it prevent wrinkles?"

He laughed. "You have no need of such a remedy. But to return to my point, it is said the Emperor Montezuma drank his chocolatl in a golden goblet before entering his harem."

She dipped a slice of orange into the bittersweet liquid, brought it to her mouth and heard his sharp intake of breath.

Lachlan took the slice of orange from her and dipped it into the drink again. The liquid dripped down his fingers as he held it up to her mouth. Amber looked into his eyes; they mirrored the dark passion she felt. She licked his fingers slowly, taking the last of the fruit in her mouth.

He raised an eyebrow. She had his full attention. Her pulse quickened as she stared back at him.

Lachlan let his breath out slowly. "I know why the monks in Italy have forbidden women this drink."

"Oh, really. And why is that?" She dipped her finger into the warm chocolate and then tasted the syrupy liquid, pleased with the primal sounds coming from Lachlan. "It tastes bitter. It could use a little more honey."

He arched his eyebrow.

She laughed. "Don't say it."

"You are all the honey it needs."

Facing him on the bed, she reached over and yanked on the hair on his chest.

He flinched, reached for her hand and held it against his skin. "You wound me, lass. Is there no way to control you?"

"Not a chance."

He leaned forward, took the goblet out of her hand and set it and the tray on the floor.

"Wait, I have plans for that."

His mouth curled up in a smile. "You can finish your drink later."

"I wasn't thinking of drinking it." She ignored the heat that crept up her neck to her face.

He stretched out on the bed next to her. "And what plans would that be, lass? The French women pour milk into their bathwater to soften their skin. What would adding an aphrodisiac, such as chocolatl, do to a woman's bath?"

Amber traced the outline of his mouth with her finger. "I'm not going to waste my drink by pouring it into that splinter-ridden tub. I want to spend as little time as possible in it. A shower would be a lot more fun." She leaned back onto the pillows, paused, and then propped herself on her hand and stared at him.

"Wait just one minute. How do you know what French women like in their baths?" The mischief reflected in his eyes caused her heart to alter its already erratic beat.

He shrugged. "Marcail must have mentioned it to me."

"You expect me to believe that?"

Lachlan tapped the tip of her nose. "Aye. Now, what is this thing you call a shower?"

Her concentration was a little fuzzy because of his proximity, and he wanted her to explain the complications of a shower? She assumed her best classroom lecture voice.

"Imagine a waterfall inside a small room in the castle and then imagine you can control the temperature of the water. A person can take a bath standing up."

The confused look on his face was worth the effort. She did not see him perplexed often. It was time to turn this conversation toward a more stimulating topic.

He tucked a strand of hair behind her ear. "You did not explain your plans for this concoction."

She traced a straight line from his chest down to his waist with her fingers. His skin was warm and the hair on his body soft. The thought surging through her mind made her feel light-headed and reckless.

"Actually, it's more of a sensual experiment."

His voice lowered to a husky whisper. "It involves this concoction you favor?"

She smiled and imitated his brogue. "Aye, laddie."

His laughter was deep and spontaneous and sent shivers racing through her. "You have captured the lilt of the Highland tongue as you have my heart. I am anxious to begin your . . . experiment."

Amber reached over and felt the other side of the bed. It still held the warmth of Lachlan's body. She stretched and wrapped her arms around her waist as she snuggled under the layers of blankets. Looking at the empty tray on the table she smiled. The oranges were gone. The warm chocolate was devoured. She felt a little like that herself.

The faint sound of metal clanking against metal drifted through the open window. Lachlan must be on the training field. Again. Maybe he was no different from anyone else who owned a castle, and was responsible for the lives of hundreds of people. Still, she wished he didn't like it so much.

She sat up, pulled the blankets around her and examined her options for the day. Amber knew what she would like to do, but Lachlan was too busy playing war games. And since her first choice, kidnapping him to a deserted island paradise without his sword, was not possible, she'd go for plan B. Gavin was down in the courtyard watching the men. Pulling the boy away for a lesson would be like rerouting the Columbia River. So much for plan B. So, she could ask Una to show her how to pluck a chicken or milk a cow. Amber looked outside. Too late for cow milking, thank goodness. Of course, she could always ask someone to show her how to weave a tapestry. On second thought, maybe she'd just go for a walk. This time she'd bring a book.

She slid off the bed. Through the adjoining door she saw the tub was filled with steaming water. A bath had been fun the first half dozen times. However, a steady dose of sitting in suds, while not feeling as though you'd rinsed off all the soap, was losing its appeal. Amber sighed loudly. She would have to figure out how to rig a shower from the rain barrels she'd seen on top of the castle. But first she would take that walk.

A soft knock ended her solitude.

"Come in."

The door creaked open and Gavin poked his head in. "Before the evening meal, we are to visit my mother. And please wear the color blue, my mother favors it."

The words were spoken as a command, but his voice trembled. Its tone tugged at Amber's heart. It was impossible for her to say no. She nodded, and before she'd finished the gesture, he was gone. She shivered, remembering the last time she'd seen Diedra. An uneasiness started in the pit of her stomach.

Amber sat on a large rock near the shore as the waters of Loch Ness reflected the clear late morning sky. She closed her eyes and breathed deeply of the crisp air. If her friends in Seattle caught a glimpse of her sitting and doing nothing except watching a flock of geese fly overhead, they'd think she had the flu. She propped her head on her hands. Waves lapped gently against the rocks. The white foam looked like the meringue on her aunt's lemon pie. She'd never realized that before. More to the point, she'd never taken the time to observe life around her.

Smiling, her thoughts strayed to last night and early this morning. As each day passed, her life here was more real, and the one in the twentieth century more like a dream. Her aunt was right; Amber had jammed her life with things to do in order to avoid facing her loneliness. She thought that if her schedule were full, she would be happy. But she'd never made a connection to anyone. Her relationships were all on the surface. Like the waters of Loch Ness, she hid the mysteries of her soul under a calm exterior. Lachlan alone had taken the time to look further.

A soft breeze blew gently through her hair. She turned in the direction of the refreshing wind and saw O'Donnell seated farther along the shore. Sheets of paper, spread over a flat board, were balanced on his knees. His smile was welcoming and he motioned for her to join him.

He had a friendly, uncomplicated face. She liked him and hoped he and Marcail had worked out their differences. He might even manage to soften Marcail's serious nature. Amber shook her head. She was becoming just like her aunt, a matchmaker.

She looked with interest at O'Donnell's drawings. In the corner of the page the face of a woman was sketched in charcoal from different angles. She had a variety of expressions. In the center he had created a picture with the shores of the loch in the background, and a woman as the focal point.

"You're an artist."

He grinned. "Not as yet, but I keep working toward that end. If you do not recognize the person I have drawn, I have many years of work ahead."

Amber glanced at it more closely. "It looks like me."

He smiled. "I am satisfied I captured your expressions, but I cannot seem to get what you are wearing correct. It is almost as though you should be dressed in a different way."

Amber felt uneasy. O'Donnell was too observant. She still felt uncomfortable in the clothes she wore. If she were going to feel as though she belonged here, she would have to reconcile herself to everything about this century, including the clothes. He was staring at her, clearly waiting for an explanation of some kind. The truth was always best.

"I'll tell you a secret. This long dress is driving me crazy. I'd like to be wearing something shorter."

He laughed. "I agree. The men in the Highlands show off their great hairy legs, but cover their women from head to toe. Maybe you can start a new fashion."

"I'd probably be burned at the stake." She forced a smile thinking that was a real possibility if they found out she was from the future.

MacDougal, with Gavin close behind, raced past her and down to the shore. The dog leaped into the water after the stick Gavin threw for him.

Lachlan followed at a leisurely stroll as though he hadn't a care in the world. The sun seemed to shine brighter as he came closer. She stole a peek at the sky. No change. It was her overactive, imagination giving him the ability to change the course of the weather. She thought of last night. Okay, so it might be possible.

He smiled and knelt down beside her. He was so close his leg brushed against her and the contact warmed her.

"Beware of O'Donnell. He has broken many a heart."

"And how many have you broken?"

He put his hand over his chest. "You wound me as deep as any sword."

O'Donnell's laughter startled the wolfhound. The animal barked with a mouthful of water.

Amber shook her head. "Men. You are all alike. A woman wants honesty, not flowery speeches."

O'Donnell frowned. "And I thought it was the other way around. Perhaps that is why the Lady Marcail will not speak to me."

Lachlan's voice sounded tense. "You two are to be wed. What has happened?"

"There was the small matter of her finding me in bed with another woman."

" 'Twas a long time ago. Explain to Lady Marcail that the woman meant nothing to you."

"I did."

Lachlan raised one eyebrow. "And?"

O'Donnell shook his head.

Amber straightened. "Married? You just met. And what about this other woman?"

Lachlan and O'Donnell both looked at her with the same blank, male expression. It spoke volumes. Amber laced her fingers together in her lap. "What other woman?"

Both men answered together. " 'Tis over."

"I was talking to O'Donnell."

"It was over a long time ago." O'Donnell fingered the piece of charcoal in his hand. "It is not something of which I am proud. I turned to this other woman because Lady Marcail and I were getting too close."

Amber patted him. "Did you tell this to Marcail?"

The lines of concern creased his forehead. "I did not think she would believe me."

"She'll believe you, if it's the truth. Forgiveness is another matter and might take some time."

"The lady is worth the wait." O'Donnell stared at the loch.

Silence hung in the air, interrupted only by the wind through the branches. At that moment Amber had no doubt O'Donnell would spend a lifetime waiting for the woman he loved.

O'Donnell nodded toward her. "Indeed, I see that the legend has come true. The Lady Amber is wise beyond her years."

Lachlan's expression was unreadable. "It is a coincidence, nothing more."

"Perhaps not."

Amber tucked her legs under her dress. "What legend?"

The ever-present breeze that blew off the water seemed to quiet. The air grew still. Only the lapping of the waves against the rocks remained constant. O'Donnell stood as if giving a speech before an assembly. He raised his arm and pointed toward Loch Ness.

Amber covered her mouth with a hand to keep from laughing. She leaned against Lachlan, who circled her waist with his arm and drew her closer. She loved stories and it looked as though O'Donnell was building toward a great one.

"There is a legend that dates back to the ah . . ." He

lowered his arm and turned to Lachlan. "When did it originate?"

"It matters not. 'Tis your tale, O'Donnell. Would it matter to you if I asked you not to tell it?"

"Not in the least."

"I thought as much."

Amber nudged Lachlan. "Be quiet. I'm interested."

He pulled her onto his lap and whispered in her ear. "Is there nothing I can do that will cause you to lose interest in O'Donnell's telling of this tale?"

His breath was warm and sent shivers over her skin. "Hold that thought."

O'Donnell cleared his throat. "Be still." He raised his arm with a flourish, once again pointing toward Loch Ness and the heather-covered mountains that framed the shore.

Through the mist-shrouded waters of an enchanted sea,
the Guardian will be summoned.
The seasons will alter their natural course.
The barriers of time will be broken.

And a woman, with hair of burnished gold,
will be pulled from the depths of Loch Ness.

It is she who will bring the knowledge
and the courage of generations yet unborn.
And a wisdom that will guide
the chosen one out of his darkness.

But the waters will reclaim her once again,
if, after the passage of one full moon,
the immortal she was sent to heal
accepts not the power of Eternal Love.

Amber felt the hair rise on the back of her neck. She did not need a castle to fall on her to recognize the similarities. But the verse sent shivers up her spine. She'd been in the sixteenth century for over three weeks. That meant there was one week left.

O'Donnell addressed Lachlan. "The Lady Amber looks a little bewildered. Would you like to explain it to her?"

"Nay, I would not." Lachlan set Amber off his lap, stood and reached for her hand. "It cannot be explained as there is nothing of substance to it. It is naught but a legend. The Highlands are thick with them."

Amber put her hand in his and let him pull her to her feet. True, her aunt used to tell her stories about a race of woodland folk who didn't share the same laws of mortality as humans. But Lachlan had grown serious. It took her a moment to appreciate that it was exactly the same reaction he'd had at the Punch-and-Judy show at the festival in Inverness.

Amber held Gavin's hand and let him guide her down the dimly lit hallway to his mother's room. She was thankful the boy was not in a talking mood, as her thoughts remained with the legend O'Donnell had told, and with Lachlan's reaction.

Gavin squeezed her hand. "Thank you for wearing blue. It is my mother's favorite color."

"I was glad to do it." Her heart ached for him. He was desperate for everything to be perfect.

He paused. "Sometimes my mother acts as though she does not like to have visitors."

"Don't worry. My mother's the same." Amber could see the lines of concern cross his face. It was important to him that she and his mother get along. She ruffled the curls on his head. "I thought my mother cared more about digging up old bones in ancient ruins than she did for my brother and me. Then one day I found a chest stuffed with things we had made for her over the years. Some people just don't know how to express their love."

Gavin nodded and led Amber into the room.

War shields and swords hung on the walls that were covered in red silk. A portrait of a woman in a suit of armor hung over the mantel. In the center of the room was one of the largest beds Amber had ever seen. Under piles of covers and furs Diedra lay sleeping. Her hands, the knuckles knotted with age, clutched the blankets under her chin.

Gavin tugged on her arm. "That is my mother."

Before Amber could answer, he released her hand and ran to the bed. He bent down to kiss his mother on the forehead. She opened her eyes and he whispered something in her ear. A flicker of a smile crossed her face as she looked toward the foot of the bed. He ran to a trunk, opened it, and began rummaging inside.

Amber felt a twinge of regret as she watched the interchange between mother and son. Her relationship with her parents was one of polite formality. Children were to be seen and not heard. No running in the house, no loud or sudden noise, no eating between meals. The list went on into infinity. She was glad Gavin had a different experience. There was warmth between these two which she had not expected.

Diedra turned and the candlelight illuminated her gaunt features. Amber drew back suddenly shocked.

It had not struck her at their first meeting, but Diedra was far too old to be the mother of an eight year old.

"Gavin has discovered a love of books, I have you to thank, and I am grateful. He also takes great delight looking through the weapons and armor I have collected in my travels. The two worlds can coexist, but it is a hard journey. Come, sit beside me."

Amber felt uneasy. Diedra's body might be shriveled with age, but her eyes were clear and her voice steady and vibrant. For some reason the contrast frightened Amber. She folded her hands as she sat down, trying to keep the tremors out of her voice.

"Is that a picture of you, over the fireplace?"

Diedra's expression darkened. "At that time I believed I could be happy only on a battlefield." Tears brimmed in her eyes. "Even after my children were born, fighting consumed my life. It was not until Subedei murdered my husband and children that I realized how much of their lives I had missed. But it was too late. I do not know how to talk to my own children."

Amber put her hand over the woman's cold fingers. Diedra was confiding in her, but then, sometimes it was easier to tell a stranger your innermost thoughts and fears.

Gavin discarded shields, daggers, and an ax to the floor, as well as an assortment of dented and broken pieces of armor. He reached for a tunic of chain mail, pulled it on and then abandoned it as he resumed his exploration of the trunk. It struck Amber that he was at ease in this room. At times small children sensed what adults missed.

"Your children know you love them."

Diedra's gaze was intense. "The Guardian chose wisely."

An image of the carving Lachlan had been working on came into vivid focus. Surely the two could not be connected.

"Lachlan saved me from drowning, that was all."

"There is more to it, my child, and from the look in your eyes you know it as well. But perhaps in your time . . . but we shall speak of it no more. I grow weary, and there is something more I wish to tell you. My son believes I am too consumed by the path my life has taken to be aware of others." She reached over to touch Amber's face.

"There are days when he is right. I believed if I showed my children a mother's love it would make them weak and vulnerable. I wanted them to be strong. They need to be strong. There are many dark days ahead for them. And I see strength in you. But to help my children, you will need to know the reason the gods have brought you here." Her sigh was little more than a whisper.

"The Lady Marcail summoned the Guardian. It is she who will speak to you. There is fear in your eyes, but it will pass. If the love you have for Lachlan is strong enough, all will be well."

Diedra's words hung in the air as she slowly closed her eyes. The room plunged into a silence so deep it rang in Amber's ears. Diedra knew Amber had traveled back to the sixteenth century. In fact that was probably what Lachlan's mother was trying to tell her the day she'd been shown Ford's grave.

Gavin shut the lid to the chest. Amber jumped at the sound and tried to calm her frayed nerves. After getting her young charge settled for the night, she intended to find Marcail.

The boy touched her shoulder. His smile was so

wide his dimples showed. In the palm of his hand he held a small wood carving of a wolfhound.

"I made it myself." He placed the small object carefully on the table next to his mother's bed.

She knew what it meant. Diedra's trunk was filled with treasures from her life and amongst the memories was something that Gavin had made for her. Amber pulled him close and gathered him into her arms.

Shadows crept over the hallway leading to her chamber as Amber turned the corner. It had been a long day. There hadn't been time to talk to Marcail. Gavin's visit with his mother had ended happily, but he'd clung to Amber, reliving each moment. After the evening meal, she'd read him stories from *Canterbury Tales*, but the entire time she was reading to Gavin, she kept going over her conversation with Diedra. Her parents had taught her that occasionally things happened which the laws of science couldn't explain. The most successful scientists were those who didn't close their minds.

Something had pulled her four hundred years into the past. There were myths surrounding the Loch Ness monster that dated back to the time of the Celts. The creature was a phenomena that had never been fully explained away.

Amber tried to ignore the trembling in her body and thought of the book *Jane Eyre*. Castles and madwomen were a natural fit. She didn't think Diedra was crazy, but the woman was far from normal. However, Lachlan's mother didn't strike Amber as the type to make idle claims. The Nessie theory was gaining credence.

She wished she hadn't left the book in Gavin's room. At least the majority of those stories were funny. She needed a laugh. Maybe jumping into bed with Lachlan had not been a good idea, but she couldn't get him out of her thoughts, and wondered if he felt the same. Amber didn't get the impression he was the love-em-and-leave-em type like other men she'd known. But Lachlan was a laird, a nobleman, and they had their own set of rules which did not take into account anyone else's feelings but their own.

Amber paused, leaned against the wall, and closed her eyes. Her thoughts were growing darker by the minute as she began to paint Lachlan into the likeness of the other men in her life.

Maybe Lachlan had stopped by earlier this evening, found she was gone, and done whatever it was he did. At least, she hoped so. After all, they had no claim on each other. She was trying to make excuses for him already.

As she opened the door, she was greeted by a crash and a loud curse. Lachlan came from the next room rubbing his head.

"Theseus assures me it will function as you describe. He saw its like when he was in the New World. However, I am uncertain how hot the water will be when finally it reaches the garderobe. It has a long way to travel once it is poured into the rain barrels on the castle roof. It will be ready for you in the morning."

"What are you talking about?"

He made a sweeping bow. "Your shower, milady."

Chapter

13

❧

Water ran unevenly through the funnel-like opening Lachlan had rigged in the ceiling. Amber closed her eyes and put her head under the warm stream and smiled. She'd once believed a shower was the best way to start the day. Now, however, it ranked second.

A small gray bird chirped on the windowsill of the garderobe. She smiled at its music as the water flowed down the back of her neck and shoulders and into a gutter that drained into Loch Ness. She felt the tension release as her body relaxed.

Amber felt a draft in the small room and opened her eyes. Light streamed in as the curtain was drawn aside. Lachlan stood in the entrance.

His claymore was strapped to his back. Several knives were tucked in his belt. Amber felt the sudden rise and fall of her chest as the rhythm of her breathing increased. Lachlan was going out to practice in the courtyard, but he had sought her out first. It was a big step for him to put his obsession with fighting second. Now, if only she could get him to forget about it . . . at least for a while. She cupped her hands and let the water gather then tossed it in his direction.

He sidestepped out of the way and smiled. "Do you mean to drown me, lass?"

"Aye."

His laughter filled the room. For some reason she felt more at ease with this man than any other. She couldn't explain it, but it was true nonetheless.

Lachlan didn't blink. His gaze seemed to be locked on her face as if he were afraid to look anywhere else, as if pretending she wasn't standing in front of him, stark naked and dripping wet. He cleared his throat.

" 'Tis a lot of trouble, merely to bathe."

Amber turned off the lever that controlled the flow of water and wiped her wet hair off her forehead. He looked as if he was having trouble breathing. Perfect. She smiled and reached for the soap on the chair.

"Isn't Angus expecting you in the courtyard?"

"I must be prepared for battle."

She rubbed the jasmine-scented soap between her hands, feeling the rich lather as she washed her arms and shoulders. She could hear Lachlan's irregular breathing. It matched the rhythm of her own.

"What would happen if you missed a day?"

A smile flickered across his lips. "The inhabitants of Urquhart will believe I am bewitched."

Amber could feel the pounding of her heart as she put the soap back on the chair and took a step toward him. She started to unbuckle his belt, but hesitated. He brushed her wet hair off her shoulder and guided her hands to the clasp. Her fingers trembled as she unfastened his belt and pulled it from around his waist. The folds of his tartan loosened as he removed his weapons and placed them on a bench outside the enclosure. He threw his tartan and shirt to the floor.

Amber turned the shower back on and drew him

under the drizzle of warm water. She reached for the soap. Lathering it into thick suds she washed his chest in slow, circular motions before moving closer to him until her nipples touched his bare skin. She heard his sharp intake of breath. His lips were wet and warm under the steady stream of water. Then he pulled her against him. The bar of soap hit the floor as her arms circled his neck.

"What have you done to Lachlan?"

Amber looked out the window of Marcail's chamber. Lachlan was playing soccer with Gavin. She smiled, hearing the two of them laugh as MacDougal joined in the game. Amber knew exactly what she was talking about and was just as surprised. Lachlan had actually skipped his afternoon training as well.

Marcail touched her shoulder. "That sounded harsh. I did not mean it so. It is seldom that Lachlan misses an opportunity to practice his skill with the sword. I find it curious."

Amber leaned against the windowsill. She couldn't read Marcail's expression. The woman was as impassive as a porcelain doll. It usually made Amber uneasy, but not today. Today she was confident and fearless.

"I told him he needed to spend more time with his brother."

"And he agreed?"

Amber could feel a wave of protectiveness. She couldn't be the only one to see how obsessed Lachlan was with fighting.

"Why wouldn't he agree? He should be spending more time with Gavin."

"We are of the same mind. It is only that you are the

first one to persuade him there is more to life than fighting." The somber expression on Marcail's face began to crumble. "But I fear that, in the end, people are incapable of change."

Amber remembered what O'Donnell had said about the woman he'd slept with. She lowered her voice. "By 'people,' are you referring to O'Donnell?"

Marcail looked up, startled, and then sank down on the bench beside the window. She nodded. "He betrayed me with another."

"He said he loves you." Amber sat down and put her hand on Marcail's shoulder.

"Those words come easily to his lips." The pain in Marcail's voice was razor sharp.

"I don't know all the details about what happened, or if you love him enough to give him another chance. But he said he would wait for you. In my experience, men are not patient creatures by nature. If someone I loved said he would wait for me . . . well, I guess I'm really not sure how I'd react, but I'd at least give it serious thought. Promise me you'll do that much."

Marcail nodded. The briefest shadow of a smile flickered across her face. "If I do not agree, I believe you will spend the remainder of the day convincing me otherwise. Perhaps you will have the strength to change Lachlan. You do not give up easily."

Amber smiled. "I've been told that before."

She glanced over at the hearth. Above it the mural of Tristan and Isolde seemed to take on a new life. The candles cast a warm golden glow on the wall. Writers were eternally creating stories of romance, because the human spirit was always searching for the perfect love. Many tales, such as the one depicted in the murals, ended unhappily.

Marcail spoke. "Lachlan told me that you were aware of the legend of the Lady of the Loch."

"Yes." Amber hesitated. "It's an interesting story."

Marcail smiled. "I have never heard it described in such a manner." Her expression grew serious and her eyes held Amber's. "I believe it has come true."

Shouts of laughter filtered into the room from below. The sounds pressed in on her. The words O'Donnell had spoken whirled through her. *Barriers of time will be broken . . . seasons will alter their natural course . . . a woman, with hair of burnished gold . . . pulled from the depths . . . waters will reclaim her. . . .* She felt dizzy and leaned against the window for support. None of it made any sense, and yet . . .

"You think I'm the woman in the legend?"

Marcail nodded. "Has Lachlan told you nothing of this?"

Amber's legs began to shake. She gripped the stone sill tightly and shook her head.

Marcail sighed. "Part of him still denies what he knows in his heart to be true. But to accept it, he must also accept that he can change. He is hardened against such a reality. I believe that you alone can guide him down that path."

Marcail motioned for Amber to follow her. "Come, there is something I wish to show you."

Following Marcail down a torchlit corridor, Amber recognized the direction they were headed. It was the hallway that led to the gallery of portraits. Shadows spread along the walls in the eerie light, their images ghost-like and watchful. She shivered.

"Where are you taking me?"

Marcail pointed to an alcove hidden in the shadows and handed Amber a torch. "His portrait hangs there."

Amber brought the light closer to a massive oil painting of a Scottish warrior. He stood on a cliff that overlooked Loch Ness, holding a two-handed claymore. It was an excellent likeness.

The torch wavered in Amber's grasp. She'd seen this picture somewhere before. She paused as the memory resurfaced. It was in the Iverness Museum. Her aunt had wanted her to see the exhibit. No, that was not exactly true. Aunt Dora had insisted she go. Once there, she remembered how nervous her aunt had become as she pointed to the man in the portrait and whispered that he was said to be immortal. At the time, Amber hadn't thought much of it. Her aunt was intrigued with the legends of Scotland.

Marcail rested her hand on Amber's shoulder. "You have seen this portrait before. Perhaps in your own time?"

Amber felt faint. "What?"

"It is she who will bring the knowledge and the courage of generations yet unborn. The legend foretells of you. There is much you must know and little time that remains. Last night the moon reached its last quarter. Only days remain until the moon is once more full. Change will have to take place, or you will return and I know not the fate of our kind."

Amber gripped the torch handle. "Slow down. Let's take this step by step. You know I am from another time?"

Marcail nodded.

"How?"

"It was I who summoned the Guardian."

Amber felt a shiver run through her. All the pieces of the puzzle were falling into place. She remembered the lightning, and how she had swerved off the side of the road into the water. Something had swum by her as she'd lost consciousness.

"The creature in Loch Ness?"

"What else would it be?"

So Nessie was real. Diedra had been right. Amber wasn't sure how she felt about being part of a legend. She straightened.

"And this . . . Guardian decided to pick me out of all the people who accidentally fall into the loch?"

"This was not a random choice; the creature chose you wisely."

Amber realized she knew exactly how Alice felt when she'd fallen down the rabbit hole.

"Okay. Let's assume, for the moment, this Guardian is responsible for my being here. Are you also suggesting Lachlan and I are linked somehow?"

In the torchlight Marcail smiled. "Precisely. And you must turn him from the insanity that holds his soul prisoner if he is to be saved. If we are all to be saved."

The moon reflected on the waters as Amber made her way down the travel-worn path toward the place where Lachlan had first pulled her out of the loch. She wrapped her shawl more tightly around her shoulders as a breeze rippled over the water. She'd gone over everything Marcail had told her until her brain ached.

Even if there really were a creature in Loch Ness, it couldn't possibly have the ability to pull her four hundred years into the past. And no one was immortal. There had to be a logical explanation that she was either too dense or too tired to figure out.

Her foot bumped something solid. Startled, she looked down. It was the still body of a wolfhound, half-covered with a pile of rocks. The animal's eyes were glazed and unblinking. Please don't let it be MacDougal, she repeated over and over. She knew what it was like to lose a cherished pet. Gavin shouldn't have to go through that.

She was twelve when Shadow had died and she had slept with his collar for months after. Her hands trembled as she bent down and touched the body. He wore a piece of tartan cloth around his neck and he was solid and cold. She remembered when she'd presented this cloth to Gavin. She stumbled back.

A flash of lightning creased the sky, shedding light on the dead animal. Blood stained the rocks. Her breath caught in her throat. There was an arrow in MacDougal's side, and dried blood caked on the wound. Her hands shook as she carefully closed the dog's eyelids. How was she going to tell Gavin?

A twig snapped behind her, but before she could react someone grabbed her around the waist, covering her mouth with his hand. Her captor dragged her to a standing position, pulling her against him. Her stomach churned and her body trembled. She tried to pry his calloused, dirt-encrusted fingers away from her face.

The man pressed the point of a knife to her neck and started to drag her toward the shore. His breath was foul-smelling as he pressed his mouth to her ear. "You have time for a prayer before you die."

The pressure of the blade burned against her skin. She concentrated on not giving in to panic.

There was the sound of footsteps rustling nearby. The man loosened his hold and turned toward the disturbance.

"Will, is that you?"

Amber seized the opportunity to shove her elbow

into his stomach. He groaned, releasing his grip on her. She lurched forward, picked up her skirts and stumbled toward the pile of stones around Mac-Dougal. Her cowardly attacker probably hadn't given the dog a chance to fight back, shooting an arrow at him from the safety of the trees. Well, she wasn't going to be as easy to kill.

She picked up a rock, turned, and threw it at the man's head. He screamed and staggered back. Amber could see blood ooze from the cut.

Lachlan raced into view, his sword raised.

From a cluster of trees near the water an arrow whistled past her, hitting Lachlan in the right shoulder. He jerked back and his jaw tightened as he broke off the long shaft. She quickly gathered her skirts and ran toward him.

Lachlan switched his sword to his left hand and pulled her behind an outcropping of large rocks. "When I discovered you were not in our chamber, I went in search of you. It appears I have been doing that a lot of late. Marcail told me she saw you walk in this direction."

Two more arrows whistled through the air, but deflected off the stone barricade.

Amber could hear shouting but in a language she didn't recognize. Here she was, in the middle of a battlefield, and Lachlan was calmly telling her he'd been looking for her. He gave new meaning to the expression "nerves of steel." Well, she had another name for it . . . idiot.

"Do not leave the protection of the shadows until I return."

She grabbed his arm. "What are you talking about? You're outnumbered. There are two, maybe more. You can't go out there. They'll shoot you full of holes. Did you see what they did to MacDougal?"

"Aye, and his death will be avenged." Lachlan cupped her face. "They gave their word they would fight man to man."

"And you believed them? They killed . . ." Her voice caught in her throat so that she couldn't finish the sentence. She pushed him away. "Of course, I forgot. They gave you their word they would fight fairly. Well, I feel much better. Exactly how many are there? Three, four, ten perhaps?"

"Do you doubt my skill as a warrior?"

She felt an overpowering desire to strangle him. "Don't you understand? I don't want you to be a hero. I just want us to be together. To do ordinary, boring things and live happily ever after."

Someone called Lachlan's name. She saw him tense.

"We will talk of this later." He reached behind him and unfastened a crossbow. Arming the weapon, he handed it to her.

"And exactly what am I supposed to do with this?" She held it gingerly. "I've never shot one of these things before in my life."

"You will use it to defend yourself."

"And end up shooting myself in the foot? I've a better idea. I could go for help."

"You would never make it to the gate."

The clouds thinned and the moon shone through as she watched Lachlan walk toward the clearing. He gripped his sword and reached for the knife as he approached his opponents. Lachlan faced three armed men in addition to the one she'd hit with the rock. Metal clashed and cries of pain rang out. Lachlan whirled around and ran the larger of the two men through with his sword. Then, turning, he stabbed the other in the neck with his knife. One of the remaining warriors charged, thrusting his sword into Lachlan's stomach.

Her fingers scraped against the rock pile. She felt helpless as she saw Lachlan double over, regain his balance, and attack. His smile was twisted and dark, his movements fluid and methodical as he turned and struck again and again.

It was apparent that the men Lachlan fought were no match for him. He battled as if possessed. The sound of clashing steel and piercing screams swirled around her. In the moonlight she could make out two men lying in pools of their own blood.

The two who remained upright were fighting to hang on as Lachlan pressed his attack. From the shadows of the trees Amber saw a glint of metal. Panic welled up inside her. Someone else was watching. An arrow came shooting through the air, from the direction she'd seen the flash of metal. It hit Lachlan in the chest with a dull thud.

The figure in the forest stepped out of the shadows and started to walk toward the clearing. He was reloading his crossbow in the moonlight and passed close to where she was hiding. Amber wondered if he even knew she was there. Most likely not or else he did not consider her a threat. Amber pushed the image of Lachlan and the bloodstained bodies from her mind. Stay calm, she thought. Don't panic. She looked down at the weapon Lachlan had given her. She had absolutely no idea how to use it.

Quite close by lay a pile of water-smoothed rocks. She glanced at the man who seemed to be having trouble loading his crossbow. Then she reached for a stone, calculating the distance. She'd thrown a soccer ball twice that far.

She stood, stepped in front of the boulder and aimed for the man's head. There was a thud, a cry of pain and then the man crumbled to the ground.

Lachlan was covered in blood, barely able to stand, yet he headed in the direction of where the man had fallen. In the meager light his face was filled with blind rage. Amber drew back. It was not the Lachlan she knew, but a man possessed. She had to do something to break this trance, to stop the killing. She moved quickly toward him, grabbing him around his arm.

"Leave go of me, woman." His voice was low and menacing.

A white-hot fear seared through her; it was as though he had become a stranger. Would he harm her? She had to trust in the man she knew. She held onto him tighter and concentrated on keeping her voice calm. "Lachlan. It's over."

Lachlan shook his head as if to protest, but the wild look in his eyes slowly faded. He gazed at her, and then at the bloody sword in his hand.

He slumped forward, dropping the blade to the ground. His voice was only a whisper in her ear. "You did well. Find Angus."

His face was ashen, but the angry mask had disappeared. Two arrows still protruded from his body as he swayed on his feet. Amber fought back the tears, wiping the moisture from her face. She needed to be strong.

"I'm not going to leave you."

Lachlan sank to his knees. "I will hold you to your promise." His jaw tightened as he tried to stand.

"Help me to the castle, before I turn the banks of Loch Ness red with my blood."

Torches on either side of the door to Lachlan's chamber cast shadows over Angus as he lay sleeping on the floor. Amber stepped quietly over him and pushed open the door. Pausing, she held her breath as the sleeping giant mumbled. When he'd quieted, she entered the room.

A single candle flickered on a table near the bed. Lachlan lay on the covers as still as the effigy of a knight on top of a coffin.

His shirt and tartan were so soaked with blood from his wounds that the colors of the plaid were obscured. The strength in Amber's legs seemed to dissolve. She blinked back the tears that filled her eyes and concentrated on remaining calm. There was no way she could help him if she became hysterical. She reached out for the bedpost to steady herself. She had expected to find Lachlan resting comfortably, his wounds cleaned and dressed with care. Instead he looked like a prize candidate for infection. She marched back over to the door and yanked it open.

Angus woke with a start and scrambled to his feet. He rubbed his eyes. "You are not to be in the laird's chamber."

Lachlan was wounded. There was no other place she wanted to be. Angus might be formidable in size and strength, but that did not bother her. At the start of each school year there were always a few of her students who tried to see if she was serious about her classroom expectations. Her methods always worked. Treat them with respect, ignore the posturing, and don't back down. She straightened and her voice rang with authority.

"I will need water and plenty of clean linens."

"Lachlan will recover in two days. The effort is not needed."

There was that blasted forty-eight hour thing again. "I'm not leaving until you bring me what I've asked for. You may think Lachlan is the kind of man who can survive being attacked by a dozen men, but even the strongest person can die from infection."

He shrugged. "I heard it was only five."

Amber couldn't believe it. They were debating the number of men Lachlan had fought, while he lay on the bed bleeding to death. She pressed the point she was trying to make.

"I will help Lachlan whether I have your cooperation or not."

Angus smiled and made a bow. "I shall have Una bring what is needed." A frown creased his forehead. "Will you be putting needle to thread, and sewing up his wounds?"

She looked over at Lachlan then down at her hand. Marcail had done a good job stitching the cut, but Amber had nearly fainted before the task was completed. She doubted she'd be able to keep her hands from trembling if she had to sew Lachlan's wounds. Amber turned back to Angus and shook her head.

"If that's necessary, I'll ask for Marcail."

Angus seemed to relax. "I shall leave my friend in your care." He turned and headed in the direction of the Great Hall.

Alone, Amber approached the bed. She took a deep breath and rolled up her sleeves as she removed Lachlan's shirt. She bit her lower lip as her stomach churned. The arrows had been removed and long, jagged wounds punctured his chest. The queasiness returned. Keep your mind busy, she ordered.

Sweat formed on her lip. She wiped it away then examined his injuries. They would need to be cleaned and bandages applied. She turned toward the door. What was keeping Angus?

The smell of blood was suffocating and the chamber was too warm. She brushed damp hair away from her forehead and willed the room to stop spinning. She was going to get through this.

Someone touched her shoulder. She flinched.

Una stood behind her carrying a bucket of water and clean linen strips. "You look as pale as a shroud, lassie. Others can tend the laird. It is not a task you need perform."

Amber felt tears burn her eyes. "Yes, it is. When Marcail took care of my hand she put a vile-smelling concoction on the wound. It looked terrible, but it worked. Could you make some for Lachlan?"

Una shook her head slowly. "The laird is to have nothing of the sort. You may clean his wounds, that is all."

Amber looked at her in disbelief. "You can't be serious. He looks like a human pincushion. His wounds are deep. I think one arrow pierced his lung, another his heart and one . . ."

Una patted Amber's arm. "The laird will be fine, you'll see." Her expression remained serious and warning was implied. "He will heal in the same manner as did O'Donnell, if you ken my meaning."

Amber rubbed her temples. "No, I don't see. Why don't you explain it to me?"

"Now, lass, 'tis not my place. I shall fetch something for you to eat. You need to keep up your strength if you are determined to hold a vigil while he recovers." She paused at the doorway. " 'Tis a hard road you have set yourself upon. Guard your heart."

Amber listened to Una's footsteps as they grew faint down the hall. The woman's words echoed in her ears. She felt as though she'd spent her life building a barricade around her heart. Just when she'd finally begun to dismantle the walls, Una was advising her to put them up again.

Blinking away her tears, she cleansed Lachlan's wounds, then wrapped them with bandages. Why hadn't Una agreed to give him the medicine? She shook her head, stepped back and looked at her handiwork. Not a bad job, if she did say so herself. Thank goodness for mandatory first aid classes in her school district.

Sitting down in a chair beside the bed, she suddenly felt very tired and very uneasy. Lachlan's coma-like behavior was familiar. Una had mentioned O'Donnell. She paused. Both men had lapsed into a deep sleep after they'd been injured. But the similarities were more pronounced. Both men lay on their backs, as though they waited for something. The legend spoke of an immortal. She'd chosen not to think too much about that possibility, until now. She shuddered. It was eerie.

The door opened. Una had returned, bringing a tray with wine and sliced meat. A cough made the old woman shudder as she set the tray down on the table beside the bed. A deep sadness seemed to weigh her down.

"Are you all right?"

"Aye. I feel my age more of late, but 'twill pass." She nodded toward the bed. "He is a good man, that one is. Teach him how to cherish life, if you can."

Una picked up the clothes and bucket of water and departed.

Firelight danced in the hearth, as if trying to lift Amber's mood. It wasn't working. Everyone spoke of Lachlan as if he were a man who was drowning, and worse, as if she was the only one to save him.

She looked over at him. His face was as pale as the linen bandages wound around his chest, but his breathing was steady and strong. She leaned back in the chair remembering O'Donnell. Both men should have had raging infections from their injuries. But they didn't even appear to have slight fevers.

Amber stood. She was too restless to sleep. It was almost the first of November in the Highlands of Scotland and the weather was balmy. She remembered the legend; *the seasons will alter their natural course, the barriers of time will be broken.*

Amber jerked awake and sat up. Rubbing her neck, she looked out at the black sky. It was the dead of night. Muffled sobs came from the direction of the window. Amber looked over at the bed. Lachlan was still in a deep sleep. But someone else was definitely in the room. She turned in the direction of the sound.

Gavin sat in the far corner of the room. He looked up at her through tearstained eyes and handed her *The Canterbury Tales.*

"I thought you would read to my brother."

Kneeling down beside him, Amber held him close. She scolded herself for not thinking of him sooner. Of course he would be worried about his brother. The adult world typically forgot about the children when something like this happened.

"Lachlan will be just fine." The words sounded

mechanical. She hoped they sounded more convincing to Gavin.

"Oh, I know he will get better." Gavin pulled away from her and fresh tears rolled down his cheeks. "But MacDougal won't. Why can't he be like my brother?"

Amber rocked him gently. "I'm sorry, Gavin."

Words were inadequate when you'd lost your best friend. Part of her had been inconsolable when Shadow died. The one thing that had pulled her through was being able to talk to her brother.

She wiped the tears from Gavin's face with a corner of her dress. "Why don't you tell me a story about MacDougal the wolfhound? Something funny he did."

Gavin pulled back and shook his head. "I couldn't do that. We are not supposed to talk about someone once he is dead."

That was the dumbest thing she'd ever heard and she almost blurted out her opinion. "Would you mind if I talked about MacDougal?"

He shook his head.

"Do you remember the time at the festival when he ate so many fruit pies the hair underneath his chin was as red as Angus' beard? Or how about the time when he tried to fish? He would snap at the water, and then look over as if to say, 'Hey, I'm trying my best. Is it my fault the fish are so slippery?' "

Gavin giggled. "MacDougal took up most of the space on my bed. Sometimes he would stretch and I'd end up on the floor."

Amber laughed. "My dog did that. I never told anyone. I was afraid they would make him sleep outside."

"Me too." He frowned. "I like remembering. Why do you think I'm not supposed to do that?"

"I have no idea, but I do know one thing.

Remembering all the wonderful things those who are no longer with us have done is a way to keep them always in our hearts. Then they can live forever."

Gavin snuggled closer. "Aye, I think so, too."

Early-morning sunlight streamed through the window onto the sleeping Lachlan. Amber bent over and blew out the candles beside his bed then sat down. She leaned back against the chair. Her eyes felt heavy. She'd slept little in the past two days between watching over Lachlan and comforting Gavin. Reaching over the bed, she covered Lachlan with a blanket. Not that he needed it but fussing over him made her feel useful.

The bleeding had stopped after the first full day. During the second, he hadn't seemed to move a muscle. If she lifted the bandages, what would she find? Scars?

She paced back and forth in front of the bed, then realized she'd worn a path in the rush-strewn floor. Pausing in front of Lachlan, she made her decision.

Amber pulled back the blanket and began to carefully unwind the bandages. This was crazy. All she would accomplish was to open his wounds and to acknowledge the fact that she'd allowed her imagination to run wild. It was a journey to somewhere in between *The Island of Dr. Moreau* and never-never land.

Her hands shook as she removed the last linen strip. His injuries had healed. She had a moment's elation at the thought he'd survived before the realization hit. Lachlan's chest was bare, the muscles well defined and . . . there were no lingering puncture wounds from the arrows. She staggered back. Impossible.

A knock startled her. Quickly she hid the bandages and covered Lachlan with the blankets.

Marcail entered. She was wearing red brocade and her hair was tucked neatly in place.

"I have heard that you insisted on caring for Lachlan."

Amber combed her fingers through her tangled hair. All she could do was nod. Her body was still shaking. She didn't trust herself to speak. Her suspicions had been confirmed. It had been the same for Gavin and now, she suspected, O'Donnell as well. No scars. She felt her knees go weak and reached over to the bedpost for support. There were voices in the hall. Before she could understand what they were saying, two serving women, red-faced and out of breath, hurried into the room.

Marcail motioned to the adjoining room. "Pull out the bathtub and fill it all the way to the top."

Within the next half hour a parade of women passed before Amber, until the tub was filled with steaming water.

Marcail smiled. She touched Amber on the shoulder. "Your vigil has tired you greatly. Please, allow yourself this luxury. It will soothe your mind as well as refresh your body."

Amber tried to smile in response to the woman's kindness. There were several things she should ask Marcail: had she made a decision about O'Donnell, had anyone heard from Elaenor, how was Gavin doing, and had they buried MacDougal. But the concept that Lachlan couldn't die dominated her thoughts. Her heart felt as though it was beating as fast as a hummingbird's wings. All she could do was to hold on. The thick, wooden bedpost was the only reality she could trust.

The women left, followed by Marcail, plunging the room into a smothering silence. Amber fought the overpowering desire to run. She needed to think this through calmly. She wandered into the adjoining room and stared at the wooden tub until her vision blurred. A bath might indeed calm her down. She peeled off her clothes, threw them on the chair and tested the water with her hand. It was already starting to cool. She climbed in and leaned her head back until it touched the edge. She closed her eyes. The world she had begun to build around Lachlan had shattered like a china plate. No matter how you tried to repair the porcelain, you'd always see the cracks.

Amber sank deeper into the bath, feeling the water swirl around her as the realization hit her full force. He was immortal. She would age, become feeble and infirm, an albatross around Lachlan's neck, while he would always look like a Viking warrior.

A slight moan came from the direction of the bed. Amber sat up and water sloshed over the sides of the tub spilling onto the floor. She heard the sound again. This time mumbled words were added, but she couldn't move. It was almost as though she were afraid to see his condition.

He was coming out of the deep sleep. He muttered the words, "Time is an illusion."

The world that had stood still moments before began to spin. The words he'd spoken repeated themselves over and over. She knew them so well. It was the first part of the inscription written in her aunt's copy of *The Canterbury Tales*. "Time is an illusion and love the only reality."

The door to the other room banged open and a

crowd of people hurried in. Amber made a wild grab for the towel on the hook. One consolation; they weren't paying any attention to her. They were all huddled around Lachlan's bed. She stepped out of the tub, made for the archway and crept out of sight.

Chapter
14

❧

$\mathcal{L}$achlan watched her flick a linen cloth over the mantel. "What are you doing?"

"What does it look like? I'm dusting."

He reached out and grasped her wrist. Beneath his fingers her pulse raced as if she had been running.

"I have servants who can accomplish that task."

"Of, course you do. But I'm really upset, and this always worked for my aunt."

He paused and knew he did not want to hear the answer to his question. "Why are you angry?"

Amber pulled away from him and backed toward the fireplace. "You should be dead, or close to it."

"You are not pleased I survived?"

She turned to face the empty hearth. "That's not what I mean, and you know it. At first no one would let me in to see you. I had to sneak past Angus and found you unconscious on the bed. There was so much blood."

He pulled her against his chest. She was trembling again. "My injuries were not as serious as they appeared."

Amber turned in his arms and looked up at him.

"It's more than being able to recover from such a terrible attack. You don't have any scars. I know, I checked."

"I am alive. Is that not enough?"

"No it's not. I need to know why."

Lachlan released her and walked over to the window. He opened the shutters and a cool breeze drifted in. Stars dusted the cloudless sky. He cursed Angus for dropping his guard and letting Amber into his chamber. Lachlan drew in a deep breath. No, he could not blame his friend. This woman would have moved the castle to accomplish her goal. And her mission had been to help him. It was important that he trust her.

"I have more than the normal ability to recover from injuries."

"No kidding. It's more than that."

Lachlan nodded. "Aye, it is more."

Amber began to drum her fingers on the bedpost. "You are immortal."

She had said the words calmly, too calmly. He turned and looked at her and read the confusion in her eyes. "I know it is hard for you to understand the concept."

She shrugged. "You'd be surprised at what I would be able to 'understand.' I'm assuming this is a family trait?"

He nodded, aware that she was building to something. He wished he knew whatever it was, so that he could be better prepared for the battle.

"O'Donnell, Angus, Marcail and all the people who crowded around your bed, are they also part of this immortal club? And while we're on the subject, why were they in your room?"

"They wished to welcome me back to life."

"Of course, silly me. That's perfectly natural." He noticed her fists clenched at her side. "But it's not natural, is it? So explain to me, in simple words, why it is that you and O'Donnell, and all the rest, can't die?"

It struck him that she would accept only the truth. Anything less, he would lose her. That was not something he was prepared to risk, and what she was about to hear he knew she would find hard to believe. But she had the courage to pull him out of the bloodlust when he'd fought those who had killed MacDougal. He could trust that she would open her mind to new possibilities.

"It began so long ago that the years number in the thousands, when human sacrifices to selfish gods were common practice. My people were gentle and peaceloving. But our island home was easy prey and frequently we were attacked. Knowing we could not stop the senseless murders, we searched for ways to help the victims survive. The ancients discovered a method to help the body heal from injury through a potion comprised of herbs and plant life from the sea. A stab wound healed in a matter of days, a broken bone within hours, and a scratch in minutes. They continued to perfect the formula and administered it at birth. The doses were continued each year until the age of seven. It was never designed to prolong life. That was never the purpose, but that was exactly what happened."

"That's an understatement." Her voice quavered. "Any chance a mere mortal, like me, could get a drink of the fountain of youth?"

Lachlan shook his head. "The formula was lost when our island began to sink back into the sea."

"I had to ask." Amber twisted her hands together. "Suppose, just for the sake of argument, I believe all of this." She paused. "I . . ." She swallowed and straightened. "I'm going to grow old, you're not. That's the bottom line. I don't know if I can do that. Every time I look at my reflection in the mirror, I'll wonder what you're thinking when you see me. Will you still love me when I'm old? Will you stay with me out of pity, or obligation?"

She held up her hand as though to fend off an assault. "Don't give me a flowery speech about how you only see what is in the soul of a person. I'm an 'actions speak louder than words' kind of woman. I'm going to have to work this through myself."

He could read the play of emotions that crossed her face and saw the deep fear. And he felt powerless to help her. "Amber, you know how I feel."

"Do I?" She sank down on the ground, as though all the strength had gone out of her legs. "I had foolish dreams that I could help you discover the excitement of our just spending time together. Of the importance of family. Time, I felt, was on my side. Because, as we all grow older and face our own mortality, we want to leave a little of what we are behind. We want to make a difference, we want to be remembered and to know that our lives counted for something." Tears brimmed in her eyes. "I've accepted that I'll never see my parents, my brother, or my aunt again, but they are always in my heart. I am who I am because of them. How can I make you understand?"

She took a ragged breath of air. "You'll never grow old?"

He crossed over to the window and watched the whitecaps form on the loch. She was right about everything, even though he was unable to change. "I am immortal. For me, time is an illusion. I cannot change who I am."

Her voice lowered. "Well, time is not an illusion for me. It's very real. Each second, minute and day is precious. Maybe I value it because I can see myself changing, whereas you will always be as you are now. Fifty days, or fifty years, you'll be the same . . . and I'm afraid we will grow apart."

Lachlan turned to face her. He wished he could ease the pain reflected in her eyes. "Please believe that I will remain with you."

Amber blinked away the tears. "That's the problem. I know you won't leave me. But I want more. I want you to stay because you love me."

Lachlan rubbed the back of his neck. He wanted to take her in his arms and kiss away her doubts, but they would still be there the next day, and the next.

"Your love made me feel whole. When first I gazed on you, your physical appearance was beyond my dreams of beauty. Now I see more. Your radiance shall never be dimmed in my eyes."

"Lachlan." Her voice was whisper-soft. She ran to him and into his arms. "Hold me. It's hard for me to think it will work out between us. Where I come from, loving a person is very complicated. The big trend now is doing things together. When I'm ninety, I won't be able to do the same things that I can now."

He cupped her chin in his hands. "And what is it that you like to do?"

"I like to run."

"For what purpose?"

She shrugged. "Just for the exercise."

Lachlan smiled. "Then I shall look forward to your being ninety. I hate to run without a reason for the effort."

*   *   *

A rooster crowed in the courtyard. Amber laid out
the ingredients on the long trestle table in the cookroom. Eggs, flour, ground cocoa beans . . . she was forgetting something. Ever since Lachlan had been
awakened by Marcail, Amber had been restless and
unable to sleep. It had to do with Una. After an hour
of tossing and turning Amber had given up and
decided to bake brownies. It'd seemed like a good
idea at the time, but she kept remembering the depth
of her conversation with Lachlan last night.

Most of it had been random thoughts spoken out
loud, the "what ifs" of their relationship. Inevitably
the subject of children arose. He had told her not to
worry. She couldn't get pregnant. Amber remembered
how uneasy she'd felt and then she recalled having a
similar conversation with Elaenor. The young woman
was convinced she couldn't have a child until she'd
wanted one.

Amber had pressed harder. Lachlan explained that
immortals were in a state of suspended sterility until
they drank a magic potion. And, of course, there had to
be a list of requirements. First, because he was the
leader, he needed permission to even talk about the
issue; the union of the person he'd chosen had to be
approved, the stars had to be in the right alignment in
the sky, and on and on. Knowing she couldn't get pregnant should have been comforting, but it wasn't. She
had never appreciated how much she wanted children
until remaining with Lachlan meant it was not possible.

She stared at the scattered ingredients on the table,
unable to move. Amber reminded herself she'd been
forced to absorb some pretty weird stuff in the last
twenty-four hours and should take it one step at a
time. Right before she'd drifted to sleep in Lachlan's

arms, she'd come to realize how deeply she loved him. Maybe, she reflected, that was enough.

Amber hadn't seen Lachlan for two whole days. She sat on a bench in the waning light of a crescent moon looking at a white rose. She pulled off the soft petals, one by one.

"He loves me, he loves me not, he loves me." She tossed the flower on the ground and stared at the sky. That was not the question. The question was whether he loved her enough. Enough to love her when she grew old, enough to learn to value life in the same way she did. She leaned over, picked up the rose and twirled the stem between her fingers. Maybe she was asking too much.

Footsteps sounded on the walkway and she turned around expectantly. It wasn't Lachlan. Marcail stood in the shadows, wearing a gown of black silk. The dress was more severe in style than usual. Maybe she should ask Marcail if she had another dress just like it. It fit Amber's mood. She returned to her flower.

The swish of material invaded the silence as Marcail approached and sat down. "There is a great sadness in your expression. And I know Lachlan to be the cause."

Amber held the stem of the rose tighter, accidentally pricking her finger on a thorn. A droplet of blood fell to the ground. She sucked on the cut on her finger.

"Tomorrow there will be a small scar where I scratched my skin. If the same thing had happened to you or Lachlan there wouldn't be a mark."

"That is true. However, do not deny the love between you and Lachlan. It shines so bright that many are warmed when they are near both of you."

"You're talking about how I feel about Lachlan.

What about you and O'Donnell. Have you resolved your differences?"

Marcail fingered the pearls at her throat. "He made love to another."

The rose petals crushed in Amber's hand. "And exactly how long ago did this happen? Five years, ten, a hundred?"

"One hundred and twenty years ago. But time does not diminish the hurt, nor the offense."

"I agree, but I'll ask you the same question you asked me. Do you love him?"

Marcail looked at her hands in her lap. "Yes, but I cannot forgive him."

Amber tossed the remaining petals to the ground. "I wish I shared your dilemma. He has traveled a long way just to find you, and is determined to wait until you change your mind." She laughed bitterly. "You have something I will never have; time. Everyone makes mistakes. However, it's how we react to them that makes the difference. You and O'Donnell have time. Lachlan and I do not."

Marcail smiled. "I have lived to see the rise and fall of many civilizations, yet you have the wisdom to remind me of a truth I had long forgotten. Time is an illusion, Lady Amber, and love is the only reality. Listen to your own advice and do not be afraid of your emotions. They are what make us feel alive." Marcail reached out and squeezed Amber's hand. "Put aside logic, and listen to your heart. Lachlan needs you but he is not able to ask for your help." She paused. "Una is dying. This has affected him greatly. He has not yet allowed himself to grieve. Indeed he does not know how. Go to him."

* * *

A single candle on the mantel illuminated Una's room. Amber, entering, saw that Lachlan knelt in the shadows beside the bed. He held the old woman's frail hand. The silence ticked by in slow motion and the similarities between her aunt and Una merged. She was glad that Marcail had told her. Lachlan shouldn't be alone. Amber had been teaching a class when she'd learned her best friend had been killed in a plane crash. The bottom of her world had fallen out.

She walked over to the bed wondering why he wasn't talking to Una. It would help pass the time, for both of them. Looking closer, Amber had the answer. Una was already dead. She put her hand on Lachlan's shoulder, wishing she'd come sooner.

"She has gone." His voice was only a whisper.

Amber knelt beside him, putting her arm around his waist and moved closer until their bodies were touching. "I know."

"I could not love her the way she wanted me to. For that, I hated myself. She deserved so much."

"You gave your friendship." Amber rested her head on his shoulder. "Do you know how rare that is? I mean, the type of friendship you and Una shared? You did not judge or try to change each other. It was pure acceptance." She felt the tears brim in her eyes. She'd shared that gift with the friend who had died in the plane crash.

Lachlan turned toward her. "What am I to do now?"

"Remember her. Keep her always in your heart. That way she will never die."

He drew her tightly against him. "The pain and regret are more then I can bear."

Amber felt his tears against her cheek as he silently mourned Una's death.

*   *   *

" 'Twas Subedei's men who attacked you and killed the dog."

Lachlan pushed away from the table and looked over at Angus. The Great Hall was empty as many had retired for the night. Now only the two of them remained. Una's burial had taken place that morning and a day of celebration had been declared in her honor. Lachlan knew Angus had delayed informing him of the identity of the men until now out of respect for Una's passing. The man was a good friend.

Lachlan nodded. "Subedei grows bold. Double the guard."

"It will be as you wish." Angus scratched his beard. "Your brother was saddened by the loss of MacDougal."

Lachlan reached for an empty tankard. "Gavin openly mourned Una as though she'd been his mother."

Indeed, his brother and Una had shared that type of bond. He had forgotten that in MacDougal's death Gavin had also lost his best friend. Until now, Lachlan had never considered the animal to be anything more than protection. Perhaps he could never replace MacDougal in Gavin's heart, but Lachlan could provide another friend. He put the tankard down.

"Come with me, Angus. There is something we must do."

The courtyard was filled with clear morning light. Amber sat beside Gavin and listened to him read aloud. He had greatly improved and even boasted that he was now reading for pleasure. She smiled, remembering how her brother compared reading to going to the dentist's office.

She heard a puppy yelp and looked up. Lachlan appeared before them, holding a black ball of fur.

"I need to find a home for this mangy animal."

Gavin shot off the bench and ran over to his brother. "Where did she come from? May I take care of her?"

Lachlan knelt down and handed the squirming puppy to Gavin. "She is from Lily MacKintosh's litter."

Amber's breath caught in her throat. There was a subtle change in Lachlan. For the first time he had referred to one of the wolfhounds as "she" instead of "it."

Gavin glanced over at Amber, giggling as he tried to avoid the puppy's licking tongue. "She likes me."

Amber smiled. Gavin had been melancholy all morning. She looked at the three of them close together. The puppy was alternating between licking Gavin's face and nibbling on Lachlan's hand. The atmosphere was charged with love.

Lachlan glanced at her and winked. "What do you think we should name this beast who is determined to chew clear through to the bones in my fingers?"

Gavin interrupted. "Amber should be the one to name her."

"Aye. But more important, the name should represent wisdom and understanding."

Amber's heart filled with hope as they included her in their circle. "Do you like the name Dora?" She knew the dear woman would like the idea.

The two brothers bent their heads together and whispered as though they were making a decision of the gravest importance. Lachlan nodded and motioned for Gavin to render their verdict.

"Lachlan and I feel Dora is a good strong name, worthy of the wolfhound she will become. But she should have a last name as well. We would like to use your name, MacPhee."

"Dora MacPhee." Amber laughed. "It's perfect."

With the puppy in his arms, Gavin stood and headed toward the cookroom. "Dora is hungry. I had better find something for her to eat."

Amber closed the book Gavin had left behind. "That was a very nice thing you did."

He shrugged. "Wolfhounds are fierce protectors of the castle, and this one was in need of a home."

"I just realized something." She grinned. "You are a fraud, Lachlan MacAlpin."

He arched his eyebrow and sat down beside her. "And why is it that you call me such?"

"You didn't give Gavin a puppy because you wanted another watchdog. You gave her to him because you knew he missed MacDougal." She smiled. "I think there's hope for you yet."

"There is indeed hope."

A soft warm breeze swirled the dust around her feet and in the distance she could hear Gavin playing with Dora. She felt better today than she had in a while. She'd done a lot of thinking since her conversation with Marcail.

"And, maybe, there's a chance for us."

He kissed her lightly on the nose. "Aye, those words are true. We are fated to be together, Amber MacPhee. One day you will believe it as well."

She leaned toward him until their arms touched. The contact warmed her. "Tell me."

He traced the outline of her neck with gentle fingers and his voice was a husky whisper. "I am empty without you."

The words soothed her aching heart. They should

have been enough. She turned away. It would be so easy to love him. Easy to live moment to moment, and not think of the tomorrows. Through the clear, warm morning air Amber saw O'Donnell and Marcail walking hand in hand toward the Loch. They had made their peace. She should be able to do the same, but something held her back.

Amber tucked the book under her arm and pushed open the door to Marcail's room. The chamber was bathed in the afternoon sunlight. Marcail, a needle in one hand, was sewing on a white linen gown.

"I saw you and O'Donnell in the courtyard earlier today." Amber smiled. "Looks as though you've decided to give him a second chance."

Marcail shook the finger she'd pricked with the needle. "Yes, but I am already regretting it. I hate to sew."

Amber laughed. "So do I." She examined the dress. It was a fitted linen gown. Celtic lettering, in gold silk thread, was sewn on the bodice and long sleeves. The gown was breathtaking in its simplicity, but not the type of dress Marcail usually wore.

"It's beautiful. If you're having trouble, why don't you ask someone to help you?"

Marcail wiped her forehead with the back of her hand. "Tradition dictates that I perform the task myself. It is the gown I shall be married in, if ever I complete the sewing of it."

Yesterday they had discussed the fact that O'Donnell did not deserve to be forgiven; today Marcail was planning to marry him. Amber pulled up a chair opposite Marcail and sat down. She decided Marcail had two rates at which she traveled: turtle slow or speed of light. Amber preferred somewhere in between.

"So, when will the wedding take place?"

Marcail looked out the window. "At the winter solstice we shall enter into the joining ceremony and drink from the cup that contains the Elixir of Life. A year from that date we shall enter into another ceremony that will unite us in marriage." She glanced at Amber. "If the gods bless our union, I shall bear a child ten months after the second ceremony. You made me understand that if you love someone, the choice is simple."

Cobwebs blocked Amber's path and clung in her hair. She brushed her face, staying in the shadows as she followed silently down the narrow corridor behind Marcail. In the pre-dawn light Amber had decided two things. First, if they were to have any future together she must be honest with Lachlan and tell him she was from the twentieth century and second, that she wanted to learn more about his people.

She'd overheard Angus and Marcail mention a council meeting at the evening meal and had made the decision to see it for herself.

Amber blew out her candle, to avoid being detected, and inched forward by feeling her way along the damp walls. She could see the light from Marcail's candle flickering along the ceiling. She was past thinking this was a dumb idea and had moved on to considering herself certifiably insane. What did she hope to discover? It was freezing in the underground tunnels and the cold air seeped through the many layers of clothes she wore. She shivered, gritting her teeth to keep them from chattering.

The light from Marcail's candle disappeared. Amber felt as though she'd been plunged into a black void so dark her eyes couldn't make the adjustment. Her heart thundered in her ears. She forced down the panic and increased her pace. The sharp edges from the stone walls cut into the palm of her hand. As she turned a corner she saw a light. Amber hurried forward in time to see Marcail step through a doorway.

Cautiously she inched her way forward and peered inside. Torches lined the walls exposing a vestibule-type room and then a larger one beyond. It was the larger of the two that Marcail headed toward. Amber entered the smaller chamber. A latticework stone wall stood on either side of the entrance to the larger room, dividing the two chambers. The designs looked Celtic. She hugged the wall and peered into the room that Marcail had entered. Candles covered a long table that shone like ebony. She could hear whispered conversations.

There appeared to be about twenty men and women. They were all talking so low Amber couldn't make out the words and the accents were as varied as their clothes. She recognized Angus and the twins, Artemis and Theseus.

A door creaked open. Lachlan entered with four men who walked behind him. She couldn't shake the feeling that the whole tension-charged atmosphere must be building toward a dark purpose. Three men and three women took their places behind a long table. Lachlan did the same.

She heard a scuffling sound. Two tartan-clad men dragged a third forward from the shadows. An old woman, her clothes resembling layers of tattered rags and her hair in wild disorder, danced and cackled around a tall slender man. He was dressed in the loose-fitting clothes of a Russian Cossack and was being held prisoner. Amber gripped the latticework and leaned closer.

Lachlan and the six people sat down and talked quietly among themselves. Amber could almost hear the sound of ticking as time crept forward. Then the old woman laughed. The shrill noise echoed through the room. Lachlan stood, his face and expression hidden from Amber in the shadows cast by the torchlight. He walked around the table to stand in front of the man accused.

"Morag, the charges against you are grave and the facts undisputed." He motioned for Angus. "It has been proven that you willingly had agreed to enter into a marriage contract with this woman, Thia, in the year 1411. Do you deny these charges?"

Lachlan's voice was clear and his words seemed to bounce off the walls, but she must have heard the date wrong. She figured she had traveled back to the year 1566, so Lachlan must have said or meant 1511, not 1411. She looked at the man Lachlan had called Morag and then over at Thia. Morag was a man in his thirties, but the woman was bent over with age. Morag must have agreed to marry Thia when she was young and beautiful and changed his mind when she started to age. Amber felt her hands tremble against the harsh stone.

Metal clanked against the floor as Morag's chains were released. He sank down to his knees and bent forward. Lachlan placed his hand on the man's head and Amber saw the muscles in Lachlan's jaw tighten.

"Thia, believing in your word and under the supervision of the Council, performed the ceremony that prepared her for the joining. When it was your turn to drink from the cup containing the Elixir of Life, you ran. Although many offered to take your place, Thia refused them, and demanded what was her right."

A suffocating silence encased the room. Amber held her breath. If what she understood was correct, not only did this elixir reverse the effects of sterility, it also started the aging process. According to her calculations, Thia had sacrificed her immortality over one hundred and fifty years ago. These immortals might age, but it was still at a slower pace than mortals.

Lachlan moved aside as Theseus mumbled a few words. He poured liquid from a glass decanter over the bent head of Morag.

"It is a credit to you, Morag, that you accept your fate. Your brothers and sisters will learn of your courage." He motioned to Angus who drew his sword and raised it over Morag's head.

Amber pulled back from the barrier, stunned. Her heart was beating so fast her chest ached. The expressions on the faces of those in the room were as emotionless as the stone walls.

Lachlan raised his hand. "The laws of our race are clear. By refusing to join with Thia, after she had fulfilled the ceremony, you robbed her not only of her life, but of the opportunity to bear children. The penalty is your death."

Silent screams rose in Amber's throat. She backed away until her fingers made contact with the stone wall of the entrance. In horror she watched as Lachlan gave the signal to Angus. The man whom Amber had thought of as a gentle bear of a man slashed the sword down toward the prisoner. The blade cut through the air and severed Morag's head.

She heard the crack of metal against bone, saw the

head separating from the body and the dark blood spilling onto the stones. Her stomach lurched into her throat, the taste bitter against her tongue. She covered her mouth with her hands and ran into the darkness, feeling her way through the passageway toward the safety of her room.

The stench of blood hung heavy in the dimly lit chamber. Lachlan watched the council members back away from Morag's body. The twins straightened the sleeves of their purple velvet coats and averted their gaze. Marcail turned to face him. She had a lace handkerchief pressed lightly against her face and her eyes were rimmed with tears. They had both known Morag, a storyteller, a poet. A man who felt intensely for a woman or a cause one moment and indifference the next. Lachlan felt it difficult to breathe.

Thia's shrill laugh broke through the stillness. All turned toward the woman who was the only one in the chamber to rejoice in Morag's execution. She danced and muttered incoherently around the stone-faced council. Marcail touched Artemis on the arm. He walked over to the woman, leading her gently from the room. Thia's intrusion into their shared grief awakened all to action. Two men, wearing the MacAlpin plaid, picked up Morag's body. A third placed the man's head in a woven basket and walked out the door. Those who remained nodded their heads respectfully toward Lachlan then filed out of the chamber.

A blackness crept over Lachlan. He denied the emotions that attempted to overwhelm him. The laws that ruled his kind had protected them and kept them safe over a history that spanned thousands of years. It was indeed essential that they be upheld. That was the gossamer thread of duty to which he was bound. For his next task he would need a clear mind.

He looked at Angus. His friend was immobilized by grief and stood where he had brought down Morag. Angus had followed the command to execute the man, not allowing emotions to engulf him until the order was completed.

Lachlan crossed to him. Times beyond counting he had questioned the fates that made him Angus' overlord. He put his hand on the man's shoulder and watched him slowly raise his head. The same look of despair had been in Marcail's eyes. Lachlan squeezed Angus' shoulder.

"There was no choice left to us."

"'Tis true, but my thoughts were also with the woman. Poor creature. For a brief moment I thought she would ask me to end her life. 'Twas unfortunate it took so long to find Morag." A dark cloud of fear passed over his face. "My sword was ready."

Lachlan placed a hand on his shoulder. "You must dispel these thoughts, lest you bring on the insanity. Come, another task will prove healing. We have much that needs attention."

Angus straightened, wiped the blood off his sword and sheathed it. The metal grated against the scabbard, echoing in the stone chamber. His chin raised, he met Lachlan's gaze.

"Subedei?"

"Aye."

Amber stumbled along the dark corridor toward her room. She should have screamed out, should have prevented the killing. Tears streamed down her face.

"Stop."

The voice was somehow familiar. Turning toward the sound she saw a shroud-like creature emerge from the shadows and she stepped back. The apparition came closer and in the torchlight Amber recognized Lachlan's mother.

"Diedra?"

"I saw you follow Marcail down the stairs. I knew what you would find. And I waited. Morag took away Thia's youth. No one will have her now. It is too late for her. You must not judge my son. He needs you."

Amber didn't want to listen to excuses. The man was dead. "I don't understand any of it. You are all immortal. So, Morag changed his mind. He shouldn't be murdered for it."

"Thia was a beautiful and intelligent woman once. I remember her. We were both to enter into the joining ceremony during the winter solstice. She gave up much only to have it torn from her."

"Why didn't she find someone else?"

Diedra looked down the long corridor. "She loved Morag and when he abandoned her all she could think of was revenge."

As Diedra's words and Marcail's slowly sank in, Amber tried to imagine the shriveled-up figure before her as a young woman. The Elixir of Life was the key. It changed them. Amber reached to take Diedra's hand. "You gave birth to Gavin eight years ago. How is that possible?"

Diedra met her eyes. "The laws which govern the mortal race are not the same for my kind."

Chapter

15

❧

A cool breeze washed over Amber's face as she lay in bed. The faint sound of the wind blowing through the trees drifted in an open window. She still tossed and turned, locked in a nightmare where Diedra was laughing and screaming that Lachlan was going insane. Abruptly she opened her eyes to see Lachlan staring at her. Relief washed over her. Then she remembered Morag.

Lachlan touched her cheek gently. "You were seen leaving after Morag's death."

The memory of the execution passed in slow motion through Amber's thoughts. She pulled away from his touch, untangled the linen nightgown she wore and left the bed. The floor was cold on her bare feet through the rushes.

"Death? You mean execution. Or better yet, murder. You ordered Angus to kill that man."

Lachlan's face was an emotionless mask.

She walked over to the fireplace and warmed her hands. She was trembling. "Your mother said I shouldn't blame you, but I need to know your reasons."

"Morag knew the penalty. He broke one of the

sacred laws. It took the council a long time to bring him to justice."

Her breath seemed to catch in her throat. She felt tears brim in her eyes. She was beginning to understand the need to punish Morag, but to her the price was too high. She tried to blot out the memory of the blade, as Angus swung it down on Morag's neck. Her stomach seemed to flip over as she remembered the smell of blood. She felt Lachlan touch her shoulder and she turned into his embrace.

"I know what Morag did was wrong, but you can't just kill someone because they broke a promise."

He held her close. "Our laws are clear. Would you have me change them?"

She pulled away to wipe her tears with the palm of her hand. "Yes, I would. What if the same thing happened to you? You could wake up one day and discover I'd grown old and you'd feel trapped." She bit her lip to keep it from quivering. "I wouldn't want you to stay because you felt obligated to me or because some law said you had to."

"We are not talking about the same thing. Thia gave up her immortality. It can never be regained, once it is lost."

"You place so much value in what you are that you have forgotten what it is to be human. I've lost something that can never be regained: my home. You've never bothered to ask me how I came into your world. I never thought about that before, until now. Actually I was relieved, because I was afraid you might think I was crazy or have me burned at the stake. Now I realize that you had a lot more to hide than I did." She cleared her throat and steadied herself for his reaction. "Lachlan, I'm from the future."

His voice was clam. "So Marcail and I suspected. What year?"

She went over to the bed and sat on the edge. Lachlan was calm, she was a mess. This seemed to be a recurring theme.

"I was on my way to the Abbey, to attend a reenactment. In my century people are fascinated with the Middle Ages. I'm from the year 1997."

"The Guardian is not confined to the barriers of time." Lachlan smiled and joined her on the bed, reaching for her hand. "If the beastie had not found someone in my century who fulfilled the legend, he would have continued his search. Your world must be very different from this one."

"That's it? That's all you're going to say? Aren't you the least bit surprised. It's not every day that someone travels back in time. Or is it?"

He arched an eyebrow. "It has happened before."

Her voice was a whisper. "I had forgotten. The man your mother calls 'Ford.' "

"Aye." He looked in the direction of the window. "It happened a day or two after my enemy had killed my father, and members of my family."

Amber remembered his telling her about the man he called Subedei. She shivered. The violence of this century was overwhelming. Senseless killings were part of her world as well, but coming from Seattle she'd lived a sheltered existence. She would have to get used to it if she was to be a part of Lachlan's life. Amber put her hand on his shoulder. The contact eased the pain in his expression and allowed him to continue.

"I was still in China, but my mother wanted a warrior to avenge the deaths of those she loved. The man pulled from the water may have had the ability to accomplish that goal. We found a metal cylinder strapped to his belt. When Angus pulled back on a lever, the weapon released an object that embedded itself in his foot." Lachlan laughed. "My usually even-tempered friend was so angered he threw the thing in the water."

Amber wondered if the Guardian had been responsible for the man's not surviving his journey through time. Maybe the Loch Ness monster had decided a twentieth century weapon in the sixteenth century would have caused more harm than good. She stretched out beside Lachlan on the bed, relishing the feeling of just being near him.

"The weapon is called a gun and it's probably a good thing Angus threw it away. But how did your mother summon the Guardian?"

"A portion of the Elixir of Life is poured into Loch Ness and the words, 'Time is an illusion' are spoken as the request is given."

"Have your people gone through this ritual often?"

"No, but as you are aware, it has happened often enough."

The pale light of dawn cast the bed in shades of molten gold. Lachlan reached for Amber and pulled her gently toward him under the layers of covers. The contours of her body fit comfortably against him. Her skin was warm against his as she snuggled closer. Lachlan was at peace. He decided he would spend the day with her. There was much he could show Amber of the heather-clad hills that surrounded Urquhart and much he wanted to learn about the world whence she had come. 1997. It most certainly was a wonderful time, if Amber was a product of it.

He pictured Amber in an isolated meadow a few miles from the castle. A mountain stream fed a pool of clear water nearby. He had used it many times to wash away the dust from his travels, before returning home. Smiling, he remembered their time together in what she had called a shower. He kissed her lightly on her shoulder. She was right. The need to fight had overtaken his life, pushing all else aside. She, alone, had reached his heart.

The door to the chamber burst open and a cold rush of air swept over the room. Angus was framed in the doorway.

Dark circles shadowed his friend's eyes; his mouth was drawn in a straight line. "Ian was found alive, but the Angel of Death is close at hand."

Lachlan eased himself from the warmth of the bed and away from Amber. He picked his clothes off the floor and began to dress. He knew Ian. He was a good and loyal clansmen and an able scout.

"Ian's assailant, is he known to us?"

"Aye." Angus' voice was barely above a whisper. "Ian would speak with you."

The light in the chamber seemed to grow harsh and a silence crept over the room. The tone in his friend's voice was like the depths of Loch Ness, cold and dark. Lachlan knew that this day would end badly. He looked over at Amber. More than ever before in his life he wanted to stay with her, but his responsibilities pulled him away. Leaving the woman ached like a physical pain.

If Ian's injuries had been caused by one of the thieving bands of men who owed allegiance to no one save themselves, they would be easily and swiftly dealt with. He motioned for Angus to follow him.

Pushing open the door he hesitated, looking back at Amber.

Angus put his hand on his shoulder. "She will understand what must be done."

"I pray you are right."

Lachlan walked into the torch lit hallway toward the stairs leading down to the Great Hall. Six men crowded around Ian, who lay on a long table. They were talking in hushed voices, but grew silent as Lachlan and Angus approached.

Lachlan drew closer. He could feel the cold stone floor beneath his bare feet. The numbing sensation started to work its way up his legs. He stared down at Ian. The man's face was the color of ash, his eyes reflected his pain. Dark red blood covered his shirt and plaid.

"Has someone sent for Marcail?"

Angus nodded.

Ian grabbed Lachlan's arm. "Subedei's brother is here."

The silence in the room deepened. Lachlan clasped Ian's hand. The man must be delirious with pain. "That is not possible. Subedei's relatives fought in the first wave of Mongols that had threatened to conquer Europe. My enemy was the only member of his family to survive."

Ian shook his head slowly. "I heard them speak of him." A spasm of pain caused him to release his hold on Lachlan and double over. Ian's voice was insistent. "At the time, Subedei's brother was attending school in London."

Lachlan turned to Angus. "What do you know of this?"

"Ian was captured and taken to Subedei's camp.

They thought they had rendered him unconscious."
Angus straightened with pride. "He is a Scotsman and
not easily defeated. Ian heard Subedei boast that his
brother was within these walls."

Footsteps echoed over the stone floor. The men
parted to make way for Marcail, who walked quickly
to Ian and felt the man's forehead. "He is burning up."
She began to strip away the bloody shirt. "Bring me
water and linens."

Lachlan watched Marcail's futile efforts to save Ian.
He knew that the man had little chance to survive and
he guessed she did as well, but while Ian still breathed
she would try to save him. His heart warmed toward
her. Her mantle of ice had melted and she was once
again the healer he remembered. He sensed Amber
was as much responsible for the change as was
O'Donnell.

Marcail drew back. "Look what that animal has
done."

Ian's chest was bare, but the skin was scorched
black. Burned into the flesh was the letter "S."

Lachlan put his hands on her shoulders to steady
her. He felt anger well inside him. Subedei had sent a
message to him. No one was to be spared.

Ian coughed, reaching out a hand to him.

Lachlan drew closer and bent down. "Save your
strength, friend. The Lady Marcail will heal you."

"You must know the name." A spasm of pain
once again took hold of him. When it had subsided
he motioned for Lachlan to come closer. " 'Tis
Bartholomew."

Amber watched Lachlan as he walked into the
adjoining room, heading in the direction of the alcove

where he kept his armor. She felt a chill as she slid off the bed, pulled a blanket around her and followed him. He wouldn't tell her where he'd been this morning, only that he had to prepare himself and the castle for battle.

He paused as he reached for a thick vest. "I would ask a favor of you, Amber. See that Gavin is kept from the battle. I would not want him harmed."

She nodded. Her voice was unsteady. "Of course."

The seriousness of what was about to happen clutched at her heart. The room seemed to darken. Amber had never seen Lachlan put on battle gear.

"Won't you be too weighted down with all that armor to be able to slaughter every man who gets in your way?"

He reached for a tunic made of chain mail. "Nay, I will not."

Amber clutched the back of a chair and held on as a drowning man would a section of his boat. She could feel Lachlan slipping away from her with each weapon or plate of armor he strapped to his body. She wanted to penetrate the barrier he'd placed between them. "I thought you were immortal. Why do you have to wear all that armor."

His gaze was black as the inside of the hearth. "If my heart is cut out, I will die. If my head is severed from my body, I will die."

She shuddered with the thought and met his gaze. "Sorry I asked. You said you wanted to protect your people, to protect me. How can you do that if someone kills you? You're preparing for battle as if you expect it to be your last."

His voice was as hard and unfeeling as the steel blade he held. "It well may be."

She pushed away from the bedpost and walked over to the window. Dark clouds churned in the sky and wisps of light were the only reminder that this was the start of the day and not the end.

"Please, Lachlan, don't do this."

"I must."

Amber was as tall as the blade he held. In the firelight it shone blood red. "I don't want you to go out there."

"If it is the will of the gods, I will come back to you."

"That's it? You're putting your future and mine in the hands of fate? I am expected to adhere to stupid medieval rules, not to mention the ones attached to your immortal race, all because I fell in love with some dolt who is perfectly content to put his life in the hands of a deity? And a deity who probably could care less."

She saw a smile cross his lips. "Angus has often remarked upon how you know your place, and obey my every command."

"Given time, it might have happened."

"Aye, time might accomplish it, but I fear even I shall not live that long."

Her heart ached with a foreboding she couldn't shake, but his dark concentration seemed to have lifted. Maybe there was still hope. She walked over to the bed and lightly touched the carved, wooden post.

"Please call it off. Arrange for a meeting with this man."

" 'Tis too late for that."

"It's not too late to fight for peace. You've asked me to trust in you. And you said that our love is strong enough to conquer any obstacle. Even time. Yet, you're not willing to do the same. Why can't you accept that anger and revenge are not the answer? Love is the answer."

His voice was withdrawn. "You ask too much."

The castle was in a flurry of activity. Windows were being closed and doors barricaded in readiness for the battle. Amber, entering the courtyard, heard voices above the clamor. They belonged to Marcail and O'Donnell.

"Lachlan is meeting with the Council. They will take all day to decide the fate of Bartholomew. Did you see what Subedei did to Ian? It was barbaric. He should not be allowed to live."

O'Donnell's voice was barely above a whisper. "Bartholomew is Subedei's brother. Perhaps the Council means to make a trade: spare Urquhart and the inhabitants for his safe return."

Marcail tapped her foot on the stone floor. "You know Subedei. He would appear to agree to their terms and then break his word. Nay, I should take the decision out of the Council's hands. Bartholomew must die."

The musty smell of damp stones and stale air filled Amber's lungs. She kept to the shadows and followed the light cast by Marcail's candle. Hushed voices drifted toward her and she sensed those she followed had paused. It was vital she stop Marcail. Maybe Subedei would go back on his word, but anything was worth a try, if deaths could be avoided. Amber ducked into an alcove and encountered a wall of sticky cobwebs. Cringing, she wiped them off her face and slid into the protective enclosure.

Marcail's voice floated toward her. The sound was

hollow and devoid of emotion as it echoed off the stone walls.

"O'Donnell, you know as well as I Bartholomew must die."

Amber backed against the wall. Marcail was a healer. She strove to save lives, or so Amber had believed.

O'Donnell's words tumbled out in a rush. "I know nothing of the kind. Leave the matter to the Council."

"I will not."

The sound of their footsteps drowned out O'Donnell's response. Amber peered from her hiding place as they turned a corner and passed out of sight.

The passageway narrowed, sloping downward. Water coated the walls. Amber paused to catch her breath. The air was growing foul and putrid She felt sick and her legs trembled. She reached out to steady herself. Instead of the anticipated coarse stones her fingers touched something smooth.

A skeleton, clad in tattered clothes, was shackled to the wall. The skull rested on one arm and the empty sockets stared back at her. The mouth was open in a silent scream. Amber stumbled back, hearing in her imagination pleas for mercy. The brutality of his death told nothing of what his crime had been. A murderer or a woman accused of witchcraft might well have died in the same manner. She shivered. Two sets of small red eyes peered at her from a crevice behind the skull, as if accusing her of being too late.

Loud, angry voices reminded Amber of her reason for being here. She heard the words; murderer, traitor, deceiver. Picking up her skirts, she headed in the direction of the sound. She couldn't let Marcail kill Bartholomew.

As she rounded the corner, the passageway opened

into a cavernous dungeon that appeared to be twice the size of the Great Hall. Vacant cells lined all four walls. In the center of the room was an enormous fire pit. Iron tools of varying sizes and shapes hung in neat rows from a wooden frame on the perimeter of the pit. All was in readiness. It only lacked for victims.

"You cannot kill me." Bartholomew's voice echoed through the corridors.

At the far end of the chamber, in the cell furthest from the entrance, she saw the tutor. The door to his cell gaped open. Marcail had him pinned against the inside wall with a knife pointed at his throat.

"I can kill you and will."

"Lachlan gave his word that I would be tried by judge and jury."

"Those crimes are nothing. We have learned your true identify."

Amber ran toward them. "Stop."

O'Donnell stepped out of the shadows to block her way. "You cannot interfere."

"Marcail wants to kill him. We can't let her."

Bartholomew turned his head. "She will not listen to you."

Marcail pressed the blade against the tutor's neck. Her voice was rich with loathing. "That is because your crimes are too many. You spied on Lachlan and his family. You poisoned Molly when she learned of your purpose and who you are."

"I admit I killed the wench. And why not? Perhaps the girl loved me so much she began to believe the babe was really mine, instead of the wandering minstrel to whom she lost her virginity."

His laughter echoed through the dungeon. "You know full well I could not father her child. She deserved to die. But you cannot kill me. Subedei's revenge would be boundless if you killed his last remaining brother."

A noise that could have been thunder vibrated through the walls. O'Donnell's voice was angry. "Cannons. They attack us with cannon." He grabbed Amber's arm and pulled her toward the entrance to the passageway. "Hurry. There is little time."

Bartholomew screamed and slumped forward. Blood coated the knife Marcail held. The blade clattered to the ground. Her voice trembled. "What have I become? I have spent all my years trying to save lives."

O'Donnell left Amber to put his arm around Marcail's shoulder. "I knew that you would not go through with murder. No matter the offense."

She twisted out of his grasp. "I stabbed him in the stomach."

"The man is immortal, Marcail. As you well know."

"That does not excuse what I have done. I must let the Council deal with him, when he recovers."

Another cannon blast shook the walls as Amber felt herself being dragged back toward the labyrinth of corridors. Things were falling into place. Molly was killed because she threatened to expose Bartholomew's identity. Tears stung her eyes. Amber felt sick inside. She'd seen no remorse on the tutor's face. As far as he was concerned, Molly's death had been justified.

As they reached the stairs leading to the Great Hall, shouts and the clash of steel drowned out all other thoughts. The battle had begun.

A flaming arrow shot by Amber's cheek. It struck the supporting post next to where she stood. A wave

of heat seared her. Lachlan shouted orders to his men
as they poured from the castle gates. His warriors
manned the turrets and were showering arrows down
on the attackers. Women and children hauled buckets
of water in a human chain, trying to slow the progress
of the flames. Amber reached down and tore a strip
from the hem of her dress. She wrapped the material
around her hand, then pulled the arrow out of the
wood and immersed it in a pail. Her fingers were
singed as she unwrapped the piece of cloth. She
blocked out the pain. Her priority, after leaving the
dungeon, had been to look for Gavin. She had to find
him before it was too late.

She hadn't seen the boy with Lachlan's men, but
that didn't mean he wasn't somewhere putting on a
suit of chain mail and strapping on a sword. He was
too young.

A scream rose above the battle din. Amber turned to
see a flaming arrow pierce the leather vest of a soldier.
He pitched forward and disappeared over the side of
the castle into the water below. She leaned against the
cold stone. Her legs trembled and her ears rang with
the man's last cries. Another shower of flaming
arrows arced over the wall. Their light illuminated the
stairs leading down to the castle gate. Gavin was there.
His sword scraped the stones as he descended the
steps, and his chain mail brushed against his ankles.

Amber could still stop him. She hurried down the
stairs and turned Gavin to face her.

"Where do you think you're going?"

Gavin raised his chin and tightened his grip on the
hilt of his sword. "I go to fight."

Amber shook her head. "No, you don't. Your brother gave you orders to stay here."

The boy's lip quivered as he looked toward the closed gate. "Only the women and children stay huddled in the castle. Lachlan needs my help to fight Subedei and his men."

It was clear that Gavin was afraid his brother would not come back alive. The same thought played like a funeral dirge in Amber's mind. She wiped away the tears pooling in her eyes. She couldn't think of that now; she had to protect Gavin. He knew only too well that Lachlan could use every man available. But Lachlan had not wanted Gavin on the battlefield and she would do her best to keep him out of the fighting below.

Amber put her hand on the boy's shoulder. "Not all of the men are out on the field." She pointed in the direction of the castle wall. "Look. Some have to stay and protect us."

Gavin followed her gaze. "My sword would be of better use defending my brother's back."

Amber knelt down beside him. "Gavin, sometimes it is harder to wait for a battle than to look for one."

Screams rang through the night air. Torchlight blended with the small fires that dotted the gently sloping hill in front of Urquhart Castle, turning the area into a vast battleground. Amber gripped the stone ledge. Marcail wanted more bandages for the wounded and Amber had returned to her room for more supplies. Now, however, she couldn't make herself move from the window. She searched for Lachlan among the blur of warriors fighting below. He was indistinguishable amid the turmoil. Men appeared to be hacking at each other with mindless and relentless purpose. They lacked any regard for the carnage they left behind. Enemy and friend, they were all the same.

The scent of blood mingled with sweat and was carried toward her on the wind. Amber covered her mouth and turned from the window. She slid to the floor, wrapped her arms around her legs and leaned her head against her knees. But placing her hands over her ears only muffled the screams, it didn't block them out. She was so afraid for Lachlan.

The sound of swords striking swords rose above the shouts of the men. She tried to put more pressure on her ears, but it did not help. Finally she released her hold and leaned against the stone wall of the chamber. She felt totally helpless.

Footsteps echoed in the hallway. She stood and braced herself. Had they stormed the castle? The door burst open and slammed against the wall.

Lachlan strode in carrying Gavin under his arm. "It was agreed you would keep him safe within these walls." As Lachlan put him down, his brother ran toward Amber.

"Is he hurt?" She reached for Gavin. Her hands trembled as she gathered him in her arms.

"He is unharmed." Lachlan's expression was remote. "Why did you take my orders so lightly?"

She wiped the blood off the boy's face and put her arm around his shoulder. "What can a mere woman do, if one of the great MacAlpins wants to fight?"

"You mock me and mine."

She straightened and met his gaze. "You're damned right. Marcail and I did everything short of tying Gavin to the bed, but he thought his place was beside you, hacking the enemy to pieces. He must have slipped away while we were tending the wounded."

Lachlan's eyes narrowed. "Would you rather Subedei and his men stormed the walls?"

She could feel Gavin pull closer to her. He was as concerned as she at Lachlan's intensity. "I'm sick to death of hearing the standard argument. You want to fight Subedei. In fact, I've never seen you so pleased with yourself. How may men have you killed? I'll bet you know the exact number. You hide your love for killing under the guise that you're defending women and children."

She took a deep breath. "From what I hear of Subedei, you and he are the same." The hurtful words flowed out of her and were said before she had time to take them back.

He clenched his fist at his side. "Subedei is insane and seeks out battles to quench his bloodlust. I only defend what is mine. Perhaps honor is not important in your time."

"It's the same as now. Men make excuses for going to war. Maybe if you tried talking to Subedei." She shook her head. "The defending part I understand. It's enjoying your work that bothers me."

Lachlan unsheathed his sword. "This is the only conversation I will have with the man. In time you will know I am right." He turned and walked out the door.

She felt Gavin tremble beside her. He looked at her. "Shall I grow to be like my brother? Shall I be as angry when I fight?"

Fresh tears formed in her eyes. She swallowed. How much did Gavin know? She squeezed his shoulder. "Your brother is frustrated, because he wants to keep us safe from Subedei."

She prayed that was all.

In Lachlan's mind the shadows that flickered on the walls were like ancestral ghosts. He sheathed his blade and ran down the torch lit passageway. Their images were illusive. Amber was from another time. She couldn't understand the fire that burned in his soul. He pushed thoughts of her from his mind.

He had to protect what was his from Subedei and his kind. The only way to purge his land was with blood. Descending the stairs he opened the double doors. He ran through the courtyard. The sound of men's screams, the ringing of metal on metal and the smell of blood, filled him. He relished the battle.

Lachlan unsheathed his sword and let out an ancient war cry. It carried to the warriors below. Those nearest the castle began to chant his name until it seemed the very air trembled. The need to join his men flooded through his veins. He tightened his grip on the hilt of his sword and forced himself to focus. He must find Subedei and defeat him. Without their leader, his enemy's men would run like rats before a flame.

He surveyed the field. Some distance away he located his enemy. Subedei carved a path through the battlefield which was littered with the bodies of Lachlan's clansmen. Anger heated his blood. Reaching down, he drew his dirk from the holder by his calf and headed along the narrow path that overlooked the loch.

A full moon shone in the black sky. Beneath it lay the bloodstained field in shades of gray. Lachlan jumped from the crest of the path to the ground below only to be attacked by one of Subedei's men. He blocked the thrust with his claymore, then stabbed the man with his dagger. Blood seeped over the man's chest. His opponent cried out before crumbling to the ground and surrendering to death.

Lachlan turned from the fallen man as another ran toward him. It took one practiced blow to pierce his assailant's chain mail. He ignored the man's pleas for mercy as he dealt the killing blow. He felt the blood pound in his veins. Turning, he welcomed the next man who attacked him.

The roar of the loch, as its waters crashed against the rock-strewn shore, thundered in his ears and drowned out the sound of screams. He pushed forward through the waves of blood-soaked men who surged toward him. Faces blurred; only their weapons were in focus. The full moon glimmered white-hot against the dark skies. With each kill he felt his strength grow.

Screams and war cries rang in his ears. They seemed to urge him to quicken his pace. He could feel his heart thunder in his chest. He had never felt this strong, this alive.

Through the deafening cries of battle Lachlan heard his name. He recognized the voice. It was his enemy. He withdrew his sword from the body of a man he had just slain. The body collapsed to the ground amongst the others.

Subedei's war cry rang above the screams of the battle. As with Lachlan, he stood surrounded by those he had killed.

"Don't keep me waiting. My blade grows cold."

Lachlan sheathed his dagger and gripped the hilt of his claymore with both hands. He held the sword out before him. He could feel the rapid beat of his heart. The need to fight and kill surged through him. He moved toward Subedei.

"Prepare to die."

The Mongol's laughter was dark. "Ah, it is clear to

me that the very thing you accused me of runs hot in your blood. After a kill the power surges through you. It is addictive, is it not?"

Lachlan clenched his jaw and felt the truth of his enemy's words. He could deny them no longer. "If what you say is true then you will know that I will not stop until my sword is drenched in your blood."

His blade clashed against Subedei's. The force vibrated through Lachlan's hands. His enemy's strength matched his own and his eyes reflected the same need that Lachlan felt.

Sidestepping, Lachlan turned and lunged forward. His sword sliced a deep gash in Subedei's chest.

The man grimaced, then growled low before he attacked. "Angus was an able teacher. I shall be sure to kill him, after I have finished with you."

Lachlan blocked Subedei's weapon. The fever inside him had built with the sight of fresh blood, and his vision blurred to all except his enemy and his sword.

Subedei cursed as Lachlan arced his blade high and brought it down with all his strength, severing the mongol's head.

The euphoria of victory surged through him. All his senses were heightened. Suddenly he could hear the rustle of the animals in the forest beyond the battle-field, the sweet smell of heather on the rolling hills and the sound of a bird's wings as it soared above. And then silence. He looked around. The battle still raged, as before. The need rose within him as strong as the need to breathe. He would have to kill again.

Lachlan heard someone approach from behind. He waited. The victory of a kill was sweeter if there was challenge to it. He would wait until he could hear the man's heartbeat. The sound of a tumbling rock, disturbed from its rest echoed in the night. His enemy was within an arm's length from him. It was a bold man to approach him so carelessly, but foolish as well.

He clenched his jaw and turned, lunging as his blade wounded the man in the chest. The man dropped his weapon and fell back. Lachlan raised his sword for the killing blow.

Someone grabbed him from behind. Blade raised, he turned toward the new enemy and heard his name through his mist-clouded mind. It seemed to be coming from a great distance away. He blocked the disturbing cry that asked more of him than he was willing to give and lunged toward his assailant. His attack was deflected. He drove this new enemy toward the edge of the cliff. It would be easy to defeat this one. The man only defended.

The cry he heard grew clearer. It was a woman's voice. She called his name. Like the haunting notes of the bagpipes it pulled him through the bloodred haze. He knocked the sword out of the man's hand and stole a quick glance in the direction of the woman. Amber. She stood on the crest of the hill, overlooking the battle. The fear he saw in her eyes made him shudder. He held tighter to his sword to keep from dropping it to the ground. She raised her arm and pointed to the man he fought.

His brows drew together. Why was she here? It was too dangerous. And why was she concerned about his enemy? Distracting him might cause his death. Lachlan forced himself to focus on the man he fought. He turned toward his attacker, who stood with his arms at his sides. The man's eyes mirrored the horror he had seen in Amber's expression. It was Angus. Lachlan stumbled back. He had tried to kill his friend.

He dropped his sword. Silence surrounded him. He looked around. The battle had ended. Subedei's men had fled.

On the ground lay O'Donnell's unconscious body. He felt the weight of Angus' hand on his shoulder.

"The lad was no match for your skill and only tried to stop you from the bloodlust that imprisoned your soul. He will survive." Angus chuckled. "But he will be as furious as the spirits from Hades."

Lachlan felt the strength drain from his body. He sank forward to the ground. He had not recognized O'Donnell or Angus. All he had seen were their weapons; all he had felt was the overwhelming need to kill.

"I have become what I feared most."

He heard Angus take a deep breath. "Aye."

Lachlan opened his eyes and stood. His arms and plaid were covered in the blood of the men he had killed. How many had been his own clansmen?

He looked at Amber in the light of the full moon. Her long hair blew free in the wind and her eyes held a sadness as deep as the waters of Loch Ness. A shadow appeared behind her, swallowing her. She disappeared from his view.

Her screams pierced the silence. Ice seemed to flow through his veins as he stood. He heard his own voice cry out her name. The sound echoed in his ears. Had one of Subedei's men sought revenge for what he had done or had the gods who had brought her to him taken her back?

A flash of lightning lit the sky. He reached the crest of the hill in time to see Amber plunge into the dark waters of Loch Ness. His cry of anguish drowned out the thunder ranging overhead.

Chapter

16

❦

Amber felt a spasm of pain as an icy chill rippled through her layers of wet clothes. It was as if she'd been struck by a battering ram. It hurt to breathe and her head throbbed. She remembered feeling someone push her into Loch Ness.

Where was Lachlan? She'd seen him turn toward her after he'd fought O'Donnell. He'd seemed like a different man on the battlefield, his face was an expressionless mask as he killed all who crossed his path. A fresh spasm of pain vibrated through her. Her teeth chattered and she clamped down on them. She wasn't sure exactly, but somehow she'd deal with what had happened to Lachlan later on tonight. Right now she was freezing and every time she moved the muscles in her body voiced their objection. What was keeping Lachlan?

A bright light clicked on and she saw the outline of people standing in front of her, but their faces were lost in the shadows. She turned to get up. The effort made her feel sick to her stomach. There was something familiar about how she was feeling, but she couldn't recall what it was.

The images of the people came into focus. A man encased in neoprene bent down toward her. He took off his scuba mask, knelt beside her and covered her with a blanket.

Scuba mask? She rubbed her eyes. The man wore a dry suit meant for diving in cold waters. She swallowed and forced herself to identify how she felt. Her body had reacted this same way when she'd traveled back to the sixteenth century. Her mind struggled to absorb what was going on. She tried to sit, but her head pounded so hard she couldn't think or make her body respond.

The ground felt cold and hard. Small rocks poked against her skin and time seemed to crawl as her eyes slowly began to focus on her surroundings. Spotlights lit the shore. A man in a dry suit emerged from the water and she could hear whispered conversations. The sky lightened to gray and wisps of rose-pink color lined the horizon. Birds chirped in the alders and a breeze rippled over the dark waters of Loch Ness. If felt as if she was observing a movie instead of what she feared. Her rescue.

The man in the dry suit motioned to a small, elderly woman clutching a wool shawl, and then pointed in Amber's direction. She recognized her aunt's purposeful walk, a sight she'd never thought to see again. Tears clouded her vision. If Aunt Dora was here, Lachlan was not.

The familiar smile lines creased the old woman's face as she drew closer. "You gave us such a fright."

A tall man in diving gear and wearing a scuba mask lifted her in his arms. Warm tears traveled down her checks as the realization struck home. She was no longer in the sixteenth century. She shivered against the cold material of his suit as a fresh wave of pain traveled through her. The ache in her muscles didn't matter. Nothing mattered.

The first man spoke to her aunt, and then motioned in the direction of the parking lot. "You'll find dry clothes in the backseat. When she's changed I'll drive you both to the hospital."

"You're such a dear to help us." Aunt Dora turned to Amber and patted her cheek. "These men never gave up. You're safe now."

Amber's tears flowed. "I want to go back."

She felt the man who cradled her against his chest tighten his hold around her. She closed her eyes. Maybe he thought she was going to make a run for the water. When she regained her strength, that was exactly what she was going to do. Risk to her life or not, it beat the alternative of a world without Lachlan.

Rain drizzled against the window in Aunt Dora's sitting room as Amber looked around. A blue, Laura Ashley print covered the walls. A fire crackled in the hearth. Crisp, white woodwork framed the door and there was a view of the River Ness through the trees.

She took a deep breath. This had always been her favorite room, guaranteed to bring her world into focus. This time it was not working. She'd endured an overnight stay in the hospital while doctors had said she was lucky to have survived the thirty-two degree temperature of the waters of Loch Ness. Then they had pronounced her fit. She wanted to tell them she wasn't fine, she still felt numb and cold inside.

Outside the warm cottage the gray morning melted into a gray afternoon. She sank into a winged back chair by the window and tucked her legs beneath her.

Her body still felt stiff and sore, but at least the headaches had lessened and soon she would be back to normal, whatever that was. A steady afternoon rain pelted against the glass panes. The smell of cock-a-leekie soup drifted from the kitchen. Since she'd returned, her aunt had fixed all her childhood favorites.

She looked at the book, *The Canterbury Tales*, on the table beside her and traced her finger over the patterns etched into the leather in gold leaf. Amber and Gavin had read "The Knight's Tale" together. The book had been new then. Now she was afraid to touch the brittle pages. She carefully opened it. On the inside page, the ink faded with age, were the words:

To Amber,
Time is an illusion and love the only reality.

L

Amber took a deep breath, fighting back the tears. She'd learned the meaning of those enchanted words as a child, but never truly understood them, until now. She straightened. If her aunt caught her crying again she'd call a therapist. This was stupid. She had a teaching job back in Seattle, there was the recreational soccer league she played in, and she'd always talked about getting a pet. Maybe she'd buy a tabby cat and each day would blend together again. Everything would be perfect. She hugged the book to her chest and felt a tear travel down her cheek. Amber loved a man who lived four hundred years ago and claimed to be immortal. She'd begun to believe him, but now . . . she sighed. Even if it'd been true, he had been a warrior. It wasn't possible he could have survived all those centuries.

Aunt Dora entered the room hunched over the tray she carried. The cups and saucers rattled as the elderly woman set them down on the table. The noise made her wince. Amber put the book down carefully, wiped her face and stood. If she didn't focus on something other than herself she'd be a shredded mess. She helped her aunt to the chair opposite hers.

"I should be waiting on you."

"Nonsense child." Aunt Dora poured the tea and added cream to each cup. "I can't remember a time when you weren't taking care of me. You were barely old enough to go to school when you first came to live here at River Cottage. Even then, you wanted to do everything on your own." She reached for a handkerchief tucked in her sleeve and wiped her eyes.

"When I heard you had fallen in the water, I blamed myself. You always hated the water which was why I never insisted you learn how to swim. I thought you'd been taken from me." Aunt Dora leaned toward her and touched her cheek. "Promise me you'll not go near that wretched loch at night, ever again."

"I promise." Amber watched her aunt breathe deeply and sit back down in the chair. It was not this room that had brought her life into focus, it was her aunt.

The old woman took a sip of tea, then rested the cup on the saucer in her lap. "While those men were searching the loch, I remembered the years you spent putting my needs and your brother's above your own. I couldn't turn on the stove or fluff a pillow without you beside me making sure I didn't overdo. Your teachers said you always went out of your way to make sure everyone was happy. I had forgotten those little snippets, until you disappeared."

The sound of the rain against the window seemed to echo in the room. "It was something I wanted to do." Amber reached for her cup and looked at the steaming tea.

"Not at the price of your own happiness." Dora set her cup down and patted Amber's arm. "Dear, we can't always control everything around us. Excitement comes from the unexpected."

Her aunt knew her too well. Thoughts of Lachlan gently filtered through her mind. She closed her eyes briefly, in an attempt to squeeze away the tears and took a swallow of tea. "Wanting predictability is not an easy habit to break."

" 'Cold Turkey,' I believe, is the expression you Yanks use. Drink your tea and I'll fetch warm soup. It will cheer you up and make you feel as good as new."

Amber did as she was told. She and David had learned early it was easier to give in. Once bent on a course of action, their gentle aunt would never change her mind. Amber smiled and sipped the cream-laced tea and watched the river from her window. She'd guessed she'd only been in the water for a few seconds before breaking the surface, but the icy currents had chilled her to the bone. She wondered how long she'd been away.

The cup rattled in the saucer on her lap. . . . *But the waters will reclaim her once again if, after the passage of one full moon . . .*

Her voice trembled. "Aunt Dora, how long was I gone?"

"Well, it is not certain when you fell into the Loch, but you were missing about six or seven hours altogether. When you did not come back, I called the police. They notified the medical team and the divers." She sighed with relief. "The lads knew exactly where to look."

A shiver tickled the back of Amber's neck. There was a knock on the door. Amber set aside her cup and hurried to answer it.

A stone-faced deliveryman waited. He held a long flower box tied with a thick gold ribbon. "Delivery for Amber MacPhee."

"I'm Amber. Who could be sending . . . ?"

He shoved a clipboard at her, pointed at the line where he wanted her to sign and then handed her the box.

"Who's out there, dear?"

Amber turned toward the kitchen. "Someone sent me flowers."

"How lovely. Shut the door and let's have a look."

The large thick ribbon slipped off easily. Amber tossed it on the chair as she lifted the lid and folded back the green florist tissue. She heard Aunt Dora's sharp intake of breath. Inside were at least two dozen long-stemmed red roses, their perfume soft and fragrant.

"Your parents did not mention they would be sending you flowers and your brother would never think of it." Her aunt stood beside her. "Do you have any idea who sent them?"

Amber shook her head. "I haven't a clue." She set the flowers on the table and reached for an envelope tucked under a rose. Inside was a ticket to a lecture by the physicist Steven Hawking. "The Nature of Space and Time" was the title of the talk. There was also a white card. Written in a bold script across it were the same words inscribed in *Canterbury Tales*. It was signed Lachlan MacAlpin.

Lachlan was alive. A mixture of joy and shock ran through her. She felt overwhelmed. Too much to absorb, too much to take in. It was true, all true. Her hand trembled. The card and ticket fluttered, turning round and round on their journey to the floor. Somewhere in the distance she heard her aunt's voice.

"Child, what's come over you? You look as if you've seen a ghost." Aunt Dora reached down and picked up the slips of paper. She read them, then put them back on top of the roses. "Odd, that it is the same phrase written in *Canterbury Tales*. And the address . . . is he a professor? The address is on the University of Edinburgh campus."

She sighed and put her arm around Amber. "Are you feeling poorly? Come sit down, dear. The soup is almost ready."

Aunt Dora guided Amber to the chair. "Your parents speak highly of Hawking. You should attend his lecture."

The images in the room blurred and began to spin. Amber reached over to hold onto the top of the winged back chair; she pressed her fingers against the cool upholstery. Everything he'd said was true. Over and over he had told her that time held no meaning for him. Even when she'd seen him survive wounds that would have killed a normal man, the concept of his immortality had never fully sunk in. It was as improbable as palm trees in the Highlands, polar bears in Africa and . . . and time travel. She looked at her aunt, noting the lines of concern creasing the old woman's face.

Aunt Dora squeezed her hand. "Are you all right?"

Her vision blurred and she welcomed the darkness.

It wrapped warm arms around her and pulled her into its comforting embrace.

A spotlight focused on the empty stage in the auditorium at the University of Edinburg as Amber looked at a program. The words printed on the front cover in bold black letters read, "Dr. Stephen Hawking, British physicist, will speak on the Nature of Space and Time." She was surrounded by the soft sounds of conversations, hushed laughter and the rustling of pages as she waited for the scientist's entrance.

In the second row near the stage she saw a couple who were wearing replicas of *Star Trek, The Next Generation* uniforms. Dr. Hawking had appeared in one of the show's episodes, playing himself. She figured he wouldn't be offended. After all, the mere mention of time travel seemed to bring out the science fiction fans.

Behind her someone kicked her seat. She heard the laughter of kids. This was reality. Hopefully, his lecture might make sense of what she'd experienced. She turned the palm of her right hand toward her. The crescent-shaped scar that Angus had given her at the base of her thumb was still visible. Amber felt a tightness in her throat and swallowed. Marcail had done a good job stitching the cut. She willed the memories from her mind. They paid no attention to her wishes. In other relationships it had been easy to say goodbye, easy to walk away. This time was different.

She heard someone clear his throat. A man stood in the aisle and motioned toward the empty seat beside her. His features reminded her of the color beige; his eyes, hair and complexion were all the same shade.

The man climbed over her and sat down. "Hawking

is a genius, you know. Crippled body, but a mind that would give Einstein pause."

Amber wondered if she had a sign, printed across her forehead, that read, "talk to me, I enjoy idle conversation." She ignored his comment, looking at the empty stage and then at her watch. There were still ten minutes left before the program began.

"This business about time travel. Can't be done, you know. Dr. Hawking will set it right."

Amber rolled her program into a cylinder and rapped it softly on the palm of her hand. "The fact he's devoted a lecture, no, actually an entire tour, on that possibility means, at the very least, it can't be discounted."

The beige man sat taller in his seat and pushed out his bottom lip. "A person would have to travel faster than the speed of light, 186,000 miles per second to be exact. Impossible."

She leaned back and folded her arms across her chest. "In water, light travels seventy-five percent as fast as in the air. If I was to travel back in time, I think my best shot would be in water."

"Never thought of that."

Out of the corner of her eye she saw him take his pen and small notebook out of his shirt pocket. She could almost hear the man's brain cells doing the mental calculation before he began to write.

She knew why she was here. The realization hit her as Hawking came on stage to a standing ovation. She wanted reassurance that it was scientifically possible to travel back in time. Her parents held the belief that many things on this earth could be manipulated, that only the laws of science were pure. If that extraordinary concept was within the realm of reality, so, too, would be her loving an immortal.

Chapter
17

❧

A car screeched to a stop on wet pavement. Lachlan nodded at the driver and crossed the street to the University of Edinburgh. He looked at his watch. His next class wouldn't start for another hour.

"Hello, Professor MacAlpin."

He turned to greet the group of students who hurried down the walkway. They were headed toward the ivy covered brick building that housed the science department. A crisp breeze rustled through the trees. He had grown attached to this campus and those who attended his classes. His goal had been to breathe life into the subject of Anthropology just as Amber had into his life. He had succeeded. There was always a waiting list for his classes.

He pushed open the oak doors and walked down the narrow hallway toward his office. He calculated he had only another ten or fifteen years left, before the faculty began to wonder why he never aged. If Amber decided against him, he might see if he could secure a teaching position on one of the islands in the Caribbean. It would be a tranquil spot to end his days. He smiled. It was unfortunate that, these days, society frowned on a man kidnapping the person he desired for an extended time, until she'd had a chance to fall in love with him. The Vikings had believed it a sound plan. Amber would not.

"Hola, big brother." Gavin sat back in his chair behind a desk cluttered with a mountain of papers and folded his hands behind his head. Morning sunlight streamed through a window.

Lachlan grinned. It was good to have his brother in the area again, even if Gavin was in the habit of turning up unexpectedly. He had grown to be a fine man. Amber would be proud of him. Lachlan put his briefcase on the desk. "I am pleased to see you, but how is it that you come to be in my office? The windows and doors are on a sensor system."

Gavin shrugged. "Do you really want to know?"

"No. Now, get out of my chair. I have work to do."

"You haven't asked me why I'm here." He pushed away from the desk, crossed the room and sank into a brown leather chair.

"I knew you would get to it." Lachlan opened his briefcase and put a pile of essays on the desk.

"It's been a week since we fished Amber from the water. The lass, however, doesn't seem to be in a hurry to rush into your arms. How much longer are you prepared to wait?"

Lachlan sat down at his desk and added the essays to a stack by the phone. "As long as it takes." The chair creaked as he leaned back. "I appreciated your help in the dive at Loch Ness. The area where she was to come through was uncertain until the Guardian showed us the location. However, I do not interfere in your life; do not tell me how to run mine."

Gavin leaned forward. "Ha, and what do you call

the time you flew your plane behind the German lines in World War II?"

"You were in need of rescue."

"I was doing fine on my own."

Lachlan took out a pen from the desk drawer. "You had taken up residence at a prisoner of war camp."

Gavin rubbed the back of his neck. "I had a plan."

"Did it involve that blonde singer in town?"

Gavin smiled but refrained from answering.

"Your trust in women, little brother, is admirable, but it may be your ruin one day. The woman you speak of turned you into the Germans as a spy. Her only interest was the reward."

"She was right. I was spying for the British, but I knew the risks." He shrugged. "It was war. People do what they can to survive. But you're a fine one to lecture me. You sit here waiting for Amber to come to you, instead of going after what you want."

"It is not that simple."

"It's exactly that simple."

The silence was so complete that Lachlan could hear the hum of the digital clock on his desk. "Amber must give her love freely if the curse is to be lifted."

Gavin stood and shoved his hands in his pockets. "It's that blasted legend again. You've only had a few lapses in four hundred years. What makes you think she is the only one who can fulfill the legend? You're doing pretty well on your own."

Lachlan stared at the silver pen in his hand and clenched his fingers around the cold metal. "You call the murderous acts that I engaged in 'lapses'?" He looked over at Gavin and opened his palm. "If I hold a blade in my hand, someone will die. I tried to kill you during one of those 'lapses.' Or have you forgotten?"

Gavin turned to look out the window. His voice was low. "No, I haven't. But you didn't answer my question. What makes you so sure Amber is the one?"

"When I recall to memory her smile, the touch of her skin, or the way she laughed me out of my dark moods, the shadows that hold my soul prisoner disappear for a time. I wait for her to come to me, not only to fulfill the legend, but for myself. I must know if her love is as strong as mine. There is a lot for her to accept. Perhaps too much."

"No shit." Gavin rubbed the back of his neck. "I think you're asking more than she can give. There was a reason the ancients forbade us to join with mortals. How's she going to handle the age difference, when she's eighty and you still look thirty-five?"

Lachlan stared at the pen in his hand and twisted it back and forth. The gray metal shimmered like the blade on his sword. He threw it on his desk. "I have taken the Elixir of Life."

"You what?" Gavin stood so quickly the chair overturned. He paced back and forth in front of the desk. "You're crazy. What happens if she rejects you? Then what? You'll spend the rest of your life . . . alone."

"Don't you think you are being just a little melodramatic? You missed your calling. You should have pursued an acting career, instead of the cloak-and-dagger business."

Gavin put his hands on the desk and leaned forward. "I may still. That's the point. Who knows, I may even teach at a university. Don't look at me like that. Amber said I was a good student."

Lachlan smiled. "And what was she going to say? You were eight years old."

Gavin shook his head, went over to the chair, righted it and sat down. "We're off the subject."

"That is my intent."

Gavin looked at him in exasperation. "Your taking the damn elixir doesn't solve anything. Mother lived another one hundred and fifty years after she drank the stuff. You'll grow old, but it will be so slowly that Amber may not see a difference in you." He leaned forward and rested his elbows on his knees. "Okay, so it's done. Can't be reversed. So, to hell with the legend. You have to go after what you want, and our task is to convince Amber that you're her one and only. I suppose I could kidnap her and abandon the two of you to a deserted island paradise until she agrees? It's worked before."

"No."

"Does she like to ski? How about a cabin in the mountains?"

"Gavin."

"You made your point. The subject is closed." He leaned back in the chair. "Angus told me you've kept watch on the MacPhee family over the centuries."

"Aye. Amber said she was born in June of 1970 and I knew during the fall of 1997 she was on her way to a reenactment when she was pulled back in time. It was a matter of waiting until she returned."

"Why didn't you just introduce yourself before she took a swim in Loch Ness? It would have saved you a lot of trouble."

Lachlan smiled. "You know our laws do not permit us to interfere with the events of time."

"I thought we were in the process of changing those outdated commandments?" Gavin sighed. "I almost envy you, big brother. You've found your true love."

The sun felt warm on Lachlan's face. He turned toward the window and looked out. Buildings that mirrored the grayness of those in the Science Department blocked the view of the park. It made no difference to him; there was a quiet beauty in the people and the surroundings that held him to this city. He need not view a tree or flower to feel it. Ever since the plague that ran unchecked through the streets of Edinburgh in the seventeenth century, his brother had sought only those cities where there were bright lights, exciting people and adventure. Over time Lachlan had hoped his brother would settle in one place, and to one goal, but Gavin showed no signs of slowing down.

The door burst open, its hinges protesting as it slammed against the wall. Angus stood in the entrance, his legs spread apart and his hands on his hips. His head was shaved and he wore a patch over one eye.

Lachlan coughed to hide a smile. "Good to see you, old friend." Gavin, he noticed, was laughing so hard he almost fell out of the chair.

Angus scowled in Gavin's direction. "Can't you teach your brother manners?"

"I have tried."

Angus rubbed his hand over the top of his head. "The young pup doesn't understand the need for disguises, especially if one is to remain in Scotland for a time."

Lachlan clenched his jaw to keep from smiling. "It is a great disguise."

Angus' eyebrows drew together. "Knew you'd understand. Any word from Amber?"

Lachlan shook his head.

"Thought as much. That's why I bugged her phone and had her house watched."

"You what?"

Angus raised his eyebrows. "I thought you'd like to know what she was up to."

Lachlan placed his palms on the desk. "I alone will determine how to handle the situation."

Angus shoved his hands into his pockets. "Somehow, I seem to remember you saying the same thing to me, when I suggested she was immortal. It worked out well. She still bears the scar. It was the first thing I checked, when we pulled her from the water. It was the mark that proved her identity."

"You did not mark her so that we could find her. You injured her, against my will, to see if she would heal without a scar. If she had died from infection, I would have cut out your heart."

Angus turned to Gavin. "I thought you told me he had mellowed with age, like a good Scotch whisky."

Gavin shook his head. "I thought so too, but his sense of humor is as lacking as ever."

"Pity."

"If the two of you have finished?" Lachlan walked around the desk. "When I need your help, I will ask. Until that time, do not interfere."

Angus looked over at Gavin and then back to Lachlan. "It's only that we want to help." They exchanged glances again. "We didn't want to tell you, what with Amber's arrival and all . . ."

He stopped within an arm's length of Angus. "Tell me what?"

"Bartholomew has been seen in Inverness. There's little doubt that he's come to avenge his brother's death."

Lachlan did not fear Bartholomew. He was ready. He felt four hundred years slip away, until he was

again on the bloodstained battlefield. He remembered
Amber's expression of horror after she witnessed him
thrust his sword into O'Donnell, and heard her
screams when she fell into the loch. Bartholomew had
disappeared that same night. It had been assumed the
schoolmaster had either died or fled when Subedei's
armies were defeated. It was curious that Bartholomew decided to make an appearance at the same time
as Amber's return. Lachlan did not believe in coinci-
dences.

Electronic bells announced that class was about to
start. It jarred him back to the present.

Angus motioned to Gavin. "Come lad, I'll buy you
a pint at the Rose and Thistle."

Gavin paused and put his hand on Lachlan's shoulder. "Remember, you don't have to do this alone."

Lachlan watched them leave. His brother meant
well, but he was wrong. He gathered up his notes and
stuffed them into his briefcase. It would feel good to
talk about the ancient digs in Egypt, instead of
dwelling on his current problems.

The com-line on his phone buzzed. "Yes, Fiona?"

A singsongy sweet voice came over the wire. "There
is a woman here to see you. Her name is Amber
MacPhee."

He cleared his throat and tightened his grip on the
receiver. He hadn't expected Amber. Sending her
flowers was his way of breaking the reality to her gently that what he had told her in 1566 was true. He was
immortal. Next week he had planned to telephone her
and set up a meeting. He smiled. It was just like
Amber to do it her way. "Show her into my office."

"But, Professor MacAlpin, your class is about to
begin."

He recognized the tone. Fiona was jealous. Lachlan had spent more times than he wished to recount explaining to her that he was not interested. She did not choose to listen.

"Have someone cover for me." He clicked the receiver down and turned to the window. Lachlan had thought that waiting over four hundred years had prepared him. Apparently it had not.

Amber followed the long-legged receptionist down the hall toward Lachlan's office. Fiona kept looking back at her, as if sizing up the competition. Amber gripped the book closer. Stop being paranoid, she lectured herself. She should be trying to figure out what to say to the man. It had been four centuries. He could not possibly feel the same. Her married friends said that after a few years passion cooled. Maybe she'd just engage in small talk.

Fiona opened the door and let Amber go in first. The large picture window behind a mahogany desk bathed the room in light. There were green leather chairs, bookshelves framed the window, and an Oriental rug carpeted the wood floor. Somewhere on the lawn of the university, students practiced the bagpipes. The sound mixed with the shrill noise of honking horns.

Lachlan stood facing the window. His hands were clasped behind him. Although he had traded his kilt for corduroy pants and a tweed jacket, he was just as she remembered: shoulder-length hair, broad shoulders . . . she couldn't speak.

He turned and she thought her heart would stop. God help her, he was even better looking than before. She reached for the edge of the desk.

"Fiona, did you get someone to cover my class?"

The deep, familiar voice sent shivers up her spine as she stood between Fiona and Lachlan. She swallowed.

"Dan said he was free." The woman glanced at Amber. "I've been meaning to ask if you like haggis, I'm preparing it tonight."

The smile disappeared from his face as he shook his head.

Amber saw the obvious disappointment in Fiona's expression. A pout formed on the woman's face. Fiona must practice that expression in the mirror. She glanced over at Lachlan. Good; he was busy straightening papers on his desk. Either he hadn't noticed the siren's come-hither look or he was immune. She hoped it was the latter.

"Fiona, that will be all. Tell Dan to show the class the video about the Pharaoh Queen Hatshepsut until I arrive."

The door shut so hard it rattled the panes of glass in the window. Amber flinched. Her nerves were shot. Visiting Lachlan had sounded like a good idea at the time. She rubbed the scar on her hand. She glanced at the door. He might not be interested in Fiona. He was not the type to take vows of celibacy . . . but he had waited.

Or maybe not. This man who stood behind the desk could be some look-a-like relative, with a voice that matched Lachlan's, familiar with an improbable story. She pressed her fingers to her temples. The walls of the room felt as though they were pressing in on her, threatening to crush her.

"I dislike haggis." Lachlan's voice broke the silence.

"Really. I think you'd better tell Fiona."

"I have." His eyes darkened. "Amber, I love you."

He looked so good to her. Tears stung her eyes. "Are you real? I mean . . . I got your flowers."

"Did you hear me?"

She smiled. "Yes, I heard you."

He vaulted over the desk, scattering papers and pencils, and stopped uncertainly only a short step away. Amber laughed, the weight of the questions that pulled at her lifted. "You're crazy."

"Aye. Did you also find the inscription I wrote in the book?"

She opened the cover to where his message was scrawled boldly across the page. She nodded.

The phone rang on the desk and Lachlan answered it. The harsh sound jarred her back to her purpose for coming to the university. Her intention had been to tell him that it couldn't work out between them. But seeing him brought back a flood of memories: the time Lachlan told Gavin that he could be whatever he wanted, watching Lachlan eat Elaenor's burnt short-bread, or how complete she felt whenever he was near. These things were more important than her concern over aging. Weren't they?

She walked away from him over to the shelves lined with books and wooden carvings, remembering the replica of Nessie that he'd carved for Gavin. She found the piece and reached out to touch the smooth wood. Memories of an afternoon in the autumn sun rushed back. Lachlan had tried to teach her how to carve and the piece of wood she'd fashioned into a nebulous bird lay beside Gavin's Loch Ness monster.

He had kept it. She wasn't just some pleasant memory neatly organized on a shelf. He still wanted her, she could see it in his eyes. But loving her and obligation were two different things. Obligation was a terrible word.

Amber glanced over at him and felt a flood of love so strong and bittersweet it took her breath away. She ached to hold him, to feel his skin against her, if only for one more time. Maybe she could go about her life with this one last memory. It would be like saying good-bye.

The door burst open and Fiona waltzed in. She glanced at the debris of paper on the floor. "Dan is losing control. The class is ready to revolt. You'd better come to his rescue."

"Tell him to pull it together or dismiss the class. I don't care which one he chooses. I am busy. And please do not slam the door when you leave."

Silence fell on the room as the door clicked shut.

Amber replaced the carving on the shelf. "She doesn't give up."

"Neither do I."

"I need you to tell me something about myself that only Lachlan would know."

"But I am Lachlan."

"You look like him and sound like him, but immortality is something you read about in books or see on a movie screen. It's hard to believe it's real."

He leaned against the desk and folded his arms across his chest. "Proof? All right, lass. So it is proof you need, to decide if the man standing before you is the same one who bedded you in the sixteenth century. Do you want me to take a bullet to the head or a stab wound to the heart? You choose."

"Neither. Just tell me something that passed between us. Something that only you and I would know. Not an event that might have been retold over and over."

"You like chocolate." He walked over to her.

The air in the room seemed to heat up. There was no way she could forget the goblets filled with warm liquid and the platter of oranges. "Many people like chocolate."

He reached for her hand and kissed the mound of flesh on her palm. He whispered in her ear, his breath was warm against her skin. "We found other uses for that concoction."

He gathered her in his arms. Her lips parted. She felt the warmth and pressure of his mouth against her skin. His searing kiss made her limbs feel as though she were floating in the air with only his strength to keep her from falling.

Lachlan reached for her hand and guided her toward the desk. He tossed the remaining items on the floor and then lifted her onto the smooth wood surface.

"On your desk? You can't be serious."

He raised his eyebrow. "Aye, lass, I am."

Amber opened the door at the end of the hallway of Lachlan's office, and stepped out on the concrete porch. She paused and smiled. She hadn't broached the subject that she'd wanted to discuss because other things had taken over in importance. It was a topic she admitted she was reluctant to talk to him about. She would grow to be a shriveled up old crone and he would look like Superman. He may not think it was a problem, but she compared it to climbing Mt. Everest without equipment.

She buttoned the collar on her coat and continued down the path. On the steps to the auditorium building was the marquee, advertising the lecture of Steven Hawking that she'd attended. He'd said the laws of science supported the theory that time travel was possible. Of course, a person might not survive the trip, and it would be a wild ride.

"Interesting theory, don't you think?"

Amber turned toward the man. He was tall, lanky and dressed in a fisherman-style sweater and jeans. Something was familiar about his smile and his eyes.

"Do I know you?"

The man made a casual salute and bowed. "Gavin MacAlpin, at your service."

She swayed on her feet and felt him grab her arm. She reached up and touched his face. The laughter and carefree spirit that had marked him as a boy still remained in the man he'd become. She shook her head and put her hands in her pockets.

"I feel as if I've walked into a world where all the laws of nature are broken."

"Maybe not broken, but certainly bent." He threaded his arm through hers and he nodded toward the picture of the physicist. "Hawking is closer than he thinks to unraveling the theory of time travel. As for the rest . . . my race did what they could to survive. Our scientists didn't set out to make us immortal. It was a violent time. We faced extinction at the hands of our enemies."

She felt his fingers tense on her arm and put her hand over his. "It's okay. That's in the past."

"Is it?"

A blistering wind stirred the trees overhead and she pulled her coat tighter around her.

"Let's talk about something else. O'Donnell and Marcail, did they ever marry?"

Gavin laughed. "Aye, and he insisted that a passage from Canterbury Tales be recited at the ceremony. He said he'd never remembered reading the book before, but he had a fondness for it nonetheless. He mentioned that you would understand."

Amber smiled and rubbed the scar on her hand. "And Angus, is he still Lachlan's right-hand man? And Elaenor . . ."

"Wait, I almost forgot." He reached in his pocket and pulled out several pieces of folded paper and handed it to her.

Xeroxed copies of an old handwritten letter crinkled as she opened them.

1789

My dearest Amber,

If you are reading this letter I hope it will mean that you and my brother are once again united. Destiny is such an overused word, but truly, the two of you are destined to be together.

Now, where should I begin? Perhaps by telling you the real reason that I went to see Elizabeth so long ago. It was to dissuade her from thinking it possible that anyone could travel through time. You see, by then I knew you were the person her astrologer spoke of.

Amber began to read the second page. Tears brimmed in her eyes. "Elaenor named one of her children after me."

"You meant a lot to her, a lot to us all. Come, let's find a place out of this wind and I'll answer all your questions. Whenever I began to take myself too seriously, you found a way to shake me out of it. No wonder my brother loves you."

Amber closed her eyes and drank in the full measure of the words he'd spoken. She opened them as a group of students passed by, no doubt in a hurry to class. Their conversation and laughter were hushed, their young faces full of hopes and dreams. It'd been a long time since Amber felt that way. But Gavin's words, casually spoken, had brought back the emotion. Lachlan MacAlpin loved her, after all this time, and God help her, she loved him as well.

Chapter

18

❦

The smell of vanilla, brown sugar, and chocolate filled the compact kitchen. Amber turned the burner under the saucepan on medium. She yawned and stretched. It was late. Maybe two or three in the morning, but it'd been worth it.

She stirred the dark liquid with a wooden spoon. Ten more minutes and it would be ready to pour into the oblong pan. In a short time after that it would be walnut fudge. She needed a distraction after seeing Lachlan yesterday. Amber wiped the perspiration from her forehead. She was incapable of rational thought when he was around. There were issues she needed resolved. An image of the large mahogany desk slowly appeared in her mind. She smiled.

The hallway door opened. Aunt Dora shuffled into the room in her rose-print, flannel nightdress. She removed the crocheted shawl she always wore and draped it over the chair by the round oak table.

"It is as warm and muggy in here as a July day in London. What have you been doing, child?"

"Baking. By the way, we're out of semi-sweet chocolate and cocoa. I'll make a trip to the store in the morning. What are you doing up so late?"

"Couldn't sleep with all the racket." Her aunt smiled, reached for the teakettle and carried it to the sink. "It's been a while since you've fussed in the kitchen." She filled the kettle with water. "Are we expecting guests?"

Amber shook her head. "No, I just made a few desserts."

Her aunt nodded, brought the pot back to the stove and then sat down. "I thought, perhaps, you might have invited your professor for a visit. What was his name?"

"Lachlan MacAlpin. No, I haven't invited him to the cottage."

Aunt Dora wrapped her shawl around her shoulders and drummed her fingers lightly on the table.

Amber frowned. "Don't give me that look."

"I can't imagine what you mean. A man sends you two dozen, long-stemmed, red roses and you don't as much as ask him over for a cup of tea. I understand perfectly. You're American. But the man should be thanked properly for his thoughtful gesture."

Amber concentrated on the fudge, grateful her aunt was not a mind reader. She hadn't thanked him, but . . .

"Is it warm in here? I think I'll let in some air."

She felt her aunt's gaze as she opened the window over the sink. A breeze from the River Ness drifted into the room.

"His name is curious."

Amber turned. "Lachlan is a common name in Scotland."

"Maybe so, maybe so. I have heard numerous stories about a man who called himself Lachlan. Such tales have long been a part of the local legends. A popular choice in a name."

Amber bent over her pot and stirred the chocolate. She did not like the direction of their conversation.

"It is said he pulled more than one woman out of the waters in his search for the lass he loved and who would save him from his curse." Aunt Dora rubbed her chin. "I can't seem to remember what that was."

"Insanity."

"Yes, that was it. Anyway, where was I? Oh yes. Lachlan of the Loch, he was called. It was believed to be good luck to name a firstborn after him."

Amber licked chocolate from her finger and looked over at her aunt. "Why are you telling me this story?"

"Your man's name is Lachlan, as well, is it not? A good name, a good man, I always say."

"You just made that up. I've never heard you say that before."

"Well, no matter, it sounds as if it should be true."

The sticky chocolate in the pan bubbled. Amber turned the burner to low. At three in the morning cooking had seemed like a good idea to occupy her time. She could not sleep. Every time she closed her eyes she thought of Lachlan. Her aunt was not helping. She was not prepared to tell her about him. Not yet.

The kettle whistled. Amber took it off the stove and reached for the cups. As she made tea she could see her aunt fidgeting.

"There is another legend. Closer to home, one might say."

Amber handed Aunt Dora a cup of steaming tea and returned to the chocolate on the stove. "Sometimes I think there are as many legends in Scotland as sheep."

Her aunt poured milk in her tea. "This one should interest you. I always assumed you were named after an Amber who lived in the sixteenth century. An odd name for those times. She was loved greatly by a man named Lachlan and it was he who put the inscription in the book *The Canterbury Tales*. I do believe there is a connection between this man and the one we spoke of earlier." She took a sip of tea before she continued her story.

"When this woman fell into the loch, it was believed she did not drown. She was taken to an enchanted place by the beastie that haunts the dark waters, until a time when Lachlan of the Loch would be worthy of her."

The wooden spoon in Amber's hand slipped into the thick fudge and slowly disappeared. She opened the drawer. The utensils clattered noisily as she fumbled for metal tongs. She began fishing for the submerged spoon. Aunt Dora was too close to the truth. Most people had relatives who had trouble with memory loss, but not Amber. She was blessed with an aunt who never forgot a thing.

Pulling the spoon out, she tossed it in the sink and reached for another one. The thick syrupy confection started to boil up the sides of the pan. Amber stirred until the muscles in her arm burned. Concentrating on the fudge, and not on her aunt's words, was the best plan. She didn't want to talk about Lachlan. She'd said good-bye to him. It was time to start over.

"Want some more tea?"

"I'm fine, dear. Anyway, as I was saying, this man put an inscription in *Canterbury Tales*. It was said to be the lass' favorite. He believed she would return to him one day." Aunt Dora's voice lowered as though she were confiding a secret. "You see, it is said the lad was enchanted and could live forever. A lovely story, just lovely. Because the girl was a MacPhee, he gave the book to the head of the clan for safekeeping. You can imagine how pleased our ancestors were that a laird had taken such an interest in them and so they named each firstborn girl after his great love."

"I've never heard that story."

Aunt Dora picked at the fringe of her shawl. "You were not to be told. It was one of the conditions."

"Conditions?"

"Aye, the laid takes good care of us."

Amber wiped her hands on a dish towel and gazed at her aunt.

"How long have you known?"

"I knew, for certain, when he sent you the flowers. But you haven't answered my question. Exactly how many sweets have you made, dear?"

Amber threw the towel on the drain board. "You should have told me."

"About being out of cocoa? How was I to know you were going to bake?"

"You know what I'm talking about. If I'd known about this stupid legend I wouldn't have been so frightened when I zipped back to the sixteenth century."

Aunt Dora laced her hands in her lap. "Dear, I've never seen you afraid in your life. I'm sure you handled it well. By the way, is fudge supposed to smell that way?"

The gentle rolling boil had escalated out of control and the pungent odor of burnt sugar hung in the air. The fudge was ruined. Amber took the pan from the burner and turned off the stove.

"Lachlan likes his food burnt. I have to know one

thing, when you sent me off to the medieval reenactment at the Abbey, did you know what was going to
happen to me?"

Aunt Dora did not answer directly. "Do you love
him?"

"It's not that simple. Lachlan's immortal." Amber
didn't mean to blurt it out, but there it was. Anyway,
she'd like to see how her aunt rationalized that concept.

"Of course he is, dear. How else could he have waited four hundred years for you?"

"You can't be serious. How can you talk about it so
casually? This is not a legend or tall tale. This is real."

Aunt Dora sat looking at her as though Amber had
announced Lachlan was good in arithmetic, instead of
the fact that he lived during the reign of Mary, Queen
of Scots, straight through the Elizabethan period,
Napoleanic wars and both World Wars. She combed
her fingers through her hair.

"Okay. Tell me why you can talk about his immortality as if it was on the same level of importance as a
person's height."

She frowned. "You are missing the point, lass."

Amber straightened. "Missing the point?"

Aunt Dora set her cup on the table. "You have been
away from the Highlands too long."

"What has that to do with it? I have a teaching job
in the States, a life there, and friends."

"Of course, and I'm sure it is a fine position.
However, don't you see, in America, you believe only
in what you can explain. Give them a few hundred
years and everything will be as it should be."

Amber took a deep breath. At least her aunt hadn't
called America "the Colonies." "Are you telling me
that immortality is an easy thing to understand, just

because Scotland has been around since before Rome invaded the place?"

"Precisely, and there are legends to prove it. There are stories of clans who had the gift of long life that date back to the Celts, and beyond."

Sheets of gray rain washed against the window. In the hall, the grandfather clock struck four times. The chimes vibrated through the snug cottage.

"I don't know what to do."

"I'll ask you again. Do you love him?"

Amber set the pan with the scorched fudge in the sink. "I can't talk about this right now." She turned the water on to soak the pan. "Raspberry chocolate butter creams and chocolate mousse are in the refrigerator. Chocolate chip cookies are cooling on the rack and there are brownies in the oven. They should be ready in about ten minutes. And, of course, the fudge. In the morning I'll make a chocolate layer cake. What do you think?"

Aunt Dora brushed imaginary crumbs off her flannel sleeve. "I remember at least two other times my kitchen was reduced to such a state. Chocolate was the main ingredient then as well. However, this time you've really outdone yourself. What I think is that you have no business traveling back to the States when you have a perfectly good man who, shall we say, has passed the test of time right here. And I think you answered my question."

Amber turned over in her bed. Her aunt had agreed that she could resume her marathon baking spree in the morning. But Amber couldn't sleep. The light of the moon cast a soft glow across her bed. She looked at the florescent numbers on the clock. 5:00 A.M. Amber wondered if Lachlan had the same problem.

She rolled onto her back and stared at the shadows on the ceiling. She certainly hoped so. Maybe it didn't matter to him that she'd grow old and he wouldn't, but it bugged the hell out of her.

A floorboard creaked. It was probably Missy, Aunt Dora's cat, exploring the house again. Amber closed her eyes and pulled the covers over her shoulder. She hear the sound again. This time it seemed to be coming from inside her room. That was odd. Usually Missy announced her entrance with a loud meow.

She felt a hand over her mouth and the point of a knife touch her throat. Startled, she jumped. Her heart raced. Sharp pain shot through her as the blade pricked her skin. She grabbed for the hand that held her. A man stood over her, blocking the light from the moon. His features were unclear in the dark shadows.

He pressed the blade against her skin. "Scream and I'll slice your throat as easy as warm butter. The phone line's cut, don't get any smart ideas."

Amber froze. The voice was familiar. Her thoughts focused on her aunt. She'd better be all right.

The man removed the knife from her neck and stared at her.

She rubbed her throat. "Who are you and what do you want?" She sat up, grateful she slept in sweats, and peered at her assailant in the shadows. Medium build and height.

He flicked on the switch to the lamp beside her bed. "Don't you recognize me?"

She stiffened as memories flooded back. "Bartholomew." She grabbed the lamp and threw it at him. "You pushed me in the loch."

He ducked. "Clever girl."

She remembered him coming toward her on the cliff. His tunic had been soaked with blood. "Why?"

His breath smelled like stale beer. "Because Lachlan killed my brother and I wanted him to suffer. I suspected you might survive and return to your own time. So I waited. When I read about your miraculous rescue by the famous Professor MacAlpin, I knew I had a second chance. I'm going to kill you in front of Lachlan and then cut out his heart."

Amber shrank against the headboard. She had to warn Lachlan.

"You, lady, are bait. Nothing more. They say the great warrior, Lachlan MacAlpin, will no longer raise a sword to fight. That will change." His laughter was high-pitched. "Cooperate and I'll spare the old woman sleeping in the next room."

He turned the knife in his hand. The blade caught the light from the window. "Don't cause me any trouble." He reached behind Amber for her pillow and stabbed it several times. White feathers floated through the air. "You can be in one piece when I present you to Lachlan or many. Either way it will have the effect I need. Get dressed. We journey to Loch Ness."

"Why there?"

He twisted the knife in his hand. "Because that is where the great Lachlan MacAlpin will be. I sent him a message that I was using underwater bombs to kill the Guardian."

Amber's legs trembled beneath her. They barely held her weight. She scrambled off the bed. Her fingers felt stiff as she pulled on a sweater. She took a deep breath. She needed to remain calm if she and her aunt were going to survive. Her hands shook as she reached for her shoes. Stay calm, she repeated over and over to herself. Think.

She stood. "I have to leave Aunt Dora a note. She'll be worried and might call the police."

He stepped toward her and grabbed her arm. "Write it plain."

Amber grabbed a pen and an envelope from the dresser.

Aunt Dora,
*   I've gone for a swim in the loch, be back in a few*
hours.

*   Love, Amber*

Jostled into the backseat of a car, which was badly in need of a tune-up, Amber lay on her stomach. Her hands were tied behind her and her mouth was gagged. Bartholomew was a dead man. Her aunt would understand the hidden message in her note. She had to.

Amber felt like the classic victim in a B movie and everyone knew how those turned out. To top off this perfect evening, her fingers felt numb, her feet were freezing, and her nose itched.

The car stopped abruptly and pitched her forward. She rolled against the back of the front seat, ending up on the floor. The words "black-and-blue" were added to her list. Bartholomew got out of the car and opened the backseat door. His big, meaty hand reached toward her. She pulled against the rope that tied her hands. Her wrists burned, but the rope held.

He grabbed her shoulders. "Glad you didn't try to escape."

If Amber hadn't been gagged, she'd tell him how dumb that was. She might be in love with an immortal, but she wasn't crazy. Although, under the circumstances, it might have helped.

Yanking her out of the car, he caused her to stumble forward, lose her balance and fall to the hard ground. A pain shuddered through her arm. Trying to block out the sensation, she rolled to a kneeling position and looked over at Bartholomew. She was no longer afraid of him. Anger had replaced the fear. She would not allow him to use her as bait to catch Lachlan.

She struggled to her feet and searched the water for signs of Lachlan. Nothing but black shadows. Maybe he'd already left. And what of the Guardian? Ripples spread across the loch as a person emerged from the water. She recognized the way the man moved. She smiled. It was her knight in shining armor. Lachlan peeled off the scuba mask and slowly approached the shore. She had to do something. Warn him somehow.

Bartholomew's back was to her. Obviously he felt she was no threat. That was a mistake. Having a younger brother had its advantages. Amber had learned how to hit and run. She slammed into him with her shoulder.

He yelled and turned on her, but she ducked out of his reach and started to run. She knew she couldn't get away, but it didn't matter. She had accomplished her goal, Lachlan wouldn't be caught off guard. Out of the corner of her eye she saw Lachlan pause and look in their direction.

Bartholomew caught her and pressed his blade against her throat. "No more of that." He began to drag her toward the shore. His voice sent a shiver down her spine. "MacAlpin, I've brought you a gift."

Lachlan's face was lost in the shadows. She couldn't make out his expression, but the tone of his voice was clear.

"Let her go."

Bartholomew pulled her closer. "I'm here to settle a score."

Lachlan removed his gloves and tossed them to the ground. "It has been four hundred years. What has taken you so long?"

Amber could feel the tension in the man build as his arm tightened around her. Terrific. While Lachlan was deliberately trying to make him mad, Bartholomew was squeezing her to death. She struggled to pull free and felt the knife at her cheek.

"Easy does it, little lady."

An icy breeze blew over the water as Amber felt the cold steel against her face. She looked over at Lachlan. He had narrowed the distance between them.

Bartholomew's voice was a sneer. "I'm told you are no longer the great warrior. The fight has gone out of you."

"Not the fight, Bartholomew, the bloodlust."

"Ah, so the legend is true. I thought as much. It's why I've brought the woman."

"If you know the legend, then you know I will not draw a blade against you."

"You would watch her die, then?"

The muscles in Lachlan's face tightened. "Leave her."

"In good time. She's the reason you've given up the sword and for her sake you will embrace it once again. Or you shall see her die, by inches."

Lachlan walked forward slowly. "It would not be wise to threaten me."

They were only separated by a couple of feet. Amber felt Bartholomew tremble. Without warning the man pushed her to the ground. She scrambled out of the way, focusing on Lachlan. His hands were loose at his sides. He circled Bartholomew as a predator would its prey, a smile curled at the corner of his lips. His eyes seemed to pin Bartholomew in place, like a butterfly in a display case.

Lachlan felt the need to fight surge through him. He ducked as his opponent swung his weapon. If he had a sword in his hand, Bartholomew's blood would be spilling to the ground. He could feel Amber's love pour over him, cooling the bloodlust that pumped through his veins. He would not kill this man. He would turn him over to the Council, for judgment.

He doubled up his fist and caught Bartholomew on the chin. He felt the jawbone crunch beneath his blow. The man stumbled back before regaining his balance. Bartholomew steadied himself, roared and charged. Lachlan sidestepped. The schoolmaster tripped and fell to the ground. Lachlan bent down, wrenched the blade out of Bartholomew's grasp and threw it out over Loch Ness. It cut through the water and disappeared from sight.

Bartholomew struggled to his feet. "What have you done?"

"Prevented needless bloodshed."

"You've just prolonged the inevitable." Bartholomew spit blood on the ground at Lachlan's feet.

Lachlan willed his anger under control. The clear image of Bartholomew in a pool of his own blood flashed before him. He pushed the vision from his mind. "I will not fight you with sword."

"Then what I've heard is true."

Lachlan folded his arms across his chest. "Aye, it is true and more. If it is a fight you seek, you will not find one with me. The Council meets in ten days. Your old room at Urquhart is still intact and awaits you."

"You will have to kill me."

A twig snapped nearby as someone approached. It was Angus.

Lachlan's friend placed a heavy hand on Bartholomew's shoulder. "That can be arranged."

Lachlan laughed and helped Amber to her feet. "Angus, I am glad you ignored my orders. What kept you?" He removed her gag and the rope around her hands.

Amber rubbed her wrists. "That's what I'd like to know."

Angus chuckled. "I received a frantic telephone call from Aunt Dora. It seems she had to place the call at a neighbor's. Something about her niece swimming in Loch Ness." He smiled. "Took me a while to calm her down. Besides you two were doing just fine on your own. I didn't want to interfere. Now, I think I'll leave you two lovebirds alone, while Gavin and I see to Bartholomew's needs."

Moonlight spread its glow over the shore and the lyrical sound of bagpipes drifted toward him as he gathered her in his arms.

She pulled away. "Lachlan, the Guardian . . . Bartholomew said . . ."

Lachlan kissed the tip of her nose. "Everything is as it should be. It was merely a way to lure me to Loch Ness."

"I'm glad the Guardian is all right. If it weren't for him, we never would have met." She shivered and drew closer against him. "I was afraid for you."

"I know, and I for you."

"I thought Bartholomew would take you from me."

"It is over."

Her voice trembled. "I want whatever time we have together, but promise me one thing . . ." She hesitated. ". . . I will grow old, while you stay the way you are. Promise me you'll leave while you still love me."

Lachlan brushed the hair behind her ear. "I have waited for you for four hundred years. What sustained me was not the image of your physical form, beyond perfection though it might be, but the look in your eyes when you gazed into my heart, and discovered the man I wanted to become. I will not leave you, Amber MacPhee. You are a part of me."

Tears glistened on her lashes as she pulled him toward her and kissed him. She smiled against his mouth and whispered, "Our love is forever."

He nodded. "Aye."

"I like that, though it has taken me a long time to accept it. However, that brings up an interesting question. What if I'm not in love with you, but with the medieval world I dropped into, complete with a battle-scarred castle, wolfhounds and a valiant warrior. And you, once you get to know me in my natural habitat, may feel differently as well."

The corners of his mouth turned up in a smile as he held out his hand to her. "I am in love with a logical woman. A more fearsome foe than Subedei's mercenaries. But as I prevailed once, so will I again. I'm the same man in any century and it is long past time to prove this."

She snuggled against him. "It will be like starting over."

"Am I to court you anew?"

Amber laughed. "Aye."

Return to
a time of romance...

**SONNET
BOOKS**

Where today's

hottest romance authors

bring you vibrant

and vivid love stories

with a dash of history.

PUBLISHED BY POCKET BOOKS

SONNET BOOKS
PROUDLY PRESENTS

The Quest
Pam Binder

Coming soon in paperback
from Sonnet Books

The following is a preview of
The Quest . . .

Prologue

❧

Scotland, 1328

In the days when magick ruled the land,
And gods fought by our side,
One stood out from all the rest,
The valiant warrior Cuchulainn.

Anonymous

"It is forbidden."

The words her mentor and friend had spoken swirled through Ana de Dannon's mind like the mists over the highlands. She gazed out the window. A full moon shone silvery white and snowflakes blanketed the Loch, clinging to the castle walls. She pulled the rolled parchment from the protection of her sleeve. A family friend had brought the announcement to her just over a fortnight ago, as well as the news that her mother still lived.

To all those who honor the treaty of peace between Scotland and England, please read on. A tournament will take place at the first blush of spring. In celebration, the prisoners in Edinburgh Tower will be freed under the following condition: To prove their innocence, their champion must defeat all who challenge him.

A torchlight cast flickering shadows on the oak beams. Ana shivered and pulled her cloak over her shoulders. Her mother was a prisoner in the tower. Tonight was the end of the winter solstice and, according to her Book of Spells, marked her last opportunity to conjure a champion. Her other attempts to draw the warrior Cuchulainn from his resting place had failed.

She heard footsteps echo down the corridor and turned. It was Danu. Years of laughter and wisdom marked the corners of her dark eyes.

Danu smiled as she drew near. "I have been looking for you, child. There is a chill in the castle tonight. You should come away from the window."

Ana nodded. "I am a woman, fully grown, and yet you fuss over me as though I were still a babe."

Danu put her hand on Ana's arm. "It is a hard habit to break." She paused. "I know you wear a heavy burden. But you should not keep yourself apart at such a time." She sighed. "I am as anxious as you. Learning your mother survived was indeed a joyous occasion. But my sister would not want you to risk so much. You should not do this."

"It is the only path open to us."

"At five and twenty you have inherited both your mother's strength as well as her stubbornness." Danu shook her head. "However, as yet you have not mastered her skills."

Ana rested her hand on the window ledge and pressed her fingers against the rough stones. "Time is not our ally. The man we choose must not only be a skilled warrior but must be more committed to freeing my mother than the coin to be made at the tournament." An icy breeze tugged at her hair. "We need a man who will defeat Roderick and prove my mother's innocence." She wrapped her cloak tighter around her shoulders. "Many able men are afraid to challenge my stepbrother."

"And for good reason. Young Jamie, and the men he brought with him, tell me that Roderick has grown more powerful." Danu tucked wisps of graying hair behind her ear. "All the more reason to reconsider. The old Celtic ways are discouraged."

Ana turned and smiled. "At first you said bending the currents of time was forbidden; now you say it is only discouraged. There is a wide valley of difference between those words. Besides, you are at fault, for you placed the notion in my thoughts."

Danu folded her arms across her chest. "I remember the conversation well. I only said that to challenge Roderick you would need a champion as strong and as bold as the legendary warrior Cuchulainn." She hesitated. "I did not mean that we needed the man himself."

"We do need him. My decision is made. You have shown me a mother's love; now I will ask for your trust."

Tears brimmed in Danu's eyes. "I give it freely. But take care, child. I sense whatever the outcome, your life will be forever changed."

A mist rolled over the water and wrapped around the castle walls. Ana felt as though it wove around her as well. She faced the wind and let it blow her hair free. This was a night where all manner of things were possible, even those that were forbidden.

Chapter

1

❧

The Present

A wall of fire rolled and churned around Kenneth MacKinnon. He fought the hot fury of the flames with a broadsword that blazed as though it were made of molten gold. He heard a woman scream. He must reach her before it was too late.

Mac awoke with a gasp. He wrenched free of the nightmare, sat up, and rolled to the side of the bed. Sweat beaded his forehead. His recurring nightmare had taken a bizarre turn. In the other dreams he'd been alone, but tonight he battled to save a woman.

Mac glanced over at the digital clock on the chrome-and-glass nightstand beside his bed. It was 8 A.M. He'd better get going.

He felt a cool hand on his back and flinched. He'd forgotten about her.

"Are you okay, honey?"

He looked toward her. "Sure, Taffy, just a bad dream."

Mac ducked as a pillow sailed past his head.

"My name is Muffy. We've dated for over a year. Why can't you remember? It's not age. You're barely thirty. Besides, you know the names of all those kids you coach." She swept her long blond hair over her shoulder. "My psychic friend tells me there's a reason you keep forgetting."

"I have a lot on my mind, that's all. Besides, those kids need me. Most of them live in shelters."

Muffy twirled a strand of her hair around her finger. "You're such a Boy Scout. You can't help every stray cat that comes your way."

"I can try." He stood and looked toward the open window opposite the bed. Sunlight drifted into the room. He could see Puget Sound and one of the ferryboats that made their daily run to Bainbridge Island. His condominium was on the top floor in one of the most expensive areas of downtown Seattle. The huge salary he was paid as quarterback for the Dark Warriors professional football team had its benefits. If he wanted to spend some of it on those kids, that was his choice.

He glanced at the clock again. "I'll be late if I don't get going."

Muffy reached for his arm. "Let's not fight." She smiled. "I need to ask you something."

The tone in her voice had the singsong quality that always signaled she wanted something. He rubbed the back of his neck. "I'm listening."

She leaned closer to him. "I realize you'd just as soon spend the evening in a sports bar, but we've been invited to the opening of that new French restaurant. It will be good for your image."

He doubted anyone cared where he ate as long as he got the job done on the field. He shook his head. "I don't care where we go."

Muffy continued in a rush of breathy words. "Terrific, but I'll need something new to wear."

He sighed with relief. He thought she was going to

reopen the subject of marriage. Mac grabbed his jeans off the floor. Enduring a night in a fancy restaurant would be worth the price. "Go ahead and charge it."

She winked. "What would you like your Muffy to wear? And don't be a naughty boy and say nothing."

He wasn't going to say a word. Mac pulled on his pants and reached for his shirt. "You know I can't pick out women's clothes. Buy anything you like."

Mac grabbed his keys from the nightstand as Muffy jumped off the bed and headed toward the bathroom. He watched her leave. No good-bye kiss, no good luck Mac, nothing; just the clinging smell of the gardenia perfume she wore.

He didn't blame her. Mac was sure she wasn't any happier than he was. She'd expected a celebrity who liked to party until dawn. He'd wanted someone . . . Hell, he didn't know what he wanted. One thing he knew for sure: he didn't believe in love anymore. The whole idea of finding a person who made you feel whole was an elaborate hoax concocted by the greeting card companies.

Fluorescent lights flooded Husky Stadium as Mac stood on the sidelines with his team. A woman with a soprano voice sang the national anthem. He was anxious for the game to start. A fog bank rolled off Lake Washington and hung in the air. It was hard to see. The weather was unusual, even for rain-drenched Seattle. He smiled and accepted the challenge. It would only make the game more interesting. The breeze was charged with electricity as though it, too, were waiting for something to happen. He breathed in the air, feeling invincible.

Once again he would bring home a win against impossible odds. He had built his reputation on such moments. That's what he was paid to do, and with it came a truckload of money and the hangers-on. He thought of Muffy. She'd disappear if it stopped rolling in and the parties ended. The familiar emptiness darkened his mood. He shrugged it away. He had to focus on the game; that's all that mattered.

The roar of the crowd echoed through the stadium as he walked onto the field. They were on their feet, chanting his name, smelling the victory they knew he would bring them. Blood pounded through his veins and thundered in his ears. He was ready.

A hush moved across the field as Mac took his position behind the center. The football was snapped. The crowd screamed their approval. He dropped back and avoided a lineman. Mac searched for his receiver. Griffin was open. It was a good way to begin. The man caught everything Mac threw.

The fog rolled in as thick as the foam on beer. A lineman hit him and drove him to the ground. The ball was still in his hands. Damn.

He was pinned against the AstroTurf. The faces of the football players blurred. He felt dizzy, sick to his stomach. Hell, he hoped it wasn't another concussion. The sound of the crowd became muffled, as though they were a long way off. The dizziness increased. He fought to stay conscious but could feel the energy seep from his body like the slow leak in a rubber inner tube.

The noise of the crowd still rang in Mac's ears as he struggled to open his eyes. It was as though he was under a pile of linebackers. The last thing he remembered was yelling and cheering. Now there was only silence. He'd probably been transported off the field and taken to a hospital. Well, he needed to let the nurse know he was awake and ready to go home.

After a few attempts, he succeeded in opening his

eyes. A fireplace and candles provided the only light in the windowless room. A table close to the hearth was littered with clay containers and open leather-bound books. There was a musty smell and something else he couldn't quite identify.

He pushed himself to a sitting position and almost fell off the bench. The football thumped to the ground. He watched it bounce on the floor. Odd. He shouldn't still have it. Mac looked around. Where the hell was he? He'd expected hospital-white walls and antiseptic smells, not a room where breathing the air might prove fatal. He tried to stand. His legs felt like over-cooked spaghetti. He braced himself against the wall.

A small, furry creature moved among the discarded food and clutter on the table. It was a rat. The rodent's red eyes blinked and stared back at him, more curious than afraid. Mac had a bad feeling.

A door banged open. The rodent jumped off the table as two women entered the room.

The younger one pointed in Mac's direction. "How can you doubt me? Our champion stands before you."

The woman had thick, waist-length red hair. She wore a long green dress that clung to her full breasts and slender body. A gold belt accentuated her hips. He gulped. Her clothes resembled the style he'd seen in a movie Muffy had dragged him to. The story was all about chivalry and codes of honor. He'd fallen asleep after the first fifteen minutes. However, if any of the women had looked like this one, he might have stayed awake longer.

The older woman, with salt-and-pepper hair piled on top of her head in a braid, wore a floor-length blue dress. She shook her head. "I have not the time for your jest, Ana. There is too much left undone."

The redhead put her hands on her hips. "It is no jest. I have conjured the great warrior Cuchulainn."

Mac rubbed the back of his neck. Conjured? That was one of the things Muffy said her psychic talked about all the time. He thought it had something to do with spells or magic. Maybe both. The fool linebacker must have hit him harder than he thought. He must be dreaming. He tensed. He didn't like dreams, even those with a gorgeous woman. They always ended the same. Mac willed himself to wake up, hoping he'd not missed too much of the game.

Nothing happened.

The younger woman frowned. "Danu, you must be aware of how closely this man resembles the description of our legendary hero. He has the size and appearance of a mighty warrior."

The older woman raised an eyebrow and looked over at him. "I have heard it said that the larger the animal, the smaller the brain. This one must have the intelligence of a flea. Wherever did you find him, child?"

He was being insulted in his own dream. Mac took off his helmet and cradled it in the crook of his arm. He tried to speak, but nothing came out.

The redhead glanced toward him as though trying to decide if what her companion had said was true. He wondered if his engineering degree would impress her, and then couldn't understand why it mattered.

She turned to the older woman. "His intelligence is of little importance. We have the plan well in hand and here he stands. He is our champion."

Mac shifted his helmet from his arm and dangled it by the strap. This was all very flattering, but he'd heard enough. It was time to wake up.

The scurrying of tiny feet across the floor caught his attention. The rodent had returned. It ran frantically back and forth in front of a closed door to Mac's right. The rat reared up on its hind legs and sniffed the air.

The smell Mac noticed earlier was stronger now. This time he recognized the odor: burning wood.

His helmet came loose from the strap and clattered to the ground. He stared at it and then in the direction he'd last seen the rat. It was nowhere in sight.

The women argued about whether Mac was zapped by magic or brought here as a joke. He lost interest in either theory. What drew his attention was behind the door. His uneasiness grew as he walked toward it. This dream hadn't started out like the rest. Of course, he usually only remembered the end.

Mac raised his hand and reached toward the door. He hesitated. Without touching the oak panels, he could feel the warmth coming through them. He took a deep breath and let it out slowly. Mac placed his palm on the wood. He jerked it away. He'd felt more than heat. The panels bulged outward.

He stepped back. The fire beyond these walls searched for more fuel to satisfy its hunger That's why the door was expanding with the heat. The flames were testing the strength of the walls. He rubbed his hand against his pants. His fingers still stung.

The fire was getting impatient. Mac combed his fingers through his hair. In his dreams he never actually felt the heat on his skin. He turned toward the two women. They were still arguing. Mac remembered a woman screaming in his dream last night. He didn't want that to happen again.

He walked toward them and slammed his fist on the table. Bottles toppled over. Green and brown liquid oozed from the containers. He nodded in the direction of the door. "Is there another way out? This place is burning."

The two women turned to stare at him as if they objected to his interruption.

The younger of the two patted him on the arm as

though he were a hysterical child. "Calm yourself, Cuchulainn. My name is Ana and I am sure these surroundings seem strange to you, but please rest assured we mean you no harm."

He thought he heard the older woman make a *humph* sound.

Mac shrugged off the younger woman's touch. "The name is Mac, not Cuchulainn. And strange doesn't begin to explain this place. But in a few moments it won't matter." He leaned closer and said each word distinctly. "Your home is on fire."

"Perhaps he tells the truth. Danu? I smell something burning as well."

Mac looked toward the door. Smoke snaked up the wood panels. "Is that the proof you need?" And they thought he was as dumb as a goalpost. So far no one had died in his dreams. He didn't want this to be a first.

He motioned toward an alcove. "Where does that lead?"

Ana's voice was low. "The courtyard."

He walked over and tested the wood panels on the door. They felt cool. He forced it open. The corridor was narrow. He'd never make it through wearing his shoulder pads. He pulled off his jersey and threw it in a pile by his football and helmet. Then he unfastened his pads and tossed them beside the rest of his gear. His stomach seemed to twist in a knot. He glanced over at his stuff. It was as though he were leaving a part of himself behind. That was ridiculous. This was only a dream.

Mac reached for a candle on the hearth and cupped his hand around the flame. "Follow me."

The door led down a flight of stairs that emptied into a dark void. The candle flickered, casting shadows on the walls.

"Ana, did you notice the strange armor your champion wore?"

Ana's voice rose against the sound of their footsteps. "Yes, Danu, it is most curious. And his manner of speech is like no other I have ever heard."

They were talking about him again instead of to him. Just as well. He didn't feel like conversation.

Sticky cobwebs clung to his face and hot wax from the candle dripped on his hand. He ignored the burning sensation on his finger and adjusted his grip. Holding on to the belief he was dreaming was proving to be difficult.

An icy breeze whistled through the dark corridors. The candle flickered.

Ana brushed his arm. The scent of roses filled the air. She was standing next to him.

She leaned closer. "This door leads to the courtyard."

Mac hesitated. A sense of paranoia seized him. He felt like a contestant on a game show. Behind the door in front of him were three possible choices: a football field, a courtyard, or a man-eating fire. He had never felt more unlucky in his life. Of course, by now he should have had a sword in his hand. Maybe the rules of the dream had changed. He shrugged and handed the candle to Ana. What the hell. No one lives forever.

He leaned his shoulder against the door and pushed. It burst open.

Damn. It was the courtyard. He was still dreaming.

Screams filled the enclosure as men, women, and children ran in terror from the flames that snaked up the walls of the castle. Dark clouds covered the night sky. Mac tamped down his frustration. He pushed Ana and Danu through the crush of people to a clearing a safe distance from the flames.

Mac looked over his shoulder. He felt the muscles in

his neck tense. The single castle tower and connecting wing were engulfed in flames. Castles were usually made of stone, but this one was mostly wood. It would be over soon.

He turned to Ana. Her thick hair blew in the icy wind and her eyes sparkled like an emerald he'd seen once. He cleared his throat. "Stay here. I'm going to check and see if everyone is okay."

Her voice was little more than a whisper. "That is commendable, but why would you concern yourself with those you do not know?"

He turned and headed toward the castle. "Let's just say I have the intelligence of a flea." He glanced over his shoulder and saw the shadow of a smile cross her face. She was beautiful and had a sense of humor. Too bad this was only a dream.

Look for
THE QUEST
Wherever Books
Are Sold.
Coming Soon in Paperback
from
Sonnet Books.